Also by
James Alexander Thom

FOLLOW THE RIVER
FROM SEA TO SHINING SEA
LONG KNIFE
PANTHER IN THE SKY
THE CHILDREN OF FIRST MAN
THE RED HEART
SIGN-TALKER

with Dark Rain Thom

WARRIOR WOMAN

Saint Patrick's Battalion

Saint Patrick's Battalion

A NOVEL

James Alexander Thom

Ballantine Books NEW YORK

Saint Patrick's Battalion is a work of historical fiction. Apart from
the well-known actual people, events, and locales that figure in the narrative,
all names, characters, places, and incidents are the products of the author's
imagination or are used fictitiously. Any resemblance to current events
or locales, or to living persons, is entirely coincidental.

Published in the United States by Ballantine Books,
an imprint of The Random House Publishing Group,
a division of Random House, Inc., New York.

BALLANTINE and colophon are registered trademarks of Random House, Inc.

LIBRARY OF CONGRESS CATALOGING-IN-PUBLICATION DATA
Thom, James Alexander.
Saint Patrick's Battalion : a novel / James Alexander Thom.—1st ed.
p. cm.
ISBN 0-345-44556-2 (acid-free paper)
1. Riley, John, b. 1817—Fiction.   2. Mexico. Ejército. Batallón
de San Patricio—Fiction.   3. Mexican War, 1846–1848—Fiction.
I. Title: St. Patrick's Battalion.   II. Title.

PS3570.h47S25 2006
813'.54—dc22   2005057171

Printed in the United States of America on acid-free paper

www.ballantinebooks.com

2 4 6 8 9 7 5 3 1

First Edition

Text design by Laurie Jewell

FOR KURT VONNEGUT, JR.

who knows a thing or two about war whoopee

and those who make it.

* * *

ACKNOWLEDGMENTS

I THANK historian Peter Guardino of Indiana University for finding insights and specific answers for me during his regular trips to Mexico, and for vetting the novel's awkward "phrasebook Spanish" to protect me from embarrassing myself.

I am grateful to Peter F. Stevens, historian, author of *The Rogue's March,* for his insights into the severe treatment of Catholic immigrant soldiers during those times of vicious Nativism.

Thanks to Linda Arnold at Virginia Tech for her data on correspondents and news transmission during the Mexican War.

For certain facts about President Polk's selling of that war in the Capitol, I thank my pen pal Andy Jacobs, Jr., who remembers what it's like to force fellow Congressmen to examine skeptically the bombast of warhawks—a lesson still having to be relearned.

And thanks to my editor, Mark Tavani, for seeing how a war story might be told more truthfully by boys than by men.

PROLOGUE

April 1861

Why does Mexico matter? Have not our Anglo-Saxon
race been land stealers from time immemorial . . . ?
When their gaze is fixed on other lands, the best
way is to make out the deeds.

—GENERAL WILLIAM WORTH

Allow the President to invade a neighboring nation,
whenever he shall deem it necessary to repel an invasion,
and you allow him to do so whenever he may choose to say
he deems it necessary for such purpose—and you allow
him to make war at pleasure. Study to see if you can fix any
limit to his power, after you have given him so much.

—CONGRESSMAN ABRAHAM LINCOLN,
DISSENTING AGAINST PRESIDENT JAMES K. POLK'S
AGGRESSION TOWARD MEXICO, 1846

Near Mexico City ✳ April 1861

ON A SUN-HEATED road to the Shrine of Our Lady of Guadalupe, a freckled young man with red hair and long legs hurries
up a hill, carrying a wooden writing portfolio under his left arm and a
knapsack slung over his right shoulder, squinting ahead, stepping
around the black-clad *penitentes* who are crawling toward the cathedral
on their knees. Most of them are old men and crones. Their progress is
excruciating to see, and they have miles to go. The expression on each
old face could be trance or torment.

After so many years away, the young man is immersed anew in the
sense of Mexico's heart: the thin air of this altitude, sunbeams leaning
through arid haze, blue mountains beyond his shoulder, and a haunt-
ing intuition that every incline in the road mounts some ancient Aztec
temple obliterated by the *conquistadors.* From shadowy doors and iron-
grille gates come wisps of speech he cannot understand, though he can
distinguish Spanish accents from Aztecan and loves the lyric beauty of
both.

As for the aged *penitentes* in the road, he glances down with pity and
awe at each one he overtakes.

The hurrying youth is looking ahead for a different kind of pilgrim,
one who is neither old nor poor. From what has been said, there will be
no mistaking him among the others. His clothing is described as elegant, his hat of glossy beaver, he is *guapo,* the people say. He might be

smoking a cheroot as he goes along, he might be singing, he might even be *un poco borracho.* He is well known to most of the people who live along this pilgrimage road. He comes by every year about this time. He is considered a bit eccentric, but is full of charm and generosity, most of the time. He is crippled and deaf; it is known that he was one of *Los Niños Héroes* of Chapultepec in the past war, and their behavior is always indulged. Many people who live along the pilgrimage road take the *penitentes* in at night to shelter them, and some of those people boast that they have been host to him. They have told the red-haired young man that it was their honor to do so, and that, furthermore, he would leave *una propina,* a peso or more, if he remembered. Also, he is said to have sired a baby or two in passing through. He carries a flask and two silver cups, but is not known ever to have been robbed along the way. To rob pilgrims is of course a despicable offense, but it happens.

In the narrow world of this holy road, this particular pilgrim is a celebrity: the deaf cripple, the laughing *penitente,* easy to follow.

The man following him is a correspondent, a writer and illustrator, who has come to Mexico on an advance allowance he wheedled out of the editor of a New York magazine known as *Harper's.* The correspondent had proposed to write and illustrate two articles of a historic nature, both pertaining to the U.S.A.'s last war, which was the invasion and conquest of Mexico. With a war of secession building up in the United States, he had argued that readers would be receptive to curiosities about that prior conflict, which had been the fiery baptism of all the new commanders, Union and Confederate alike. The new president, Abraham Lincoln, as a young congressman had opposed that invasion. The correspondent had suggested to the editor that his readership might now have matured to a more sympathetic view of the Mexican cause. And in that preceding war as in this new one, the role of the slave states had been pivotal. His spiel had convinced the editor to let him try.

The American strides along through the traffic of the road, peering ahead, weaving among farmers with their loaded burros, carts whose iron-rimmed wheels rattle and rumble, graceful women in rebozos carrying bundles or pots on their heads or babies on their hips, boys wearing sandals and loose white cotton, their dark eyes furtively glancing at him, horsemen riding in pairs, their faces and shoulders shaded by broad sombreros. And all these people, going both ways along the shade-dappled road, maneuver around the hunched little black-clad pilgrims who creep tediously onward along the roadsides, all going his way. Hooves clank on stone, soles shuffle, voices murmur and laugh, somewhere a tenor is singing and somewhere else there is a flute, somewhere else the bleat of a goat, languid strumming on guitar strings, birdsong, a crying baby. Yellow dust drifts, full of sunrays, and the correspondent smells hot meat grease, baked cornmeal, charcoal, horse manure. He is thirsty, but not hungry. His feet are sweaty, blistered. He limps, but is ashamed that his trifling discomfort vexes him so much while the ancient pilgrims go on and on upon their suffering knees, their toes dragging through grit and pebbles behind them.

The man he is pursuing has no feet to drag. There he is, it must be the one, a few hundred paces ahead, almost in the middle of the road. He looks more like a toddling dwarf than a crawling *penitente.* The journalist studies him as he catches up. The pilgrim is actually walking upon his knees, which are his extremities. There are no shins or feet. Closer, it appears that the stumps are fitted into some sort of padded leather device, hoof-shaped. His black trousers are cut off uncuffed to reach the tops of the bootlets. The journalist slows a bit, intently observant. Unlike a dwarf, the man is not squat or burly, but rather slender, with a trim waist, and his arms and hands are long. His suit is neat and well cut, black, but dusty. A leather satchel with buckles hangs at his left side, its strap crossing over his right shoulder. He looks like a stylish traveler, but appears to be less than four feet tall. He tips his hat now and then to people coming toward him, showing a head of thick, wavy hair, and some salute him in return. This is not the demeanor of a *penitente.* Some of the people coming down the hill look at the journalist, that quick, polite appraisal a red-haired foreigner gets in these parts.

The cripple senses that they are looking at someone behind him. He stops, turns his head to reveal a long-nosed, delicate profile, neat mustache, then a pair of nearly black eyes, looking up from under the brim of the beaver hat. He notices the writing portfolio, the red hair, the other peculiarities of this foreigner.

The journalist stops beside the cripple and bows slightly, touches his forelock in salute, then draws from his pocket the handwritten note he has prepared for this moment.

Con Perdón. Esta tu Señor Agustin Juvero? Espero que sí.

If the cripple is surprised, his eyes do not reveal it. A sardonic half smile twitches at the corner of his mouth. He says, "Clearly it will be better if I speak in your tongue, *Señor Gringo.* Why do you come to accost Agustin Juvero in the sacking and ashes of his *penitencia*? What do you want of me?"

The red-haired one writes another note, this one in English, explaining who he is, the magazine he represents, and the topics of the last war that he hopes to cover in his interview. That is, if *Señor* Juvero will be so kind. He apologizes for interrupting him on his pilgrimage. The young Mexican reads the note, his lips moving. He looks up, eyes glittering, smile mocking, and says:

"*¿Y luego?* You want to hear the war story about me. And you want to hear about Don Juan Riley. What a remarkable coincidence, *me parece* . . . But my question to you, *Señor Reportero,* is:

"Do you bring me anything good to drink? If so, I might pause for a refreshment, even with a *Yanqui.* And of course, it would strengthen my memory. I have forgotten as much of all that as I could."

BOOK I

The Northern Campaign

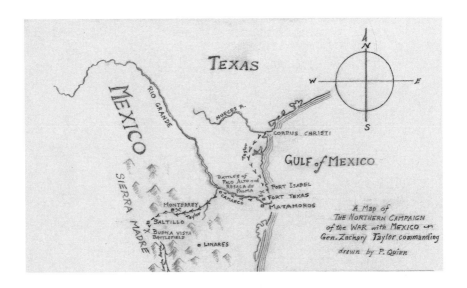

CHAPTER I

AGUSTIN JUVERO
SPEAKS TO THE AMERICAN JOURNALIST
ON THE PILGRIMAGE ROAD

THERE IN THE shade by the wall is a bench. Let us sit on it so that I need not look up at you while I talk. Eventually looking up hurts my neck. And as you can see, I cannot stand as tall as you.

¿Bueno, y qué? Please let me taste what you carry in your flask. Thank you.

¡Uf! This *Norteamericano* liquor is so bad, I might almost leave some! But no, I will drink it all, in order not to insult you in my country. *¡Salud!*

What you want from me you will have to take in the way I give it. I will talk, you will listen. You may not mitigate my story with quibbles or protestations, for I cannot hear them. As you know, I am deaf. From your guns, when your soldiers came here. The one good part of deafness is that I can say all I want without hearing interruptions. All I hear since your guns fourteen years ago is inside my head, like the scream of an eagle and the roar of the ocean. I can feel church bells, but not hear them.

So, *Señor Periodista.* Here is what I tell people like you, so that you can be comfortable looking at me, and we can smile and be at ease together:

When I was small boy, I was taller than I am now as a man. *¿Aunque parezca extraño?* Funny enough? It goes better if we are amused. If not, it goes nowhere.

So! A new war is beginning, up in your country! It is a matter of much interest to us, if not all a matter of delight. We are satisfied that you deserve it. No, forgive me. Your President Polk deserves it, but he is already dead anyway. Your new president does not deserve it, I suppose. It is to be seen whether he will earn such desserts. *¡Vale!* Providence sees to it that there are enough wars, say two or three in a man's lifetime if he lives through them, that the human race doesn't forget how to murder on a grand scale. Practice is always needed. God forbid that wars should be fought by beginners only, or that weapons should rust, or wounds fully heal, or that women should be denied the rich emotion of lamenting lost sons to compensate for the pain of giving them birth.

Your war now gathering up there promises to be an enormous event, which will solve some long-festering problems, and create new ones. We in Mexico know that is always the case. I have read in your newspapers of your armies forming under generals who learned war right in this Valley of Mexico. Many of them who fought shoulder-to-shoulder against us will now fight face-to-face against each other. How they must be remembering, dreading, anticipating! *Señor,* I am a scholar of American wars. But we were to talk of me.

You were told that I am one of *Los Niños Héroes* of Chapultepec, eh? True. I was one who survived. Thirty-five cadets were captured. Three of us were severely wounded. Five boys died on your bayonets, and one leaped from the castle with our flag to prevent its capture, and died far below.

I meant to die with those. Unhappily, I lived. As I did not expect. As no one expected. It was not God's will for me to die that day. That is a mystery. I was deafened by shell bursts, I was bayoneted, my legs were shot off.

I received *el viatico sacramento.* After the rites, however, I failed to die. So it would seem that I am prepared to do so if it occurs, and I have no fear, therefore.

Si, *Señor Reportero,* some say I deserve to be honored among those who gave their young lives, because I earned the last rites. That would be *una cuestión formal,* a technicality of law.

Likewise it was a technicality of law that determined the fate of our beloved *Coronel* Don Juan Riley, he of your other story besides mine.

What a remarkable coincidence it is that in seeking those two differ-ent stories you came to me! Or did you somehow learn from someone that he is in my story, as I am in his? How could that be? To my knowl-edge, no one still lives who remembers. No one told you then, eh? No?

Take a drink of your awful whiskey, so I don't have to drink it all by myself. Heheh! You drink like a soldier! I have heard that *Yanqui* jour-nalists do drink like soldiers. Excuse me while I climb down from this bench and go piss against the wall. Uh! I do not piss noisily from a height. My *pene* nearly drags the ground. For you to say such a thing would be boastful, with those long legs. Ah.

I am told by persons who have been in the United States that many of your Mexican War veterans, trimmed down as I am, have to beg in the streets to live. That some go out on a little cart into the street crowds every day and plead for alms. And perhaps sleep in crates in the city alleys. In particular, the veterans who are Irishmen. You *Yanquis* do not love the Irish as we in Mexico love them. Don Juan Riley told us that is why he deserted your army.

Mexico does not abandon me to beg, or to sleep in a crate in an alley. Though a short crate would suffice for me! I should fit comfortably in an artillery caisson. One would suit me well for a coffin, too, if that time ever comes. I would be honored to be buried in a caisson box from *Coronel* Riley's own cannon battery. I have in fact reserved one for that eventual purpose. You appear to doubt. But no, *Señor.* It is in a military museum in the city honoring his battalion, the *San Patricios.* At my re-quest, an uncle of mine made arrangements with the curator, a man who had served under him against the Texans. *Tío* Rodrigo, my excel-lent uncle, didn't scoff at my fancy. He said that he, too, would be hon-ored to be interred in a caisson upon which *Coronel* Riley had ridden to battle in defense of our country. But of course *Tío* Rodrigo died too tall to fit in such a thing.

Whenever I say the name of *Coronel* Riley, *Señor,* I think I see your ears grow. And your eyes brighten. I suspect that you are more inter-ested in him than in me. Of course! Mexico loves the memory of the *San Patricios* as much, perhaps even more, than that of the Heroic Chil-dren. And your nation cannot forgive them.

I am a scholar of the history of your nation, *Señor,* as well as that of mine. Since that war, half of my country has been yours. I have ancestors who were buried in their homeland of California when it was Mexico. And now, though their graves were never moved, they are buried in the United States. So, how could I not study your nation's history?

I know that your American army for a long time called *Señor* Riley the most hated man of America. Even though he never was a citizen of your country!

And that your Department of the Army is so ashamed of their deserters in that war, that your army historians now deny that he ever existed. *¡Ay de mi!* How confusing for one's reputation, eh, to be the worst traitor ever, but never to have existed? *Coronel* Riley must be laughing!

I have finished sprinkling this place. Now, *Señor,* I need to resume my pilgrimage. This has been an interesting visit for me. I think you will have to come along and talk with me on the road if you hope to hear more of my knowledge and wisdom.

You come? Good! It's long way yet. And if your *Yanqui* whiskey makes me fall down, you can help me up. Heh!

I was speaking of *Coronel* Riley. In your army he was only *un soldado raso,* a lowly private. But in General Santa Anna's army he rose to *coronel.* He might have been an officer in your army, too, had he not been an Irishman and a Catholic. That is not my bias only, *Señor Periodista.* It was the opinion also of his own commanding officer in your army, who admitted it to journalists. I read it in some of the New York newspapers. And some of the Catholic journals as well. The officer said those words at *Señor* Riley's court-martial.

I am addicted to your *Norteamericano* periodicals, *Señor,* for I try to understand your country.

Yes, I have even read articles written by you, and I have seen illustrations by your hand. They are not bad. Some, in truth, are excellent. Only last year I saw your reportage and drawings of the last days of the insurrectionist, that John Brown. Time and again I marveled at the story. A great and terrible man, eh? You were near enough to see and hear him? He looked quite like God. That is to say, God as you *Yanquis* imagine God. Or as even Michelangelo imagined God! It thrilled me, his shaming of your slavers! I memorized his words, from your article: *I, John Brown, am now certain that the crimes of this guilty land will never be purged away, but with Blood!* You said that those were his last written words. *¡Magnífico!* What a people you *Yanquis* are, at your best and worst!

And *Señor* Brown spoke true, I believe. The blood to be spilled in this new war of yours, it will purge your crimes, not only of slavery, but your crime against my country. You cannot like to hear me say it. But you came to hear me. Just as the crime of the *conquistadors* was purged away by the blood of our *revolución* against Spain.

¡Perdón! I am a man of strong opinions, *Señor*, in matters of what is right and what is wrong. But I was speaking of your work, and you did a fine thing when you told the world of the righteous and defiant heart of that insurgent *Señor* Brown. Your portrait of him is engraved forever in my mind, as are the words he spoke at the end of his life, at the gallows: *I am ready at any time. Do not keep me waiting.* A man who looked like God could speak that way!

What I would like very much to see is a portrait of *Coronel* Riley. None was ever done, to my knowledge. No painting, no daguerreotype. If only I had one to refer to for my memory! It has been so many years, and, *sí,* he was a familiar to me. You did not know that. Maybe you don't believe it. Many wanted to claim familiarity with him, who never knew him. I can tell you. *¡Un hombre guapo!* Of stature and vigor, strong as oak. And the eyes of that man! One would trust him at once and put oneself under the protection of his arm.

¡Ay de mi! Alas, even trust well deserved can lead to disaster for the faithful, for we do not know God's designs. *Coronel* Riley never betrayed our trust, but we who loved him were to suffer, as he did. We cannot presume to know what God intends. Unlike you *Yanquis,* who believe God meant you to seize the continent. You called it Manifest Destiny. The end of that is yet to be seen.

But God perhaps has other plans than those we presume. It is said, if you would hear God laugh, tell him your plans.

Don Juan Riley, a good Catholic and honorable man, put his body and soul to what he thought was God's purpose. Many followed him to their doom. Likewise, many followed General Santa Anna.

Perhaps it is well, *Señor Periodista,* that I am on my little stumps now and cannot follow anyone. Following has not done me well. But I don't regret.

You have followed me, and found me, to ask questions. I am on a pilgrimage of atonement. To listen to me answer your questions, you must now follow me on this road of atonement to Our Lady of Guadalupe. You *Yanquis* have much to atone for, God knows. Can you stay along? It will take a long time. Can a *Gringo* go so slow?

You are a Catholic, are you not? Look, *Señor,* what a good Catholic I am:

Permanently on my knees!

PADRAIC QUINN'S DIARY

New Orleans ✳ June 15, 1845

SINCE GOD AND my mother saw fit to make me literate, I have made up my mind to keep a diary. This is the beginning of it. Nothing much is happening to write about at this time, but it appears the United States Army will be going to Mexico pretty soon, and I'll be going along with it. I ought to keep a diary.

Here it is about me and the Army. I was with the soldiers in the last year of the Seminole campaigns in Florida. I was an errand boy in camp. Mostly I did servant work for the officers who didn't have their own personal slaves. Officers are pretty helpless, so many of them being gentlemen and too good to shine their own boots or empty their own chamberpots, or go fetch anything they need, so there was always something for me to do to earn my keep.

You see my handwriting is pretty good. Soldiers who can't write asked me to write letters home for them, and I earned some pennies from them. They would tell me what they wanted their families to know about the Indian campaign, and I came to like writing it. It's like storytelling, and I practiced making the stories sound the way the soldiers would have told them if they had the gift of words. Or what my mother called Blarney. It seemed to me that a man soldiering against those Seminole Indians in their great swamp, a man doing that would want to seem like a heroic sort of fellow back home. So I sometimes wrote some flourishes and maybe little exaggerations to make their folks back home admire them.

I never wrote any outright lies, such as, a fellow had been awarded a medal for bravery. But I might suggest in the letter that he deserved one.

Sure and they did deserve medals just for being down there in that mucky, prickly swamp with all the poison snakes and those mosquitoes. And officers who were meaner than alligators! The Seminoles themselves were scary, being cunning and in their own kind of countryside, where white folk don't really belong, not having webbed feet. The Seminoles don't really have webbed feet, either, but a body could believe they do, the way they get around in there.

I don't think we really won that Swamp War, but a couple of years back the government said it was over and we moved back into garrison on solid ground. What I am getting at here is that I regret I wasn't writing down all those interesting events and occasions, so that I could remember them better. I was only nine then. I write much better now. I teach myself by reading everything I can get.

Lately our country and Mexico got to squabbling about their border with Texas, and pretty soon our Army moved here to New Orleans where we can load on all kinds of ships and go straight over to Mexico, if it comes to that. It seems the President is pretty determined to have a war against Mexico. You don't do this much getting ready if you don't really mean to do something. This city is all a-stir with soldiers and officers. More ships here at the wharves of the Mississippi than I would have believed there are in the whole world, and the docks are piled high as a house with the stuff an Army uses.

In this old city there's every kind of people you ever could imagine. Merchants who talk all kinds of foreign languages, fancy men and ladies, sailors and pilots and pirates, stage actors and gamblers off the steamboats. You can't quite tell the whores from the other ladies. There are churches about every hundred paces, and they have religious processions and parades and carnivals. The land here is so low and wet, they can't bury dead people in the ground, so their big cemetery is above-ground, looks like a whole city of tombs and crypts, like little stone houses.

It's a steamy, lazy place where just about everybody sweats and drinks all day and all night. Most of the work gets done by negro slaves. I never knew there were this many negroes in the world. You can go to auctions and buy people if you can afford them. Soldiers like to go to those auctions, not that they can afford slaves, but can sometimes see the slave women stripped. Some of the slave men have been flogged so much their backs look like the backs of the alligators I saw in Florida. Lots of our soldiers likewise have whip scars, so I'm used to the sight.

I followed some officers to Chalmette, near the city, where General Jackson beat the British Army in 1815, before he was president. Our officers like to go there to see the place because they learned about it at West Point army school. From the way I hear them talk, it raises their pride. It makes them cocky for what might come with Mexico. You hear them say that since America whipped the greatest Army in the world, Britain's, it should be real easy to whip the Mexican Greasers. That's what they call the Mexicans. In fact, that's what they call most of the people here in New Orleans. Greasers, Creoles, and Frogs. All the same, they sure go after the tan and brown ladies. They figure they'll be easy to conquer, too, because Catholic ladies don't have the same high virtue that their wives and sisters at home have, they like to say. I don't know how these officers know such things, but they talk as if they have the wisdom of experience. The more they talk to each other, the more sure they sound.

They sure are eager to conquer anything that's in their way.

About half of all the soldiers are Irish immigrants, or Catholics from Germany and other places in Europe, a lot of them are veterans of armies over there. The officers grouse a lot that they don't have more real Americans in their companies. Last Sunday a troop of Mississippi Volunteers taunted some Irish soldiers coming out of Mass. Big mistake. Half those yokels are now halt and lame.

This is my first writing in my diary. I like writing in here. I like saying whatever comes into my head.

What I'd like to write in here next is some of my adventures before this. Things I don't want to forget. I have had an interesting start, and probably there aren't many boys my age have so much to remember.

New Orleans ✳ June 18th 1845

I HAVE BEEN thinking how to start writing about myself. I thought, I'll just tell it like a story, not a real happy one.

Saint Patrick's Curse is what I call it.

I have been under Saint Patrick's Curse from the first day of my blighted life, & sure through no fault of mine. I wasn't even born in Ireland. I was born . . .

Sure, why not start right at the start? Never mind that about the Curse. Mark that out. Start over.

I was born in the state of Michigan, by chance. It was Michigan instead of some other place only because my sire—I can't bring myself to call that vicious bastard my "father," for "father" has a fond sound to it—he was a veteran soldier of the War of 1812 and living in Michigan when he set himself upon my poor Ma.

I don't know whether she tried to resist him; probably not. But if she'd known how mean he was, maybe she'd have kept him off. But to hell with all that; it was before my ken.

He was not Irish, that's all I know. He was some persuasion of English Protestant, and my mother won't even speak his name, that's how much she came to hate him. That's why I've carried the name Quinn. It was her maiden name.

By giving me that Irish name, she put Saint Patrick's curse on me. If I'd had my father's Protestant name, whatever it was, my youth'd not have been near so rough and thorny and low.

She was overweening proud of being a Quinn. You'd have thought it was Queen, she was that proud of it. Tell me, if you can, how a laundress and seamstress following Army camps gets pride.

Aye, well, she was proud she was no barbarian heretic like the brute who begot me, I guess that was enough for her, and so, I'm a Quinn like her. And like her, I've been following the soldiers all my life, what little there's been of it so far. I can't guess what any other career would be like. And I reckon I'll become a soldier myself when I get to the manly age. If God willing I do get to that age. The Seminoles in the Swamp War never got me. God willing the Mexicans won't, either. Sure and there's no other tolerable work for any Irishman in America. Well, shoveling muck and breaking rock to make canals, or hammering spikes on a railroad, or toting loads onto a steamboat. Those are hard, and no one's ambition, but at least they're honest labor and no shame.

But I've only been an Army camp boy, and that's why I think soldierly, and don't know much else until I read of it.

I am grateful that my Ma saw to it I learned to read. Many of the soldiers I write letters for say they regret they didn't have mothers to make them read. You get to know a soldier well when you write to his family. You don't get to know officers that same way. They write their own letters. It's about the only thing they do for themselves. A camp boy can stay busy fetching for them and cleaning up after them, polishing their boots and brass. But they can write. That's one reason they're officers. That, and their not being Irish or German immigrants. Or negroes.

I swear half this Army is Irishmen. More of them can read and write, taught by the Church, than the U.S.-born soldiers. But being able to read and write won't make you an officer if you're an Irish Catholic, especially one born in the Old Country. There are a few Irish officers in this Army, but only if they were American-born, maybe two generations or more, you see, established, educated somewhat, own land or a business. Those like that, they can get in West Point. It helps if they've had the foresight to unIrish their names a bit. Or have one of those names that aren't too plainly Irish. Some quit the Mother Church and pretend they're Scot, or Ulsterman, and they might get by.

Now, that man who fathered me. Ignorant brute he was, to be sure. A sutler at one of the garrisons up there. He had been born a Virginian, moved to Kentucky, and could just barely write and cipher, but that was all enough to make him a captain in the militia cavalry, and that's how he'd got up to Michigan. He went up there in the War of 1812, and there he stayed when he was mustered out. Ma wouldn't tell me what his name was, but she told me some about him. He used to knock her about. In truth, that is the first damned memory I have in this world, all that thumping and outcry of beatings. And the rum smell.

I myself was barely toddling when he found some fault with me and took his razor strop to me. I should tell you about that strop. It was his most treasured object. Two thicknesses of brown leather, the backing side cowhide, the other side being, he said, skinned off the back of the Indian chief Tecumseh, the evening after the Battle of the Thames River in Ontario, year 1813. Said he'd flayed Tecumseh himself. Told Ma all this, that he'd been the one, not Colonel Johnson, who'd shot Tecumseh down. Well, that could have been so, as far as she knew. I know that strop hurt so bad, it might well have come off a warrior chief.

Once he whipped me, though, Ma got us out of there, and carried me away. She settled at another garrison and did washing and mending. And then when the Seminole campaigns drew some regiments down to the Florida swamps, I was just big enough to do some camp errands. So rather than go to the priests' school with Indian tykes, I stowed away with a company of garrison soldiers who went clear down to Florida. By boats and ships, then by marches, and by dugout canoes in those swamps. Ended up with Col. Harney. I'll write more later about that flaming red devil, who was I guess the most vicious son of a bitch I'd ever have the honor to meet. Made all his men carry nooses, he did, to hang Indians, runaways, anybody he told them to.

It would be hard to judge who old Harney hated most: Negroes, Indians, or Irishmen. Got him in trouble sometimes. Even in an army of tyrants, he had a bad name.

Harney was Irish himself, but one like those I spoke of, the third generation in America, and so he was especially vicious to the immigrants. The littlest offense and he'd lay on with the flat of his saber. Very severe that is, if you've ever felt it. Once in Missouri he'd beaten a poor slave woman to death, it was said because she resisted him. But for his acquaintance with President Jackson, that would have been the end of his Army career.

I myself saw enough to make me believe the rumor about that poor slave woman. In the swamps our soldiers often caught Indian women and girls. Harney had a special lust for any dark-skinned damsels, and the power to do with them as he pleased. And sure he would demonstrate the contempt he had for Indians.

There was one morning outside his tent the awful sight of a naked Indian girl, bruised all over. Her mouth and cunt were bloody and fly-blowed. She had been strung up unconscious by her thumbs from a tree limb.

Being as we were in conflict with Indians, the soldiers passed many a fearful night, near smoky campfires to baffle the plagues of mosquitoes and listening for splashes and rustlings out in the darkness, whispering of the stealth and the murderous skills of the savages. The cunning of the Seminole Osceola put me in mind of legends I'd heard of Chief Tecumseh up north. Already at that age I'd gotten good at cadging at least one dram of a soldier's daily rum or whiskey ration. One night I got giddy on it and started telling some of the soldiers how I had used to get lashed with a razor strop made of what but Chief Tecumseh's own hide. Plied for more fact by those side-squinting soldiers, I told them the truth as I knew it, that my father had killed and flayed Tecumseh. Thereupon an old veteran, a sergeant, winked at me and asked, "Would ye mind tellin' to me, Quinn lad, how come I never heard that the great chief was killed by somebody named Quinn, which I should have, as I was in that battle?" "Well, see, Sergeant," said I, too besotted or slow to think it out, "my father's name wasn't Quinn." The laughter that rose up, I was afraid it would attract every Seminole that lurked in the Everglades. And when he asked me what *was* my father's name if not Quinn, I was embarrassed bad, wishing I'd never said anything, for how could I say to a circle of rogues like them that I didn't know my own father's name? I thought as fast as I could. I remembered the jingle I'd heard in Michigan:

> *Rumsey dumsey! Rumsey dumsey!*
> *Richard Johnson killed Tecumsey!*

And I said, "My father's name was Johnson." For all I knew of it, that was as good a guess as any.

The sergeant's eyes gleamed like a devil's then, and he sucked the stem of his dudeen pipe twice before saying in a tone of theatrical lewdness, "Oho, then! So 'twas Colonel Johnson that knocked up Quinn the washerwoman! Ha! An old mystery resolved! Well, lad, if . . ."

They say I attacked him then, though I don't remember just what I did. A hellish light flared in my head. Later I was wakened by one of those maniac swampfowl calls and found myself alone, lying near the campfire embers with my face in my own puke and drool, and daybreak just beginning to pale the swamp.

I hoped that would be the end of it. But the next evening I was summoned to another gathering at the same campfire. The sergeant sat there with his dram, and as far as I could see, my assault had not left a mark on him. Beside him, one on each side, sat a pair of veterans, a private and a corporal who were the oldest soldiers in Harney's unit. There also was a young private who hadn't sat in the group the night before.

"Lad," the sergeant began, "ye jumped on me last night like a rabid bobcat, set to kill. Now I want ye t' say y'r sorry for that."

That did get me hot again. "By God never!" said I. "You insulted my poor faraway mother, and if I could get a sword I'd put it through your guts!"

"Only if I allowed it, and I'd not," he said. "Rather, I make you a gents' bargain right here and now: Apologize to me, and I'll apologize to you about what I said. And then you and me, we'll drink to that. I shall provide th' rum. And more than just a dram. I've on hand here more rum than ye can hold. I should be intrigued t' see how much it'd take to slake y'r thirst, Quinn lad. Not much, I'll wager, as one little dram turned ye into a banshee last evenin'. I thought Irishmen could hold it better, but o' course, y'r not really no Irish *man* yet."

They all laughed. They were having a lark at my expense, and I knew that whether I accepted or not, whichever way it went I would be their goat. Maybe I should say their kid.

So then we traded our apologies. I shook his rough and filthy hand, and accepted the cup of grog he handed me over the fire. In a still moment as we sipped and nodded, looking into each other's eyes, I recall there were two cries I heard not far away in the night. One was some sort of owl, sounding like a child talking in a foreign language. The other was a girl's voice sobbing and protesting pain. I knew, we all knew, it came from the tent of old Horny Harney, our commander. He had in there a waif of a Seminole girl the scouts had drug in from a fish camp, she being not more than a year or so above my age. To be plain about it, Harney was ravishing a child. Again. It was right unsettling to glance about at the faces of the soldiers around our fire, all of them knowing what their "superior" was up to, and sure I suspect every bedamned one of them both condemning and envying him at once. I had seen the worst of his men go after his leavings. I had seen them drag off some half-dead girl and line up to get on her.

But the sergeant and the newcomers to our fire circle plainly had an issue with me, and I'd been summoned for that. The sergeant forthwith turned to the toothless corporal beside him, who resembled a twisted length of beef jerky, and said to him:

"Mister Barton, this fine lad regaled us all with a yarn last evenin' that I thought would prick up y'r ears, since you was at the place and time that it happent. Quinn, lad, tell Corporal Barton here about that razor strop y'r pa had. Corporal Barton, y'see, lad, was there in Colonel Johnson's Mounted Kentucky Rifles at the battle where Tecumsey was kilt and skinned."

The grog wasn't diluted hardly at all, and I was half sotted even before I started retelling the story. When I'd finished, the old corporal and the other two were laughing and tilting their heads toward each other. The old corporal said to me, then:

"M'boy, listen. Of all the soldiers in that battle, I reckon half went home with strips o' redskin hide they peeled off the dead Injens lyin' about. And I further reckon that about every one of them soldiers bragged at home that his trophy come right off Chief Tecumsey hisself. They must have been an acre o' skin carried off that bloody place. As big as ol' Chief Tecumsey was, he wan't *that* big! Here by me sits Private Grainer, who was in that battle, too. He used to wear a hatband, didn't ye, Lloyd, that he believed was a strip off the chief's thigh. He bought it off one of Johnson's lieutenants for a month's wages. Lieutenant swore that it was off the chief."

The man named Grainer nodded, sneered, said: "Later I heard that popinjay lieutenant brag all drunk that he'd made four hunnerd dollars off selling the skin of one dead Injen to 'bout forty innocent soldiers like me who'd not got near where th' action was at." He spat into the fire and wiped his nose on his shirt cuff, which from the looks of it had been his snotrag since the War of 1812.

Corporal Barton said, "Lloyd meant to go home and show off his Tecumsey hatband, but all he could claim was, it was *some* mis'ble savage kilt that day. Right, Lloyd?"

"I admit. Hell, I could of said it was Tecumsey. Who'd a knowed? But I never was no liar, so I didn't."

My head by then was bullroaring from the grog, but I was sensible enough to see that the only grand myth I'd ever had a hand on had been yanked out from under me.

With the insult to my Ma still rankling down in me, that made me feel lowly and glum, instead of the way liquorous spirits are supposed to make one feel. It was just then that the young private on the other side of the fire, maybe eighteen years with a red, round face and a pouty underlip that stuck out as far as his ears, pointed at me with his grog cup and said:

"Boy, y' ain't the only one ever whupped with a Tecumsey hide. My Pa come home from that same battle with a long brown strip o' leather like that, he glued it on one side of a cutoff oar blade, an' when he paddled us with it, he'd always tell us it was Tecumsey's Vengeance, so as no generation of palefaces would ever fergit how mad he was at us all. Well, I used t' believe Tecumsey's skin had stung mine, just like you thought, till Lloyd and Corporal Barton told me the truth. Fact is, the Shawnee themselves, after they got tamed, always said old Chief Tecumsey never got skinned nohow, on account o' his braves carried his body off the battleground before the skinnin' started! It just shows, anybody'll lie to ye, even your own kin, to biggen 'emself in a war story. But stories like them git found out."

My head was spinning and roaring so much by then that I wouldn't have been able to reply even if I could have thought of what to say, and the last thing I remember of that evening was him saying that he aimed to cut the whole hide off of some Seminole chief, but if he didn't get to, he'd take home any old piece of leather, even raccoon or alligator, or one of those Indian wenches Harney hung out to dry in the mornings, or if nothing else he'd skin an Irish camp boy and take the pelt home as a trophy from this goddamned swamp war.

Well, menacing as that threat was, it just managed to hang in my memory. But the rest is, mercifully, oblivion. I say "mercifully" because, upon waking from my rum stupor sometime before daylight in the bilge of a pirogue, I hurt so badly at both ends that I knew that those authorities on the flaying of Tecumseh had, one or all, used a besotted camp boy as shamefully as they'd have used a girlchild of the Seminoles and Mikosukees. It is one of the hazards of being a camp boy, and a good reason for a lad not to get fond of liquor. But I am fond of liquor, I'll admit that. I have a weakness for it.

Well, that was a tale of glory from the Seminole War!

I do mean to keep a journal in Mexico. A journal is supposed to tell of a day at a time. Jour in French is Day. But I wanted to write about

myself before the beginning of my diary, and what I just wrote, that was it. So I have begun to write of myself, instead of just writing for illiterate soldiers. Sure and that's worth doing, too!

Best things I know are writing and drawing. I'd as soon have a big, new piece of paper as a dram. Ma always saw to it I had a pencil. I drew before I could write. I'm content when I have a pen or pencil, or a stick of charcoal in my hand, and I practice and copy good writing and drawing. I gather up the newspapers and magazines that the officers have finished, and I study them, hoping I can learn how to tell stories so you can hear what people say to each other, with the quotation marks. I found stories by someone named E. A. Poe in newspapers and magazines. I would like to be able to write as he does so that a reader sees a picture in his mind instead of the letters and words on the page.

It seems that Mr. Poe doesn't illustrate his own stories. I expect I can do that, if I keep practicing. To go with what I wrote here's a pencil portrait of old Corporal Barton.

This Army soon loads on ships here at New Orleans to be transported to the Texas Coast. Gen. Zachary Taylor will command. The amount of equipment going onto the sailing ships and steamers is past imagining. The Seminole War was little compared with this.

What I'll miss of New Orleans is there are books and papers and magazines here from everywhere. Most of what I know about this Army going to Mexico I read in the newspapers. One thing is, not everybody agrees it's a good thing to do. But I guess a President can start a war if he wants to.

Now that I look this over, I think my Ma would be proud that she made me learn to read and write. Sure and I ought to let her see how good I've got at it. I should also let her know what I've been doing since I ran off from Michigan.

I think I should write her a letter, maybe copy some from this, but leave out parts that might vex her. I'll send it to the last place she was in Michigan. The Army up there should be able to find her. If she's still alive. If she's still around the Army.

Writing this has felt like a Confession. Confession is necessary for the soul. I'll feel better if I write to her. I should have a long time ago. I guess I was afraid she'd be too mad that I ran off.

A body does owe his Ma that much, the news that he's still alive. What good is writing if it doesn't tell somebody what they'd want to know?

PADRAIC QUINN
New Orleans

CHAPTER II

Corpus Christi Bay Nueces River ✳ Sept. 1845

Padraic quinn, beginning my diary—
This camp is Purgatory: sand, wind, bracky water. We're on a
desolation of grit and grass. Rancid pork bacon and wormy biscuit to
eat, bowels boiling, even seagulls shit more solid than we do.

I thought Florida was a prickly, vermin-ridden Inferno. At least it
had some shade! Not a tree or bush here from one horizon to the other.
The drill field is about two hundred acres. When the sun shines the
field is like a hot skillet.

Officers here as bad as Old Harney, but in a different way: fresh from
West Point, imagine themselves Napoleons. To them, soldiering means
strutting. Drill all day, every day. They're like shepherd dogs yapping to
make their herds of soldiers turn this way and that. They go berserk if
they see a food stain on a soldier's coat, and will punish him all day for
it. Sloppiest soldier in the whole army is Gen. Zachary Taylor, but of
course they can't punish their commander.

Taylor a famous old Indian fighter, looks like the town drunk,
dresses like a trail drifter. Nickname is Old Rough & Ready.

Fronting the drill field the camp is rows of little white tents, supply,
medical, mess tents, corrals, and cannon parks. I myself camp under a
broken wagon with about ten thousand bugs and ants.

Corpus Christi Bay
Army of the Observation Camp Nueces R. ✴ *Sept. 1845*

I RAN AN errand today that made me a good acquaintance among the officers, one who treats me like a real person. 4th Infantry, a lieutenant named Sam Grant. We talked about the newspapers, which he reads every free moment. I asked him to save me the one he was reading and he seemed pleased a camp boy could read. I told him how I copy the drawings from the papers and that surprised him, too. His real name is Ulysses, and I ventured how I could see why he preferred being called Sam. That made him laugh, which he doesn't do much. Talked to me like I was a regular adult, said he hopes no war really comes of this because we have no business down here provoking Mexicans in their own place. Most of the young lieutenants act like they can't wait for it to start. Not many dare say what he said about it.

He's somber, not much polish. Handsome when he does smile. Has a fiancée he means to marry soon as this is over. Had a miniature of her in a locket, a very pretty lady.

I expect I'd like to draw a picture of him. If I can look at a face awhile, I remember it well enough to do a good likeness from memory.

He is from Ohio, son of a farmer, sure not fancy like so many of the West Pointers. Sure and a body can see he doesn't care much for prancers and popinjays.

There in the 4th Infantry camp I saw a famed fellow I remember from the Seminole campaign. An Irishman he is, and sure he's a one for us to have pride in, a true legend for bravery.

Sergeant Major Maurice Maloney is the man, but no one dares to call him Maurice. He wants to be called Mick. That's a name the West Pointers call all Irishmen to slur them with, but the Sgt. insists on being called that. He says any man ought to be proud to be a Mick, especially in the Army, where the business is fighting. He was Limerick-born, and calls himself living proof that a native Mick can earn rank even in this bigot Army, if he's soldier enough.

Mick Maloney claims to be the highest-ranking Irish-born noncommissioned officer in the whole U.S. Army, and Lt. Grant says he believes that's so. Lieutenant Grant admires him. The lieutenant is no bigot, and I think really likes Irishmen, so he deems Mick Maloney to be a good example for the other immigrants.

Frankly, they need all the morale they can get, for the officers belittle and mortify them without mercy.

Mick Maloney is a giant, red-faced, bright-eyed. I never saw any man sweat so. Seems to be either jolly or fierce, nothing in between. I heard him harangue a whole company, said "Stand tall, goddamn ye! It's no wonder them officers look down on ye! If y'r backbones were as stiff as y'r fondlecocks are all night, they'd have to look up at ye Irishmen!"

I was a good part of the whole day at the 4th Infantry's camp, watching the sergeant, much in awe. I hoped he might recognize me, but he didn't seem to, even though he saw me. Well, though, it's more than three years since I saw him in Florida, and sure I reckon I don't look like the urchin I was then. Maybe a foot taller now. And sure I was no more important to him than a gnat, so why would he remember me?

But he saw a Lt. talking to me today, so maybe he'll think I'm at least somebody. I'd sure like him to, being a fellow Irish. Sure and he could guide me up as a man fit to soldier.

After today I've got Lieutenant Grant and Sgt. Maloney much in mind. Really not the same kinds of men, but both braced me up and I'm glad I went over to the 4th Inf. Compared with Mick Maloney, the Lt. looks like a boy. Small wonder; he's maybe ten years older than I am. He was only 17 when he went to West Point, he said. The sgt. appears to be near 40, been in the Army 12 years or so. To put it elsewise, the Lt. could be my older brother, while the Sgt. Major could be my father.

Faith, and that would be fine family, it would. Except that the Lt. is a Scot, not Irish like me and the Sergeant.

Mr. Grant's face is so clear in my mind, I ought to start a sketch of him. Gives me a pleasure, drawing faces of people I like. It's as if I am in their company while I draw them. When I draw or write, I'm not so lonesome.

Corpus Christi Bay Nueces River Camp ✳ *Sept. 30, 1847*

WELL, I HAD never thought people could do things like this to other people, not on purpose! Their excuse for it is they've got to keep disci-

pline. What it seems like to me is they enjoy punishing. The more humiliating it is, the better. Here are a few of their favorite cruelties I've seen here already.

Flogging. Saw plenty of that under Col. Harney, but usually for serious causes. These West Pointers do it for hardly any reason at all.

Barrelheading. Make a soldier stand on a barrel all day in the sun. If he faints they throw water on him and make him get back up. For anything, even so little as stepping off wrong in drill, or for not having brass polished bright enough.

The Horse. Put a man a-straddle of a narrow rail with irons on his feet, all day long. Maybe for not saluting a lieutenant properly.

Buck-and-Gag. Set a man on rocky ground bound up hand and foot with a pole passed over his elbows and under his knees, and a stick tied between his teeth, leave him there all day rain or shine. A man can scarcely breathe scrunched down like that.

It's plain to see that the soldiers who bear most of this are the immigrants. Irish Catholics especially. The officers call them "Mick apes" and "cod eaters," and "nun fuckers," and "catamites."

The worst officers for this kind of sport are the southern dandies. It's like they don't have their negroes here to punish, so they take it out on the Catholics, mostly the Irish. I don't quite see how this makes for good soldiers.

Corpus Christi Bay Nueces R. Camp ✳ Oct. 17, 1845

A GRAND PARADE and a showing-off was staged for the Inspector-General, & sure it was impressive. Rank and file marched and maneuvered for hours, brass bands and fifes and drums. Cavalry troops swooping and circling, yelling, waving sabers, raising so much dust they all but vanished in it. Then the artillery, the "flying batteries," dashed about as nimble as the cavalry itself, wheeling hither and yon, unlimbering in minutes and shooting off volleys and salvos. Then hitched up again to race around and repeat the performance in another part of the field. If an army was ever ready for action in the field, this one appears to be it. One must admit the results of the training here are plain to see. After a show like this, the force of a modern campaign is so evident, it can make one's legs feel weak.

Every bit that amazing, I beheld something I never thought I'd see. It was about Gen. Taylor. It's the talk of the whole Army now. I saw it from as close as 30 or 40 paces. I was on an errand for a lieutenant when Gen. Taylor rode by on his nag "Old Whitey." I angled over to get a close look at him. Just then there came some fierce and profane yelling, uncommonly shrill and furious. A company of infantry stood there, all wavery in the sunheat. Two soldiers lay on the ground where they had fainted from standing at Attention in the heat.

The general rode to a place where a lieutenant was screaming, real tantrum screaming, at a big lout of an Irishman, one I took to be just fresh over from the Old Country. This private was scowling red-faced at the lieutenant, a-hulking with his chin jutted forward, holding his musket at a slant in his left hand with its butt on the ground. The poor oaf was standing a few yards from the rest of the company, which was at Attention but all watching this scolding wary-like. When General Taylor rode upon that scene, his shadow fell over the lieutenant, who turned and saw him, and saluted. I was still catching up and too far yet to hear all their hubbub, but the gist was, that lieutenant was complaining that the private wouldn't obey his order of drill. Sure and it's no wonder, for the lieutenant has one of those southern accents that sound like a jew's harp. Some lieutenants from nearby companies were strutting over, likely hoping to be noticed by the general. That seems to be the real day-to-day ambition of these West Pointers, is to have Gen. Taylor notice that they exist. I think some of these Peacocks might just perish outright if Old Rough & Ready didn't nod their way once a week or so.

General Taylor swung down from his saddle just as I caught up, and he strode up in front of the poor brute, declaring, "You, soldier, you will obey any order you are given!"—at the same moment grabbing the soldier's left ear with his right hand, one of those humiliating liberties the officers are wont to take with soldiers to impress their authority on them. It is really painful, as I can say from my own experience, having often felt as if my own ears were being yanked out by their roots.

Thereupon came the spectacle that is already become a legend in the rank and file:

The Irishman blew up out of his sullen humiliation with a great rising blow of his fist, which struck the general so hard under his jaw that his boots left the ground, and he landed on his backside in a flurry of dusty sand.

Yes, I saw that with my own eyes, close by. What other sight could have been so stunning! All the dandy officers within sight of it froze for an instant, and soldiers groaned.

Then the officers recovered from their paralysis with shouts and curses. Most all drew their swords in the same instant. There were so many blades shining in the sun I'd have sworn that every lieutenant must have had three hands, with a sword in each hand. All of them were poised as if to run the red-faced Irishman through, in punishment of his unthinkable crime against authority. He turned like a bewildered beast, his left ear all bloody, where the general's talons ripped it when he was sent a-flying. I waited for them to skewer him. A growl came from the ranked soldiers of the company, who surely sensed his jeopardy. I felt that some of them might jump out and kill any lieutenant who would have taken the sword to their fellow Irishman. There is about that much hate built up in this Army.

Gen. Taylor, amazingly, after such a blow, was still conscious! He clambered to his feet. He stood swaying, examining his jaw with one hand. Then he yelled at the lieutenants, "No, damn you all! Harm that man and I'll have your guts for garters!" It was several breaths gone by before all those officers seemed to hear him. They turned from the soldier to look at the general, all with their mouths hanging open. Gen. Taylor said, "Leave that man alone. I reckon he didn't obey your order because he just couldn't understand you screaming at him like a parrot. Leave him alone! He'll make a good soldier, a man who can hit like that."

Then Old Rough & Ready dusted off his sleeves and his seat, and got back up on his nag, and rode off to wherever he'd been going to.

Soldiers in this camp are talking more about the General's fall and rise than about anything else.

As I was a witness, I enjoy a certain popularity I'm not used to having. Another important person is that Irish soldier with his bloody left ear and his swollen right fist, who is beginning to understand it's a miracle that he's still alive. And many are a-wishing that the officers of this army were more like Old Rough & Ready than like the little Napoleons they are.

Well, they can scoff at me for thinking I was ever whipped by a piece of Chief Tecumseh's hide. But when this thing today gets to be a legend, by the holy fist of Saint Patrick, they can't say I'm giving them blarney! I know what I saw! And scary though it was then, I reckon I'll enjoy remembering it, by and by.

Nueces River camp, Corpus Christi ✳ *March 7, 1846*

THE ARMY'S READY to march for the Rio Grande. Going southward. Why couldn't we have headed south five months ago? That ungodly winter might have been a little milder down there. I scarcely remember a night we didn't lie shivering in rain or sleet and every man dribbling snot and hacking his lungs up. Half the Army, any day, unfit for duty. But no duty possible anyway for the camp was usually knee-deep in floods and icy puddles. So, now that it's warming up, we'll march south.

That wretchedness drowned the last of anybody's civility and respect. We're suffering an epidemic of sullenness. There's hardly an Irish soldier I know of who wouldn't kill his lieutenant and light out from this Army if he thought he could get by with it.

Wagons mostly loaded, & some already on the road down the coast. The vendors' slum, the laundresses, bootleggers, and all those, all breaking camp, too. "Little America," it's called. Also known as the "Whores' Nest." Soldiers who were daring enough to sneak out of camp and go there mostly added clap and crabs to their ailments. Only thing that went on unabated all winter was punishment.

Those awful months of inactivity could have been a fine good time for me, to read and write and practice sketching. But there was seldom a day dry enough or when I wasn't too shivery to put pencil to paper.

One hopeful thing is, it's hard to imagine anyplace we're going to that could be as bad as this Nueces River camp. We don't mind turning our back on this!

On the other hand, from here to the Rio Grande is all country the Mexicans say is not Texas but Mexico. Once we're on that side of the Nueces, we're provoking. According to the newspapers, that's President Polk's aim. Lt. Grant shared his *New York Herald* with me. He said the newspapers' call for war makes him have to grind his teeth. Confessed that he wishes he had the moral grit to resign his commission and go home.

But, he *is* a West Pointer! If that place teaches them anything besides strutting, it's that birds of a feather must indeed flock together.

Sure and he'll do what the President wants, even if he thinks it's wrong. That's what soldiering is, and it's one thing that makes me wonder about my ambition to soldier.

But I'm merely an ignorant camp boy, and should I even dare weigh such big matters? Should a flea on a dog's rump say what the dog ought to do?

I reckon if I didn't sit alone and write, I'd never even ponder such things.

The one thing wrong with writing that I can see is, it makes you think.

CHAPTER III

Fort Texas, on Rio Grande R. ✳ *March 2, 1846*

DAY BEGINS WITH the bugles here in camp. Then we hear a very different music, the bells of the Catholic churches in Matamoros, just across the river. I wish I could write well enough to compare the different feelings those two sounds set up in my soul. I see in the faces of Irish soldiers a kind of troubled longing which must be like what I feel. Bugles and bells. Arms and faith. All those churches are Catholic.

Well, we are all just laborers now. Moving dirt to make the fort. Rest of the time it's drill and maneuvers and target practice. No rest. The West Point officers treat the soldiers like slaves. Camp and corrals around the fort, what used to be Mexican cornfields. Town and fort in gun range of each other across the river. Mexican girls bathe naked in plain sight over there. Our soldiers can hardly keep their eyeballs in their heads.

Also over there is a big portion of the Mexican Army, digging in. I am setting myself up for business, running errands and doing letter writing. Paper hard to get. My diary so far is a wad of sheets and scraps, tied with twine.

Fort Texas, Rio Grande R. ✳ *March 5, 1846*

GOOD CLEAN PAPER to write and draw on is hard to come by here. Sutlers and camp followers, hucksters and bootleggers are already setting up around the fort & you can buy about anything, but not decent paper.

Part of my diary and a few drawings got ruined by a rain leak. Everything in ink faded and spread. That did get me low in spirits. Guess I'll rewrite what I can read or remember of it.

I quit lodging in the soldiers' tents. If you're in there with them, they have you do the chores free. And they pick on a boy where they'd be more careful about picking on each other. Sometimes you get fondled in the dark. So I found a hollow between dirt piles banked against the fort's wall, on the river side, and here I've rigged up a canvas roof over willow sticks, and moved in. I dug niches into the dirt to put my papers in, and one to hold a candle. It's better than a tent when the wind is cold.

But it did leak the first heavy rain. I think I have it fixed now so that won't happen again.

The Mexican Army and Gen. Taylor's Army strut around on the two sides of the river, marching, maneuvering, like trying to scare each other. They might not be doing that very well but they're scaring me.

Ft. Texas on R. Grande ✴ March 19, 1846

FORT ALMOST DONE, walls 15 ft. thick. Bomb shelters dug inside.

Company K of the 5th Inf. has Michigan men in it mostly, so I went to their camp to look them over for familiar faces. Also to scout up more errand work. Capts. Chapman and Merrill were names I remembered, but never saw them in Michigan that I remember. Both were already drunk at noon today!

Many of their men are Irish, some of them veterans of the British Army before they came to America by way of Canada.

One of those fellows I got drawn to by hearing him laugh. I heard it among the tents, and had to go see who would have a laugh like that, that could make you feel good just by hearing it. I went over and there was sure the finest-looking man I think I ever saw in this Army, a big Irishman, looked hard as oak, broad white brow and dark curly hair. About a squad of men were laughing at whatever he'd been saying. My thought was, I would wish to draw that man just as he looks, but I doubt I'm artist enough to come near it! He saw me gaping at him and leaned toward me and pointed, and said, "Lad, tell me y'r not my own son, for I left wee Johnny in Galway! Come tell me who y' be!" I felt he wasn't trifling with me, for he'd gone somber as one who's seen a ghost.

Here it is about him. John Riley is his name. Told me he joined the bedamned British Army a dozen years ago, so his family wouldn't starve in the famine. Learned gunnery, was in some scraps in parts of the Empire, was sent to Canada and mustered out a sergeant. Loaded Great Lakes ships with lumber, sent money home to Ireland for to raise his son, whose mother had died. That's the son he'd thought I favored. He meant to save up and buy his boy passage to come to America. When the U.S. Army sent recruiters to sign up men for President Polk's war plan, Mister Riley went and talked to one, told him he had been a British gunner & a sergeant. The recruiter led him to believe that a man of his abilities was sure to gain that rank at least, especially in artillery. Instead, he's a private in Infantry.

I stayed awhile. Listened to those Irishmen grumble how they'd been duped, how they'll never get up to their former ranks in this Protestant army, how they're humiliated and tortured by West Point coxcombs who have never lifted anything heavier than a teacup.

I heard them mutter about that feeling I'd had, about the church-bells and cantatas we hear across the river. Why were they down here menacing a country of their own religion, some were asking. It was close to mutiny the way they were talking, and plainly that Riley fellow was the center of their whole persuasion. For a man who laughs like an archangel, he is more like a powder keg with a fuse burning to it. I could see that they all were watching each other's eyes and listening to who said what. Any soldier sure might take such talk to the captains, with names, and there would have to be discipline of the hardest kind. Those Irishmen all looked to Private Riley as if he was their leader, not those captains, not Old General Rough & Ready Taylor.

Well, I came away troubled, but I have got that man's face and his laughter in me. I will be for trying to draw what I've seen, for I get a strong instinct, somehow, that something's going to happen to him. He seems like a magnet to the Irish soldiers, not just of his company but the whole 5th Regt. Any officer would envy the kind of admiration he gets.

Pvt. Riley is handsome, but not in a pretty way. Has a high, broad brow, a proud bearing. A look in his eye like an eagle, but they'll go merry in an instant, too. It's plain he's lived a hard life, but it's left no coarseness in his face, nor any nastiness in his manner. By his complexion and blue eyes you'd say he should be a redhead, but his hair is almost black. Long and curly. I guess I might sound like a poet trying to praise someone he loves, but no, I'm just trying to reckon out what it is about him. I think too much.

Well, sure and he won my heart a bit when he took me for his son. I will say he makes me proud to be Irish, and I would fancy sometime becoming such a man and a soldier. Sure and I'd rather have had a man like this as my sire than the unknown scoundrel who was. I expect I'd have a father yet, if he'd been someone like this.

Two kinds of soldiers I've noticed, those who just try to serve out their time without ever getting noticed, for getting noticed often means getting hooked out for punishment or real bad duty. Then there's the kind who want to be esteemed as good soldiers because soldiering is their trade and they're proud men. Pvt. Riley and those around him are such men, I believe. They believe promotion in rank is their due. I heard them doubting they'll ever get their due in this Army where all the officers are rabid against Catholics. I could sense mutiny. Maybe that's why I felt he's important. I'd better not let anybody see what I've written here.

Fort Texas, Rio Grande * March 22, 1846

WAS OVER TO 5th Infantry again. Got newspapers from Lt. Grant.

That Private John Riley of K Company sure has given me a lift in my spirits. He's the one who said I favor his boy over in Ireland, and by heaven he treats me as kindly as if it were so. Invites me to sit nearby to him at the fire, and asks my opinion of things just as if I were a man. Asks me to talk of the Swamp War sometimes, for him and those of his company who weren't in it. Sure and he makes me feel like I'm a veteran myself, and doesn't mock me the way Harney's dragoons always did. John Riley would not let me get drunk and buggered like they did.

He himself doesn't drink, though he's Irish in every other regard. He knows I do, but I don't do it when I go to visit him. I know he'd likely wean me of it, if I was just in his company only. His own men do taste the spirits, and he doesn't condemn them for it, but when they're gathered with him, for whatever occasion, the drinking is but a wee part of it. Whether he's got them in a debating match or a boxing match or wrestling or footraces, they have a good time liquor or no.

And those debates are really something, I mean to say! Those educated lieutenants and captains, up in their area, don't have any better sense of the world, or of our peculiar situation in it, than John Riley and his immigrant soldiers have got. What he learns from the journals and papers, they get from him, in turn, and do they have their talks! When officers hear the voices and the laughing, and come around, why then his men all pretend like they're dumb as donkeys who never had a thought more interesting than a pot of ale, or how to keep a musket dry on a rainy night. As Mister Riley confided to me, the officers don't believe an Irishman can think, and would be alarmed to find out that one did.

Some of these fellows have soldiered in parts of the world that their West Point "superiors" have only read of in a geographical book. Mister Riley told me, they've been everyplace Marco Polo ever went, but since they didn't learn to read and write, they can only talk and sing. And he let them know that his young friend Paddy Quinn could write like a bard, and that I would write home to their families for them, and that if they couldn't afford the few pennies for my service, he'd pay it himself. He tells them, I don't make any more soldier's pay than the rest of you, but I don't drink my wages away, and one thing I will pay for is a letter home!

So he's helped my business. And even gave me a name for it. He said "Paddy, you are the amanuensis of Company K." He taught me what the word means, one who writes for others, a most important position in any field, and he taught me how to spell it.

And I told him, why, sir, I've been an amanuensis for several years, and didn't even know what I was!

So all those fine rough fellows around laughed and came to shake my hand, and I did feel bigger than I was accustomed to. Thanks to him.

Fort Texas on R. Grande ✳ *April 4, 1846*

A SENTRY EARLY this morning shot a deserter in the river trying to swim over to Matamoros. He went down and wasn't seen after he sank.

This is getting to be a problem for our Army. Several soldiers have left their units. Some have been seen swimming over and shot at but got away.

Hearsay is that the deserters are losing their heads over the Mexican girls who wash and swim naked over there in plain sight of our fort. There might be truth in that. I hear soldiers talking about that all the time. Hear them gibe each other about "climbing the flagpole" all night, which means stroking their cockstands. There has always been plenty of that in the tents, but never like this now.

Those girls and women might have something to do with it, but there are other causes. The meanness of the officers is one, sure it is. Maybe the main cause, though, is the church bells. This Army doesn't have one Catholic chaplain, even though near a half the soldiers are Catholic. Those people over in Matamoros are all Catholics. It was something I heard those soldiers murmuring about to Pvt. Riley, that maybe they're in the wrong army.

I made $3.28 last week writing letters home for soldiers, $1.03 in other errands. Best money for the effort though is in fetching liquor in from Little America. Of course this has to be done at night, and past sentries. I'm developing my skills at sneakery. Some of the things I learned from the Seminole War prove useful. But I know this could get me in real trouble. Made $4.05 smuggling bottles.

I determined one thing about Pvt. John Riley, that he may well be the only Irishman in 5th Regt. who doesn't imbibe. One reason may be he sends every penny he can send home to support his little boy in Ireland. The one he said I look like.

Across the river the Mexicans keep building emplacements for troops and guns outside the town, by the river, facing us. We see new earthworks when we get up in the mornings. Means they have the commonsense to work at night when it isn't so hot.

As for our defense, a moat around Fort Texas has been finished. Most of our cannon emplacements are dug in, guns covering Matamoros.

Many Mexican soldiers over there, sure and it's a bigger Army than ours here. But it's a town, and our place is a fort. Pvt. Riley said it angers him, seeing cannons pointed at a civilian town. He said he recalls that the English Redcoats went to Ireland and drove Irishmen out of their homes at gunpoint for the good of the landlords. And when he was a Redcoat, he had to aim guns at native villages in their own countries. That was when he decided not to reenlist as a Redcoat. Said he didn't mean to join the United States Army to go on being a damned Redcoat pointing guns at towns full of people.

But said he feels like a Redcoat again. But now without the sergeant's chevrons.

CHAPTER IV

Y OU HAVE BETTER luck than you know, *Señor Periodista*. I
have in me much of the knowledge you would like to obtain
about those *temas melancólicos* from the last war.

So it seems that you came and found me so that I might tell you
about the last battle. *Sí,* I can tell you that. I was among the doomed
cadets, *Los Niños Héroes,* in the Citadel. I can tell you of that day because, unlike some of them, I did not quite die there. Yes, I shall tell
you, perhaps, if you demonstrate proper respect, if you do not irritate
me with stupid *Yanqui* statements—and if you keep me from becoming too thirsty—I shall describe for you that day of wrath and shame.

But the reason I say you are lucky is because I know not only the last
day of that unholy war, I also know it from the first day—yes, even before the first day.

Your other realm of inquiry seems to be of the *San Patricios.* The
newspapers of your country, in that time, condemned them as vilest
traitors. And in particular Don Juan Riley, the more they spoke of him,
the more they relished the vitriol on their tongues. This is a trait I have
observed in you *Norteamericanos:* the more unspeakable you deem a
thing, the more you love to speak of it.

So, *Señor* the *Periodista,* let me tell you how fortunate you are to find
me, Agustin Juvero, the sawed-off hero. Now the surprise:

I can state in all truth that Don Juan Riley—*¡Viva Riley!*—came to abet the holy cause of the defense of Mexico in part because of me. I am personally a part of that great man's glorious history in my nation.

You are startled to hear that, no? I see in your face that you do not believe me, not at all. You do not even put your pencil to paper to write the most remarkable thing I have said, because you think that I made it up to enlarge myself in your story. *¡Oye!* The people of your country think Mexicans don't tell the truth, because what we say is so unlike the lies you tell yourselves. Or you believe, perhaps, that since *Yanquis* lie, everyone must be lying also.

I am making you angry. *Bueno, ¿y qué?* If I make you angry, maybe you will go away and leave me alone. I could bear that with ease. And then perhaps, as they do, another journalist will find his way to me, one who does believe me, and then the story will be in that journalist's name, not yours, and in his periodical, not yours. It is all the same to me, your story or another man's story, or no story at all. If no one believes me, no matter. Just as if you do believe me, and write the truth I tell you, that will do me no good, either, unless you pay me well for what I know and tell you. I will not have my legs restored to walk on, even if you write a good and true story.

¡Como! So you do want to listen? You do, eh? Is it worth a bottle of the best tequila to hear of my peculiar insights?

Then come back, *Señor,* with such a bottle. Also, *por favor,* go to the fruit seller in the street and get lemons. When you return, we will share the lemons. But if you want to drink tequila with me, you should buy a bottle for yourself, and we shall each drink our own.

Ah, you are back with tequila and lemons! *Gracias, Señor,* for this bribe. Here, in my satchel, I have a silver cup for each of us. On a *peregrinación,* one must be prepared.

I raise my cup to the memory of our great *compadre, Coronel* Riley. *¡Viva Riley!* Or will you, a *Yanqui,* drink to the worst traitor in all your historic memory? Worse even than Benedicto Arnold of your *guerra de independencia!* I see you are surprised that I know the name of *Señor* Arnold, eh? But in the military academy we studied the heroes, and the traitors, as well, of all nations. We took especial relish in reading of *Yan-*

qui traitors, for they troubled your armies. And the great Riley not only troubled your army, he did it in *our* cause. ¡*Viva!*

Señor, I shall tell you that true story of that Irishman and me, including a part of the story that only I know: an element of romantic love! The readers of your periodical will hunger for that part.

Prepare your little desk, then. What a clever device it is, with its little clamp to brace it to yourself. You must have devised that for yourself? Yours is a nation of such clever *mecánicos.*

Now, *Señor,* here is the way it was from the beginning. It was in Matamoros. One of the towns where I had lived when I was a boy. I had lived in many towns, for my father was an army officer before he was killed fighting your Texans. I was a boy living with my mother in a small house when your General Zachary Taylor arrived on the other bank of the Rio Grande—the Rio Bravo del Norte, we call it—to build his fort, to threaten us. We were angry and alarmed. We held that the Nueces River was the border between Mexico and Texas, and when your general crossed it and came down to the Rio Bravo, with cannons and wagons and regiments, what then could that be but another *Yanqui* invasion? Many of the people in Matamoros were refugees who fled ahead of your army when you burned their coastal village of El Fronton. My mother gave some of the refugees shelter in our house. It was crowded and difficult to care for so many.

They could not stay in our house long. When General Ampudia marched to Matamoros with his troops, he put his headquarters in our house because it gave a fine view of your fort.

Our house became headquarters. Thus I met General Ampudia, and the General Arista, and General Mejia. So many generals! General Ampudia took notice of me. He spoke of the military academy, and offered to arrange for me to go there as a cadet, if I were a good reader and a brave boy. I read for him from one of my schoolbooks to show him how well I could do that. I told him that I thought myself brave, but how does one know? The general told me there was a way to learn how brave. I remember, as he told me that, the general sat on a bench in our house, very splendid with gold and silver braid and epaulets on his dark blue coat, a man of much presence, and he leaned close to me with some kind of bright fire in his eyes, like a priest's eyes when he is doing sacra-

ments. He had silky mustaches, and a small beard, shaped like an ar-
rowhead, just on the point of his chin, and I must have been staring
right at his mouth as he told me how I could prove my courage, so that
no word would escape me.

What an intense and important memory it is, that moment when a
general of the army is speaking directly to a boy on the matter of
courage.

"*Niño,*" the general said to me, "you can do very good service for
Mexico, in this troubled time, if you are not afraid to go across the river
to the *Norteamericanos'* camp and their fort, like a secret messenger.
One your age could go safely near them, while a grown man, if he were
seen, might be shot or captured. Do you know the river and its shores
well?"

"I have lived here long enough," I told him.

He said: "Do you swim well?"

I told him I was a strong swimmer. It was true, then. Now I would
be no swimmer, no more than a piece of floating debris going where the
river took me, because of what your *Yanqui* soldiers did to me. Then,
though, I swam well. And I was able in boats, also.

I was excited by what the general was saying, but mystified. What
messages I would be taking to the *Yanqui* side I could not yet imagine.
And to whom would I give messages? And then General Ampudia
asked, "*Niño,* do you know why the government of the United States is
coming against Mexico? It is for two reasons, and you should understand them. First, they want land, to make new states where they can
own and sell slaves. They have a law that they cannot have slave states
north of a certain line. And their other reason is religion. That government is against the pope, and against the Catholicism of Mexico, the
true religion, against the Virgin Mother. Did you know those reasons?"

I had not understood why the *Yanquis* were invading. I told him that
I thought those to be bad reasons for them to hate us or come and
threaten us. The general agreed that those were very bad reasons. He
told me that many of the people of the United States also knew it was
wrong and were opposed to the president for invading Mexico. The
general knew quite well about your United States, eh, *Señor*? Then the
general went on and told me:

"Many of the soldiers on that side of the river, building that fort, about half of them perhaps, are Catholic soldiers. Many of them are new immigrants to the United States, from Ireland, and some from Germany. We believe that they would not want to come and invade a Catholic country, a country of their own sacred religion, if they thought about it very much at all.

"Therefore," said the general to me, looking straight into my eyes, "we want to make them think about it very much, very seriously. Before war actually begins, we must propagate in them a great reluctance to attack their fellow Catholics. If we can turn their minds thus, it might weaken their resolve to serve their officers, who are nearly all *herejes* and mockers of *La Santisima Virgen.* We would like to encourage them to desert that cause, which is not their own cause. Most of them are not even citizens of the United States! We expect it should not be difficult to entice them to desertion, if not mutiny, to come and live with us, even to fight for the peace and honor of Catholic Mexico! Here, *niño,*" the general said to me with great fervor, "here is the way you, and other brave boys like you, can help do that:

"On the march here from Mexico City, I wrote a broadside in English language, for the *Yanqui* soldiers to read. It implores them not to come and make war on people of their own faith. It reminds them of the old affection between Mexico and Ireland. It offers them pay, and land, and citizenship, if they come to us."

Señor Periodista, it was stirring and convincing, what General Ampudia told me, sitting on that bench in my mother's house. I could never forget it. I know not how it sounds to you, a *Gringo.*

The broadside was on a printing press at that moment, and thousands of copies were being made. I was to find boys in Matamoros who would want to help carry those leaflets across the river, where the soldiers could find them and read them. He said that we who delivered them would be paid in *centavos,* but also in honor and the gratitude of our country. Some of us who so served might be admitted to the *Colegio Militar.*

"There is some danger, a little," he said. He said *Yanqui* sentries might shoot, not knowing we were children. And if we were caught carrying such propaganda, we might expect to be whipped. But danger is a reasonable expectation in the patriotic service of one's country.

And so there you have that part of the story, *Señor.* You have yourself seen, I am sure, the leaflets, of which we delivered many thousands in enthusiastic and ingenious ways. Your General Zachary Taylor's army was not great in numbers. We estimated five or six thousand at that time, and a half of them were not United States citizens, but alien immigrants who were in your army because they could find no other work in your country due to the terrible prejudice against Irishmen and Catholics. From the walls of Matamoros we could see scores of those poor soldiers being punished on the parade ground by your Protestant West Point officers. It did seem reasonable to believe that we could reduce your army considerably with the appeal of words and truth. And the town of Matamoros itself set about enticing your soldiers across the Rio Bravo. Church bells, music, parades! And the usual religious processions moved in the north part of town into your soldiers' view. Nuns strolled, and the women of Matamoros, they never sang as much as they sang in those days, even though their hearts were dark with dread of the *Yanqui* army . . .

And what does this have to do with me and Don Juan Riley, you must wonder.

I shall answer that question, *Señor Periodista,* and tell you of our adventures as propagandists to the enemy. But at this time, I must get myself back onto the road of penitence. There are yet days of traveling on my knees. See, the old pilgrims crawl by us even as we sit and drink. *¡Vamonos!*

And you, too, should be on *your* knees, *Gringo.* You *Norteamericanos* all should come down here and crawl to Our Lady of Guadalupe to atone for your sins in that last war, before you dare to march against each other in this present one.

Now watch this, how nimbly I dismount from a bench!

PADRAIC QUINN'S DIARY

Fort Texas, Rio Grande ✳ *April 2, 1846*

I LEARNED THIS tonight: if you prowl at night, nothing is more scary than finding another prowler!

Sure and I'm a prowler. I live by errands, and some of them are wildcat errands. Soldiers are no saints, and they will want what they're not allowed to have. If they don't want to be shot by a sentry for going after it themselves, they'll send for it by an errand boy. And I dare go about in the night, for if caught, I'd not be shot as a deserter, for I'm not a soldier, just a camp boy. I smuggle liquor into camp, if I'm asked, and collect my pay, which might be in pennies, or in a dram of the contraband. There's my confession: sure I'm a bootlegger, in my own wee way.

A corporal sent me this evening to a bootlegger outside the camp. As I was returning, with two jugs muffled in sacking, edging through the willowbrake along where the river sentries are, damn if suddenly I wasn't face-to-face and not two arm's lengths from someone faint and light as a haunt! He was no bigger than I. Even with no moonlight, for it was foggy and cloudy, I saw that he was coming from the fort, mere yards from the pickets. Plainly a Mexican lad, in those cotton breeks & shirts they wear. He dropped something. Sure and I near strangled to keep from yelping aloud. Being sure he was Mexican, I backed off in case he'd be for carrying a knife at the least. It was awhile we stood looking at each other, and if his heart was pounding like mine, I should have heard it. Or the sentries should have. Just that heartpounding of mine, and the sound of the river water running, and some faint string-and-rattle music from the town beyond. You really hear keen when it's too dark to see much.

It was soon enough we both saw that each of us was too furtive to accost the other. He sort of raised his hand to his temple like a little salute, and began to edge away. He must have been too scared to pick up what he dropped. He vanished toward the river. After a while I started worrying more about the sentries than about him. I picked up what he had dropped. Just a cotton bag with a strap. Mostly empty, but some scraps and torn-off corners of paper in the bottom.

I can use a bag like that, so I kept it. Delivered the jugs to the corporal, who gave me not just ten cents, but a good sip from the contraband, for he said I looked very pale and needed some blood in my face.

I didn't mention the person I'd encountered down by the river, hardly knew what to say anyway. For all I know, the Mexicans themselves might be bootlegging.

Anyway, I know now that I am not the only one sneaking about an army fort, and I hope I don't come onto one that's got a cutthroat knife like the officers say Mexicans all do.

I can use this bag to tote bottles and contraband in. On the other hand, I could sure use it to make patches for sewing up my clothes. In the old times my Ma never let me be seen raggedy.

Fort Texas, R. Grande ✳ April 4

THAT DEARTH OF paper I have lamented, it's been relieved, by an unexpected deluge of good paper suddenly arriving in our camp, thanks be to the enemy, I guess I'd have to say.

I write this on the back of a document that showed up in thousands of copies. I bet every soldier has a copy. I got myself about fifty. Sure and I'll be for using every piece!

You can see what it is by turning over this page. It is a handsome pamphlet, all neat and well printed as a newspaper. It's written in grand English, adorned with signatures and seals and escutcheons. From what we've been told about Mexicans, one wouldn't think they could produce such an elegant thing. A body wouldn't think they could write so well, either. It is highflown language that makes a body get to thinking, "do something."

Sure and one would think the Mexican General who wrote it was reading the minds of our Catholic soldiers!

If I can gather another bundle of these, I'll bind them with twine and make me a diary book of some considerable thickness.

Turning this page over shows what that Mexican boy was delivering when we met in the dark by the riverbank.

THE COMMANDER-IN-CHIEF

OF THE MEXICAN ARMY TO THE SOLDIERS UNDER THE ORDERS

OF THE AMERICAN GENERAL TAYLOR:

Know ye: That the Government of the United States is committing repeated acts of barbarous aggression against the magnanimous Mexican nation; that the government which exists under the flag of the Stars is unworthy of the designation of Christian. The American Government is provoking to a rupture the war-like people to whom it belongs, President Polk boldly manifesting a desire to take possession, as he has already done Texas.

Now then, come with all confidence to the Mexican ranks, and I guar-

*antee to you, upon my honor, good treatment, and that all of your expense
shall be defrayed until your arrival in the beautiful capital of Mexico.*

*Irishmen, Germans, French, Poles, and individuals of other Catholic na-
tions! Separate yourselves from the Yankees, and do not contribute to defend
a robbery and usurpation which, be assured, the civilized nations of Europe
look upon with utmost indignation. Come, therefore, and array yourselves
under the tri-colored flag, in confidence that the God of Armies protects it,
and it will protect you, equally.*

> *General Pedro de Ampudia Francisco R. Moreno,*
> *adjutant of the Commander-in-Chief*
> *April 2, 1846*
> *Composed upon the Road to Matamoros*

Fort Texas Rio Grande ✳ April 6, 1846

FAITH, WHAT THAT Mexican boy smuggled in to our Irish soldiers, it was sure as intoxicating as what I had been bringing! And will
be for causing more trouble than any booze, I can see it coming.

I was around the 5th Infantry today, and I could see slips of paper
everywhere. Not that they were lying about loose in plain view, indeed
not. But every man seemed to have one about him, either taking it out
of a pocket or putting it slyly back in. And wherever a gaggle of soldiers
stood, or sat, there in the middle was someone with that sheet of paper
in his hands, reading or talking, in whispers or low-voiced, looking out
over his shoulder. You could just feel something in the air, all about the
place. Some of that was the usual bitter fury these Irish gents have in
them all the time, for the way the officers treat them, but this of the papers is a thing not so much sullen but like to make your hair raise up.

I kept my eye on Private Riley himself mostly. For as I said before, he
was the center of that company, regardless of rank. Today the man was
different from his usual demeanor, I mean he was scowling like a thun-
derstorm. Usually when a soldier's deep in the miseries, John Riley will
buck him up with some clever words and a warm hand on his arm. But
today he looked short-necked and thin-mouthed, and there was lightning in his eyes. I soon enough heard why. A West Point artillery Lt.
named Bragg, one of those southern slavemasters, hooked him out in

passing and called him to attention for not saluting him briskly enough, then proceeded to impugn the good soldier for the dastardly crime of being Irish-born, for having naught but snot and earwax in his Irish head, and for worshipping a Gilded Poobah in Rome instead of the proper Anglican God who rules in any civilized whiteman's Heaven. The harangue continued a half an hour, witnesses said, and in all that time Pvt. Riley stood at strict attention, not even moving his eyeballs in any response, until the lieutenant apparently grew hoarse and thirsty from his tirade, and having been unable to provoke one flicker of insubordination that would justify corporal punishment, strutted away to his own unit, which is reputed to be one of the unhappiest in the whole army, with him in charge of it.

I remember writing that Mister Riley seems like a keg of gunpowder with a lit fuse a-burning to it. There's power waiting in a keg of powder; who can calculate how much? What matters is the length of the fuse, and whether it gets snuffed out before it blows the powder. I reckon that Mr. Riley's fuse is long. I'm not sure why that is so, but I suspect it's because he's a long-seeing sort of a man. He said that he enlisted in the American Army with the long goal of attaining such rank of sergeant as he'd held in the Redcoats before, or even becoming an officer. He believes that should come if you're a competent soldier, and he holds him-

Lieutenant
Braxton Bragg,
U.S. Artillery, in his
usual mood.
Drawn in pencil
at Fort Texas April, 184
by P. Quinn

self to be such a one. Mister Riley does not get harassed quite so often as the average Irish soldier, for he's an exemplary soldier and seldom gives an opening, even to an officer looking for a body to torment. His comrades look to him to see whether he will suffer it or explode, and from what I hear, many would like to see him explode, as it would ignite themselves and give them release to their seething angers. He is doing the Army a service with his forbearance, I'd wager, but of course the officers haven't a notion that it's so. A few days ago, by what I hear, Mister Riley had quietly dissuaded some fellows from knifing Lieutenant Bragg some dark night. Two days later that same Bragg, not knowing that Pvt. Riley had likely saved his life, cursed him out as a Mick moron.

I've heard it said, some of the officers conspire to provoke good Irish soldiers like Pvt. Riley and Sgt. Maloney till they blow up. That would prove all Irish are bad as they say. It seems much of the endless drilling is little more than a means of tormenting the Sons of Eire that they've got at their mercy. How they come to hate us so much I don't know, but I guess any man has got to be able to look down on somebody, and we Irishmen have been given more chance than just about anybody to squint up into everybody else's nostrils. As I wrote when I first started up this diary, that's the curse of being Irish.

The way Riley is today might be on account of that Lt. Bragg who humiliated him so roundly. But that little printed sheet of paper from Mexico that he is keeping on his person, I suspect it is more on his mind than any particular West Pointer.

Ft. Texas, R. Grande * *April 9, 1846*

I HOPE NEVER again to see a man be burnt like a steer with a branding iron. I saw it today and once is too much for me.

He's an Irishman, what else? Three times before, he had been punished for drunkenness, made to stand all day on a barrelhead in the middle of the parade ground, and that had not cured him. Nothing cures us of it. Liquor is the only escape from our misery here that we can obtain, and of course the obtaining is easy. It's the business and the concern of most everyone here, meself included. The officers themselves are a lot of drunken jackanapes in their own right, but of course they never get punished for it. I've seen their own debauches.

The poor sot they branded is Hanley by name, a nice, droll fellow who is as foolish sober as when he's drunk. If you said Hanley is drunk, somebody could reply, How can you tell? His signature remark is, I'm thirsty clear down to my breeks. He first said it, and now it's in the lingo.

I delivered the bottle to Hanley last night. I rue my part in it. I expected he'd be lucky enough to have no more punishment than his usual shakes and aches, or, at worst, a day spent groaning and tottering on the barrelhead. But this morning he was too ruined to turn out. He was dragged to the drill field. A little fire was built, a branding iron heated red, and poor Hanley was held down to the dirt by one soldier on each limb. A soldier with near as many drunk offenses as Hanley himself was ordered to apply the iron to Hanley's forehead. When he balked at the deed, he was threatened with the same iron, and saw fit to comply.

Though I've been my whole life around soldiers, I can't fathom the deliberate inflicting of pain and mutilation on helpless people. These dandy officers, who profess to be the Army's gentlemen, are in general the most heartless class of people I have ever seen. Soldiers like Mister Riley, who formerly served in the British Army, complain that only American officers *torture* soldiers in the name of discipline. There was much harsh discipline in the British Army, but malicious torment was not done. Even Pvt. Morstadt, a veteran of Prussian service which is famously brutal, said Prussia didn't have many officers as vicious as these. The victims are just about all immigrants. The officers seem to hate them for having been born on Irish soil, as if it had been their choice to get born in the evil Green Isle, as I heard an officer call the Old Country. As for the branding:

The soldier was gingerly with the brand; he was weeping, and he made a quick touch on Hanley's brow with it, and jerked it back at the sound of Hanley's first scream. The lieutenant snatched the brand from him and knocked him a-sprawling. "Damn you, I'll show you how to mark a drunkard!" the lieutenant yelled, and he put his boot on Hanley's throat for to hold him still and pressed the glowing brand—HD for Habitual Drunkard—down hard as if to push it through his head, and O God but it hissed and smoked. Hanley thrashed so hard he upset two of the soldiers who were holding him down. I smelled the roast skin and burnt hair. The expression on that lieutenant's face was something like a demon. If I'd had a gun I'd have shot him dead, I do believe. There, I've put it in ink: a homicidal thought from my own head. And if a thought is as bad as its deed, here is the evidence that I would gladly have killed an officer of the United States Army. I looked across at the ranks of Irishmen in that company, all a-standing there with their muskets, and I was thinking, There you all stand letting him do that to your own countryman! Any one of you stout lads could break that popinjay's neck with your bare hands! Why do you just stand there?

I was thinking mutiny, plain enough. But no one did anything. Even John Riley stood there in the rank with his eyes aimed straight off at the Mexican horizon and not a hint on his face of what he was for a-thinking or a-feeling. That was what finally brought me down so low I began to cry and had to get away from there before I was seen at it. A good thing I wasn't a soldier in ranks. They had to stand there and see it & couldn't even turn their heads, for if they had, some little prancing fiend out of West Point would have branded them HT for head turner!

I needed to calm myself down after the branding. So I got around to finishing my portrait of Lt. Grant.

Lieutenant
U.S. "Sam" Grant
4th Infantry
Drawn in pencil
at Fort Texas,
April 1846 by P. Quinn

CHAPTER V

Monday April 13, 1846 ✳ *Fort Texas on the Rio Grande*

JOHN RILEY HIMSELF is gone! For me this is more important and more distressing than the absence of one private soldier ought to be. The most part of his company is worried and sullen. Some go about looking fierce and smug.

Captain Chapman of the 5th Infantry recorded Mister Riley's absence from muster this morning. The men already knew, by then. This afternoon Capt. Merrill told the assembled regiment that Pvt. Riley had left the camp yesterday morning with his permission to go to a Mass. There was a priest from Matamoros a-holding the Mass at a farm near here. The Captain signed Pvt. Riley's pass because of his steady good conduct. The day passed and he didn't return. It was cold and rainy all day and the men were out of their tents only for chores and mess. The rest of the day they stayed mostly in the tents, muttering and reading the Mexican leaflets. The officers and the Protestant soldiers, those who professed faith, went to services in the camp chapel. No Catholic soldiers go there.

The captain hasn't yet said Mister Riley deserted. He is said only to be missing. It could be that Mexicans waylaid him out there. But there is suspicion. Captains Merrill and Chapman have been calling in some of Mister Riley's messmates one at a time and questioning them. They come back and say they played ignorant. The captains asked them about the propaganda leaflets, and the soldiers pretended not to know about them. The captains must know that's not true, as those papers are everywhere in the camp.

I think the soldiers know all the truth of him leaving. They don't think he got lost or captured. They noticed that he didn't leave much of his kit in the tent when he went away. He took his Bible and Missal, as a body might well do on going to a Mass, but also took his pen and pencil and notebook, his spare underclothes, mess tin, canteen, and his whole issue of cartridges and gunflints. They say he had his blanket over his shoulders against the cold rain, so he must have hid all his gear under it. They won't say whether he told them if he would be back. But you can about see in their faces what they know. You can even see in their looks how they feel about him leaving. Some are glad for him, or envious, or resentful. Each man takes it his own way. But when the officers are about, you'd think every one's a card sharper. No sign.

As for me, I'm not for appreciating his absence, and I sure would like to see him back here where he belongs. But I reckon Mr. Riley doesn't think this is where he belongs.

Damn, but this upsets me something awful. It makes me have to think. If a man like him thinks it's wrong to be here, why would lesser ones stay?

Ft. Texas, R. Grande ✳ April 15, 1846

IT GROWS MORE dreadful here. Any day, some petty thing could start the cannons a-shooting.

Mexican Army reinforcements keep coming into Matamoros. They surely have us outnumbered considerably by now. They throw up new gun emplacements over there about every day. Priestly processions parade down with music and bless the guns. Some of their artillery is angled up and down the river to put us under threat of crossfire.

More desertions night and day. Those Mexican pamphlets made up many a mind. I think Pvt. Riley did, too. Several more men gone from the 5th.

To put fear into anyone who might think of going over the hill (I should say over the river), the officers are up to their old vicious discipline. Worse than when we were camped at the Nueces last winter. They will damn near kill a private with brutality for the littlest cause:

hanging by the thumbs, sword whipping, ride-the-rail, barrelheading, buck-and-gag. West Point must have a torture school. They don't seem to understand—the more torment, the more desertions. One private took so many punishments he gave up and killed himself yesterday with his own bayonet. He was buried in the same funeral with two men who had got sick and vomited to death.

I punched a hundred leaflets and stitched together a diary book, covered with oilcloth. Open it one way, it's my diary. Turn it over, it's a book of Mexican propaganda calling for Irish Catholics.

Well, I'm still here on this side of the river. But I thank their general for all this nice, white paper.

CHAPTER VI

Padraic Quinn's Diary

Ft. Texas, Rio Grande ✳ *Apr. 15, 1846*

I NEVER THOUGHT I would rue the day I took up the pen, but at this moment I regret, profoundly, that I did write a certain letter. I cringe when I consider the consequences of something so ordinary and well meant as a son dutifully writing a letter to his mother. I mailed it from New Orleans, before we sailed.

It was written from a guilty feeling that I had surely left her wondering if I was dead or alive. I had never written to her in the months of the Swamp War against the Seminole Indians. I had not written to tell her I was faring as well as might be expected of a camp boy in a coarse and brutal Army. I suppose that the sentiment was confessional, as much of my writing has been; I wrote to her to confess that I had been negligent in easing her apprehensions, and I tried to atone by composing one letter of considerable length and substance, a veritable history of my travels with the campaigning Army. I related as vividly as I could the dangers and discomforts of the Swamp War. I confess that perhaps I was showing off for her the facility of my improving penmanship, and the burgeoning erudition of my prose. In that letter I discoursed on all manner of topics, such matters as the mythical Tecumseh-skin strop, with which I had been disciplined, and the veterans' refuting thereof. I doubted it would surprise her that my sire had been a liar. I did not reveal to her of course the buggery our brave soldiers had inflicted on me when I was unconscious. But in the true confessional spirit I did tell her of my precocious fondness for liquid spirits. That seemed a proper thing for an Irish mater to concern herself with, if indeed she concerns herself with her son at all.

And it seems she did concern herself with me, much more than I expected, or desired. For, more promptly than I'd have expected my letter even to follow and find her in the Army garrisons of the Great Lakes, I received her reply with this appalling news:

She was setting out to come and join me.

Of course she knew our Army was on the move. That was the talk in the garrisons. She intended to make her way, with patronage of some unspecified sort, down to New Orleans, where she would find me if I would remain there until her arrival. Odd it is how she presumed that a lowly camp boy should go or stay at his own whim and convenience when armies are moving.

She made no comment upon the quality of the writing in the letter she had received from me. That was a disappointment, for that was the foremost thing I had hoped to elicit by my letter, a bit of a mother's praise for an accomplishment. Especially since it was she who insisted I be literate!

So my letter to her, as literature, seems to have been wasted upon her poor sensibilities.

As to the matter of literature: Some periodicals were passed to me by a Lieutenant Wallace, who aspires to write novels. They contain more by the writer Poe. Also serials by an Englishman, Dickens, recommended highly by Lt. Wallace. I only hope that there won't be a war breaking out here before I have leisure to read some of the stories. Besides reading, and the evening dram or two, there's nothing much to look forward to with any pleasure. Especially as John Riley has removed himself from our presence.

This evening I surprised a very large rattlesnake in my shelter. Fortunately I heard it or I'd have sat on it. By a maneuver learned in the Swamp of Florida, I pinned it and cut the head off. Not having had supper, I skinned and cooked him over a little driftwood fire. I learned by the Seminoles that reptile meat is much better than a body would presume. In fact, it's as good as any other flesh, and better than most. I

could have told Ma in my letter, if I'd remembered to, that I've eaten alligator tail. I don't doubt she'd have had something to say about that,
for I remember as a child eating beaver tail that she would sometimes
obtain up in Michigan.

This is a large rattlesnake skin and I expect I can cure it and sell it
with its rattle to one of the officers. Then he could take it home after
this campaign and brag of killing it himself.

Like Chief Tecumseh's hide.

AGUSTIN JUVERO SPEAKING
TO THE JOURNALIST ON THE PILGRIMAGE ROAD

It is discomfort, is it not, *Señor*? And we are young. How do the *viejos*
bear it? I can see that you will have to stop more than you go, ha! More
likely, you will give up. But if you don't come along on your knees, I
won't continue with our interview.

Yes, we can sit a moment. There is a good place, in the shade of that
wall. You have a question? Then write me a note and ask.

Do you doubt I really was at Matamoros? That I really was one carrying the leaflets over? You wonder if I am making up my part in the desertion of Don Juan Riley? You think I would do that to enlarge my
importance in your story? How can I prove what I say? I don't know. But
I can show you, *Señor*, a piece of paper written in the hand of *Señor* Riley
himself. It is one of my treasures and I always carry it. Look, *Señor*.

> *In the month of April 1846, listening only to the advice of my conscience for
> the liberty of a people which had had war brought upon them by the most
> unjust aggression, I separated myself from the North American forces. Since
> then I have served constantly under the Mexican flag.*
>
> *John Riley*
> *A native of County Galway in Ireland*

Of course you may doubt that it is authentic, in his own hand. And
how I obtained it, that is a later part of my story. Now what we were
speaking of was my role in delivering pamphlets to Fort Texas.

There is no denying it was dangerous, and I might have been shot by a sentry at any moment, or caught and beaten. I hardly ever thought of that, however. It was like a game to me, and probably I smiled in the darkness, even as my heart beat fast. That is how boys are, if you remember.

There was also the danger of the river itself. *Sí.* There are places where the water sucks you down. But we who lived in Matamoros, we knew where we could cross with little fear. And we were strong swimmers, also, we who volunteered to take the leaflets across. The *Norteamericanos* were generally poor swimmers, afraid in the water. Perhaps this is because they do not bathe much. I suspect that many would have deserted you during the occupation of that fort if they had been able to swim at all. Some would try to come over by hanging on driftwood, if you remember. Some of them got sucked down, and drowned, trying to cross at night. We would find their bodies farther down. The ones who were afraid to go into the water at night, they were easy for the sentries to shoot, as they drifted down. For them, I suppose, it was not like a game, as it was for us.

We had various means of bringing the propaganda across the river without wetting it. Sometimes we floated it across in ammunition boxes sealed with pitch to keep the water out. Other times it was taken across in fishermen's boats and hidden for us on the north bank. Some pamphlets were carried by *rancheros* and *vaqueros,* even by the priests. Transport is easy in one's own country; preventing it is nearly impossible. Everything is like a game when *extranjeros* occupy one's country. No matter how strong occupiers are, they are weaker by their ignorance of one's country. They do not understand how strong we remain by being rightfully in our own land, where they do not belong. Even if an invader wins, we are stronger because we are right. Invaders are almost always wrong.

Now if you have anything to ask me, write it. The deafness, ah, well! There is so much foolishness that I don't have to hear. What I wish I could hear are birds, and laughter, and music. I remember this curiosity about music: When we crossed the Rio Bravo to carry the leaflets over, the music of Matamoros would fade behind us, and we would emerge on the other side into the music of your soldiers. So different! We heard *Yanqui* songs. I remember a war song about the battle at New

Orleans. Almost every night we heard it. With handclaps and the noise-maker you call a jew's harp. There was a song about giving one's sweet-heart an apple. And a song about a dying soldier. Even at that age, I knew your tongue.

But the best music in your soldier camp was the singing of the Irish soldiers. Oh, their songs, and those voices! Sometimes I would linger beyond prudence if they began singing the one about "the last glimpse of Erin," or the one about "green grow the lilacs," which must have been their favorite. It was always being sung somewhere at night . . .

Your question? When and how did I first know John Riley? Listen . . .

CHAPTER VII

AGUSTIN JUVERO
SPEAKING TO THE JOURNALIST
ON THE PILGRIMAGE ROAD

IT WAS THAT Monday, April 14, 1846, in my mother's house in Matamoros, when I first set my eyes upon Don Juan Riley. I shall never forget!

Two soldiers brought him in, two of our Mexican soldiers, one on each side of him with their bayonets pointing up. Those soldiers were not as tall as to reach his shoulders, I remember.

General Ampudia was in our house drinking hot chocolate that my mother had made for him, because the day was dank and cold. The soldiers presented themselves and their prisoner before the general and reported that he had come ashore out of the muddy river with his gun and blanket floating on a driftwood bundle. They said he had saluted them and handed them a wet piece of paper, which was the leaflet that the general himself had written, and I myself had delivered to the *Yanqui* side of the Rio Bravo. Ha! I was proud! And this is true, *Señor*.

I must tell you how we were struck by the presence of that Irish soldier. He seemed not in the least frightened or abject. He was proud and cheerful, although soaked and smeared with mud. His eyes were wonderful to behold, glittering with zeal, and his face was like the pale portrait of a saint, framed in black ringlets of his wet hair. I am not embellishing, *Señor*. We all stood as if we were dumbstruck by that beautiful giant. The general actually rose to stand as if in the presence of a peer, though I am sure he was unconscious of doing so. And my mother! She put her hand over her heart and swayed where she stood.

I remember that *Señor* Riley quickly bowed his head to my mother and saluted General Ampudia. But, strangely, I cannot remember which gesture he made first. I have wondered often how memory works upon significant moments!

I do remember what came next. From where he stood inside our door with a soldier on each flank, he was looking out the window and across the Rio Bravo toward the huge brown earthworks of Fort Texas, whence he had come. I have already told you that it was due to this prospect that General Ampudia had made our house his headquarters. I will not attempt to describe his expression as he stared at that place, but the soldier said,

"Excellency, I am John Riley, an Irish citizen. I offer my services as a gunner in defense of Catholic Mexico, if that army over there commences hostilities. I am trained in artillery by the British army beyond the skills of those people over there. I ask only for ranking authority to serve that way. I accept all the terms offered in the advertisement that was delivered to us. I have crossed the river on the advice of my conscience."

He made that declaration in English, presuming rightly that some or all of us in the room would understand him, as we all did—excepting his two guards—although his odd, rolling dialect required attention.

General Ampudia resumed his haughty composure and put on a skeptical expression, and asked him whether he had not sworn fealty to the American army from which he had come, and asked why Mexico should trust him not to be a spy. It was a query that might have daunted someone in that circumstance, but the Irishman's gaze did not falter, and he replied,

"Excellency, sure and I did give my word when I enlisted, but, sir, they broke their bond at once by treating us like dogs, not soldiers. As I understand contracts, if one party breaks faith, the other's no longer bound."

"*Verdaderamente,*" the general agreed. Then he sat down. He told one of the guard soldiers to find the captive's blanket and wrap him in it. He told my mother to make a cup of tea for this Irishman. She blinked and took her eyes from his face and went to the *chimenea* to heat the kettle, and I noticed that *Señor* Riley stole a look at her. All men watched my mother; I was used to that. Men who knew she was a widow all had a way of looking at her. Of course, *Señor* Riley in that moment did not know it. Perhaps he surmised that she was the general's wife, though he learned otherwise soon enough. Men looked at her but she would not look them in the face. She was a virtuous woman, of proper modesty. Thus it was unusual to have seen how she looked at this newcomer. She did so several times as he sat in his blanket that morning and talked with General Ampudia.

The general, you see, had presumed that *Señor* Riley must have been an officer. He was astonished to learn that such a man had been only a private in the American infantry. By then, they were already sitting together like peers, having their tea. But the good general did not look down his nose at him even then. He was interested in what the Irishman might become in serving Mexico. He was pleased to learn that the Irishman had been an artillery sergeant in the British army. The Redcoats are held in esteem as soldiers by the officers of Mexico. I imagined that the general was appraising the deserter for the fit of an officer's coat. Or perhaps I did not imagine that then, but only *después,* after he did become an officer.

The general and the private talked at much length about many matters that were of deep concern to both of them, and I listened and learned much. They spoke most often of two things: artillery, which the general admitted to be a weakness in the Mexican army, and the *Norteamericanos'* religious prejudice against the true church.

"Give me guns, caissons, and strong soldiers, and I will make for you the best flying batteries in all the Americas," *Señor* Riley told General Ampudia. It was a big thing for a private to say.

"Mexican soldiers are tireless," the general said to him. "They are brave and obedient. Also our army is rich in cannons and horses. We know the science of gunnery. What have you?"

"Gunnery is a science, but the tactic of gunnery is an art," *Señor* Riley told the general, and the general was intense with interest. Even I, a young boy, wanted to understand the meaning of that statement, for as a student I was in love with words like *táctica* and *arte.* And that day I was falling in love with that Irishman, as well. Though not, of course, in the way my *mamá* was doing. I mean, as a boy making a hero in his heart. That sort of love was growing in me. The other kind, it seems, was growing in my *madre*. Ha! You like that in your story, don't you, *Señor Reportero*? *¿Una historia de amor?* But surely you expected it. There are many legends of women who loved the *San Patricios*. Of women who loved him specifically. If he had been loved by so many as is said, he would not have had time to become our hero in battles. So this is another truth that you can learn only from me: the only woman *Señor* Riley truly came to love in Mexico was she, my *madre*. Ah, this love story makes you skeptical, I see by your face. But it is true, and it is a matter of importance and pride to me.

But we are getting in advance of the story of that day. I was telling you of what Private Riley and General Ampudia spoke while talking in our house on that day of his arrival. The Irishman was convincing the general to entrust him with great responsibility and authority in the Mexican army. One reason why the general could believe his sincerity was the Irishman's bitter anger toward the *Norteamericanos,* for their prejudice against the Irish and other immigrant peoples. That was well known already to literate Mexicans, for your newspapers and books were full of unconcealed contempt and vitriol. In those days, one read in your newspapers that priests and nuns held orgies, sacrificed babies on the altar, that they drank human blood in church, that they copulated with demons and boys and beasts. They alleged that the popes were scheming to assume control over all the world's peoples and governments. We knew such things were lies, and we wept to see so many such lies being told in your powerful and aggressive nation upon our border. We already had been afflicted by *Norteamericanos* in the form of Texans. The Texans were loco, most of them, but all in different ways. What we read in your books and newspapers made us think that the rest of you in your country were all loco in the same way.

General Ampudia was about to be replaced by General Arista in command at Matamoros, but we did not know that yet. He was planning as if he would be in command if a war started there. It was important. My *madre* and I were listening, but trying to seem as if we were not listening. *Mamá* made tortillas and stewed some rice with *pollo,* and made more tea for the general and the private. Our friend Francesco Moreno, the adjutant, admitted officers who came with their issues for the general's attention. To such officers the general introduced *Señor* Riley, and told them of his great knowledge as a gunner, trained by the British, and the officers were polite. Some were impressed and seemed glad. Others seemed suspicious and only looked warily at the deserter. Some of them I could see were displeased by the general's enthusiasm, and were only as civil as the general's rank required them to be.

In the Mexican army, *Señor,* you see, most officers are unsure whether they are in favor or not. It frightens them to hear their superiors praise other officers, or to see their general being warm to someone else. And this man who was spending so much of the day in General Ampudia's company, why, he was a foreigner, a prisoner in the muddy clothes of a *Yanqui* soldier! You may presume what was in their imaginations! If this was interrogation of a prisoner, why was there no guard, or any scribe writing down the deposition? Of course, there on the table lay the leaflet that the captive had brought with him across the river, and the sight of it explained enough, one would think. But subordinate officers are usually worried for themselves.

Some of the officers who came, the general treated them brusquely, and did not even explain the Irishman or introduce him to them. This you can say for General Ampudia: He knew well each of his officers and treated them accordingly.

As for the officers in your army, the West Pointers that most of them were, those officers were very much a subject of the conversation over the many cups of tea. Often when *Señor* Riley was speaking of them he would rise from the table with his blanket over his shoulders and stare across the river at that fort they were building over there. His anger and his contempt were plain to see in his eyes and hear in his voice. It is said to be a trait of Irishmen that if one earns their enmity, it will endure for a long time, perhaps forever. You are Irish, yes? So you understand how he bore the resentments of his fellow soldiers for their sufferings at the hands of those officers over there across the river. Soon there was no room to doubt the sincerity of his passion. He offered to do whatever he could do to lure more of the immigrant soldiers across to the Mexican ranks. The general was aglow with eagerness. Plainly to him, a man of great potency had been delivered to us.

I learned much of *Señor* Riley's life that morning, as I sat in a corner pretending to study my schoolbooks. In case you don't know it, or have

heard it from sources that don't really know it, here is the great Irish patriot's *biografía* as I heard it from his own lips. Please pick up your pencil, *Señor,* for the history of your Greatest Traitor does not begin on the
day he swims across the Rio Bravo del Norte.

He was from a country where people dead of starvation lay rotting
on the roadsides, as the British soldiers had torn or burned down their
hovels because their English landlords meant to graze sheep on their
land for the wool trade. This is not the first you've heard of their trouble, *Señor.* All the world knows of it. You know this to be true, yes?
Thank you. The poverty and suffering were beyond endurance. The
Irish have never been a tame people, and they tried to rise against the
English, here and there, only to be crushed by Redcoats, and by harsh
policies. As they weakened with hunger, their will ebbed. The only sal-
vation they could see was to flee to better places. The Americas were
seen as a better place. They came to all parts of America, not just the
United States. Some came to Mexico, and found themselves welcomed.
But Mexico is a poor and troubled land also. After this country freed itself from the Europeans, those who wanted to rule were like crabs in a
tub: climbing up and pulling each other down. Our Santa Anna would
be in and then out and then back in. Everyone would be the savior of
Mexico. There came theorists and reformers, and *reaccionarios,* and always only one thing was certain, *Señor:* Almost everyone would be
poor. To bear poverty, it helps to be Catholic. In this, Mexicans and
Irishmen *son muy semejantes.* Thus it was poverty that sent the Irishman
into the broader world as a mercenary soldier.

Many young men of Ireland who could find no work, they were
brave and tough. The English army was always at war and needed brave
and tough young men. If one could earn a living in no other way, one
could become a Redcoat, even if one hated the Redcoats. Such was the
way of that Irishman of whom I speak. He lived in one of the poorest
corners of that stricken country, and had a wife and a son to feed.
Therefore he became a Redcoat soldier. He meant it to be only a while.
But he liked soldiering. Soon the army promoted him to corporal. It
sent him among the colonies. He became an *artillero.* Then a sergeant.
He was literate, and considered himself fit to be an officer. But Irishmen had little hope of becoming officers in the English army. They are
not of that class, you understand. Being in Canada when an enlistment

expired, he therefore mustered out, meaning to seek his fortune in the
United States and send home for his wife and son. He labored on docks
in the Great Lakes. He learned in a letter that he had lost his wife to ill-
ness. My *madre* gave a soft cry of sadness when she heard him tell of
that, and though it was surely evoked by true sympathy, I suspected
that she was, beneath it, relieved that this man had no wife. Or did I
imagine that because I expected her to feel so? As I have said, we have
strange ways of remembering our emotions.

General Ampudia was a despot, feared as too ambitious and cruel an
officer. He was soon to be replaced by General Arista. But it was nevertheless General Ampudia who lured the great Irish soldier to Mexico,
who gained his confidence, who took it upon himself to offer him a
commission in the artillery. That was a boldness.

But consider, too, the part that I had played in it, equally or perhaps
more bold—taking the leaflet to the enemy camp. That was a very important service done by this brave *niño* for Mexico! Maybe it was the
best thing I have ever done, or that I ever will do . . .

Or perhaps, *Señor,* it was a terrible thing. When one looks *hacia
atrás.*

PADRAIC QUINN'S DIARY

April 19, 1846 ✳ *Fort Texas, R. Grande*

MORE MEXICAN REGIMENTS arriving at Matamoros.

More of our Irishmen than ever going across the river. John Riley
seems to have inspired more and more to go.

Some of our deserters now stand on that side of the river and call
over to their messmates by name, exhorting them to cross over for the
wine, women, and song, and good rank in the Mexican Army.

A patrol went out from the 4th Inf. to search for Col. Cross, our
Quartermaster. He rode out more than a week ago, like a fool, alone,
and has been missing since. The patrol of 10 men went out under Lt.
Theo Porter, a friend of Lt. Grant's. I had carried a letter over to Lt.
Grant, from his fiancée, that had got shuffled into 5th Inf. mail, and
saw Lt. Porter's patrol go out. Mr. Grant shook his hand as he left. Of-

ficers seem like they almost hope Col. Cross's disappearance will spark a real fight. Lt. Grant is grim about such talk. He said in my hearing that we are striding toward an unholy war, that our presence here in the disputed country between the rivers is "a deplorable aggression." He argued the matter with other officers and I would not have been surprised to see them come to blows with him.

Seeing and hearing a fine fellow like Mr. Grant makes me ponder.

It is that when shooting begins, even those that don't believe in the cause will have to fight in it! It is that notion, in the back of my mind every day, that makes me question whether I want to be a soldier someday, for a soldier has no choice except of course by deserting, forever disgraced. An officer can resign his commission, on the principle of it, but there's disgrace in that too, and an officer's got more to lose by it, as he has more to begin with. Soldiering is all I ever meant to do in my maturity, but being here on this dubious mission, and hearing everybody divided on it, has set me to questioning on the whole matter of soldiering.

All those who have deserted, and got across the river without drowning or being shot in midstream by the sentries, they have given up their souls as far as the United States Army is concerned, and they're doomed beyond pardon if they're ever caught. But sure and I know that they've settled it all down inside themselves by the time they go. The inducements are mighty and many, enough to tempt either the good side or the bad side of any kind of a man. Every day there's the sound of church bells—Catholic church bells—across the river, and most days more faint comes the chanting and singing of the faith. And other music, too. Those Mexicans make music even more than Irishmen do, and at all hours. To hear them, one might think there's no such thing as an unhappy Mexican, nor do they ever sleep.

And as if the faith and the music were not enough to pull on a man's soul, there's the earthly inducements. When the wind's right—as I write this, in fact—the smells of cooking come across the river, so savory as compared with the steamy stench of our rancid and slimy keg-beef and bacon boiling in kettles, something a buzzard would find repulsive, I daresay.

And then there are those girls over there, who come to the river to wash their clothes, and bathe themselves and frolic all bare within plain

view of our panting wretches, as if we were no more than so many cat-
tle gazing across at them. Our soldiers are sick with longing, and a mix
of longings it is, both sacred and profane.

And even if there were no such enticements, many of our soldiers
would be happy to risk the crossing just to get away from the humiliations and cruelties of their officers, which grow ever more malicious; as
an example, Lt. Bragg, who lately made one of his artillerymen ride the
rail all day in a cold rain. It was explained that Bragg was in a foul mood
because the weather prevented battery drill that day. I myself heard one
of his gunners to say that if he abandoned all to cross the river, he
would kill Bragg in his tent before he swam away.

If he continues with his ways, the lieutenant might become a casualty before a war even starts!

Ft. Texas R. Grande ✳ *Apr. 21, 1846*

MUCH GRIM NEWS.

Col. Cross's remains were found under a gathering of buzzards. A
bullet hole in his skull, his watch and horse missing. The buzzards not
thought to be responsible for the loss of those, as one low jester put it.

Also Lt. Porter of the 4th and one of his soldiers out looking for the
Colonel got killed in an ambush by Mexican ranchers.

Lt. Porter shot three Mexicans before he fell, and is being called the
"first hero" martyred in this confrontation with the "Papist Greasers."

Officers are ranting that when the report of Porter and Cross being
killed reaches the U. States it will suffice as a reason to declare the war.

Funerals with all honors to be held right away.

I finished preparing the hide of my rattlesnake and sold it with its
rattles to a captain of the 5th Regt., for $4.50.

Before I could read any of the Dickens serial another rain leak ruined
the papers.

Too much fretting to read anyway. I can't think of much but what's
sure to happen next.

Also heard this day that John Riley himself was seen drilling a battery
of guns outside of Matamoros! An officer watched him with a spyglass

and was sure it was he, that although he was decked out fancy in a Mexican officer's uniform, there was no mistaking him.

The officer said that Mr. Riley's battery was performing with great skill and rapidity, wheeling and unlimbering as well as anything he had ever witnessed. That if anyone had doubted his claim that he had been an artillery sergeant in the British Army, they wouldn't doubt if they saw him.

Most of the gunners in his battery looked like Americans or Irishmen, not Mexicans, the officer said, though he didn't recognize any of them.

Lt. Grant commented with some sarcasm that if those Irishmen had been treated by their officers like men instead of dogs, they might now be doing excellent gunnery for our Army, not the other. I was glad to hear him say it, for it was like my own notion of the matter.

Like everything else in this idle camp, it's being talked of by everyone, even as much as Col. Cross's death, and Lt. Porter's.

Private Riley is on my mind, far too much. I never saw a soldier I liked more, and like fools we just threw him away!

Sure and I don't like being on the opposite side from him in a war. I miss going over to talk to him when I have things in mind.

I think we're past averting a war. The Mexican commander at Matamoros sent Gen. Taylor a letter telling us to pack up and move back to the other side of the Nueces River until the governments settle the Texas border question. Advised that if we don't, we will be removed by force of arms. Old Rough and Ready wrote back that he was sorry to hear that threat, but he wasn't afraid of it. General Taylor's letter was read to the troops, and they gave the expected huzzahs.

I wonder how many of our soldiers really want to fight, or how many just don't want their fellows to know they're scared.

April 24, 1846

A BIG HULLABALOO and clamor over at Matamoros at mid-morning. All the church bells tolled, an uproar of yelling, cannon salvo, and bands playing. Mexican troops parading wherever we could see up their streets into town. Rumor is that more reinforcements arrived. Their newspaper *Matamoros Gaceta* has been reporting that a higher-ranking general is taking over from the one named Ampudia. They already outnumber us all to hell.

I think our officers are deluded. Call the Mexican soldiers Greasers and nigger Injuns, and monkeys in blue suits. Mexican officers they call Gypsy Dancers.

Contempt, I guess, is what you have to feel for your enemy in order to keep your courage up before a fight. I saw that in the war with the Seminole Indians. Swamp niggers they called them. Hunting swamp niggers would be like 'coon hunting, all a lark. Until they outfought our soldiers for a number of years and earned respect.

I look across the river and see those Mexicans all in their dark blue with their shiny muskets, all drilling and showing off to impress us, and I am damned well impressed. They have cavalry troops that look like so many princes. Lt. Grant said they ride like centaurs. Had to ask him what a centaur was, and then I understood what he meant. A centaur can't fall off of his horse. Mister Grant is as good a horseman as any and he was impressed.

Same with their artillery, at least the flying batteries with all their light cannons and horse teams, the ones they suppose Mister Riley is training over there. I watched them from the riverbank a day or two. Didn't have a spyglass, but think I could tell Mister Riley even at that distance in all the dust and smoke they made, by the way he moves and carries himself. We have some of the best artillery in the world, our officers like to brag. Funny I used that word *brag*. Lt. Bragg strives to be the very best, and he can really make his gunners scamper. But I wouldn't argue that he's better than Mister Riley and his gunners over there, if that really was him.

And I've seen something else that would make me bet on Mister Riley over Mister Bragg.

It is the priests in their robes who come down with water and incense, and put their blessing on the Mexican cannons.

I just think of those prayers and those chants, so pretty and mystical, and I believe it works. It's supposed to be that all Christians have the same God, Protestant or Catholic, and what little I understand of God, He would favor a kindly man like Mister Riley, with blessed cannons, over a nasty, slave-whipping villain like Braxton Bragg whose cannons may be all polished and painted but never blessed by a priest.

That's why I would bet on John Riley.

This seems odd: Here at Fort Texas, waiting for war, we get a newspaper from their side. The *Matamoros Gazette.*

They print an English translation, and make sure we get it. Just like getting your hometown paper, same day it's printed.

We read all about ourselves. Pretty accurate, I'll say.

Well, they can see everything we do.

Our army is their big news. Their generals are always quoted in the paper. They are pretty cocksure.

They report the number of deserters who show up over there. They say if the shooting starts, most of Gen. Taylor's infantry will pop over onto their side, good Catholic Irish eager to defend a country of their own faith from an invasion by heretics. They say "Old Taylor" as they call him will desert, himself, because there'll be no one to stand with him but Protestant officers who have come fresh from the West Point academy and never fought. That newspaper knows more about us than we do, I'd say.

It seems sort of like reading your own home newspaper every day and finding out everybody in town considers you the village idiots.

What is the truth? I gather from reading newspapers, the Mexican ones & the ones we get from the United States, there seems to be two versions of this Texas border thing, the U. States version and the way everybody else looks at it. The U.S. newspapers say the Mexicans are attacking Texas all along the border and President Polk is trying to protect America from Mexican aggression. But the Mexican paper says that most of the civilized nations of the world, in particular Europe, are scolding America for aggression. The European countries accuse us of what they call "imperialist designs" on Mexico.

Well, I'm a camp boy and I don't know much. But this sounds to me like any argument over anything. You just tell your own side.

If I read just the *Matamoros Gazette,* I would be pretty sympathetic to Mexicans. If I read just the U.S. newspapers, I would be raring to invade Mexico.

By the time I get the Matamoros newspaper, it's so worn and limp and smudged I can hardly read it. The officers cut out parts of it to keep. I retain what scraps of it I can, and read them at night and think. I read about people with their Mexican names, and about things like commerce, and mining, and diplomatic things. But also I read about Mexican people getting married, and about funerals. I read about their farming, about shipping, about such things as operas and orchestras. The *Matamoros Gazette* makes Mexico seem like a really interesting place. It sounds as good as anyplace I've ever been in. Better than most. But I've only been in Michigan and Florida, and awhile in New Orleans. People who have been in Mexico say those people are decent. But our papers say they're throat cutters who worship the Pope and have rituals where they drink babies' blood, and sell their children to the priests to copulate with, and all such as that, which I tend to doubt.

I would like to think that everything I read, I could count on to be the truth. The only written thing said to be wholly true is the Bible. But both Catholics and Protestants use the Bible. If the real truth is there, why do they disagree?

When I write in this diary, I would like it all to be true. But the only things I know are true are what I see with my own eyes.

If all the Bible is true, it must have been written by people who saw what happened themselves.

But I hear tell that is not so, either.

Sure and I wish that this war thing would get over with so that I could spend more of my time thinking about this whole *truth* matter. If I could ever figure it out, I would write it down.

One thing it said in the *Gazette* was that seven slaves of the American officers were among the deserters who turned up in Matamoros. It said they are free now because slavery is against their law over there. Now that's interesting to think on. That might be one reason why slaveholders like Lt. Bragg hate Mexico so much and can't wait to start shooting.

Pres. Polk, too, is from a slaving state, North Carolina, they say.

Some old Co. K messmates of Pvt. Riley staged a boxing match, as he used to do for them. It attracts the West Pointers, who place bets and yell at both fighters, Kill that Mick! While the match was distracting officers and sentries at dusk, several Irishmen sneaked down to the river. I saw them slip into the willow brake. But didn't report them. I suspect Mr. Riley might have thought this up before he left. Or maybe after he left. There's a rumor that he still sends messages over, and even that he comes back across the river in fishermen's boats at night and slips into the camp to encourage more deserters. That sounds like a yarn to me. I'll believe that when I see him. But I wouldn't put it beyond him for boldness.

CHAPTER VIII

DON JUAN RILEY soon convinced our officers that he had not exaggerated his talents as an *artillero*. In a well-tailored uniform of first lieutenant, he went out to the walls of Matamoros to supervise the placement of cannons, facing General Taylor's vast dirt pile, Fort Texas, across the river. I went with him everywhere, as interpreter. Thus I know what he said about the artillery, as I had to translate it for our officers.

Teniente Riley was not flattering about our artillery defense at first. He told the generals that the earthen walls the Americans were building were too thick to be affected by our cannonballs, the largest of which were twelve-pounders. Our defenders had two mortars. "But you cannot expect them to achieve much against the fort," he said, "because they built bombproof burrows within the fort. They learned in their 1812 war how to hide from the excellent British gunners."

He told our generals: "There is little that can be done to save Matamoros from their batteries if they begin bombarding. We can make it expensive for them, by accurate shooting into their batteries. And by praying for the safety of Matamoros. By praying that someone in their capital is wise enough not to declare war."

Our officers of course disliked his assessment, and some asked General Ampudia why he had put so much authority in a foreigner who could deliver no more promise than that. Then it was that *Teniente* Riley began to put new ideas into their heads.

"Tell them this, Agustin," he said to me, his translator. "That it would make no sense for the *Yanqui* cannons to try hard to destroy the town of Matamoros. A wooden town they could ignite with heated cannonballs, but Matamoros is adobe. The civilians can leave the town and get out of harm's way. But the *Yanquis* will not likely shoot much at the town. Instead they will be shooting at the artillery. The town cannot hurt them, the artillery can hurt them. So they will be shooting at our guns, and we will be shooting at their guns.

"The real purpose of our cannons will be to cut their army to pieces if they attack across the river anywhere. For this reason, we must have most of our guns ready to move quickly wherever the *Yanquis* come at us. Our bigger guns and the mortars will remain strongly emplaced and bombard the fort unceasingly."

It was heartening, to see the officers peering at *Teniente* Riley with growing interest, and to be the translator who was passing such important words to them. Some of the officers looked doubtful, but most were nodding as if that made sense to them. Of course it was not the fort that would attack into Mexico if the war started, it was the soldiers! The fort was there only to protect their soldiers! And then he told them what he had observed to be the great weakness of the Mexican artillery: that it was *muy pesado, muy lento*. Too slow! He said the old way of moving cannons on the battlegrounds was ponderous. The new artillery must be agile, he said.

"Who brings your cannons to a battlefield?" he asked them, and they replied that it was teamsters, of course. It is the teamsters with their oxen and mules and horses who move everything that is too heavy for soldiers to carry. The baggage, the cannons, the cannonballs. Of course, *¡trabajo pesado!*

But he said, "No! *Soldiers* should move cannons, not hired men! Soldiers and gunners know where the artillery is needed! *Artilleros* must be their own teamsters. They must always have the horses and mules nearby in harness, and ready to move to a better place at once. This is called a flying battery, and it must be able to arrive in minutes!" I translated it for him: *batería móvil,* and the officers murmured and pulled their chins. Military men do not leap eagerly to new notions, *Señor,* as you might know. But they were listening keenly.

And so that splendid-looking Irishman, who had been a mere private a few days before in the United States Army and now was a Mexican army lieutenant, offered to transform Mexico's ponderous artillery corps into a swift, self-reliant force that could race in minutes to any front in a battlefield where it could smash an oncoming assault. It was audacious! And I, a boy who could translate languages, was a part of that transforming, because I helped him convince them! *Señor,* I was changing history! Fill my glass, *por favor,* and we will drink to that!

Soon, *Señor Periodista, Teniente* Riley created a "flying battery" of his Irish gunners. He showed in the field how fast they could be.

General Mariano Arista arrived very soon to replace General Ampudia, and brought with him reinforcements. At once *Teniente* Riley was granted audience with him. General Ampudia, though bitter at being replaced, endorsed the Irish gunner to his successor because of his enthusiasm for the flying batteries of artillery. *Señor* Riley had more to say to General Arista even than he had said to the others. It made one dizzy to stay abreast of that Irishman's thinking! He told General Arista:

He wanted his flying batteries to be made up as much as possible by Irishmen. Or at least, by soldiers who understood his tongue, as that would make them more efficient. He noted that deserters from the other side were coming, a few every day, and that more propaganda should be carried over to encourage them. He said there were some skilled European gunners in his former infantry unit, and that he wanted them, and expected they would come eagerly, knowing that he was established with a commission in the artillery. That they would gain rank by merit.

General Arista agreed it was a fine plan. The general had lived outside Mexico, a political exile. He had seen and admired the soldiers of European and British armies. He admired Irishmen and Germans in particular, for their courage, their strength, for their *iniciativa.* Of this last, *Teniente* Riley was a stirring example. The general granted him authority to form and train two flying batteries, and more if good *artilleros* became available. And he told him to oversee also the placement and fortification of the stationary batteries of heavy guns protecting Matamoros. General Arista had already been composing a *folleto* of much eloquence to be sent among *los soldatos immigrantes* of General Taylor's army. He invited *Teniente* Riley to embellish what he had already written, to make it more appealing to the soldiers who had so recently been his comrades. Here, *Señor,* is a copy of the pamphlet, for you to read at your leisure. I apologize that it is so brittle and yellow. It was so many years ago. Once again I began crossing the Rio Bravo at dusk, to deliver General Arista's new propaganda, as I had a few weeks earlier with those of General Ampudia. See what it says here, that "the United States Government, contrary to the wishes of a majority of all honorable and honest Americans, has ordered you to take *forcible* possession of the territory of a *friendly* neighbor, who has never given her consent to such occupation. . . . It is of no purpose if they tell you that the law for the annexation of Texas justifies your occupation of the Rio Bravo del Norte; for by this act they rob us of a great part of our country. . . ."

You see, *Señor,* it was to tell the *Yanqui* soldiers that they were not in their own country, but in Mexico as unlawful aggressors.

Then it harangued the soldiers, saying, "I warn you, in the name of justice, honor, and your own interests and self-respect, to abandon their desperate and unholy cause, and become peaceful Mexican citizens. I guarantee you, in such case, a half section of land, or 320 acres, to settle upon, gratis. Be wise then, and just and honorable, and take no part in murdering us who have no unkind feeling toward you. If in time of action you wish to espouse *our* cause, throw away your arms and run to us, we will embrace you as true friends and Christians. Should any of you render any important service to Mexico, you shall be accordingly considered and preferred." Such persuasion, *¿sí?*

I was very successful again in crossing to the *Yanquis* and distributing the pamphlets. I did it better than before, even, because *Teniente* Riley knew the camp and told me where to find certain persons—bootleggers, launderers, fortune-tellers, whores, and such—who could help distribute them into the right units of the camp. He sent me to seek certain Irish soldiers within certain units, with unwritten messages from him! In the fewest soft-spoken words, passing by a particular soldier, almost invisible to him, I could convey the most compelling message, such as:

"Mister Dalton, yes? Your friend John Riley invites you to join him and be a sergeant in his artillery. To the honor of Saint Patrick and the Trinity."

Yes, *Señor,* imagine the effect of those words upon an Irish soldier, fresh from barrelhead punishment or the buck-and-gag: a furtive waif addresses him by name, speaks also the name of his missing countryman—and those allusions to higher ranks, and the Mother Faith as well! Add that to the persuasive new writing of General Arista, which was in every soldier's hands!

The result was as one should expect. Irishmen who had long been poised to turn their back on the cruel officers, they suddenly disappeared in the darkness and went down to the river to cross over. Even those who could not swim came down, and they were led by whispers out beyond the sentry posts, where Mexican fishermen came to shore in boats with muffled oars, and murmured in the darkness, *avemaria,* and the soldiers would get in the boats.

You are astonished, *Señor.* You did not ever hear about the men in the boats, did you? Your officers always thought the deserters had to swim or float on driftwood, or find the fording places up the river! Oh, so many would have drowned! And we needed them! Once we organized the ferrying, no more had to drown.

I, Agustin, was one of those whisperers in the dark along the river paths through the willows. Sometimes I could greet those soldiers by name as they got in the boats. They were startled to hear their names, you may imagine! Sometimes I would say, *Lieutenant* Riley waits to take your hand.

What came of this? It was that General Taylor's army got smaller, as everyone waited to see if war would begin. Scores of his ablest veterans crossed the river and took the hand of Mexico in warm friendship. And even before the shooting began back and forth across the Rio Bravo, my friend Don Juan Riley had already collected forty-eight of his old comrades to make a company of *artilleros,* and he began to transform them into the best unit, it is said by many, that ever served in the defense of Mexico—a country that has had to be defended over and over against invaders.

As you see, *Señor Reportero,* I was important in the making of the *San Patricios,* even though a mere boy. *Para siempre,* I have the pride of that.

PADRAIC QUINN'S DIARY

April 24, 1846 * *Fort Texas, on the Rio Grande*

I'M DAMNED! As if being Irish wasn't perplexing enough. A body finally gets something sort of worked out to go by, when up comes something else to block your way.

I probably oughtn't even try to write this down. But it's important. Probably one of those things that make a difference in the whole rest of your life. My life. Shouldn't say "probably" one of those things. Sure as anything it makes the whole difference.

It was that Sgt. Mick Maloney. Hero of the Swamp War.

Here's how he fuddled my head today.

Mister Riley and so many others being gone over to the Mexicans, it's affected everybody like a plague or some such thing. You know you've caught it, or you expect you will. Everybody looking at everyone else and wondering if they've got it. Men getting out their pamphlets and reading them over and over. Looking over at Matamoros town with one eye, and with the other eye seeing who's watching you watch Matamoros. Of course Matamoros is the place to be watching, because that's where "the enemy" is. But you feel like other people can tell what you're thinking. The officers in particular. They probably presume that every Irish soldier has made up his mind to swim over, or is so close to making up his mind that he'll likely not be at muster next morning.

Odd how it is that I got myself included into those kinds of feelings. I'm not a soldier, just a camp boy, never took a soldier oath. Say, now, I made up my mind to go over there, follow Mister Riley and whatnot—that wouldn't break any oath or law. Nothing I could be punished for, not officially. When I think on it, in fact, I am maybe the only "free" person in this whole place. Soldiers have their oath binding them, and if they go, they break it and they're in big trouble. Slaves, like those officers' servants that have gone across, they aren't under any soldier oath, but they're their officers' property and the law of the U. States forbids them to leave. So sure and they're not free. Maybe it could be said that some of the camp followers are as free as I am, the laundresses and their children. The whores. That one wryneck woman who is both a laundress and a whore. Some of those people might be as free as I am. Except the ones that are married, and have their own kind of obligation, so it's hard to say how free anybody else really is. But soldiers aren't.

Private Riley and most of those other Irish soldiers who went over, and the immigrant Germans, they had their Army oath they broke going over, but they weren't deserting their *country,* because they aren't U. States citizens, and wouldn't be for years yet. I am a U.S. citizen by birth, and so maybe that's a kind of bond or obligation on me. But it would still be no wrong for me to quit this Hell Place of a fort and swim over to Mexico, because if the Mexicans accepted me in, I'd be breaking no law that I can think of, since the fact is that no war has been declared with Mexico yet, not to my knowledge. Mister Riley and those other deserters, they are really still citizens of Ireland, and sure there's no war between Mexico and Ireland.

So whatever way I look this thing over, every angle of it comes out that if I want to just walk out of here, if I can get past the sentries without getting myself shot, there is nothing else to stop me. That is that. And I have been full ready to do it, and my conscience was at ease with it. That Matamoros town does pull on me, with all its bells and music, and the laughing, and the smell of food. And most of all, Mister Riley himself is over there, one man I'd be for following anywhere. I'm not obliged to "follow" any man, but being around soldiers all your life you do tend to get sort of "followish." I was ready to go over.

Until Sgt. Mick Maloney, just today.

The sergeant is a fine soldier, as fine as there is. Folks say if he'd not been born Irish he'd be a colonel or a general by now. I wrote some about him awhile back in this diary so I won't repeat it all here. I drew a portrait of him a few days ago. He didn't "sit" for me, but I drew it when he wasn't looking.

Well, to go on, the hero's here by the Rio Grande. Some of the Protestant officers think he's too proud, and torment him like other Irishmen, though not quite so much, because he is a hero by repute, and of course a sergeant. He's as severe on our Irishmen as the officers themselves, almost, but for a different reason, being that he wants Irishmen to be respected, not scorned, and says they have to earn it the way he did. By being better soldiers than anybody. Some soldiers claim they owe their pride to him.

Today for some reason his attention fell on me. I was moping along

Sergeant Major Maurice "Mick" Maloney of the 4th U.S. Infantry drawn in pencil by F. Quinn at the fort on Rio Grande April, 1846

between errands. It was near the parapets facing Matamoros and maybe he saw that I was more over there than here. Which I suppose was plainly so.

Well, he'd never said anything to me ever before, and I'm sure no soldier, but he yells, Paddy! and I turn and see the famous Mick Maloney crooking a finger at me and his eyes staring into me.

There was nothing for it but to go to him. I was no little reluctant, though, as a body is when his woolgathering's disturbed. I stood before him almost like a soldier expecting a scolding, but I was surprised and maybe feeling honored that he knew my name.

He looked over my head toward Matamoros, and said to me, "Lad, what d'ye make of those people over the river?" I said, "How should I know, sir, as I never met any Mexicans." "Mexicans hell!" said he, "I mean those deserters!" I told him I was sorry to see good men leave us, that some of them had been good to me, but he pointed at me and stopped me with a loud curse. "Good, hell! They're low, they're a disgrace to the Mother Country! They are everything people say bad about Irishmen! Goddamned traitors and cowards! That John Riley's the worst of them!"

Those words hit me like a pole ax! Someone I look way up to was damning somebody I hold even higher!

Sure and I was so mad for a moment, I couldn't see. But of course a whiffet like me does not talk back to a big sergeant major like Maloney, so I kept my mouth shut and let him go on, which he sure did.

"Every Irish scut who sneaks away from duty, he earns us all the slurs we get back in the States!" said he. I admit I saw it could be so. But I knew the other face of it, too, and so I piped up & said, "Sir, don't you feel some of them were driven off? By these officers here?" I saw in his face that he caught my drift, but he didn't pause for it. "M'lad," said he, "I am now twelve years in this Army and every day of those years I have pinched my nose and swallowed their shit, and given them better sol-dierin' than they deserve. I owe it to myself as an Irishman. It's raised me to a sergeant major, and I mean to come out of this war an officer, God willin' I come out alive. I don't like shit, but the shame's theirs, for givin' it. But I would have shame for betrayin' my oath to the Army. Now, m'lad, I know about the charms of Private Riley and that pretty Mexican town yonder, and being true to the Faith, and scornin' the motive of the President and the slavemasters for this venture. Sure and it's no better than houndin' the Indians in their swampland. But I swore to do my duty and I do it. Riley ate officer shit less than a year. Then he gave up and betrayed all his fellow Irishmen and gave the offi-cers cause to feed us more of it! I say this, lad, mind who y'r heroes are!"

Then he walked off, for to leave me thinking more confused than I was. Either one of those gents is a hero by my lights.

And yet they're opposite in what they think and do.

If this gets to be a war, they might well kill each other.

Now am I to be on one side or another?

Thank the Lord I'm not old enough to soldier. I'd scarce know which way to aim my gun!

CHAPTER IX

Ft. Texas, R. Grande ✳ *April 28, 1846*

DIARY NEGLECTED A few days because of alarms and fracases hereabouts. A goodly number of Mexican soldiers crossed the river upstream and caught a unit of our dragoons in ambush. They shot 14 dead and captured the rest, about 40 or so. Killed a lieutenant. Captured the captain, a Marylander named Thornton. Got our officers in a state of fury.

Then we couldn't believe our eyes when a Mexican ambulance wagon came to the fort and brought Capt. Thornton's wounded dragoons back to us! They said the Mexicans had been real kind to them after the skirmish was over. Don't know what to think of that. Maybe it's true what we hear of them being decent folk. But sure that won't matter. This is sure to help President Polk get his war declared. Half of our officers say this was American blood shed on American soil, but others argue it's Mexican land here and we shouldn't be here. Lieutenant Grant is one arguing on that side of the issue.

I don't know just how they palaver in Congress, but I expect that the argument there sounds just like the argument here. Most of the officers spoiling for war are southern.

By the time of that skirmish, there'd been about two hundred Irish soldiers and some Catholic Germans deserted. More sharpshooters are being posted on the parapets facing the Rio G. to shoot deserters dead in the water. But most get away.

Mister Riley gets blamed for inspiring most of them. Many of them get across alive by going at night. But some I guess have more fear of going into dark water than being shot at in daytime. One thing is pretty certain, they're getting plenty of help and encouragement from the Mexicans. And rumor is that the deserters who already went over are helping them, too.

Something big is going on here in the camp and I can't make out what it is. Officers are packing their stuff. I've got the fluvial shits too bad to go a-finding out.

Fort Texas, Rio Grande ✳ May 2, 1846

STILL GOT THE spews. I could call this the Diary of Diarrhea. But I found out what the big stir was all about, and it's dreadful.

This fort is almost empty. Gen. Z. Taylor marched most of the Army back to the coast three days ago when he got a rumor that the Mexican troops were going up there to destroy our supply depot at Port Isabel, which would ruin us for sure. Took more than ¾ths of the army and left only the 7th Infantry and Lt. Bragg's artillery to guard this Fort. All the camp followers are in the fort now, scared pale. Maj. Brown of the 7th in charge here now. He is an 1812 veteran of the Battle of New Orleans and a real solid officer, as good as anyone could ask for. But here we are with only 500 men, and no sooner was Gen. Taylor out of sight than here came scouts saying the Mexican army's crossed the Rio G. upstream from us. We don't know whether Gen. Taylor's chasing the Mexican Army or it's chasing him. It could be both. The Mexican force around Matamoros is big enough it could be both ahead of Gen. Z. Taylor and behind him.

I get all this from the yammering of the officers in the 7th, but am trying to think for myself on it, too.

Twice today, officers claim they saw Mr. Riley over there go from battery to battery. I wish I had a spyglass.

Judging by the sounds, the people in Matamoros are much happier than we are here. Some of the troops are joking that this fort might be the next Alamo, and wouldn't that be an honor.

Think I finally have conquered the flux. But any bite of these rancid rations could start me going again. And a look in the latrine tells me any number of us have got worms.

Would rather be just about anyplace other than here. If I'd stayed in New Orleans my Ma might have caught up with me by now.

I can hardly remember what it was like to have somebody looking after me, instead of looking down on me. I remember it could be a comfort. I could use some comfort.

AGUSTIN JUVERO
SPEAKING TO THE JOURNALIST
ON THE PILGRIMAGE ROAD

General Arista continued to use my mother's house as a command post after he replaced General Ampudia. It was plain even to me as a boy that he was more bold. One could sense *más energía*. His predecessor went out sullen but General Arista was polite to him and listened respectfully to his advice. He had scribes in the house writing everything down. Like General Ampudia he kept sending the propaganda across the river to the unhappy immigrant soldiers of the enemy force. He had me continue my work as a courier of those pamphlets. He assured me he would honor the arrangement by which I might be admitted as a cadet in the *Colegio Militar* as a reward for my service and to prepare me to be an officer. My mother gave the impression that this would be an honor, but I could see in her eyes a fear of it. She was a woman of good education, and such women do not like to see their sons become soldiers. Later we spoke of it in private and I told her that although I did not wish to be a soldier, I could learn in the Citadel the science of engineering, and could then become an engineer instead of a soldier. That seemed to cheer and comfort her, and she urged me to ask if I could return to Ciudad Mexico with General Ampudia's party when he departed. Thus I would be far from Matamoros if the war began here.

And so we made that suggestion to General Arista, but he said no, he wanted me to remain as a courier and a translator. That was more danger for me and my mother was displeased, but she acquiesced. An educated person understands that it is dangerous to protest what generals want. Even widows of soldiers are to obey orders.

And so it was, *Señor,* that I continued to cross the river with my *brigada.* We called ourselves with pride *Los Serpientes del Rio Bravo.* Or as you *Yanquis* would say, the Water Moccasins.

It must seem most unlikely to you now, *Señor,* as you see this poor hobbling wreck of a pilgrim laboring along the road to Our Lady of Guadalupe, that in another time I was a runner and a swimmer, a fencer, a wrestler, *un atleta* of uncommon swiftness and suppleness. But in those times I could run like a deer, swim like an eel, and go anywhere without fear.

In the days following, many more of your Irish and German soldiers came across, and more slaves of your officers. Many of the soldiers, General Arista made available to *Teniente* Riley, and they reunited with a beautiful heartiness. He trained them at once in the maneuvers and firing of his swift artillery, the "flying battery." Those who already knew gunnery became corporals and sergeants at his request, and those were ranks they would not have achieved in the *Yanqui* army because of your officers' prejudice against Catholic immigrants. It gave them splendid spirit, and they responded with alacrity. They were also overjoyed with the welcome they received from our soldiers, and our citizens, and in particular the young women.

There was an excitement among our young women because of the sense of danger and the suspense of coming war. They were curious about the big Irishmen and Germans, so tall and fair and deep-voiced. These men were being treated like saviors, come to help defend Mata-moros. Some had curly red and golden hair, and magnificent side-whiskers and coppery mustaches. Many had blue eyes and pale skin, traits like those of the *hidalgo* class in Mexico. When they were fitted with the dark blue coats of the Mexican army, they all seemed like offi-cers. They were less reserved than most of our officers, and laughed among themselves with a great sort of camaraderie. And of course they could not keep their eyes off the girls, who were most flattered by such overt attention. When *Teniente* Riley's cannoneers were not out in the field training, flirtation was strong in the air like springtime. And when they were out in the field, wheeling about in formations of horse-drawn cannons and caissons, creating clouds of dust, then firing their rows of cannons at targets, *estampido, trueno, ¡boom! ¡retumbar!,* with the billowing smoke and the fire flashing from the cannons' mouths, and shells bursting like blooming flowers in the air, so much power and thunder, all the townspeople would go to that side of the town to admire them, especially the young women. Though women love peace, they are excited by force, and the cannoneers were the very image of force.

And in the evenings, the Irishmen sang songs from their Mother Country. They were so happy to be free to sing without being stopped and scorned by their officers! They sang most often "Green Grow the Lilacs O." A beautiful sound, but so unlike the sound of our songs. "Green grow," they would sing. And our people would smile and say to each other, *"¡Gringo!"* They would laugh. *"¡Está balada de los Gringos!"* It was their joke and they never tired of it. The war was almost always in their minds, the dread, the anger, and they loved the joke because they feared and hated the *Gringos* across the river, but loved these *Gringos* who had, by coming over, shown the enemy *Gringos* their backside.

The deserters were in heaven. Suddenly they were praised and adored, after being reviled and punished. The young women they had seen bathing across the hostile river were now close enough to speak with, to touch. It was springtime, also, the season of rising desires. With the danger of war looming, passions were even more urgent. As you may imagine, *Señor,* many a romantic dream was fulfilled in those short days before the shooting began along the Rio Bravo del Norte— the Rio Grande, as you know it.

General Arista was considering two large matters. The first was the removal of General Zachary Taylor's army from the Mexican land between the Nueces and the Rio Bravo. The other was the well-being of the people of Matamoros, and their safety when the *Yanqui* soldiers and guns came to bear on the town. Always beyond the window of my mother's house there loomed those huge dirt walls of your fort, like a bank of dark storm clouds building.

General Arista talked many strategies, there in that room. He spoke of drawing the *Yanqui* army away from Matamoros by going down to attack its supply base at Port Isabel by the Gulf. He talked of placing our force between Port Isabel and the fort, to cut them off from their supplies. Our army could ford the Rio Bravo upstream from the fort and surround it. I remember, too, that *Teniente* Riley proposed a bold plan to cross the river up there with a battery of artillery and emplace it close to the fort, to dominate the weaker northwest side of the fort. He knew the fort well, and said that a crossfire would create a severe demoralizing of all the *Yanquis* within. He also pointed out on the map that a battery in that place would guard the road from Port Isabel to the fort. None of the batteries based around Matamoros could even sight on that road, nor would their shells reach it from so far back. Being a bold officer, General Arista was zealous for *Teniente* Riley's plan. He would tie it to his larger strategy. He would first try to decoy General Taylor's army off on the road to Port Isabel, and then he would let *Teniente* Riley cross the river and build his battery. That is, after the force within the fort was too diminished to send out an assault against the battery.

My mother, plainly to my eye, was distressed to hear of this plan, for all such reasons as would alarm a woman in her circumstances. If much of General Arista's army did move away toward the coast, she feared, the *Norteamericanos* might be emboldened to come over and assault Matamoros. She feared that. And she feared that any movement of either army might precipitate the war, whereas sitting still might postpone it forever.

But I was no naïve child, and I understood that what alarmed her most was the danger to *Teniente* Riley himself. Day by day since the moment of his arrival, I had seen and felt the passion building between those two. It could be felt, like lightning in the air before it flashes. My mother and the Irishman were in straits of propriety, however, and not free to indulge their desires like his soldiers and the girls of the town. They were in the presence of each other only when he was at our house, under the eyes of General Arista and all the high officers, and the officials of the town. She was of station, and the widow of a highly esteemed officer. Her virtue was guarded as if it were the sacred flag of Mexico. *Señor* Riley was esteemed, but only a *teniente*. And having come as a deserter, he was as if a man on parole, earning trust by the strictest protocols. There was longing, but only longing. I myself, *Señor*, was of mixed emotions. They were bewitched by each other, and I loved them both. But the honor of one's own mother is sacred to a young gentleman. Perhaps you understand. Sometime when I am not in the

process of a narrative of war, I shall ask you about how a *Yanqui* journalist deems the honor of his mother. Ha, ha! Forgive me. I should not
mock any man on that matter, not even a *Gringo.*

My concern for my mother's honor and happiness was a major pre-
occupation for me. More than one might expect, as boys of that age
think mostly of themselves only. But there was no other family. I remember her being a woman almost without fault. I have no memory of
any unfair word or deed from her throughout my childhood. She was
devout in her religion, and *la Santisima Virgen* must have been the example by which she guided herself.

But she was not a nun, no. It was her nature to love a man, one who
was worthy. His own Catholic faith was evident to her. It was observed
by us that when his men were in the *tabernas* and the *burdels,* he was
not with them, but in the *catedral.* Such information came to my
mother through the women in Matamoros who saw and knew everything. She was known to disdain gossip, yet almost everything note-
worthy came to her. For their reasons, good or malicious, they told her
what they knew, and what they thought. But whatever she was told, she
weighed its source. I remember she taught me, one must always understand why people say what they say. She was wise, my mother, *la viuda
de Juvero.*

There were Mexican officers there attending upon General Arista,
caballeros, proud and vain, who gave my mother unwanted attention.
They preened and flirted about her. She was merely polite with them,
and they grew frustrated. She did not slight them but they felt slighted
because she remained aloof. Certain of such gentlemen observed her
demeanor in the presence of *Teniente* Riley, and their envy focused
upon him. One of those, a *Coronel* Ramirez, began trying to plant seeds
of suspicion about *Teniente* Riley. Subtly he raised doubts about the
wisdom of letting him and his Irish gunners take a battery of valuable
cannons across the Rio Bravo to the vicinity of the *Norteamericanos.*
The *coronel* wondered if the Irishmen could be trusted not to turn those
cannons over to General Taylor. How clever they would have been to
come across the river in the guise of turncoats to steal cannons from our
army! General Arista listened but said nothing about it. My mother had
overheard, and she urged me to warn *Teniente* Riley that there was such
intrigue. But I was not to tell him which officer had raised the doubt,

for it could not be good to set one off against the other. The Irishman thanked me for the warning, and implored me to convey his thanks to my mother. He said only that, but in his eyes when he said it there was intensity that he did not try to hide from me. I could feel him restraining himself from saying more. Try to understand, *Señor,* how delicate were all our sentiments in that time when the *Yanquis* were in their fort and their cannons were pointed at our town.

General Arista seems not to have taken the *coronel*'s alarm seriously, for he approved *Teniente* Riley's plan, and gave him laborers and horses and infantry support for it. He made it a part of his own strategy to divert the force of General Taylor.

Again it became our duty, we the "Water Moccasins," to cross the river again, and to kindle a fire of excitement. We began subtly, around the camp followers.

"*Se rumorea que . . .*"

It is said that the Mexican army is going to Port Isabel on the Gulf, and destroy your supply base! You will be cut off from everything you need!

In the way that rumors proceed, this soon was on the lips of all three thousand of General Zachary Taylor's soldiers, and no one knew where the information had started. And then, very soon, General Arista sent regiments of soldiers out marching, making great clouds of dust, with the bands playing and the trumpets squealing and blaring.

On the first day of *mayo,* we looked across the river from Matamoros and saw a remarkable sight. White tents were folding down, wagons and oxcarts were going out of the fort, hundreds of wagons! And we watched the *Yanqui* soldiers leave their fort and the deserted campground, and march away in the dust, going down the road toward Port Isabel. We counted and counted. Most of General Taylor's army was leaving. Scouts came in and said they had counted more than two thousand of the *Gringos* on the road, nearly the whole army! The rumors had succeeded, and the *Yanquis* were out from the protection of their great fort, marching away from Matamoros! There was such joy and mirth in our town. We rang all the church bells.

But all was not celebration, for General Arista had formed up the rest of our army and it moved out that same afternoon, marching downstream along our bank of the Rio Bravo del Norte. He might catch the *Yanqui* army out in the open somewhere, and defeat it, for ours was the superior army, and we believed that God would surely favor our forces, as we were rightfully protecting our own homeland from the invasion of the heretics.

Of course, one believes such things. Before one learns the lessons of war. We have come to understand much, eh? Let us moisten our throats, *Señor,* while we consider that war which was beginning on its own, as yet undeclared. My country's official stance was a defensive war. Your army by coming to the Rio Bravo had invaded Mexico, and those of you who were between this river and the Nueces were facing patriots. When we crossed the Rio Bravo to go anywhere around your fort or to your supply depot at Port Isabel, we were not in your territory, but our own. I know, *Señor,* I know. Your government interpreted the Texas solution as it wished, to its own advantage. Your officers were told that Texas bordered on the Rio Bravo. Perhaps some of them believed that, though not all believed it. We have read much of those debates in the years since. Your whole country, not just your government, not just your army, was divided. You are a journalist, *Señor,* but I am a scholar. For more than a decade I have studied that war which so disabled me that I am able to do what else but to study. As I have said already, you were fortunate to come to *me* with your questions about the war, and about *Señor* Riley, not just because I was so close to the events that concern you, but also because I have studied every detail of the war. I can help rid you of misconceptions.

You must understand something about my country, *Señor,* if you are to understand what happened in that war. Mexico is very old. All through its centuries, conquerors came. They all supposed that they were bringing to us something superior to what was already here. They tried to change our country to meet their vision. They came, full of zeal to better us. When they controlled us, they became corrupt. Then the next conqueror would come with his own kind of zeal to destroy and reform that of the one before. We the people of Mexico always accommodated the new conquerors. Some of their notions we embraced; some were put upon us with force and cruelty. Through the centuries we were changed, but the people of Mexico changed more slowly than the succession of conquests, and beneath it all, something in us never changed at all. Each new conqueror said he was bringing enlightenment, but they all had to keep us ignorant in order to control us. Each new conqueror reached down into Mexico and hauled the wealth upward to himself, and the rest of us remained as poor as we had always been, and as ignorant as we had always been.

But a people, *Señor,* contain their own long wisdom, whether or not they are kept ignorant of the conquerors' doctrines. In the long course, the old wisdom is greater than the new doctrines.

Do you comprehend, *Señor?* It has been a long, flowing river. The ancient kingdoms were dominated by newer kingdoms. When the Aztecans were on top of us, the *conquistadors* came. New ideas came from Europe and liberated us from the Spanish king. Then came a succession of class wars. Always there was the turmoil on the surface. But the old wisdom continued to flow quietly beneath, always enduring.

Then, in that period of which we speak, your United States came to conquer us. Your enlightenment you called Manifest Destiny, as you remember. You had a president who told lies to make a reason to invade my country, and although half of your people did not believe him, and resisted the assault, he sent his armies into the Mexican territories from Texas to California. Your armies succeeded swiftly, for various reasons, including their great courage and uncommon initiative, but also because of the failings of our own leaders.

General Arista underestimated your army. He believed it would disintegrate by desertions, and that it would be helpless against his forces when he caught it out from its fort. General Arista had come to know some American officers during his years in exile from Mexico. He admired them. But he did, nevertheless, underestimate their abilities.

In war, you must presume and presume. But to presume only one thing is fatal.

It was very quiet all the next day in Matamoros. Most of the soldiers and officers had marched down the river. It was quiet but it was busy. My mother made me stay in our house and help her pack our small belongings into trunks and crates. We stacked all that inside the door to the street, where a man with a carriage was to come and load it.

Teniente Riley came up from the artillery redoubts with a warning for our defenders. I think he came also to pass eye messages to my mother.

They did much glancing at each other while we translated to the officers the information that the *Yanqui* artillerymen in their fort were preparing incendiary shot. He told an officer to take his spyglass and look at the hot smoke rising from the gun emplacements over there. "Those are furnaces," *Señor* Riley said. "They will be used to heat roundshot before they bombard the city. A glowing-hot cannonball can start a fire in wooden buildings. They are heating the furnaces now so that the incendiary shot will be ready whenever the shooting begins. Everything that will burn must be removed, wood buildings abandoned."

General Arista looked with the glass, and thanked him. He said, "As of now, the civilians in Matamoros begin leaving by the Linares road. They all should be safe from those cannons by nightfall. As for our cannons, the priests will come through the batteries and once again consecrate them. At daybreak tomorrow, we begin bombarding the *Yanquis* who stayed in their fort."

Teniente Riley said, "Then, Excellency, is it the Americans have finally declared their war?" General Arista replied that he did not know whether the Congress had done so yet, but that President Polk had declared war by sending an army into Mexico, and Mexico was in a state of defensive war. "Blood is already on the ground. Declarations are the formality. President Polk has already decided. Therefore we will destroy his fort tomorrow, and catch his little army out in the open. *Dios mediante,* this war will be over as soon as it begins."

My mother was bringing tea to the officers. I remember that the tea set was the one item she had not yet packed. In giving *Señor* Riley his tea, she caressed the back of his hand. I saw it, and I saw that they both closed their eyes and inhaled. Later she told me that she did not know at that moment whether they would live to see each other again. That was why she had been so forward.

PADRAIC QUINN'S DIARY

Fort Texas on Rio Grande ✳ *May 2nd 1826*

IT IS AN ODD feeling here, with most of the Army gone away. Good not to have so many people crowded in a place. But after being used to so many, the absence is scary.

Only about 500 left here, being Maj. Brown's 7th Infantry. Lt. Bragg's artillery makes up the rest. Some of the camp followers gone with the Army, about a dozen laundresses and children still here, and moved their things into the fort where there is more than enough room now.

I have to worry what will become of us here if Gen. Taylor and the Mexicans have a big battle down by the coast. What if we were to lose that battle? The Mexicans could just swallow us up here then. And they wouldn't be very kindly disposed toward us. A little comfort is the kindly treatment Capt. Thornton's dragoons got after they were captured, but one could hardly base one's hopes all on one example.

Can't sleep at all. This afternoon had to tote several barrows of firewood to Lt. Bragg's gunners. They have little ovens there to heat cannonballs. Tired me out good. While I was up there we got a view of a procession of priests with their tall crosses, over around the town, saw them go down to the gun emplacements. One of Lt. Bragg's gunners cussed and called it popish mumblejumble. That made me mad but I know better than to talk up for the Pope among such people as them.

Lt. Bragg reckoned the benediction might mean shooting was about to start, and said he'd knock down and burn down their damned churches if they did.

It is a hard thing to think about, I mean blessing a gun that's made for killing and destroying. Does it mean God's help killing and destroying, or does it just mean keep the gunners from harm? I hope it's only that. If Mister Riley's to be on those guns, I would pray he doesn't get hurt.

Nothing but water and wormy biscuit for supper tonight. Gen. Taylor left us with just 2 weeks' rations. Wonder if we will be for living even till that's gone.

I shouldn't have let myself get in a place like this. Should have crossed the river when I had that chance. If that Sgt. Maloney hadn't got his ideas into my head.

Maloney is down there with the troops that went to the coast. I might never see him again, either. Or Lieutenant Grant.

I wish I was someplace else.

*May 3rd, 1846 * Fort Texas, Rio Grande*

HAIL MARY FULL of grace the Lord is with Thee; blessed art thou among women and Blessed is the fruit of thy womb, Jesus. Holy Mary, Mother of God, pray for us sinners now and at the hour of our death. Amen.

The Mexican cannons opened up on us this morning and they're playing hell. Whoever invented cannons is the worst sinner ever!

This day could well be my last day alive and so I ought to make note of it in this diary. This wad of pages is the only thing I have ever made, to leave any trace of evidence that I Padraic Quinn ever lived or had a thought, except in Michigan where there's a record of my christening.

It is my wish that if I get scattered in pieces by one of these Mexican cannonballs or buried under the collapse of this bombproof, that this memorial be sent to my mother, Moira Colleen Quinn.

That might be difficult, as she is probably somewhere between Michigan and Mexico. She would be for making her way by any means she thinks of. She does get to where she intends to go. Wherever the headquarters of this Army may be, if there be an Army left, that headquarters is where she will make her way looking for me. So on reflection I suggest this be kept at such headquarters for her arrival.

If on the other instance, as seems likely, there is nobody to find this except Mexicans, I pray they will put it in the hands of someone who reads English. I would ask that such person would then put it into the possession of the gunnery officer John Riley, formerly of K Company 5th Infantry and now in the Mexican Army. He will remember me, I'm sure.

I write this a bit at a time. When a cannonball or mortar shell lands inside the fort the earth shakes, and things fall, and then there is so much dirt sifting down and so much dust in the air. Then a time passes before my hand is steady enough to write. People in and out, screaming, needing water, some beshitten out of fear. A cannonball coming over sounds like, I imagine, some old tomcat being pulled apart. The shellburst is a kind of clanking boom and if it's close enough you hear fragments hissing around and smacking into anything near. Everything in the fort is nicked and tattered, and smoky little fires burning on the ground. I write to describe it because I can't think of anything else except being in this. Everything gets very interesting when you think it may be your last thing ever. So if any person ever reads this he'll understand how keen and awful it is, without having to be in it actually.

It has passed through my mind many a time since this began at daybreak, that these shells are being shot at me by Irishmen I used to run errands for, and listen to them talk in their tents. That a soldier I liked so well, I'd cross the camp just to see him and hear him talk, is over there shooting at me.

Well, not at me.

I had rather think that he's shooting at Lt. Bragg. Sure and it is like a duel between those two. Bragg is a mean son of a bitch as no man will deny, but sure he's a brave gunner and has stayed up there on the parapet without cover, returning cannon fire on the guns around Matamoros all day. If a ball took off his head I doubt anyone would weep except maybe his mother, if ever he had one. No one could deny he's brave. But as I wrote here some days ago, I doubt he and his cannons can prevail against a better man whose cannons have been blessed.

If those cannons got holy blessings over there, they're sure getting unholy curses from our fellows here. Hardly any of our soldiers have ever been under cannonfire before, not even the Swamp War veterans, since Seminoles didn't have cannons.

The Mexicans, though, have no cannon shortage! Their shells come from three angles. Our parapets are crumbling in places. My head is aching and my ears ring. We have no one killed in the fort yet, though a few wounded. If not for these earth-roofed shelters where we can burrow like moles, we'd have many dead, sure. Most of the infantrymen are down here. No one is of much use aboveground except the cannoneers.

My God, what a noise, that! There it is again.

And again. It's our big guns shooting back. Heated cannonballs, whitehot, meant to set their town on fire. That would be the firewood I pushed up there in barrows. So I help burn a Catholic city?

Not good to think of this. Those Mexican civilians over there have no bombproof shelters. Hope they moved the townfolk out.

Evening coming on at last, but yet bombardment continues. I really don't like this. I wish that President of the U. States was here cowering as the shells come in. He'd have shitten britches.

Here's something awful that happened today, so close by: I heard a private of the 7th Inf. say that his understanding is that President Polk never soldiered. He opined that no man who has not faced cannonfire should be elected to the authority of sending men to war. He had just finished saying that when a shell fragment tore through the opening of our shelter and sheared his left cheek and chin away to the bare bone. I was sprayed by his blood, and got wet by more of it while helping other soldiers drag him over to the surgeon. I pray never to have anything like that again.

Midnight now. Cannons stopped. The soldiers sleeping with their muskets. More likely, lying awake. We keep hearing all sort of noises out in the dark, voices, digging tools, metal clinking and scraping. Mexican sappers ditching or tunneling, maybe? Oh this is scary. After all the boom and roar. Can hear the river running. Matamoros dark, just a glow now and then, like somebody lighting a cigar or a pipe. First night the town has been all dark. Most of the people must have left before their artillery opened up on us.

I should put out my candle, quit trying to write. Exhausted. I am not the only one writing. Soldiers are scribbling despite the discomfort. One who can't write came and asked me to write a letter to his family. I put him off until daylight. He went back to his burrow and I could tell that he was crying. I haven't cried. I've written instead. I probably would be crying if I couldn't write. I guess that's why I don't want to put out my candle.

May 4th, 1846 ✳ *Fort Texas on Rio Grande*

HOLY MARY, MOTHER of God, pray for us sinners now and at the hour of our death. Amen.

All I know to do is burrow deeper, pray harder. We who'd slept at all awoke to more bombardment, and worse. Some shells coming in from northwest of the fort, over our weaker and lower parapets: that is, from our own side of the river, not the Matamoros side. Maj. Brown our fort's commander in Gen. Taylor's absence discerned that Mexicans now have artillery dug in upstream of us, much closer than the batteries around Matamoros. It would explain the activities we heard in the night. They crossed and dug in under cover of night.

We are trapped.

Some of the soldiers no braver than the camp women under this shelling. Crying and praying with their faces down in the dirt. Some near losing their wits.

Had to leave my hole in the ground to go to the sinks. Also, to find food to bring back. Got to the latrine almost the same moment a mortar shell from Matamoros reached it. Lucky it was for me it got there a moment earlier than I, or I'd not be here to tell of it. Memory is uncertain whether I really saw the missile, but heard it screaming in and then everything rose up with a burst of noise and spraying matter. I woke some time later full covered in wormy shit and blood. I ached everywhere in my head and body and still do, ears ringing like carriage bells. Whose blood I don't know, but not mine, heaven be praised. Was it that some poor soldier was down there as I arrived I don't know, and don't care to think on it. Forgot caution and went reeling down the path to the river and in, clothes and all. Across the river Matamoros was all smoke, from their cannons and from fires set by our incendiary shot.

There I stood in the river washing off, shaky and puking, cannonfire pounding in my head and shot howling over. I doubt anyone could see me, or would have cared if they had. It came to my mind that if I started swimming across, there were for the first time no sentries posted above to shoot deserters. I could be off to Mexico and no one the wiser. I was for making my mind up whether I had strength to do it, and doubt my brain was in much balance to be deciding such important matters, when I saw askance somebody moving on the bank. I wiped water from my eyes and saw it was two soldiers in their dirty blue coats going at full run into the water, all a-splash, then just their heads and shoulders visible as they swam for Mexico. In the light of day like this any other time, sentries or snipers would have killed them by now. But on they went, one paddling like a dog and the other thrashing his arms.

I could swim better than either of them. I doubt they wanted out of Fort Texas any more than I did. They were grown men, sworn to soldier. I could follow with impunity, was my thought. I was leaning down to go with the current, thinking to meet John Riley and starting to pray for a safe crossing, when, damn me, who comes into my head but Sgt. Maloney. And my feet sought the muddy bottom. And I stood there remembering what he'd told me, shot and shell still screeching over and banging like all thunder. I just caved in, it felt like, and I'll admit I cried and cussed at the same time. Then I waded out of the river and came back up to the fort. I might have been too numbed to be as scared as I should. I went finding a sack of hardtack and brought it to the people in my shelter. Need something to show for all that.

I doubt I'll ever get so close to crossing over as I did today. Don't know how I'll feel tomorrow about staying here.

Not ashamed to admit that some of the shit I washed out of my breeches after the shell blew up the latrine was my own. Hope that doesn't happen again.

A dismal thought, that Gen. Taylor's got attacked by the Mexicans down by the coast, and we're all doomed, both there and here.

Writing calms me. But must quit. Candle about gone.

May 5, 1846 ✳ Fort Texas, on Rio Grande

TODAY, WHAT I would call a milestone. I became a "combatant." Of a sort, anyway.

A gunnery sergeant from Lt. Bragg's battery grabbed me at dawn and impressed me into service as a powder monkey. That is, fetching powder charges from the magazine to the cannons. One of their privates was hurt bad by a piece of bombshell yesterday and I took his place.

I never had a harder day. Had I known yesterday this would happen, I would have gone on across the river when I could. This entry will be short. I am too spent out to write much but thought it seemly to commemorate the milestone.

The closer I get to cannons the more I hate them. They're monsters made by men to kill other men and shatter anything erected by men.

They are hot and filthy with black powder and soot. They stink of death and they're deafening. And they are like magnets for drawing enemy fire. The cannoneers are in love with them, though. Sure and it's terrifying to go near and about all that fire and blast while carrying enough explosive powder to sunder a stone house. Cannons kick up as much dust as smoke. My eyes and throat feel like they'd been scorched.

I can say I am surprised to find myself still alive tonight.

I did one fool thing that earned me a mighty thump from the gunnery sergeant, but it was the one fine moment of a dismal and terrifying day. Here follows how it happened:

One battery had been moved from the parapet fronting the river and Matamoros, over to the northwest parapet, to face the nearer battery erected by the Mexicans this side of the river, and counter its fire. I had brought up as many bagged powder charges as I could carry, and was resting, when I heard a gunner yell out "There's the son of a bitch Riley!" It sure brought me up straight. The gunner had a spyglass aimed on the Mexican battery, while keeping his head down as low as he could. I skipped over beside him and asked if I might use his glass to see such a villain, and it was the right thing to say, I reckon, for he handed it to me and went to the cannoneers to sight their gun, I suppose, right on Mr. Riley. The gunner yelled "The dog is right under that second banner!" It took me some squinting to get the glass where I could see aught but smoke and dust, and a ball or two screamed over even as I was peering, but then through the smoke I saw a banner, and there below it sure as I'm Padraic Quinn there stood John Riley himself, in a dark blue Mexican officer jacket and black kepi hat, not a bit cowered down, but full exposed and signaling orders to his cannoneers, who were fair dancing around their guns with ball, swab, and rammer, that's how spry he had them working!

Then he turned our way and raised his own spyglass onto us. And that's when I just got that mad leap of the heart and forgot about the shooting. Up I scrambled to the top of that parapet, and waved my arm at him, wild as a lunatic. I didn't yell, not that I remember, though maybe I did. And I got the glass back up and on him again, and there he was with his glass on me, sure as hell, I know he saw me and knew me, for he raised a hand and waved it at me, two, three times. Then he signaled me to drop down, I suppose, but it wasn't necessary because the gunner grabbed my ankles and pulled my legs out from under me and brought me down on my face in the hard dirt of the parapet. That instant both batteries, Riley's over there and Bragg's here, opened up on each other, and it was all head-splitting thunder and red muzzleblasts and flying clods and whistling metal, ball, grapeshot, and shell.

The next thing for me was I was lifted off the ground by the back of my shirt and spun about face-to-face with the gunnery sergeant. He wasted no time expending every known profanity upon me, and one great wallop with his forearm the size of a leg of mutton left me un-winded and upside down at the gunners' feet. But it didn't hurt me too severely to be sent back to work hauling powder.

The gunnery sergeant never got me aside to explain what my crime was. Sure and I'm thankful for that.

My first day as a combatant. It was worth it, to hail Mister Riley. But tonight I've found another hole to lie in, and hope the gunnery sgt. won't find me again.

I can't find a place on me that doesn't hurt. Well, I guess my earlobes are all right.

CHAPTER X

Fort Texas on Rio Grande ✳ *May 18, 1846*

D ON'T KNOW WHETHER Congress ever declared a war yet, but with or without their say-so we've got one going here. And damned if we don't seem to be winning it, in spite of the odds!

The Mexican batteries were shelling us from two sides whilst our Army and the Mexican were out chasing each other between here and Port Isabel. What they say is, Gen. Taylor clear down there could hear the bombardment of his fort, as it's only twenty miles. So he started his Army back this way. Well, then it was about ten miles up from here he ran up against the Mexican Army at a place called Palo Alto. I kind of remember it from when we came down, a line of trees. The Armies faced off and then in a long fight that we could hear from here at the fort, both sides held till dark. The cannons started a big grass fire up there that we could see lighting the sky red.

Next day the Mexicans drew back about five miles and forted up in a dry riverbed for protection against Taylor's artillery. But our Army fought through, as we discovered by seeing the Mexican troops come willy-nilly down the road past the fort and tumble down the bank of the Rio Grande trying to get away. What a spectacle that was! Even the artillery northwest of us, where Mister Riley was, abandoned their cannons and headed into the river. Awful lot of Mexicans drowned. God-almighty, you just never know! Our troops came in victorious, but they were dazed and tattered something awful. Most of them, it was their first combat. Many had been hurt bad by bullets and canister shot, or blade wounds, or just cut up by fighting through thorny thickets and suchlike. There were plenty of wounded that couldn't walk and were in the wagons, along with dead comrades that had to be buried here. All that meant work for me. I've been a gravedigger now, 150 killed and wounded. Some died after they were brought into the fort, including an artillery major hit in both legs by a Mexican cannonball.

I heard more awful tales than I could ever remember. I saw Sgt. Maloney, who was slashed up something awful but had done himself proud leading a charge in the arroyo with some of his Seminole War veterans who captured a Mexican cannon crew and its gun. He is bragging that half the casualties were Irishmen like him. Most of the wounded aren't even American citizens yet but good soldiers for the U.S.

There had been several reporters at the battles and it was sure interesting to see them writing notes. It seemed to me like the officers spent too much of their time going after those journalists and telling the stories in ways that made themselves look good. Some of the reporters were foreigners, from Europe and South America and the like, very strange and interesting fellows, to my mind, but the officers wanted to talk only to American reporters, who could I guess get their names in the newspapers close to home. Gen. Taylor is said to have hopes of being the President sometime soon. This victory over General Arista might help him. But this seems to be just the start of a war. I guess he'd have to win the whole war to earn the presidency. I really don't know about all that, the politics and the ambition. But I do eavesdrop on the officers, and they talk about such things most of the time. That is, they did until now, and all they talk about now is battle and glory. Their favorite term I've heard over and over is that they've "drawn the claret." It took awhile for me to understand that, then a soldier explained that claret is a sort of wine just the color of blood.

Yesterday it looked like General Arista's whole army fled from Matamoros, and the people of the town, too, with everything they had in wagons, heading westward. Gen. Taylor sent scouts across, and the whole town was deserted, nobody left but those too wounded or sick to move. Lots of them, I hear. Today our army is on the move to occupy the town. Rumor is that Gen. Taylor means to go pursuing the Mexican Army into their country. That Congress will sure declare war now, if they haven't already. General wants us moved away from this low land before the sick season starts. We remember from when we first got to Corpus Christi in the heat of last summer how bad that is. Inland more than a hundred miles there are hills and mountains, where the air is healthy.

I guess it's healthy if you don't get killed by another Mexican Army. There's got to be a lot more Mexican soldiers in this whole country than just the ones Gen. Arista had here. And although the officers tend to scorn them, some of our soldiers were pretty impressed. I guess our dead ones are impressed.

Matamoros on the Rio Grande or Rio Bravo as the Mex call it
May 20, 1846

I AM IN a foreign country! Another milepost in my life, first time outside the U.S. Here we are in Matamoros, that we gazed at so long.

(Though the Mexicans would argue that I was already in their country, there at Ft. Texas.)

First time since Michigan that I've had a real roof over my head instead of tent canvas, or palm leaves like in Florida during the Seminole campaign. And four walls around me. Actually about 3½ walls, as the north one was half ruint by Lt. Bragg's artillery. Found the very cannonball here in the rubble inside. Returned it to the gunners, hoping for a penny or two reward, but Bragg cursed me for a little Mick beggar and aimed a kick at me. I dodged it and think he threw his back out a little. I got that satisfaction if not a penny.

So I have a room of my own, unless some other beggar moves in, the first room I've ever had. For company I have at least one rat—though it may be several appearing one at a time—and a number of scorpions. I have furnished my place with straw for bedding, a broken chair I found and fixed, and a table made from a plank laid over one crate and one keg. The room reeks of smoke. The cannonball was one of those incendiaries and had ignited the wainscot and part of the wood floor. Looks as if there wasn't much damage from incendiary rounds. Most of the town is built of mud brick instead of wood, and the floors dirt or tile. The shelling beat down lots of north walls though. Streets are full of cast-off things I guess the people had to leave. Soldiers had already picked it over before I came over so as usual I get hind tit.

Most of the camp town is now on this side of the river, some in the half-smashed buildings. The bootleggers already in business. Boats of contraband already coming up the river, with fear of the Mexican Army gone. There are still hostile rancheros and guerrillas along the river, both banks, but hucksters and peddlers of all kinds are arriving. Whores are already here. I had to threaten one with my knife to keep her from taking over my room. Don't know how long I'll live here before the Army moves on. I'll probably go on with them. But I mean to enjoy this room long as I'm here. It is a treat to sit and write on a desk instead of my lap or the floor. Have about eight inches total of candle stubs. Found base of a lamp in the street, with a wick in. If I can get some whale oil I might just sit here and write a whole book, ha ha.

The most wondrous part of all this though is the quiet after all those cannons. I do not want any more cannon fire for a long time yet, if ever, even though a cannonball did provide for me the ventilation I have in this little room of my own.

May 21, 1846

THIS MORNING I went to a house that was the headquarters of the Mexican generals. Not much left of it, too good a target for Lt. Bragg to leave standing. That particular pile of rubble is a curiosity place the officers and some of the men stop in and see, I guess so they can say they stood where the Mexican general had been. It had the best prospect of our fort over there, sure enough. Nothing much left for keepsakes. If there had been any inkstands or map cases or other kind of officer equipment, it was all taken away before I got there. I did see a gleam in the rubble over by a fireplace, and dug out a brass tea kettle still serviceable though dented deep on one side and no sign of the lid anywhere. Sure I reckon somebody used the kettle to make tea that Gen. Arista drank, and his staff officers. It's my souvenir and I can imagine what I want to about it. Nobody seems to know whether any Mexican officers got killed when the house was hit, but it is pretty certain the general wasn't here anymore by that time, as his army had gone out after ours before then. I found some bloodstains on walls but most of the floor and walls were too heaped up with mud brick and rafters and roof tiles to tell what happened.

Other places I went to see today were some of the earthworks where the Mexican cannons and mortars were, the guns that gave us such a pounding over there in Ft. Texas. Nothing much left in those places, either, but a broken rammer and shreds of powder bag cloth. Sure and it smells like the true hell in those gunpits, even after a morning rain. I mean that sulfur smell from all the powder they shot up there in those pits. I hung around there awhile and thought about Mister Riley being there as he must have been, in some of them anyway, shooting away at us. I also walked in that battery on the other side of the Rio where I know I saw him that day and we waved at each other. I walked out and walked over it before we crossed the river to here. Had to help with burial detail burying an awful lot of dead Mexicans. Sure and every buzzard in North America must have flown in for the occasion.

What with the Army mostly over here in Mexico now, I need to find where the units are that know me, and get me some errand work. Sort of like to hear some of the stories, like from Mick Maloney the sergeant, and what he did, and how he feels now. Saw Lt. Grant on my way back here and he still damns us for invading Mexico. I heard him tell an officer, This is naked aggression! This is a damned unholy adventure and we ought to be ashamed of what we're doing! Regardless of those sentiments, I hear it told he soldiered real brave in the battles on the road.

Most of the officers are sort of giddy about routing the Mexican Army, saying they won two battles in two days, which I guess sounds better than saying one two-day battle. Since the actions were a few miles apart I guess you could say two victories. Most of the officers don't want to stay here but rather chase the Mexicans down and whip them good before they can get reinforced and rebuilt. So no one knows how long we'll stay here. Gen. Taylor will be for making up his mind on that I guess any day. Has to figure on our supply road from the coast, and rumor has it there will be some steam packet boats used on the Rio Gr. for that, too. Also to bring troop reinforcements.

There is always a townful of vendors and whatnot built up as soon as the army moves into a place and stops. Army privates make 7 dollars a month and have no place to spend it except near camp. The officers call these places Little America. I am a sort of a part of it.

Now that I have this desk, and a place "of business," I am again writing letters for the soldiers who don't know how to write. Now that they've been in battle, they want many letters written. Most just tell their families they are alive. Some want to tell what they did in the battles, and therefore I get to write some really good stories, and I am learning a lot about the battles, and how men in battle feel. One thing they never say in their letters is how it felt to kill somebody. One private from the 5th Infantry, Company K, wrote to his sister in Michigan and said that the Army had made him violate the greatest of the Commandments, that he would not have gone forward in the battle and done it, but he would have been shot by his own officers if he had disobeyed. He told her that a lot of what passes for bravery is that the enemy fire might miss you but your lieutenant wouldn't. I wonder if that could be true.

That K Company was Pvt. Riley's company. I asked that soldier what he thought about Mister Riley being in the enemy artillery. He said he was sorry he had not gone across the river with him. But he asked me not to put that in the letter. He said that nobody could understand unless they had been bucked and gagged by one of these Army officers. He had been through that torment twice.

The soldiers who have been bucked and gagged made up a song about it. He remembered part of it and helped me write it down.

> "Sergeant, buck him and gag him," our officers cry
> For each petty offense them lieutenants espy,
> Till with bucking and gagging of Mick, Pat, and Bill,
> Faith, the Mexicans' ranks they will sure help to fill!
> Derry down, down, down, derry down.
>
> A poor soldier's tied in the sun and the rain
> With a gag in his mouth till he's tortured with pain.
> Sure, I'm damned if the Eagle we show on our flag
> In its claws shouldn't carry a buck and a gag!
> Derry down, down, down, derry down.

Their song goes much like that. It was hard to follow his words just quite, as he was drinking. For that same reason, I might have got part of his letter to his sister wrong, when he said, I think every day of you Dear Sister as I suffer through this—I couldn't tell whether he said "sojourn" or "soldierin'." I asked him which, and when he repeated it, I still couldn't tell, in fact, it sounded more like "soul journey."

So I just wrote it Sojourn. It's all the same.

I won't be surprised if that soldier vanishes from K Company, too.

Matamoros, Mexico ✳ June 12, 1846

NEWS ARRIVED BY boat from the States: War was declared by Congress May 13. (Though that was after the shooting had started.)

Also a letter from my Mother. It had been sent in Care of Colonel Harney's battalion. I have stayed away from his outfit because I had way too much of him in the Seminole campaign. Maybe some clerk in that unit remembered me and found out where I am now. No matter. The letter told me that she was in New Orleans and would find a means of following me to Mexico if I will confirm that I'm here. That I should please write back to her at once. She gave no address as such, but that of Army headquarters at New Orleans, care of a Maj. Williams. That's enough information to tell me that as usual she is supporting herself on the Army, and the Major would be her "liaison," that being the fancy word she taught me to use, and to spell.

I have spent much of this day thinking what I should do about her letter, as a good son. It does not seem to me that a good son would encourage his Ma to travel into a theatre of war.

I could write to her and say that, but if I do so and reveal that I am with Gen. Taylor's Army, she will certainly come following, even if I ask her not to.

On the other hand, I could write to her and tell her that I will come to New Orleans if she will wait there until I find passage, as I could do, on some supply ship.

It just doesn't make sense a mother would want so much to follow a son who has run away. It would make sense for her to try to persuade her son to return to her.

I never thought I would be thinking about things like this.

Sure I am glad I started keeping this journal! I am learning not just how to write and draw, but also to think. To write, you have to think.

Have to do some errands for the soldiers now. I wish there was somebody I could ask advice about this letter. Mister Riley was the only soldier I would have asked about things like this.

Sometimes I wish I had followed him over. In spite of what Sgt. Maloney said.

Maybe I could talk to Sgt. Maloney about my mother's letter. But he's such a hero now that you can't get near him for the reporters.

Matamoros, Mexico * *June 15, 1846*

I DECIDED, in good conscience, not to answer Ma's letter, not yet. Good conscience because rumors are we'll be moving up the R. Grande toward Monterrey in a full offensive. She should stay in New Orleans, and probably will if she doesn't hear from me.

Sure I could go back to New Orleans myself. But our Little America is stirring for the move & now I've a kind of a place to fit in. An Irish soldier, John Doherty, mustered out with a wound he received at Palo Alto, says he will be doing business with the Army and could pay me a little to assist him when we next set up. I asked him what would be the nature of the business, and he replied we'll be for providing an ever-needed product for the thirsty soldier boys. There is good money to be made in that, he said. I know that to be true. My own dear Mother once told me that in all the years she worked near the Army, laundering, sewing, letter writing, and whatever else, the only time she prospered to speak of was when her liaison was a bootlegger.

Very much excitement here among the soldiers, as the rumor grows of invading deeper into Mexico.

For a short while after the Army did so well in those two battles, the Irish soldiers simmered down about deserting. Now with the invasion talk a-building, they're murmuring about it again quite a lot. I believe they'd be for ducking out in droves by now, if they knew where to go. But nobody really knows where the Mexican generals went after they left here. When they were right in sight, one might have to swim the river to get to them, but they were there to greet you, and so were the senorita girls. Now you look off into Mexico and see nothing but grass and sand and shrubs to all the horizons. And you reckon that any Mexicans you'd run into out there would be those bands of rancheros like them that ambushed Lt. Porter, and Col. Cross, back in April. Those would not be likely to inquire of your sentiments before shooting.

And if you didn't meet up with them, your only company would be rattlesnakes and scorpions and wolves.

Matamoros, Mexico With Gen. Taylor's Army * June 20

HERE I SIT at my table in my own nook, some whale oil burning clean in the lamp. Have my diary notes and sketches all in a stack with a hatchet as a paperweight. I'm like a scribe of old, or a monk in a cell. Well, maybe not so like a monk, though, as the monks probably didn't have two gills of rum inside them making them think in whimsical philosophistry the way I am now. The rum came from Mister Doherty. He invited me to help him test his first shipment of the commodity we'll be dealing. We agreed that it is good enough for Irish soldiers, as they are not picky-like or fastidious and would sooner swallow it right down with gratitude than waste their breath complaining. As Mister Doherty joked, "They'll have the rum gone before they realize it ain't whiskey."

The rum sort of makes me want to say important things. Here I am with a pencil in my hand, pretty comfortable, and the whole world running through my head. Maybe I can write down how this war looks to a person in my situation, being rather caught up in it like a bit of chaff in the wind. What I really feel is, if I couldn't put words down on paper, or didn't care to, I'd be just about nothing at all.

Sure and by the holy fist of Saint Patrick, we are truly off to war! All because some particular mortal man in the President's chair got it in his head that we must do it, and somehow, however presidents do such things, persuaded the Congress that it has to be done. From what we read in the newspapers that come down here, not everybody in Congress saw a need for it. I try to imagine just how such things come to be. The newspapers said that the President warned Congress that Mexico is a danger to the United States, and was attacking Texas. I read that one congressman got nicknamed "Spotty" because he kept demanding to see the "spot" on the map where Mexico was attacking. "Spotty Lincoln," they call him. I think I would enjoy hearing an argument like that, in a great, important place like Congress must be. I wonder if they threaten each other when they argue. I wonder if they laugh at each other sometimes. If they give each other nicknames, they probably laugh at each other sometimes. Most of the arguments I've seen and overheard, they got around to laughing now and then. In fact, the one who made them laugh usually won. Though apparently Mister Spotty Lincoln didn't win.

It comes to my mind, that it would be pretty awful to make up one's mind to send anybody off to war. I don't think I could do that. Soldiers and officers talk about this President, that he never was in military action himself. Some say they wish he had been at Palo Alto to catch a bit of case shot, just enough to make him think twice about sending men someplace to kill and to die. Some of our older officers and soldiers were in the War of 1812, and some of the immigrants were in the wars of Napoleon. (I hope I spelled that right. I can almost always spell a word if I've seen it printed. But I haven't seen Napoleon printed for a long time.) I hear many of them say that a man who has never faced gunfire should not send others to face it. I think that sounds right. But does that mean nobody can be a President unless he has been in battle?

I remember when our army was fighting the Indians in Florida, some of our old soldiers said they admired the Indian leaders because they never stood back and ordered their warriors to fight, they always led them. I remember old soldiers, who had been in the war in 1812, saying that Chief Tecumseh was always right out in front where you could see him. But no one could ever kill him with a bullet. He was wounded a time or two but kept on fighting and leading his warriors. That's what those soldiers said about him. But then in that last battle he was killed finally. That was when the battle just stopped and all his Indians disappeared. They said Indians would do that sometimes, just vanish, and then attack you again when you weren't expecting it. I heard about that sometimes in the Seminole War. But the old soldiers said it was different when Tecumseh was killed. He had been yelling like a bugle, and when his voice stopped, they just all vanished. Eerie, they said, like a witching kind of thing.

General Taylor was an Indian fighter back in those years too, so it is said. And a brave man. He's faced gunfire a-plenty, it's said. He could be a president who could send men to battle.

They also say he's conniving to be president if things work out in this war down here.

Having some rum, a body is likely to write just almost anything that comes to mind, and just almost anything does.

Here I am, sure nothing if ever there was nothing, a boy camp follower and bootlegger's helper, polisher of others' boots and brass, an amanuensis, here am I writing about presidents and wars, and about courage and loyalty, and all suchlike.

I do like that word amanuensis. It makes me sound like something important.

Private John Riley taught me that word. One of the things that man gave me, that I will always have.

May he be safe and well, wherever he is.

Hail Mary Mother of God, blessed art thou and blessed is the fruit of thy womb, Jesus.

That is really pretty language. That I'd say is Poetry.

That story writer Poe is a good poetry writer, too, by what Lt. Wallace tells me. "I guess his could be called Poe-try," is a joke I told Mr. Wallace. He shook his head and grinned at me.

Lew Wallace is an Indiana Volunteers officer who shares newspapers with me. He's been trying to write a novel but says the Army doesn't leave you much free time to write. Maybe if he was a camp boy instead of an officer, he could write well and plenty like me.

Seems to me I write better when I have some rum.

Or anyway, I enjoy it more.

CHAPTER XI

Agustin Juvero
Speaking to the Journalist
on the Pilgrimage Road

¡OYE! SEÑOR PERIODISTA, for a few, war means to be a soldier, and to be in battles, a few hours of rage and terror. But the most part of a soldier's life is to be like a refugee, in fatigue and desperation. Swept along, *una astilla en un torrente.* For the larger part of the people, war is like that: being a refugee.

When the cannons began shooting between your fort and our Matamoros town across the Rio Bravo, we became refugees. First we made camps out of the range of your guns. Then, when your army routed ours, our soldiers came fleeing across the river, true panic seized us. We fled nearly two hundred miles on a terrible dry road southwestward to Linares. We had to keep leaving everything along the roadside, except what we wore. We scarcely paused to bury those who died—the old, the babies, the wounded soldiers.

Your scouts followed us at first, and we thought it was your whole army; the Texans especially we feared, for their vengefulness. We even discarded some of our food, to lighten ourselves in flight. And then of course we starved. Our soldiers left cannons and equipment along the way. Some in misery and shame shot themselves to death.

Many people of Matamoros resigned themselves to their fates and returned to their battered homes. My mother and I went west, under the care of Francesco Moreno, who had been the adjutant. I was destined to go to the *Colegio Militar,* in reward for my services as a carrier of propaganda into the enemy lines. As I have described to you before, you remember. It was a terrible journey for us, as for everyone. My mother was strong in spirit, and maintained her dignity and good cheer, but in body she was not hardy. She was of the *hidalgo* class and was not inured to fatigue or hardship. After the first days the carriage broke and was abandoned. Our horse became lame, was killed and eaten raw by soldiers, and so we walked the rest of the way to Linares. All but the highest officers were afoot by then. My mother's feet were bleeding. She fainted several times. One time when she was unconscious, some Irish soldiers made a litter by slipping muskets through the sleeves of their jackets and carried her until we reached a water hole and she could be revived.

I see the question in your eyes, *Señor,* and will answer it: *Sí.* The man in charge of those soldiers was *Teniente* Riley. During the march all the way, he kept us in sight, though he did not march with us. He had responsibility for all his gunners, who had their own difficulty in keeping up. European and American soldiers are brave and strong, but no one can keep marching without food or water the way Mexican soldiers can.

Teniente Riley could not let his gunners fall behind. He knew that if the *Yanquis* were following and caught them, they would be executed as deserters and traitors.

Thus we and the army struggled to Linares; earth was the anvil, the sun the hammer. Late in *mayo* our remnants staggered into the plaza and fell down at the town well to drink.

In the days of our recuperation, we awaited orders from the capital. Our officers prepared elaborate excuses for our defeat. There was a terrible anxiety about being disgraced. I suppose it is the same in any army, but in ours it is more extreme. One never knew who would be ruling the nation until the next edition of the newspapers came, and by the time it was read, that could be changed again. Among certain officers there was always hope that General Santa Anna would have returned from his exile. Among others there was perpetual dread of that.

Teniente Riley was solicitous of my mother's health in those days at Linares, where she was recovering in the care of the *alcalde's* wife and sister. Those *señoras* chaperoned her severely. Only two or three times was she permitted to sit with *Señor* Riley upon a bench in the shaded courtyard, and on those occasions the old *señoras* were at the window, guarding as if she were their own daughter. I in my turn watched the old women, to make them uncomfortable in their spying. But, too, I watched my mother and *Señor* Riley with keenest concern.

I know little they spoke of, not being near enough to hear. And so I remember only what I saw. He had become unshaven and very dirty during the retreat, and burned by sun, but immediately in Linares he had got himself shaved and clean, and his uniform washed out. Thus he was most presentable, and of a gallant manner. Their conversations seemed intense. They must have poured torrents of words into each other. Even if they were not *enamorado,* the discussion of their circumstances would have been from the depths of their hearts. How much they must have tried to understand, and to make understood! How they must have wondered about their fates, the fates of all of us, the fate of Mexico! Together they had seen a war begin, and they were swept up in it, as was I, her only son.

I can imagine how they must have spoken. Their common language was English, but hers was hardly fluent. His tongues were his native Gaelic, and English so dense with brogue as to require close listening. He had learned but a little of our language by then, and even those phrases he spoke correctly were obscured by his accent.

One matter was of so much concern to the Irishman. He spoke of it fervently to her, and she told me of it. But he also spoke of it when I was his interpreter to our officials and messengers. It was this:

That he and his Irish soldiers were very brave and very honorable. He was anxious that some might doubt this. He felt that the loyalty of deserters would always be suspect, even in their adopted country. And he was mortified that he and his gunners had retreated from their battery and left their cannons on the other side of the river. Even though most of General Arista's army had fled in just such haste, *Señor* Riley was most pained by the memory. It was he who had influenced so many other Irish soldiers to come and serve Mexico. They were sure to be executed if the *Yanquis* caught them. He deemed himself responsible for their lives. He told my mother that he would justify Mexico's faith in him if it cost him his life. That his Irishmen would prove themselves the bravest of all soldiers in the defense of Catholic Mexico, if given the opportunity on the battlefield. He said they had vowed never to abandon any of their compatriots if they were wounded in battle. For the honor, he said. My mother said that he was desperate to prove the courage and integrity of these Irish brethren of the good Mexican people. She told me that he believed himself on the verge of disgrace, that he prayed for opportunities to redeem his honor. She was deeply touched by his fervor.

I myself, *Señor, yo mismo lo vi.* To convince her of it was a sign of his ardor. She, as well as Mexico, must believe in him. I know not what else they spoke of in the shade of that tree in the *alcalde*'s courtyard, but I know they spoke of honor.

And I believe, *Señor,* that while they awaited orders from the commanders, they both wanted the orders and dreaded them. For the orders of war would surely separate them one from the other.

I believe that was the feeling they had, because it was the feeling I had.

¡Ay de mi! Of course the orders came. Now we would be separated from *Señor* Riley. There was no time for the sentiments of leave-taking, nor privacy. My mother and I would go by wagon road to Mexico City, where I was to apply as a cadet at Chapultepec Castle. *Teniente* Riley with his gunners would march with the army's remnants, northwestward into the Sierra Madre of the East, to take up the defense of Monterrey, where your army was expected to go. Major Moreno would go with him.

Our good General Arista bore the blame for the recent defeats and was expelled from the army, we heard with sadness. In the army of Mexico, as in other armies perhaps, someone must be dishonored so that others may assume honor.

Those assuming the honor were General Francisco Mejia and General Pedro de la Ampudia. They had been replaced at Matamoros by General Arista, and now in their turn they replaced him. So you see how such matters devolve, *Señor.*

We stood in the gate at the house of the *alcalde* and watched our poor army march away toward Monterrey. Many were without shoes, yet going into the stony mountain paths. That was a minor hardship for the infantry soldiers from the Indian class who had never had shoes before, their feet already like leather. For the rest, we could imagine what an ordeal it would be. We watched the Irishmen march out, in their tattered uniforms, artillerymen without cannons or caissons. But *Teniente* Riley would not let them be seen as abject, *¡ni una miaja!* He made them, eh, *pavonearse.* What is your word? Strut! If you could have seen it! My mother with her chin up watched them, smiling; perhaps they could not see her tears of pity, for dust rose thick off the sunbaked road. The last we could see of them was the white crossed belts on their backs, growing more faint in the yellow dust. I remember that sight, even so many years later: the dust full of sunlight, the mountains looming clean above the dust. And I remember the distant noise of the bands. Our army lost many weapons when it retreated across the river at Matamoros, but it did not seem to have lost any horns and drums.

And then soon came the time for the rest of us to leave the town of Linares. Wagons and an escort were assigned to carry us, and the officers who were too badly hurt to serve in the defense of northern Mexico, and a few other civilians.

We had more than three times farther to go, and in the opposite direction, than the soldiers going to Monterrey. From Linares to Mexico City, *Señor,* was a steep and perilous journey along the backbone of the Sierra Madre, three hundred miles if the road had been straight, but it was not straight anywhere of course.

In the summer it was good to climb up from the plains and foothills into the mountains. Up from the unhealthful air and *los mosquitos,* into the fresh smell of trees. But the roads were bad, the wagons nearly shook apart, the nights were so cold I felt my mother shuddering all night although we slept against each other to keep from freezing. I recall even now how close the stars seemed to be, and also the howling of *los lobos* in the mountains. Sometimes we spent the nights in tiny towns, where the children would stand back against a wall and with wide and fearful eyes watch the officers who were missing arms and legs. They knew the word *guerra,* but this was the only evidence of it they had ever seen, for they were too young to have known all the constant wars before.

The road took us through Ciudad Victoria and Ciudad Mante, both in Tamaulipas State. Then a hundred miles farther on, in San Luis Potosi State, we arrived at Ciudad Valles, at the crossing of the road between San Luis and Tampico. There we heard of messengers who had gone through, telling of the ships of the *Yanqui* navy seen patrolling in the Gulf. We rested and our wagons were repaired, and we traded our limping horses for mule teams before going on for many days, down into the valleys of fast rivers, then climbing ever higher, and at last crossing to the western side of the mountains in Hidalgo Province to reach Pachuca. There again we traded for good horses and mules to finish our journey. South of us was the great *volcán,* Popocatepetl, and ahead to the west spread the grand Valle de Mexico, the heart of my beloved country. You yourself, *Señor,* have come to Mexico City from the east. Surely you have never seen anything so magnificent anywhere. I have told you of our journey because I love to remember it in the eyes of my memory as I speak of it.

And coming down into the Valle de Mexico was a return home, for me and for my mother. She was born in the great city, and in my turn I was also. It was because of the military life of my father that we ever were in other parts of Mexico. I am grateful that I have seen much of my country, for it swelled my heart. But here in the *ciudad capital* I am at home. Here live the families who enveloped my mother when she was a child and a young woman. When we came down from the mountain roads and into the sight of the great city, it was to her a sanctuary. Though the nation was being invaded by foreigners, she said to me that their invasion could not come this far.

When she said that, I reminded her that three hundred years before, the Spaniard Cortés had come with only five hundred soldiers and conquered Aztecan Mexico, in the very place. I was only showing off for her my education. But I should not have done so, for my words dampened the joy of her homecoming.

We were greeted in our home city by my mother's relatives. They made much over her, for she was thin and very fatigued.

My uncle, Rodrigo, who had formerly been a soldier, he took me in his carriage to Chapultepec to enroll me in the *Colegio Militar.* We brought with us the paper that General Arista's clerk had given me, with the general's signature on it. It was a fine, bright day, I remember, and I wore a new black suit, which had been tailored for me to replace the torn and faded clothing I had been wearing since Matamoros. In the carriage we rode across the great plaza, the Zocalo, for a look at the cathedral where I had been christened. After centuries of construction the cathedral had been proclaimed complete. You have seen it, *Señor,* how magnificent it is. The horns and drums of a regimental band were echoing in the vastness of the Zocalo between the cathedral and the government buildings, and many companies of soldiers in their blue coats and white belts and black shakos were being drilled. It was the *movilización de ejército,* the grand patriotic calling up of armies, a reminder that our country was being invaded. Though the cities were alive with their usual markets and festivals and bullfights, there was the feeling of sadness and yearning and self-righteousness that prevails when your country is being attacked. *Tío* Rodrigo kept talking of it during our long ride, out through the city walls through the Belén gate and westward toward the castle. It is about two miles, and riding on the causeway you see the castle looming above the roofs and the trees. I as a Mexican cannot look up at that high place without imagining the king Montezuma and the seat of Aztec civilization there, for it remains in our national spirit, despite the efforts of the *conquistadors* to erase all traces of it. I do not have to describe to you the magnificence of the castle on that precipitous hill, for I know you have seen it, *Señor.* But if you have not gone up the steep road to the castle, if you have not seen from there all the *valle,* the city, the lakes Xochimilco and Chalco to the south and east, the Pedregal of lava in the south, a desert within a paradise, and the mountains beyond it all, *Señor,* if you have not seen all that from up there, you cannot know one's eagerness to prepare for the service of one's sacred land.

As we went up, my good *Tío* Rodrigo showed me the grove of old cypress trees on the western slope, trees said to be hundreds of years in age even before Montezuma was upon that hill, and I remember he said to me, as we left the carriage in the care of cadets, he said, Agustin, you feel as if you are in the center of the world, that nothing exists before or after your lifetime, but the truth is that your life is a spark in size and duration, but Mexico is eternal. You must enter here in humility.

¡Son habas contadas, Señor! I don't need to tell you that I could not have felt more humble, as even the lowly cadets who tended our carriage looked at me with contempt, for I was not yet even a cadet, but surely would come in even beneath them!

On Chapultepec also is the summer home of the *presidente.* Therefore it swarmed with gentlemen and officers whose gravity and splendor and air of importance made my uncle and me seem almost invisible, which helped assure that I would feel humble. I did not know at the time that some of them were ambassadors of other countries, that another crisis of national leadership was in progress. I did not know that General Santa Anna was returning from exile, in hopes that his reputation would invigorate the patriotism needed for the national resistence to your invasion. The discussion was frantic in the government, about the need for him to come and lead, and the dangers of returning him to power. Thus, Chapultepec was teeming with advisers.

My uncle led me to a room where a captain looked at the letter I had carried from Matamoros. I stood waiting, not as humble as my uncle had said I should be, but proud to have brought a paper signed by a general. When the captain looked up from the paper his expression was not impressed or friendly. He put his finger on the signature and said that General Arista had been expelled from the army in disgrace, and so, what good was this piece of paper?

I had not expected such a challenge. I was stunned. I imagined my entire career suddenly swept from my reach. But *Tío* Rodrigo must have expected it. He pointed to the date of the document and said that it was written while the general was still in command, and was thus still valid as an application. Then he menacingly hissed a demand to see the director of the *Colegio,* who was, he said, an old comrade-in-arms.

The captain took the letter into an inner room. There were voices. Then the captain returned. With politeness he showed my uncle into the other room. But not me. He led me down a dark hall where an older cadet was writing at a desk. He told the cadet to take the usual information and then to take me to the *comisario* and then the *residencia.* It meant I was admitted. I was flooded with joy, and I told the cadet of my good fortune in having such an uncle. The cadet listened with arch interest as I explained. I should have seen that I was telling more than I should have told. I should have deduced from the jealousy among our army's officers, that army cadets might already be cultivating the traits of suspicion and envy.

Though untrue, it was presumed by all the academy's cadets, almost from the moment of my arrival among them, that I had been admitted to the *Colegio Militar* only because my uncle was an old friend of the *commandante.*

At first of course I did not know that was the rumor about me. I presumed it was only tradition that the newest cadet was to be snubbed and abused. They called me *un niño pera* in whispers as I passed. A spoiled rich child.

Eventually I learned of the false rumor. I could have laughed, as I was perhaps the only cadet who had *not* gained admission through the influence of relatives or politicos. I had been recommended by an officer in the field, in reward for helpful service. How many of *them* had been? Not one.

But I could not allow myself to be diverted from my education by such *mezquindad.* The education required three years. I had arrived only a little late for the beginning, and applied myself to come abreast in the first term. My earlier education had been acquired in spite of many disruptions, but I was adequate in mathematics and physics, which my mother had made me study from books no matter where we were. English was a course required at the *Colegio,* and I was already fluent in it. The education also required French language, because much of the curriculum had been derived from the Napoleonic arts of war. Chemistry was my realm of severest ignorance, but I was at advantage in astronomy, which had been a fascination of both my parents. I knew most of the celestial bodies and the constellations, as well as the mythology pertaining to them.

Like most of the student cadets, I was impatient to proceed to the military subjects—fortifications, artillery, and tactics—but those would prove to be slow in coming. First were the academic studies, and, in large portions, drill, discipline, and the meticulous maintenance of uniforms, quarters, and accoutrements. One might have presumed at that stage in our education that the sole criterion for being an army officer was to look like one. We spent much of our time being inspected or preparing to be inspected. Fortunately, our frustrations with the routine, and with each other, could be vented *en la esgrima,* with the fencing swords. Many of us developed a passion for it, and I was already adept. In fact I became so adept that the antipathy of other cadets toward me became tempered by their respect for my skill with epee and saber. Perhaps some foresaw that their boorishness to me in school might someday be recompensed at maturity by an invitation to duel. I confess that now and then I entertained such a fancy.

Although there was no official course in cavalry, except as a section of the course in tactics, we cadets were much exposed to the equestrian arts, racing and jumping, lancing, mounted combat, and the care and training of warhorses. Among the duties that filled all our waking hours were stable cleaning and the grooming of military horses kept by the Citadel. I grew to love and admire the beasts, which are essential to the military, and my affinity for them inclined me toward the eventual purpose of cavalry or dragoons, or perhaps to the horse-drawn artillery. I often remembered the élan and the efficiency of the flying batteries I had seen demonstrated in *Señor* Riley's training maneuvers outside Matamoros. I could with gusto imagine myself, like him, commanding units of such importance in modern warfare. The Irishman was an inspiration to me in ways he did not even suspect. I thought of him every day, and prayed for his safety and success.

In your travels in Mexico, *Señor,* have you seen Monterrey? Yes? *¡Bueno!* It was a favorite city of my father and mother, for its beauty. For the sweet nature of its people. For its great cathedral, and for the wide plaza along the Rio Santa Catarina. High on a crag where it gleams in the sunrise is the bishop's palace. And dominant on the north of the city stands the Citadel of Monterrey, where my father was stationed briefly when I was quite young. It is a formidable place made of dark stone, with embrasures for many cannons, and it guards several roads to the city.

Soon after I arrived at the *Colegio Militar* in Mexico City, the news came that your General Zachary Taylor was marching on Monterrey. Our instructors talked to us in class about the tactics and the possibilities of the imminent campaign. They thought they knew what had gone wrong in the battles by the Rio Bravo: that General Arista's courage had failed in the face of an inferior army. That was of course the official judgment. Such a thing would not happen at Monterrey; it was not even in the realm of the possible, because General Ampudia was returned to command the defense, and Monterrey's defensive posture was unassailable. With such hope and pride we listened to those discussions! We loved the instructors' appraisals of General Taylor's inferior army, of his undisciplined volunteers, and the prospect that as many as half his army, the Catholic Irish and other Europeans, would soon desert him and come over to Mexico.

It all made sense to our young and supremely patriotic minds. We believed that God was on Mexico's side because of our righteousness. The instructors inflamed our hatred and dread of the *Yanquis.* They told us tales of atrocities done by the Texan barbarians, who shot civilians for sport, who raped girls on the roadsides, who looted churches and smashed the altars. The instructors assured us that such beasts and vandals were condemned by their own *malevolencia.* One of the advanced cadets, a mathematician, had the audacity to question whether God's righteous indignation could be calculated into our plans for the defense of Mexico. Ha! His impertinence earned him considerable demerits. But his punishment was reviewed by the *commandante* General, who adjudged that the cadet's challenge was in order: that God could *not* be calculated into battle plans in the art of war, even though he well might determine the outcome in some unforeseeable way. The cadet's demerits were removed.

I will say, *Señor,* that I took great pleasure in such speculations and arguments. Here were philosophy and theology made urgent by the onset of invasion. We carried the arguments out of the classrooms and kept them alive wherever we went, even into the dining hall and the stables. The heretical religion of the *Yanquis* was a factor in the fate of our country, we believed. Catholic nations everywhere were condemning the United States, and some of their military leaders were volunteering to come and aid Mexico with their service. Our generals and politicians in the meantime were writing measures of every sort to entice General Taylor's disgruntled immigrant soldiers to our side.

Although I was too low in status to express opinions in the lecture rooms, the cadets became aware that I had experiences far beyond theirs. I had prowled the *Yanqui* camp on the bank of the Rio Bravo, even stealing among their sentries, to spread our propaganda. My own home had been the command post of the generals, and it had been demolished by the *Yanqui* bombardment from across the river. I myself had endured the hardships of our retreat from Matamoros to Linares, and had seen our soldiers die along the way, and had seen them slaughter horses to fend off starvation. I was, in a way that impressed them more than they cared to admit, a veteran even though I had not been a soldier. I was clever to let them know these things, but without boastfulness. I gave small hints and let them ask me for more details. The tactic of not being a braggart is greater and more effective than one would expect. To have someone come seeking to learn, that is a kind of importance that will compensate for one's insignificance. Ha ha! Look, after all, *Señor Periodista,* did it not bring you all the way to me now? Ha ha!

But, *Señor,* the one experience of mine that most drew the cadets, those young students who had never been near war, only in lecture rooms, what intrigued them most was that I had, my lowly self, moved among those very brave and mysterious figures, those strong and principled Irishmen who had come across to help defend Mexico against the heretics! I had walked among them and translated for them with our own generals and *coronels!*

The name of Don Juan Riley was not yet known widely in Mexico City. But it soon became known in the Citadel, and I modestly—oh, yes, modestly—predicted that, if that Irish warrior kept his safety, at Monterrey or wherever he might serve, he would become a giant among us, a beloved hero in our sacred cause. I described his grand and noble appearance to them, because they asked me what he looked like. I told them of his gentlemanly manners and his boldness.

And I was sincere. I believed in him. I never doubted my intuition about *Señor* Riley. And was I not right?

One important truth, though, I kept to myself, for, among ignorant youth such as they were, it would have changed their entire perception, and would have eventually brought mockery back upon me, or, reaching the ears of officials of the academy, might have harmed *Señor* Riley himself.

I did not mention to anyone that the Irish gunner and my mother the widow of an officer had given their hearts to each other. Of that truth, *Señor,* I dared not speak.

CHAPTER XII

Monterrey, Mexico ✳ *September 26, 1846*

AFTER A LONG delay, back to this diary. This was a day of note!

This is a new diary book. All my writings and sketches hereto have deteriorated to a big, ragged wad, too unwieldy to handle on the march and under the living conditions of camp life.

I therefore rolled it in oilcloth and bound it with twine. It covers all the time from the beginning of my journaling, with all my awkwardness of writing. It tells the campaign of Matamoros and then the progress of Gen. Zachary Taylor's Army up the Rio Grande by boat to the City of Camargo at the mouth of the San Juan River. It contains my account of the riot aboard a troop steamboat, between Irish soldiers and a contingent of Protestant volunteers. At that point I quit writing for some weeks because of our approach to the city of Monterrey, and the battles which defeated the Mexican Army here. I summarize that part of the first diary here, in the event that something might separate me from it, and as a prologue to this volume, which as the reader can see is more compact and tidy, actually a true book under stiff covers. This is a ledger book I found in the ruins of a government building here in Monterrey after Gen. Taylor took this city.

I might not have resumed this journal at this time, except that today I saw Mister Riley for the first time in several months, under heartrending & awful circumstances. I felt that I ought to observe this day by beginning the new journal.

We are just plain astonished that Monterrey fell to us. It is a beautiful city defended by strongholds on several high hills, giving the Mexican artillery every opportunity to catch our soldiers in crossfire. Cannons were emplaced in a fortress, the Black Citadel. Their headquarters stronghold was in the central Plaza, their powder magazine the cathedral. The city was defended by other gun batteries, and by infantrymen, and snipers on rooftops. I shall not try to describe the whole battle in this diary, as I am ignorant of battle tactics. All that will be described well enough in the newspapers & the military reports. I'll recount only the part of the assault in which I participated. But not by my intention. I was drawn into it as an errand boy, which is turning into a more dangerous occupation than I ever expected.

Because of such defenses, our casualties were severe. Canister shot and snipers did us the most harm. Some officers say that we never would have taken the city but for two things, one being that Gen. Taylor divided his force to attack the city from both east and west, the other being that the Mexican general in command, Gen. Ampudia, gave up while he could have held. He is reputed to have no stronger instinct than keeping himself safe from harm. He was the commander at Matamoros before being succeeded there by Gen. Arista. Now both of those generals have had their chances to lose cities to Gen. Taylor. Underestimating Old Rough & Ready is a common error.

Now to relate here the part of the action that I saw. It was on the third day. Gen. Taylor had already lost a tenth part of his army through casualties attacking the east side of the city. Fighting through the streets was costly in lives because the Mexican defenders were set up to sweep those streets with musketry and shot. Some of our veterans knew a tactic which denied the defenders that advantage. Instead of going up the streets in plain sight, they would fight their way into the first house in a block, and then with pickaxes they would batter through interior walls into the next house, and so on, pitching hand-bombs into the rooms ahead, one by one, then going up and killing the snipers on rooftops. Thus they simply mined their way from street to street to approach the Mexican barricades and their main stronghold in the central plaza.

It was my fortune on that day to carry picks and other tools to replace those broken, which were many. I cannot remember how many trips I made through rubble, half blinded by brick dust and gunsmoke, knocked down several times by hurrying soldiers. They soon had me fetching water in canteens as well. I hope I never have to go among fighting men ever again, especially in such close and blinding circumstances. Bayonets scare the stuffing out of me when those carrying them are milling and lurching about. And even inside the house walls I heard musketballs whiffling and smacking around, breaking windows, fired by the Mexican soldiers and snipers on roofs. As for cannon shot, it throws chunks and splinters in every direction. Even a thick wall is not much protection. I could hardly see, from all the grit in my eyes, and got a cut on my shoulder from something, either a fragment of shell or being grazed by someone's bayonet. I cannot even remember exactly where or when I received the wound, in all that jarring chaos. Afterward I found myself scarcely able to walk from twisted and sprained feet and ankles. I would not have been much use helping soldiers the next day. Fortunately, the battle ended that evening when Gen. Ampudia gave up.

It was by the unusual terms of surrender that I saw John Riley today. It was like this: Monterrey's civilians were trapped in the plaza with the Mexican Army. Gen. Ampudia appealed to Gen. Taylor to spare them from further bombardment by letting the Mexican Army withdraw. Gen. Taylor agreed to that, because his own Army was so spent, and had suffered more casualties than the Mexicans had. I heard Lt. Grant say it was a good surrender because we probably would have failed to take the plaza anyway; one more day and we'd have lost instead of won.

Other officers faulted Gen. Taylor for not having the grit to make a real victory. But what I heard among the soldiers was mostly relief and gratitude.

I doubt if I'll ever be able to write well enough to say how I felt today when I saw Mister Riley. I went up west of the city, to the road that leads out of Monterrey toward the Sierra mountains. That road runs parallel to the Santa Catarina River and it is just about the prettiest stretch of land I ever saw. Mountains west of us, & Monterrey to the east, such a beautiful city despite much artillery damage. I followed the 5th Infantry out there. Our troops were lined up along the roadside to watch the Mexicans march out toward Saltillo. It was their reward. The 5th Infantry was the regiment that Mister Riley had been in before he deserted. I sort of trailed along near Capt. Merrill, Company K's commander. When he turned and saw me he winked, so I guess he remembered me from Fort Texas, where I had used to run errands for him and his men.

Much of our Army got lined up out there, and we were so filthy and tattered, and limping and bandaged up, that old Gen. Taylor's decision made sense. These soldiers sure didn't look as if they could have done much more fighting. I thought, if this is the Army that won, the losers must look like whipped dogs. But at midday when the Mexican troops came up the road out of Monterrey, I saw how wrong I was. Those Mexican troops sure did not look like a defeated Army. I couldn't take my eyes off of them. To see the enemy up close really gets one's attention. Their infantry were generally short, Indian-looking fellows, but wore tall black shakos that gave them a taller look. They had English muskets, what was called the big old Brown Bess, and wore blue coats and white trousers. They marched erect and smart. The Mexican cavalry looked proud, with their long lances and banners, and shiny helmets. They went by, and kept going by it seemed endlessly, not looking to either side, not letting any feelings show in their faces. Our men might have meant to jeer or mock them, but for the most part kept still and just studied them, respectfully, I think. After all the blarney from our West Pointers about our superiority to "stupid little brown Greasers," our men were seeing something different.

When a Mexican company would march past, I could see our troops on the other side of the road, over there through the dust, and just opposite me there was Sgt. Mick Maloney, and he saw me and grinned and waved to me. There was a brave man who knew who were and weren't cowards, and he sure wasn't mocking those Mexicans.

Now up the road came the Mexican artillery. Gen. Taylor had agreed to let the Mexicans take just one battery of six cannons out of Monterrey. Here they came, raising dust, a team of horses pulling each cannon and its caissons. On each caisson rode the gunnery officers, with the gun crew marching behind. As they came rattling along our soldiers by the roadside began yelling. I edged out past Capt. Merrill to see better. And just as I saw the first gunnery officer on the first caisson, Capt. Merrill exclaimed, Goddamn! John Riley!

Sure by the gnarly great fist of Saint Patrick it was indeed the very man! There he rode, looking straight ahead with his jaw set hard, all got up in blue coat and gold trim, a kepi hat with a shiny bill, looking splendid as a general. I heard Sgt. Maloney's voice roar:

"John Riley! Ah ye faithless, wormy Judas! Turncoat! Hop down and I'll rip y'r black heart out with this true Irish hannnnd!"

Others were yelling, too, a good half the regiment, but the sergeant's voice roared above them all. "Y'r a disgrace to y'r Mother Country! Y've drug us all down, bastard!"

And men were shouting other names, Murphy, John Little, Jim Mills, calling them curs and traitors, all of them fellows I knew before they swam the Rio Grande from Fort Texas. It looked like Mister Riley's entire battery was made up of Irishmen! But sure it was Mister Riley himself that had all my attention, and my heart was up my throat, or was I about to throw up from every kind of emotion at once. I wanted him to jump down and go silence Sgt. Mick Maloney, but I also wanted

Sergeant Maloney curses
John Riley & deserters
on the road out of
Monterrey, September 26th, 1846
Drawn by P. Quinn, an eyewitness

Mick Maloney to drag him down and thump him likewise, for leaving us Irishmen who had loved him so. None of that happened, though, and his caisson was abreast of me just then, and I was looking up at him, close enough even to make out the artillery sign on his high collar, like a gold sun with rays, but meant to be an exploding shell, so I've heard, that's how close I was. I heard Capt. Merrill yell to someone, "Damned if he ain't a captain I do believe!" I just felt I didn't want Mister Riley to have to withdraw in defeat with only curses being heaped on him by his old comrades. And so I yelled his name, calling him Mister instead of Private or Captain, and lunged into the road waving my hand.

And sure mine was the only voice he responded to, and he glanced down at me, just his eyes, not turning his head a bit, and he sort of smiled, or grimaced, I don't really know, but it was just the most pained look I think I ever saw. I choked on it, sure I recall I did that, and went weepy so bad I could just see the shapes and colors of things. Somebody grabbed my arm and pulled me back off the edge of the road, Capt. Merrill I suppose it was. I heard somebody bellowing, "Ye sons of bitches kilt and maimed us by hundreds, goddamn you! Your own old messmates!" I guess the deserters knew better than to yell back.

So then I just stood there in the sun sort of like I'd been poleaxed, and the guns and caissons clattered past. I'd guess I saw maybe a hundred soldiers in Mexican uniforms who had been poor tormented privates on the other side of the Rio Grande. Now they rode by with faces set like stone and looking straight ahead and hearing the awfulest things said that a body will ever hear. Captain Merrill told a lieutenant,

"To think of it! I signed the blackguard's pass that morning, and look at what's come of it!" And I remembered it then, indeed the captain had given permission for Mister Riley to leave camp to attend a Mass that morning and he'd never come back. I looked up at Captain Merrill then, he's a tall, kind of likeable, round-faced veteran, side-whiskers down to his neck and a kind of cheerful fool's look most of the time, but now he had an expression that looked rather much the way I felt, his chin crumpling and eyes glassy. And I remembered that once back in Texas he had told other officers that if the damned Irish haters wasn't running everything Pvt. Riley would deserve to be a captain or maybe better, they just didn't make better soldiers. Sure and it was Capt. Merrill himself who had recruited Mister Riley, and it was he who had permitted him to go over the river to the enemy. So I guess if there was anybody on that road this day who felt as worked up as I did it would be the captain.

Well, I'll take that back. I guess Mick Maloney, too. But I don't reckon his feelings were mixed up—just plain hate.

I've started a drawing of him cursing Mister Riley.

Tonight I sat thinking. Though I am just a camp boy and not even a soldier, sure not an officer or a diplomat, I see how smart these Mexican generals are. Now it's true, as I see it, that General Taylor won this city against awful odds. He's some general, no doubt of it. But here's what that Mexican general Ampudia did: He saved the civilians, maybe thousands of them, from being killed and hurt by our mortars and artillery. Then he bargained to have his Army march out with their small arms and a battery of cannons. He spruced them up so they didn't look like a defeated Army at all. I think that had a sort of humbling effect on our own troops who thought they had won but could hardly raise up to a slouch. And he got the Irishmen out of there, who would have been hanged for desertion if he had surrendered them over. I don't know how he drove that part of the bargain. Probably Gen. Taylor just didn't know that so much of the artillery was made of our deserters, so one battery didn't count much in the negotiating. Anyway I am glad Gen. Ampudia is that shrewd.

But as awful as it was for those renegade gunners, they got out alive. Our soldiers had the satisfaction of yelling hate at them. But there was something else going on along that road. I saw it, being Irish. I doubt the West Pointers noticed it.

All along that road stood our raggedy, worn-out, sick Irish soldiers, doomed to abuse and humiliation from their officers, watching their Old Countrymen ride by smart and proud in a Catholic Army, wearing rank they'll never rise to in the American Army. I saw their faces.

Monterrey, Mexico ✳ *September 28, 1846*

THE AMERICAN FLAG is up over Monterrey now. For weeks our Army can't chase Gen. Ampudia (by terms of the surrender), so here we will sit for a while licking our wounds and getting to the business of governing a city. Our Little America is already arriving by boat and road. Mister Doherty is here with his bootleggery and so I have a job. Most of our soldiers are either wounded or halfway crazed from all the hell of taking the city, hundreds sick from dysentery and wanting to drink anything that will stupefy them out of their misery. More than a thousand, maybe closer to two thousand, died from dysentery and related sicknesses since we came up the river. Now around this city it's the bone saws and cauterizing irons day and night in the Surgery. And delirious men screaming like babies, waking up screaming and crying.

Now the fighting's over, the West Pointers start to abuse the Irish troops again for discipline.

For this we could have stayed in Texas.

CHAPTER XIII

AGUSTIN JUVERO
SPEAKING TO THE JOURNALIST
ON THE PILGRIMAGE ROAD

To BE A cadet in the Citadel, *Señor Reportero,* was to be like a
monk, cloistered from the world. The regimen of study, drill,
and work was severe and exhausting. In that high place we were surrounded by beauty we could not reach. We could hear the deep-toned
bells of matins and vespers in Mexico City, and from more distant Churubusco, and from San Angel, as much as five and six miles away. The
air was filled with their reverberations. If you are on a high place,
sounds rise to you, and so we could hear the band music, and festival
music, and the voices of singers, singers of joyful music and longing
music, the chanters of holy songs. The ancient cypress trees down the
hill were full of singing birds. But up in the Citadel, all was echoing
stone, where no one sang. We heard only ourselves and our instructors.
Little came to us from outside and below.

Yet our country was at war, and we were learning to be warriors. Each
of us at the end of his three years was expected to emerge with the rank
of an ensign and begin a life of military service. Thus we hungered for
knowledge of that particular war, not just for studies of the art of war.

And there were ways we learned, *Señor.* Some you might expect,
some that would surprise you. Newspapers and journals of all sorts,
even those from the United States, were smuggled into the school.
Some of the instructors themselves would want to bring us some item
of news from the war that they felt would help them teach a point.

Thus we learned with astonishment and despair that General Taylor's army had conquered the impregnable Monterrey! That although the Mexican artillery and the snipers had inflicted enormous harm upon them, the *Yanquis* had encircled the city and then compressed its defenders ever inward toward the plaza, until General Ampudia called for a truce in order to spare all the town's civilians, who were trapped there with his soldiers, there in the plaza.

The general had negotiated the truce so skillfully, our instructor told us, that it was in itself worthy of study, aside from the tactics of the battle. He was able to gain some very favorable conditions because he knew how spent General Taylor's army was. If the fight had continued another day, the *Yanquis* probably would have failed. But too many of the townspeople were imperiled. General Ampudia negotiated wonderfully. We were to study what he achieved:

He would yield Monterrey to the *Yanquis,* with the safety of the citizens assured. The Mexican army would march out in peace with all its small arms, and would not be pursued until two months had expired. With them would go, unmolested, a battery of six cannons and its artillerymen. This was indeed a coup for General Ampudia, because most of those artillerymen were the ones who had earlier deserted from General Taylor's army, and had fought under the command of the valorous *Señor* Riley. Such a prize they would have been for Taylor's vengeful men!

But General Ampudia did not intend to give up those deserters. They had proven themselves above value. With their heavy guns on the Black Citadel, under *Teniente* Riley's superb command, those very cannoneers had inflicted more damage on the *Yanquis,* it seemed, than all the Mexican infantrymen and cavalry. It was said that his cannons had killed and wounded a tenth of General Taylor's whole army, among them at least forty officers! One might imagine that the Irishmen's revenge for their suffering under the West Pointers was richly satisfied in that battle!

And one might imagine as well what their fate would have been if General Ampudia had surrendered them. But he did not!

As for the city, it had no further strategic importance. We learned that our army marched south to San Luis Potosi then, and were met there by their new supreme commander, General Santa Anna himself, returned from exile and mobilizing the greatest army Mexico had ever seen. He had convinced us all that only he could be the savior of Mexico. You cannot comprehend the appeal of that man, *Señor,* unless you are Mexican. It was said, Santa Anna *is* Mexico!

I know, *Señor,* I know. To *Yanquis, Santa Anna* is a name for gigantic villainy and ruthlessness. He was merciless against your Texans in their secession from Mexico. But is General Santa Anna the only commander merciless in war? Who *is* merciful? I have long studied the histories of nations at war, *Señor Reportero.* I have found few instances of mercy shown by your own commanders. Your nation is but three-score years in existence—eh?—but already is notorious for the slaughter of its native people.

Forgive me for digressing, *Señor.* I was telling you of the ways by which the news of the war came to us in our cloister. Among the vessels of information there were our own families.

My mother wrote letters to me in the *Colegio,* though she could not come to visit. Her letters were long and well composed; to read them was to hear her speak across a table of all and any matters, as she had always done when we were together.

In the autumn of that year she sent to me a letter full of excitement. It became so much a treasured part of my family's history that I translated it for correspondents elsewhere. This copy is in your tongue.

> *My beloved Son Agustin—*
>
> *I write to say that I miss you severely, but that I have much pride that you study to become a soldier for your country. It is of course my prayer that this conflict shall be over, and peace shall come, before you are graduated as an officer, for I want you never to be in harm's way.*
>
> *My dear son, I do believe you will be pleased to learn that the good Captain Moreno, who was General Ampudia's adjutant at Matamoros, is now assigned to oversee and promote the Irish artillerists. Captain Moreno wrote to Rodrigo and explained how this circumstance came to be. You will recall the Captain's enthusiasm for the Irish gunner Señor Riley, and the respectful friendship that grew between them.*
>
> *Both Capt. Moreno and General Ampudia credit the Irishman and his*

gunners for the best part of the defense of Monterrey. Upon meeting with General Santa Anna at San Luis Potosi, they presented Señor Riley to him. Captain Moreno writes that General Santa Anna warmed to Señor Riley at once, and gave him authority to form and train a full unit of artillerists comprising the ablest gunners from among all the defectors, and to supervise the training of our own gunners in the maneuvers of which he is such a master. His unit is called Los Voluntarios Irlandeses. Our friend Captain Moreno will be their translator. They call themselves San Patricios, after the saint of their native country.

Rodrigo believes it is certain that Señor Riley will soon receive a promotion in rank in keeping with his growing authority. General Santa Anna intends to glorify the Irish artillery, with an aim of inspiring still more hundreds of Irish Catholic soldiers to defect from the invading army.

The commandante also authorized the San Patricios unit to serve under its own Irish banner. Imagine that! Captain Moreno said that Señor Riley and some of his gunners designed the banner themselves, and asked the nuns of the San Luis convent to stitch it onto a field of green silk. Captain Moreno described it: Depicting San Patricio, with his staff upon a snake; on the other side, a harp, the symbol of Ireland, and these words, "Erin go Bragh" and "Libertad por la Republica Mexicana."

Those are beautiful symbols and words, most touching to the heart in times like these. The newspapers are enchanted with the Irishmen, as a part of the general patriotic fervor. General Santa Anna has taken a loan of two million pesos offered by the Church to help him fund the building of the army. Morever, he has committed much of his own personal fortune.

This letter begins to seem more like a news dispatch than a missive of endearment, my son, but such are the times, and I know not whether you hear or read much from the world beyond your school. My prayers are always for peace, as that is the nature of woman's heart. Perhaps emissaries and diplomats may yet forestall the necessity for further bloodshed and persuade the North Americans to withdraw beyond our borders. In all the rumors and gossip and in the printed journals, the will of the citizens in that nation is said to be bitterly divided on the matter of the war. Most of Europe condemns it, we are given to believe. Adventurers and idealists from neutral nations are taking up Mexico's cause independently, and have been arriving to serve.

Our Catholic clergy in the vicinity of the enemy are employing themselves

actively in luring Catholic soldiers away from that army. They offer guides,
money, and transportation to bring deserters down from the north. As the
enemy's bases and routes of supply now extend some three hundred miles,
from the Gulf to Monterrey and Saltillo, the Yanquis are thinly drawn out,
and surely they hold little control over the loyalties of the soldiers whose con-
science is troubled. Deserters are said to be arriving from everywhere along
that line. Clergymen and rancheros work in harmony to bring the deserters
primarily to San Luis Potosi where our army is forming. Not all of the de-
serters want to serve in the Mexican Army, of course. Those who do not are
provided kindness and passage. The ones who enlist with us of course are met
with the most warmth and honor.

To be a citizen of a nation which is on the honorable side of a dispute,
that, my dear son, is inestimable, however chance resolves the dispute. Even
should we lose on the battlefields, in the eyes of our Lord and Savior, Mex-
ico shall be hallowed.

Be content in knowing that I am in good health, serene in spirit, and
constant in affection for my good son,

Your mother,
Gloria Estrella de Juvero

Such was the correspondence from my beloved mother, *Señor.* Her
letters came sometimes two or three a week, and the news they relayed
to me was welcome. It was notable to me how much of that news per-
tained in some way to the valorous foreigners, and in particular the
Irishmen. It was no less interesting to me, as my own idealism had been
inspired by the courage and the principle of those men. Of course the
personificación of this gallantry was Senor Riley, that *hombre guapo y*
fuerte. Many brave and able soldiers served with him in the defense of
this grateful country, most of them but not all Irishmen. But as you
have heard me say before, *Señor,* it was Don Juan Riley himself who
won our hearts, when we first saw him wet and muddy in our house at
Matamoros, and it was he who continued to rise in our esteem and our
affections. My mother's love for him was of a nature too sacred for me
to relate to you even if I had known every corner of her heart. I know
it was a great and noble dedication, sustained over long absences and
great anxieties.

In one of her letters to me, one that no longer survives except in my memory, she asked me to envision in my imagination the meeting of the Irishman and the *Gran Commandante General* Santa Anna. Often I did envision it, *Señor,* and with the pleasure and excitement of a fervently patriotic *niño ingenuo.*

I have described to you often and in many ways this Irishman, whom I have seen with my own eyes in close proximity.

The other man in the picture, the supreme general, I have seen him only fleetingly and never close. I know him by his reputation, which is controversial and is studied by every Mexican. It has been said that in whatever crisis in Mexico, he is the solution but he is also then the next crisis. You have studied him, too, *Señor,* if you have studied Mexico at all. Yes, he is vainglorious, and cunning, and extravagant. He is the demigod in my country.

Even now, *Señor,* although I am *desvalido,* many times dashed, *cínico,* and a mocker of fools, no matter, the image of *el Presidente General* Santa Anna brings my spirit to attention. To mock him I should have to be able to mock Mexico herself.

In appearance and stature, nature blessed him. He was born *criollo,* with the high, long head of the European but the color of a native. A tall man, he seems even taller by virtue of his bearing. He is *guapo,* and unmatched in charm. He affects a deliberate gait in walking, to mask the pain and awkwardness of an artificial leg. And so, when he walks among gentlemen and officers, you would remark on the thoughtful dignity of the whole retinue, as they slow to his pace. The leg, his left, was shattered by a French cannonball when he drove the French occupiers out of Vera Cruz. The general is always bedecked in the fullest splendor of medals and braid, shining like a sun. He is the object of the loveliest and most opportunistic women, of course.

So, yes, *Señor,* I tried to envision that meeting of our supreme *commandante* and the gallant Irish cannoneer. With pride and pleasure I imagined them standing face-to-face, regarding each other. I would think of General Ampudia relating the boldness and the terrible skills of *Teniente* Riley. And then I would see the *commandante* reach for his hand, look straight into his eyes with the appreciation one true hero surely has for another. Then, soon, they would be speaking of artillery. The Mexican army in those times was well equipped with cannons of all grades, but still deployed them in old and cumbrous ways. Even as a first-year cadet, I was critical of the gunnery tactics as they were being taught at the *Colegio,* for I had witnessed the new methods of the flying battery in manueuvers at Matamoros. And so I would imagine those two paragons talking with enthusiasm about making the gunnery more modern. And it came to be as I had imagined. The Irishman's units were supplied with enough powder and shell, and good horses and manpower for support to train brilliantly, there at San Luis Potosi. Captain Moreno wrote about it several times to my *Tío* Rodrigo. The Irishman was promoted to be a captain, and Captain Moreno was promoted to be a major, and the *commandante* of those units. I have spoken of the jealousy that prevails in our corps of officers; plainly, it would have created consternation if the Irishman had been promoted over our native gunnery officers, and thus did Major Moreno become *commandante* of the unit even though in actuality it was Captain Riley's charge. You see. Our generals must work cleverly with niceties over their officers. Politics taints everything.

De este modo, my nation's Army of the North was formed, there in the beautiful city of San Luis, growing to more than twenty thousand. Once again, as so often before, General Santa Anna was seen by Mexico as her savior in the face of an enemy invasion. He had drawn five or six thousand of the ablest horsemen in Mexico for his cavalry, twice that number of durable and obedient infantrymen under the bravest generals; also engineers, transport, musicians, priests. And shining in his expectations there was his artillery, revitalized with flying batteries, and with his most powerful cannons, the sixteen-pounders and twenty-four-pounders, to be deployed under the *San Patricios'* green banner. Several more especially well-trained gunners had found their way to San Luis after deserting the *Yanqui* army, and were assigned as *Capitán* Riley's subordinates. The supreme *commandante* himself interviewed one Patrick Dalton, who had deserted at Camargo and had ridden a burro all the way to San Luis. He assigned him a lieutenancy. He did not know the two gunners were already friends! Ah, such stories! Another example was formerly of the Prussian army, one Morstadt his name was, who had deserted after Monterrey and had been led to San Luis by a priest. Major Moreno also told of one called O'Leary, also trained by the British. He had deserted from the British army before joining and deserting the Americans. But listen: He stayed true to Mexico to the day he died fighting.

For that matter, *Señor,* I say with pride and gratitude that none of those Irishmen who had deserted other armies ever deserted Mexico! She became their homeland, and almost all of them were to die for her. But that is getting in advance of my tale. There was to be much glory and much shame before they became our martyrs. The glory was theirs; the shame was yours.

Not yours personally, *Señor.* But it is gratifying to see you on your knees, on behalf of your country.

CHAPTER XIV

PADRAIC QUINN'S DIARY

Monterrey, Mexico ✳ *December 2nd 1846*

THIS WAS A day of real hatefulness and injustice. It started bad and got worse. It all sprung from the black heart of Capt. Tom Sherman, an artillery officer. I had a little role in the cause of it, but was a mere observer of the outcome.

All I did was deliver a bottle of whiskey from the bootlegger John Doherty to one of Capt. Sherman's men. Mr. Doherty is an Irish soldier who was wounded in battle at Palo Alto, and was mustered out. As I may have said in the earlier diaries, he employs me a bit to deliver for him, as he can't get about easily since his wounds.

Captain Sherman ordered the Corporal of the Guard out of the camp to arrest Mister Doherty. The corporal, one Sam Chamberlain of the Dragoons, expressed doubt that the captain had legal right to arrest a civilian, but obeyed the order and went out and brought the protesting Mister Doherty in. Being one of the Catholic haters, Capt. Sherman saw this as an opportunity to punish an Irishman. He ordered the corporal and another guard to strip Mister Doherty to his waist and hang him from a tree limb by his wrists. Mister Doherty not being a docile man, or without wits, kept challenging the captain's authority to treat a civilian that way, but the captain persisted, all the while cursing him with every epithet the Sons of Erin ever were subject to, all interspersed with profanity of a more general nature, and accusing him of the crime of bootlegging. Mister Doherty, being no longer a soldier subordinate in rank to a captain, had cheek enough to inquire by what authority Capt. Sherman enforced the laws of a country where he was an intruder. Mister Doherty has no more genteel a mouth than the captain's, mind you, & was righteously indignant at being hung out in such painful manner, which certainly hurt his war wounds, and the air was blue with their volleys of vituperation. Capt. Sherman's face grew wet and red and he was all but chewing off his own muttonchop whiskers. Mister Doherty was earning himself no mercy by such defiance, and the captain was doubly embarrassed by the guard squad looking on with veiled mirth. It was then that Capt. Sherman shouted his order for a guard to fetch the rawhide lash. The captain extended it to Cpl. Chamberlain and ordered him to apply fifty strokes to the bootlegger's bare back.

Chamberlain held his carbine with both hands and did not release it to take the whip. Instead, he asked the captain whether he had authority to inflict a whipping on a civilian. This corporal is something of a hellraiser in his own right—a drinker, a dandy & a diarist and sketch artist like myself. No officer's puppet, he. The captain gaped for a moment at such effrontery, and then he fair screamed the order again. The corporal shook his head slowly and backed away, or seemed to, and also seemed to tip the muzzle of his carbine toward Capt. Sherman. Some say he aimed it at him, though I did not witness it like that. Of course we remember as we're inclined to remember. It seems there are as many differing accounts of an incident as there are eyewitnesses.

All witnesses agree, though, on what followed. Capt. Sherman in a full rage ordered the guard squad to seize the corporal, & buck and gag him. They did so, jamming a thick tent peg between his jaws with a gag to tie it in place. They sat him on the gravelly ground with knees up and wrists bound together over his shins. Then they shoved a pole under his knees and over his elbows, which, if you have ever been unfortunate enough to be so situated, you know utterly immobilizes the victim, locking him into place for as many hours as the punishing officer chooses to leave him there, be that in scorching sun or cold rain. It saddened me to see the fair corporal so humiliated and in such discomfort. My anger toward the captain was so strong that I would have walked away, but I knew not yet the fate of my employer Mr. Doherty, who was still strung up to the tree and his face betraying every emotion by turn, excepting happiness or brotherly love.

The inflamed captain next summoned one of the privates of the guard, thrust the handle of the whip at him and ordered him to lay fifty lashes on the prisoner. The private glanced at Cpl. Chamberlain just for an instant, beseeching, I imagine, and whatever he saw in the corporal's eyes caused him to brace up his shoulders and declare, No, sir, I'll not!

The captain's eyes nearly jumped out of his crimson face, and with a profane tirade he ordered the rest of the guard to buck and gag that man on the ground right beside Cpl. Chamberlain. By that time, these activities were attracting soldiers passing by from other units, but when they saw the intensity of Capt. Sherman's fury they quickly went on, surely for dread of being drawn into his little domain of tyranny. The captain now flung the whip to the next guard, screaming an order for him to whip Mister Doherty, but that private dropped it on the ground, and calmly refused to do the deed likewise, and likewise was trussed into the torturous position.

By that time, had there been a wagering partner near, I would have begun betting whether the next guard, or the next or the next, would finally take the lash and do as told, or whether one would, on the other hand, refuse to help buck and gag the next one who refused the whip. Some of the guards seemed to be resisting the captain in support of Cpl. Chamberlain; and some, Irishmen, might have been simply refusing to whip Doherty because he is a countryman. I believe some were motivated, rather, by a resolve to thwart one of those arrogant and cruel martinets, and this was the first means they had ever been given to do so.

Whatever was in their hearts, Capt. Sherman was near apoplexy by the time five guards sat bucked and gagged in a row, and at last a big guard who was not Irish, but a backwoodsman from some southern state, almost snatched the flail from the captain and went scowling to stand spraddled behind Mister Doherty. I heard him mutter, To hell with all you sorts o' fools! and he went to work on poor Mister Doherty's broad, white back, the rawhide soon slashing it into bloody strips, and the poor whiskey man screaming in his agony. It was about twenty-five strokes before he sagged in a faint, and the backwoodsman noticed, and paused. But Capt. Sherman demanded, You're but half done! and the lashing continued, the man with the whip fully fatiguing himself by the count of fifty. A crowd of men and officers had gathered to watch and wince, and the captain appeared to be both ablaze and frozen with some crazed triumph, which was so unsettling a demeanor that the victim's shredded flesh was no uglier a sight than the captain's face. I must confess that this is the first time I consciously wonder whether a military officer is sane or insane. My conclusion is that Sherman is insane. He's as crazed as Lt. Bragg, or Col. Harney.

But many of the officers who came to watch seemed to be in accord with him. Are they insane as well?

It feels to me as if we in this Army are descending into some pit of madness, the farther we go into Mexico. The more violence we see, the more we condone.

Nobody in this Army fought better than the Irishmen, either at the Rio Grande or here. All acknowledge that. Their casualty rate is higher than any others'. And even yet, they are ever more sought out for punishment, once the battle's over.

I can't help wonder if the sight of John Riley and his gunners going free, after the fall of this city, was more than these officers can bear. If something's more than you can bear, I guess that's when you go crazy.

This I write a few hours after the incident. The corporal and the other guards have been released from the torture of the buck-and-gag. Capt. Sherman demands, I hear, that the corporal be court-martialed for mutiny and sentenced to death! If that isn't crazy, what is?

I pray there's someone up the command who isn't crazy enough to execute a man for refusing to flog another man.

As for Mister Doherty, he was cut down from the tree and dragged out of the camp, and flung out in the road still unconscious with no treatment for his lacerations. I think soldiers were afraid to come to his help, for fear of becoming Capt. Sherman's next whipping boys. So as soon as Capt. Sherman's attention was elsewhere, I went out to revive Mister Doherty and help him back to Little America where his hut is. Washerwomen took to him with salves and linen to start him healing. Mister Doherty thanked me through clenched teeth and had me pour us some painkiller from his stock. And some for the ladies who nursed

him. After a while he said to me, "Paddy, lad, I'd like to make Captain
Sherman a peace offering, a bottle of me best whiskey, if ye'd deliver it
to him with my compliments." Before I could protest that I didn't want
myself whipped next, he got up and pissed in a whiskey bottle. "Here
we are, lad," said he, "my piss offerin' to the cap'n."

It was a relief to me, knowing that he was joking.

Monterrey, Mexico ✳ *Dec. 10, 1846*

HAIL MARY MOTHER of God. They won't hang Cpl. Chamberlain
for defying Captain Sherman's order!

The court-martial judge sentenced him to hang, but Gen. Wool
changed the punishment, reduced it to hard labor. Rumor is that the
general feared there would be too much outcry back in the U. States, if
a good soldier from a good family got executed for refusing an order
given on a captain's whim, particularly an order that was probably ille-
gal. I mean, the whipping of a civilian.

Mister Doherty continues to sell liquor now that he is recovered
from his punishment, but he is more careful about being found out.
That is to say, he is now a sneaky bootlegger rather than an overt one,
and a result of it is that soldiers can patronize his place more discreetly
than when he operated in plain sight of the camp. This has been very
good for his business, and he told me he wishes he had been this sneaky
before, for he'd be richer by now and wouldn't have suffered that awful
lashing.

As for the soldiers the captain bucked & gagged for refusing to whip
him, why, Mister Doherty had me smuggle a bottle to each of them in
gratitude, and they've since become some of our best customers.

Another outcome of Capt. Sherman running Mr. Doherty away
from the vicinity of the army camp is that more soldiers are now deserting, even more than were before. The soldiers go farther to get their
whiskey. When they drink up to the point of courage or recklessness,
they're farther from camp and closer to the Mexicans. Sometimes I hear
drunk soldiers in the dark, in the brush along the road, when I am making my own secretive errands in and out of the camp, purveying Mister
Doherty's liquor to those in the camp who need it but are reluctant, or
afraid, to skirt the sentries. I hear them whispering and shuffling

through the sand. The ones who have already obtained drink are louder: giggling, retching, farting, arguing, sometimes, about whether to go back to camp or strike out down the Saltillo Road and deeper into Mexico. Few know anything of the geography of this country, but they remember that's the route Mister Riley and their other old messmates went when the Mexican Army left.

A rumor is, priests are helping our strays find their way, and providing food and shelter as they go.

But there are guerrillas all over, and gangs of rancheros that kill any American without asking him any questions. We're in the middle of somebody else's country and they don't like us being here. There would sure be more men deserting if they thought they could do it without getting killed, or perishing in the mountains.

Monterrey, Mexico ✳ *Dec. 14, 1846*

I'VE BEEN WORKING at a sketch of Mister Doherty's flogging. And now I found out that Cpl. Chamberlain is doing one also. He's drawing it at night after labor gang work. Has his sketch kit right there in the lockdown with him. Sounds pretty bold to me. Like to see it and

Capt. Thos. Sherman oversees the flogging of the bootlegger John Doherty at Monterrey. 1846
Drawn in pencil
by P. Quinn

compare it with my sketch someday when his sentence is up. He's a brash character.

I don't envy him. It's uncomfortable enough in this camp these cold nights without a ball and chain on your ankle.

I sure do get tempted sometimes to just take my drawing book and go do pictures of that city over there. Sure a beautiful place. But it's full of its own Mexican people and they don't like us much after all the damage we did to their town.

Awful lot of our Army is sick all the time. One Irish soldier gone almost batty with the idea that the Mexicans are putting a curse on us.

Then the officers use that to ridicule the Irish for being superstitious Pope worshippers.

Seems like they have nothing else to do but wake up in the morning and go find some reason to ridicule Irishmen.

If they didn't spend part of their time talking about how backward the Mexicans are, they'd be on us *all* the time.

Monterrey, Mexico * *Dec. 16, 1846*

SOME SOLDIERS TRIED to blow up Lt. Bragg in his sleep! Sure I'd expected somebody would, as he is thought by many to be too nasty to live.

But he lives! More's the pity, some say. An artillery bombshell with a lit fuse was rolled into his tent, by somebody. It could have been anyone. I doubt there's many in his unit that haven't thought of it. It's the talk of the whole Army almost: That it likely was his own gunners, as it was a shell they used. He's flogged, or buck & gagged, most everybody in his battery, and certainly every Irishman.

They rolled the shell in and ran. His tent and most of his baggage were destroyed. He was taken to hospital scorched, bruised, and lacerated, but nowhere near dead or maimed.

Great many desertions from the camp in the last week. More of the printed leaflets in camp, with their generous promises. I suppose many a soldier also remembers the sight of Mister Riley's proud battery on the Saltillo Road out of Monterrey after the battle.

We aren't even being told anymore by our officers what the number of deserters is. But it's sure for shrinking Gen. Taylor's Army. When he finally moves to the next campaign he might have nobody left in his Army but Protestants. Then of course those Texas irregulars, who don't have any faith that a body can see, except their holy duty to kill Mexicans.

I would reckon one reason to desert to Mexico might be just the sight of this country. In spite of all this Army camp, and the peddler slum built up around it, there surely could not be a prettier place than this anywhere.

And what little I've seen of the Mexican people—well, I'll phrase it this way: Put Mexicans on one side of me, and West Pointers and Texans on the other, and say, Choose, sure I truly believe I would turn to the Mexicans. Imagine a people who smile and nod to you even if you're just a scruffy camp boy!

They don't act all that friendly to the soldiers. But they don't seem to resent me, those few I see of them out here.

Monterrey, Mexico ✳ *Dec. 18, 1846*

THIS MORNING I awoke to the sound of a birdcall. It was repeated several times before I recognized the notes, as the Death March our regimental bands play for funerals. Then it was that I understood, the bird was a mockingbird. It was mimicking that dirge which it hears just about every day, as the soldiers die of dysentery, infections, and el vomito. Rumor is that as many as two thousand have died of dysentery since the Army came into Mexico. That's two or three times as many as the battle dead, I believe.

Nothing much worth relating this day. Mister Doherty paid me enough for deliveries that I could buy a pair of shoes. My others were falling apart and also I had outgrown them so far I had to cut the toes open. Had them since the Swamp War. They had been through mud and dust a-plenty. May keep what's left of the soles to make sandals, like all these Mexicans wear.

Monterrey, Mexico ✳ *Dec. 20, 1846*

BOUGHT A KNIFE, two pencils, and lamp oil, got them at the sutler's. Better quality than out in Little America, but barely worth the trouble of convincing the sutler's clerk that he can sell to me although I'm not a soldier. I think he was trying to extort a few more pennies from me. When I turned to walk out he called me back and made the sale.

I found a Mexican Army pack in the brush of the riverbank. Used leather from my old shoes to repair a broken shoulder strap. This pack will hold my two diaries and all my writing and drawing implements. Thinking like a soldier: Be ready to tote your needs when the generals say you're moving.

I have been thinking of walking into the city of Monterrey one day soon. If I am here I ought to see more than just soldiers and tents. I would like to sketch things I see.

Monterrey, Mexico ✳ Dec. 22, 1846

THE MOCKINGBIRD SANG the Death March again this morning. I was abed, listening, feeling a bit sad but also a bit amused, just waking up. The bird then sang some notes that were like other birdcalls. And then he sang some notes that I recognized from music I've heard. He was singing one of those songs the Irish soldiers sing most every night in the camp, I mean those nights when they get a chance to sing around the fires. It was that real pretty favorite of theirs, "Green grow the lilacs." That damned little bird in a tree was singing an Irish ballad and the Death March, both here in Mexico! Maybe he sings Mexican music, too, but I just don't recognize it. God works in strange ways, as they say. If I really listen I might learn some good tunes.

That mockingbird might not learn much more Irish music. The 3rd Infantry just lost many more of its good Irish singers in a week, ten in one night, by desertion.

Monterrey, Mexico ✳ Dec. 23, 1846

THE U. STATES newspapers are writing about Mister Riley. He is a famous traitor. I heard officers talking about it, and hung near them, finally asked if I could see the newspapers. One laughed, said, "Irish tyke, pretending he can read?" But Lieutenant Wallace of the Indiana Volunteers was there, who has shared reading matter with me and knows I write.

He called me over to sit with him and other officers looking at the papers. He said the newspapers back in the States had finally come to hear about the desertion problem. Some of the papers are using it to malign all Irishmen as cowards and traitors. One of the newspapers from New York was demanding that the country must close its gates to the immigration of perfidious Irish Papists who were already infesting the slums with criminals, and now were betraying the war effort. The *National Police Gazette* was one of the newspapers harping on Irish character. Mister Riley was mentioned by name, in the *New Orleans Picayune.*

It wasn't long before Mister Wallace saw I was agitated. He kindly led the talk onto other things. Said he was happy to be in Mexico because he had a romance book in his head about the Spanish Conquistadors bringing Christianity to the savages of Mexico, and here he was, seeing the country. That would help him write his book when he got home. If he got home, he added with a laugh. There would be more battles all too soon. Maybe thinking I was shamed by being Irish, he talked about how the Scots, his people, had been scorned and driven out of the isles, too. He got me sidetracked, and by and by I was bragging about the deep thoughts in my diary, and all that.

Then all at once, I got a cautious feeling and thought I'd better be quiet about all that, because I had written so much that might seem treasonous. Like weighing John Riley and Mick Maloney against each other. He might not abide that. But he did deplore the impugning of religions, in the newspapers and in the Army. He told of an Army surgeon who had visited the Cathedral in Monterrey and had stolen the skull of some old holy patron from the reliquary, by slipping it under his cloak while the priest's back was turned. The surgeon had thought it quite a lark and mocked a religion that would worship some old rich man's skeleton. Two other Indiana officers, there sharing the newspapers with us, took up for the doctor's prank, and soon Lt. Wallace was in an argument with them. The officers, ignoring my Catholic presence as insignificant I suppose, questioned the faith of a people who would use their cathedral as a powder magazine. Lt. Wallace retorted to that by asking into the piety of an Army which would damage a Christian cathedral with cannonfire. The others then scoffed at him for calling Catholicism a Christian religion. Thereupon he launched forth with

his scholarship on the Christian missionary zeal of the Catholic conquerors, who brought their fair god to the heathen aztecs, at the risk of
their own lives. The others laughed at his notion, arguing that the Conquistadors were not after souls, but gold for their Papist king. Lt. Wallace countered that he knew better, from his studies for his book.

My presence forgotten in the heat of their debate, I slipped away.
Under my shirt I carried away the New Orleans newspaper in which
Mister Riley's name is printed.

I cannot honestly say that officers squabble on a higher plane than
the soldiers generally. Nor are the officers a more sober people than the
enlisted men. I carry Mister Doherty's whiskey to both classes. The
only difference I see is that man for man the officers do much more
drinking than the others. They can afford more, and have more free
time to get drunk. And don't get punished for it.

Right here it is, a real keepsake for me: a big-city newspaper with the
name printed in it of a friend of mine who is famous all over. I consider
him a friend of mine. He said I look like his son! This souvenir is my
Christmas gift to me.

Monterrey, Mexico ✳ Jan. 3, 1847

YESTERDAY I WALKED into Monterrey and looked around. Sure
and it looks different from when we were fighting in the city.

An uneasy feeling, and now and then got a little scared, by being followed by gangs of Mexican boys. They were just curious about me,
though. A lad my age, alone, puzzled them. Only U.S. Regular troops
are billeted in the city. Volunteers have to be kept outside, particularly
the Texans. After a while I realized I was probably safe. They could see
I'm not worth robbing.

I carried book and pencil, to make notes or sketches. It was the best
part of it. Not only did I preserve some of my impressions and some of
the sights, it drew friendly interest, wherever I stopped to write or draw.
Children shyly circled me at a distance, as I drew or wrote. Each time I
looked up they were closer. One might rise on tiptoes to see what was
on the paper. All I had to do then was smile, and they came like bee to
flower, and crowded me, fingers in their mouths, cooing and giggling at
the pictures.

An old man in Monterrey drawn in ink by P. Quinn, Monterrey, Mexico January 1847

I'd finished a profile sketch of an old man in white with his hat hanging down his back. I'm pleased with it. The children were, too. A boy pointed his finger at his face and said, Me! Me! and then pointed at the pencil. I understood that he wanted me to draw his picture, as plain as if I understood his language. So I began. But it was impossible to draw him when he kept edging around and trying to look down at the page. At length, one of his friends apparently persuaded him to hold a pose. His friends laughed as I made the picture, and his little face grew dark and sullen from their mockery. I wanted to tell him to smile, but didn't know the word. That is a shame, to be in someone's country for a year and not know their word for smile, of all things. So I decided I would learn that word if no other before the day was over. With a bit of grinning and gesturing I learned the word. It sounded like sonreez-a. I'll find out for certain later, but think of that. The word for smile sounds like sunrise.

When I showed them the picture, they laughed and carried on, and then started talking all fast and eager at me. After a while I got the idea that they wanted to buy the picture but had no money. Sure I wanted to keep it, but people were gathering around watching. So I thought it might be good if I just cut the picture out of the book and gave it to him. So I did. That seemed to make everybody like me, which is comforting when one is among strangers.

But then something unwanted came of it: The children, boys and girls alike, all wanted their portraits done. And, making it harder to refuse and slip away, the adults wanted to see them, too.

It felt good to have all those cheerful Mexicans around me. Sure they didn't seem to resent me for being with the invaders of their country. Another shy little boy came forward to pose for me and I started drawing him. He had the blackest eyes I ever saw and was as pretty as a girl. While I was drawing him a woman gave me something to eat, a kind of floury sweet. I did know the word to say—gracias. I finished that drawing and the boy held out his hand for it and said gracias. Then the woman who had given me the sweet put forward a little girl for me to draw. I guessed it must be her daughter. She kept wiggling and putting her head down but I got a good likeness of her and it made everybody happy. They kept putting children up to pose, and I drew and drew, maybe seven or eight. The sun was going down, and I knew if I didn't quit the drawing, the day would be over before I could even go to see the cathedral. I pointed at the sun, and at myself, and then away in the direction of the Army camp, and then back to the sun again. I think they got the idea that I needed to go. I also needed to pee awfully bad, but would have been embarrassed to try to mime that out, since there were more women and girls in the crowd. I drew another little girl, but kept glancing at the sun and acting impatient. Then the people began to murmur and shuffle about, and when I looked up, there stood three officers, among them Lt. Grant. They had wandered over to see what the crowd was about. The people began backing away, and pretty soon were all gone. The lieutenants were no little bit drunk. Lt. Grant seemed to like what I had been doing, and made a fuss over the drawings in my book, how good they were, and wanted to see the whole book. But then I remembered things I had written in the diary, favoring John Riley, and other comments that I wouldn't want them to see. So I just tore out the picture pages and showed them to him. Decided that from now on I will not carry this book around with me, or draw in it. Will try to find a separate book to do drawings in.

Lt. Grant and the other officers told me to walk back to camp with them, to keep me safe, as they had sidearms and swords. So I did walk back with them, but had to stop in an alley and pee. So did two of the officers, having been drinking a good bit.

Back in camp Lt. Grant said my drawing of the Irish gunners leaving Monterrey was so good it should be sent to the States and sold to one of the illustrated weekly journals. He said, That is Riley riding the caisson, isn't it? I said yes. I told him I didn't know how to send a picture to the U.S. He said maybe he could advise me later. I doubt he will remember saying so when he wakes up tomorrow. He holds it well, but really had a skin full.

I write this as my candle grows short and I am getting a pretty good skin full myself. This was a day I won't forget for a long time if ever. It was like being in a family among those Mexicans. If the officers hadn't intruded I'll wager somebody would have fed me a supper, maybe found me a place to sleep. I doubt anyone would have cut my throat, as one of the lieutenants kept saying on our way back to camp. I guess they believe they were saving my life.

On the breeze I hear now and then, very faint, some of the kind of music I was hearing there in the plaza while I was drawing. Sure it's very different from Irish or American songs, but very pretty, both cheerful and sad at the same time. They use guitars and trumpets both, and the men sing so high they sound like girls.

Here is a song our Irish soldiers were singing at their campfires earlier this evening, it goes,

> *She is far from the land*
> *where her young hero sleeps,*
> *And lovers are round her, sighing,*
> *But sadly she turns*
> *from their gaze, and she weeps,*
> *For her heart in his grave is lying.*

That one is sure not sad and cheerful at the same time, it's only sad. That is a dead soldier song and nothing more.

Looking at my pictures here in candlelight. Lt. Grant was really impressed by them. I reckon they are pretty good. They get better with practice. I draw best when I work fast.

Sure those Mexicans are nice folk. Sad, having a war with them. But maybe their high-up leaders aren't so nice. I remember what Mister Riley said once while talking about officers:

Shit doesn't rise, it falls.

Monterrey, Mexico ✳ *Jan. 5, 1847*

SOME NEWS HARD to believe.

Some of our Irish soldiers said the Army has brought in a Jesuit priest! Father Rey is his name.

I have not yet seen him. Rumor is that the President sent him and another Catholic chaplain down to mollify the Catholic soldiers, after he learned of the desertion problem.

Some of the soldiers really want to go to a priest. But most don't trust him any more than they trust the president. Think he's here just to keep Catholics from deserting. He is good for last rites.

Drinking, sickness, and desertions, nothing new. I bought some good white paper in a shop in Monterrey and will punch and bind the pages together to make a sketchbook.

I got to the cathedral yesterday. Never saw such a glorious building! Has paintings of saints and heavenly scenes everywhere from the lower walls to the highest ceilings. Some of it looks to be painted with real gold. I followed some of the Mexican old folks in and did what they did, getting a candle and setting it up front. I sure don't know much about being a Catholic. What little I learned in Michigan I've forgot, running with this Army since I was little.

Saw the damage our cannons did to the outside of the cathedral. Mexican stonemasons are already up there repairing it.

Mexican people in the streets still seem startled when they see me. Mostly they act polite and smile, and go on.

On this sojourn into town I didn't make the mistake again of drawing pictures of the children. I would like to have some such pictures in the sketchbook. But they want them. I would feel wrong about drawing their image and not letting them have the drawing. If I could speak their language, I would draw two pictures of a child and tell him I wanted to keep one to remember him by.

I would like to learn some Mexican language. No wonder people have trouble, when they can't understand each other.

*Monterrey, Mexico * Jan. 7, 1847*

A FINE DAY of news for the Irish soldiers. Mick Maloney is now a lieutenant, promoted for his valor at the battles of Resaca de la Palma and Monterrey. Disproving the belief that no man born in Ireland could ever become an officer in the United States Army. Some soldiers joke that if it hadn't been for the newspapers back in the U.S. he would still be a sergeant.

I learned some Mexican. Por don day say va me ar? Where can I go to pee? If they start telling me in words, I just say, sen oo lar con el dead o, and they point. This would have helped me that day I almost wet myself drawing pictures all day.

*Monterrey, Mexico * Jan. 9, 1847*

I WENT TO look for Lt. Grant to ask him about sending my best drawings to an illustrated gazette. Not surprised that he doesn't remember speaking of it. Must have been really drunk.

Anyway, something is happening that has all the officers in a cat fit. President Polk is taking the Army away from Gen. Taylor and putting Gen. Winfield Scott over this war. That's the rumor now.

The officers think it is because Gen. Taylor could get elected President if he keeps winning battles down here.

One would think President Polk would want battles won, since he started the war.

But some of the officers say that politics is more important to politicians than war is. I don't know about such things, but it seems it must be so.

I have awful shits. Por don day say va me air tha? Where can I go to shit?

*Monterrey, Mexico * Jan. 11, 1847*

MANY TIMES I wonder that so much misery is in such a beautiful place. The view of this city is like a scene in a legend. The white buildings, red roofs, fountains, avenues lined with dark trees, and the hills and mountains all about. But there is always death and sickness. The chaplain Father Rey was sent here to discourage Catholic soldiers from deserting. But he spends most of his hours giving last rites to the ones who die every day from disease and infected wounds.

Today went up on Black Citadel, north of the city, to draw a picture looking from there. Below me was the city, which I could see in its entirety, and the Rio Santa Catarina beyond it. This is a grand vista. It was here where Mister Riley's cannons were. He could see the whole battle from up here. But our attack that went around west of the city was out of his range, and behind Federacion Hill, out of his sight. Otherwise, the invasion likely would have failed. A strange feeling in my bosom to look on the scene from his high place, and remember my own lowly scrabbling through the dusty rubble, carrying house-breaking tools, as I was doing while he was up there blowing our soldiers to bits.

I am not very satisfied with my picture of Monterrey. What I see and feel is too big to get down onto a sheet of paper. I would need paint and color, but don't know how to use those. Probably I should limit myself to small scenes, and to people.

Monterrey, Mexico ✳ *Jan. 13, 1846*

THE NAME OF Santa Anna is in the war now.

The one Mexican everybody's heard of. Big villain!

What it's all about is that he came back to Mexico from exile in Cuba. He says that only he can rally the Mexicans to defeat the American invaders. And so he is in charge again.

These are all such big doings, I can't even picture them. But as I wrote down before, if you write you have to think, and if you're in the way of a war you have to try to understand what it's about.

I heard a big commotion out where the Texas irregulars are encamped, yelling and shooting, way more rowdy even than usual for them. They had got newspapers that said General Santa Anna is back. They hate him like the very devil himself. He was their enemy ten years ago in their war of independence, and did the massacre at the Alamo that we heard about all the time even up in Michigan. In Michigan our big massacre tale was the River Raisin where the Indians killed a lot of soldiers in the War of 1812, and the American battle cry after that was Remember the River Raisin. Likewise after the Texas war it was Remember the Alamo, and that was one thing the Texans kept yelling in their camp when they found out Santa Anna is back.

Sure I think the Texans are really happy about this, for it makes them hungry for revenge. They're awfully vengeful against Mexicans as a whole, which is why there's so many Texas volunteers in this Army. With it being Gen. Santa Anna himself they're rabid for vengeance.

It said in the newspapers that Gen. Santa Anna has been the president or dictator of Mexico off and on many times, as they no sooner set up a government than it gets overthrown.

Gen. Santa Anna they say is a real elegant sort of man, and a battle hero who limps around on an artificial leg made of cork, where a cannonball took off the real one. I guess it's easy for a one-legged man to remind people that he's a hero. Especially if he can talk really patriotic. He is famous for that, by what the newspapers say.

There was an engraving of him in a paper. I copied it in my book.

So now I can picture him and I can picture with him Mr. Riley and quite a number of the other deserters. It is something to think about at night, the faces of the people that are officially your enemy.

General Antonio Lopez
de Santa Anna
drawn by P. Quinn
from his portrait
in a periodical

It makes it feel kind of personal. I can imagine that sometime down there where General Santa Anna has his headquarters, he'll salute our Irish deserters in a parade or inspection or something of the kind. Now that I've got both their faces in my mind, I can actually imagine the two of them face-to-face.

Monterrey, Mexico ✳ *Jan. 15, 1847*

THIS ARMY IS confounded. General Scott is taking most of the regulars and veterans bit by bit back down to the coast. It's opposite the direction Gen. Taylor meant to go, which was southward toward Mexico City. The rumor is, Gen. Taylor refuses to resign, and intends to march south anyway.

But everything is rumors. As usual.

Another rumor is that the chaplain Father Rey was murdered along the road near Camargo. That is to say, they think he was murdered. He was alone and his body wasn't found.

Why would someone murder a priest in a Catholic country? Some Irishmen think he was killed by American officers. Others reckon it that he was killed because the Mexican Catholic order threw out the Jesuits. Lt. Wallace, the officer who is writing his book about Mexico, guessed it that way.

I was thinking: U.S. against Mexico. Americans against Irishmen. Protestants against Catholics. And even Catholics against other Catholics.

If this is the way adult men run the world, I'm not sure I care to come to maturity.

Monterrey, Mexico * Jan. 17, 1847

A NASTY LIEUTENANT today grabbed me by the left ear and cursed me for a little Mick monkey. I thought he would tear my ear off. He went on to call me a son of an Irish whore. There was not much I could do, hanging there by my bloody ear, to respond to that obscenity, except stomp on his foot and bite his arm until I tasted blood. At that point he lost hold of me, but he was getting set to come back on me with the side of his sword when Lt. Grant and another officer got him cornered and grabbed his arms. They told me to leave so they could get him calmed, but I was for spitting in his face, so they had to fend me off, too. Finally they had him explain why he had wooled me. It was that I had stolen his newspaper when I was there a few days ago.

All I could say was, I thought you finished your paper. It was true I'd carried it off. It was the one that told of Mr. Riley by name. Well, then Lieutenant Grant said I should return it if I still had it. I said Yes I still have it but I'm damned if I give it back to some little popinjay who rips my ear and calls my mother what he called her. That started him up again and he said he knew damned well my mother was a camp follower. It came to me he might well know that. But a camp follower isn't always a whore, I retorted. He said, Your Ma is. There was nothing left for me to do but kick him in the groin, and I did that, and fled, so mad I could hardly see.

I doctored my bloody ear the way my mother used to treat my wounds, by boiling a rag in water and holding it on until it is bled out. Mr. Doherty sponged it with whiskey. That stung something fierce, but he said it would keep it from festering.

I don't know if that officer knows where I camp, but I think I should keep on my guard. His name is Milton.

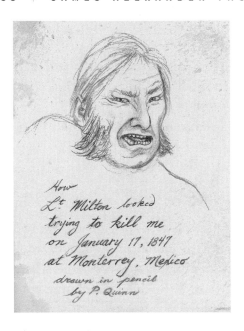

How Lt. Milton looked trying to kill me on January 17, 1847 at Monterrey, Mexico drawn in pencil by P. Quinn

Monterrey, Mexico ✳ *Jan. 18, 1847*

I THOUGHT IT over and decided Lieutenant Milton can have his damned paper back. I shall let Lt. Grant give it to him, to avoid another fight. I don't want to fight a turdbrain like him. He might also think he can whip a civilian, like that Capt. Sherman did to Mr. Doherty.

I made a drawing of the nasty lieutenant, in such a way that much of the bile was out of me by the time I'd done it. I think the word for this is caricature. Lt. Milton is one of those West Pointers who devote much time to the cultivation of displays of their facial hair. Here he is, drawn as I saw him while he was trying to pull my ear off.

I think I shall even draw a copy and post it one night in the vicinity of his company. It might lighten the misery of his poor soldiers.

Monterrey, Mexico ✳ *Jan. 20, 1847*

LIEUTENANT MILTON AND his company have left for Tampico, so I can quit watching for him to ambush me. The caricature of him that I put up did create much amusement in that quarter, so I hear. He knew who drew it. I'm getting famous for caricatures.

Gen. Scott is moving the best of Gen. Taylor's Army back down the

Rio Grande to the Gulf and from there by sea to Tampico. That port will be the staging point for his campaign toward Mexico City. I've heard this from officers, and by rumors.

Many soldiers expected to be sent home when they boarded the steamers at Camargo, but found to their dismay that they will instead go down to invade south Mexico.

So the number of desertions is surging again. The Mexican government offered a generous grant of land for any American soldier who defects to Mexico.

Lt. Wallace of the Indiana Infantry is all excited thinking of the prospect of Gen. Scott's campaign. I sat near a saloon table in the city and listened as he taught some fellow lieutenants the history of the conquistadors, as he so loves to do. He believes that Gen. Scott's campaign will follow the same route that Cortez took, that is, from Vera Cruz on the coast, west through the mountains to Mexico City. Lt. Wallace laments that his unit will remain here in northern Mexico with Gen. Taylor, and not be a part of that glorious campaign "to Montezuma's temples," as he keeps saying. I enjoy listening to these educated gentlemen. A hundred years of hearing their highfalutin talk and I could be an educated gentleman myself, I reckon.

*Monterrey, Mexico * Jan. 22, 1847*

TODAY COMING FROM Mister Doherty's at dawn I saw a thing that I'd heard was happening but never saw till now.

Four of the Texan volunteers drinking Mister Doherty's liquor on the riverbank saw an old woman and I guess it was her granddaughter on the road above going to market with baskets of vegetables balanced on their heads. The old woman and the girl had walked past me just before. The Texans grabbed the girl and dragged her down into the thicket. They tore her skirt off even before they had her off the road. The old woman started screaming and one of them hit her with his pistol. I started down the road toward them but he aimed his pistol at me and so I turned about and ran. I went to their camp to tell one of their captains. The only officer up was drinking coffee by a fire and he made no move, just said if I wanted to accuse the men, to give him their names and be ready to testify if they were brought up. I said I didn't know who they were. He said no Mexican slut ever needs to be forced anyway, and no Irish ragamuffin better make accusations against good fighting men.

Gen. Taylor keeps these Irregulars camped outside the city for the peace and safety of the townsfolk. Only some Regulars and their officers are billeted in town. The local folk keep Gen. Taylor's office crowded, coming in with complaints of battery and thieving and rape and vandalizing done by soldiers. Some by Regulars but more by the Irregulars. I reckon there is something to be said for strong discipline. I just wish it was given out fairly. I mean by that, it would be good to see some Texas raper "ride the wooden horse," not just Irish micks who fail to salute briskly enough.

I spent most of the day uneasy, ashamed I couldn't help those women. This rape thing bothers me more now than when for instance in the Seminole campaign Maj. Harney had his way with any Indian girl he caught. That was a long time ago. I reckon I had not learnt to think things through very far, back then.

Sure and I suppose the time will come before too long that I myself will be like menfolk and have the, whatever it is, and maybe understand why they act the way they do about females.

Before I get that way, right now, I make a vow to myself, and to God, and to Mary Mother of Jesus, that I will not ever do anything to hurt or disgrace a girl or woman, like those things I have seen.

One thing I can remember about such things, from up in Michigan, was Mother with a swollen hand from breaking the jaw of a soldier who tried to get too free with her. She was madder than I ever saw her, about that, and said if she'd had a knife at the time, that soldier would have to squat to pee from that day on. I didn't really understand what she meant, but I do now.

Monterrey, Mexico ✳ *Jan. 23, 1847*

I HAD A case of the mopery last night because of the rape thing. To cheer up I sat drinking & started drawing funny pictures of the officers' mustaches, side-whiskers, and other shrubbery. Had a good time, and still make myself laugh today just looking at them.

Variations in facial shrubbery of certain West Pointers. drawn in pencil by P. Quinn

As I was thinking last night about becoming a man, and all that, I thought a sign of it would be some whiskers. No sign at all yet. I wondered what I would look like with some kind of whiskers. So I drew my face by looking in a piece of mirror I salvaged, and then just drew on whiskers.

Also drew one picture of my face as it is now with no whiskers.

So there it is. My first self-portrait. As true as I can make it, no flattering embellishments.

This then is what people see when I appear before them. Sure and that's an odd notion. It would help explain why they treat me as they do.

Monterrey, Mexico ✳ *Jan. 24, 1847*

I FINALLY GOT a look at the god of War, Mars. Faith, is he ugly!

Mars is what some officers call General Scott. Most call him Old

Self-portrait
in pencil
by P. Quinn

How I would
look with
whiskers.

P. Quinn

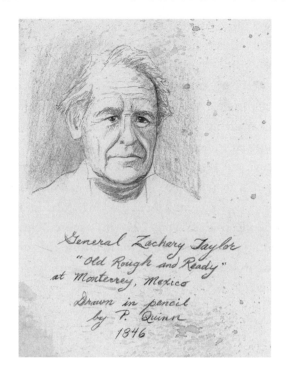

General Zachary Taylor
"Old Rough and Ready"
at Monterrey, Mexico

Drawn in pencil
by P. Quinn
1846

Mars himself—
General Winfield Scott
drawn in pencil
at Monterrey, Mexico 1846
by P. Quinn

Fuss & Feathers. Either name fits. His face looks like war itself and he is a giant tall and fat. But he wears enough decoration and glitter for about three emperors.

He is a reputed hero from 1812. Officers follow him about as if for wanting an order to lick a shine on his boots. For the life of me I can't imagine anyone more an opposite from Old Rough & Ready. Gen. Z. Taylor would appear to be his scarecrow.

Though I have not seen the two generals together and sure I never will, very likely, I can put them together by drawing the two on one page. I am doing so. I sketched Gen. Taylor before, and now copy his image alongside this one of "Mars." For my amusement.

Maybe I should post the drawing, for to amuse the soldiers as well as myself. They are in low spirits from the dividing of the Army. More deserters every day.

CHAPTER XV

Saltillo, Mexico ✳ Feb. 16, 1847

GEN. Z. TAYLOR ignoring Pres. Polk's orders to retire! He expects Santa Anna is coming up this way & wants to oppose him. This place is about 60 miles down from Monterrey on a road that goes south through the mountains toward Mexico City.

Not pretty here like Monterrey. All brown and scruffy, all the plants stick or cut you. Cactus, scrub, and tall, spiky things called Spanish Bayonet. Also a big plant the Mex. make a clear liquor out of: agave. Mr. Doherty remains at the city, so I am out of the bootlegging business for a while. Wallet flat.

I earn a little by killing rattlesnakes. Most soldiers are scared of them. So some officers pay me a bounty to kill them anywhere near their camps. Lt. Wallace of the Indiana Volunteers calls me Saint Padraic, ridding Mexico of the snakes. I use a forked stick to pin them to ground, and a crude kind of long knife, or short sword almost, that the Mexicans call a "mashetty," I use to cut the heads off. I sell the skins and rattles as keepsakes. I like the meat sure a lot better than Army pickled pork, or even the stringy tough ranch beef. I learned to like snake meat in the Seminole swamps. Most soldiers won't eat it.

Lt. Wallace is that officer who is writing a book about the Conquistador Spaniards. He wanted to go down with Gen. Scott's campaign, along the Cortez road, to help him imagine his book, was sure disappointed that Scott left his unit here, to sit idle.

Lt. Wallace has ridden back to Monterrey, carrying dispatches. He is an ambitious fellow in the military way, too, and would like to make a name in battle. If Gen. Taylor somehow went down through those mountains toward Mexico City, Mister Wallace might get his chance. But it's not likely Gen. Taylor can do it.

Lt. Wallace read law. Came down with a regiment of Indiana Volunteers. He is a handsome fellow easily flattered. When I gave him a portrait sketch of himself some time ago, he insisted on paying me a dollar for it. He's delighted I write & draw both.

He asked to see other pictures. He was impressed by my drawing of the Irish artillery leaving Monterrey, and in particular Mister Riley. He asked me to make sketches of some Indiana officers. Said he'd send them to an editor he knows in the state capital city, Indianapolis, who might publish them in the war news. He said I should draw troops and cannons in action, like a real correspondent, if there is any action. I'd have to think that over pretty hard.

When Lt. Wallace gets back, and I continue with the portraits, I ought to discuss with him a small price for each one of the portraits. Sure and I'd rather earn my daily pittance as an artist than a bootlegger. And I'm like to run out of rattlesnakes.

This evening an Indiana officer asked me whether I've the Irish grit to go out on the field and make drawings of combat, if ever there be some. If there had been no one else there to hear the question, I might have weaseled out. But there stood several Indiana officers and soldiers a-smirking at me and waiting for my answer. So I feigned a careless shrug and answered him, "Sure, if I'd not be in anybody's way." Well, they laughed and one said, "Feel free to get in Santa Anna's way, Saint Padraic." Someone else said, "Old Santy Anny himself would run from a man that eats rattlesnakes." Then they drank me a toast and gave me a gill of whiskey to drink with them, and I felt good.

Buena Vista Ranch near Saltillo, Mex. ✳ *Feb. 22, 1847*

HOLY MARY MOTHER of God, pray for us sinners now and at the hour of our death.

Faith and that very hour might be near. Sure we are in for a drubbing!

General Santa Anna himself is here in front of us with an Army of maybe fifteen thousand Mexicans. He was said to be way down south preparing to defend Mexico City from a southern attack. Instead here he is, with a glittering Army that looks to be filling up the whole mountain pass!

Here we stand, Gen. Z. Taylor and the few regiments Gen. Scott left him with. Amounting to a third of the Mexican force, from estimations made by our scouts. Three to one!

A body would expect Gen. Taylor to back away, and wait for better odds. But unless he is bluffing, he means to fight Santa Anna here. He's no bluffer.

I hear musketfire, a mile or so up there where the San Luis road goes up the pass. Not much. Now and then a bugle. The sounds echo between the mountains. This place is a sheep ranch. Sometimes the sheep seem to be answering the bugles. I don't know what's happening up there.

If Lt. Wallace doesn't get here from Monterrey soon he is likely to miss his chance for that battle glory he wants.

A very dreadful evening. There were bugles and gunfire in the afternoon for several hours, south of us. It was explained to us that there were skirmishes as Gen. Santa Anna arranged his Army on high ground. Getting ready for tomorrow. Officers coming back from up there look grim and scared. They don't let themselves talk scared, but gray faces don't inspire courage.

A cold drizzling rain has started. Hard to keep our campfires going. Way up the valley there are so many Mexican campfires it looks like a glow all across from one side of the world to the other. Everything stinks of smoke, wet ashes, sheep and horse manure. I'm of a mind to disappear before morning. Sure I wouldn't be missed.

Faith and it's hard to feel brave when you're cold and wet, and the bad rations make your innards bubble like a tea kettle. If I'm up shitting all night, it is sure I won't be up for drawing sketches of those Indiana Volunteers tomorrow. Maybe by eating rattlesnakes I've come to think like them. A rattlesnake will crawl away from danger if he has a chance to.

La Encantada Ranch, near Saltillo Mexico ∗ February 23, 1847

RECKON I'M GOING to go on the battlefield today. I could still get out of this. Could tell the lieutenants I thought they were joshing and didn't mean I'd go. But no. I will go onto the field. Taking my sketch-book. As if my hand will be steady enough to hold onto a pencil! I could hardly hold my cock still to piss straight this morning.

As for that . . . I will mention here that I had a dream during the night, and I never had such a one. I don't know whether it means I'm to die today, or that I'm to become a man. I write it here because it seems important, and it might be the last thing I write of. So I don't care if it's embarrassing. I dreamt I was sucking a tit. It woke me up in a fit. It was like I had wet my bedding but felt good in a strange way. I guess I know what it was. But does it have something to do with dying today? Why did this happen on the beginning of such a day?

Army forming up. This is a magnificent place, so big and harsh I could cry. Here at a sheep ranch two dry riverbeds join together and there are irrigation ditches, and gullies sloping up into tremendous mountains south of us. There is a narrow pass through the mountains. It was through that pass that Gen. Santa Anna brought his army up from the south.

This is the grandest and awfulest sight I ever saw. And if it is the last thing I see, I guess I should be glad I saw it. In my whole life, I've never seen this many people in one place all at once. And they're all fixing to try to kill each other. On high ground about a mile away, there is not a place to be seen that isn't solid with Mexican uniforms, all a sort of bluish gray. They must have a thousand flags and banners. Sky's clear now. In this first sunlight the whole Mexican Army glitters, their weapons, helmets of their cavalry, and the cannons. They have bands playing, a march slow as a dirge, as they move about. Also a religious procession in front. Tall, shiny crosses. As if it was the Pope's own army! Our officers mock it, trying to act brave.

∗　∗　∗

Buena Vista, Mexico
February 23ᵈ, 1847
The Mexicans overrun
a U.S. battery
Drawn in pencil by
P. Quinn,
an eyewitness

A hubbub of excitement about a concentration of enemy batteries on a rise above the road. It appears to command the whole field. Our officers got their telescopes up and someone cursed, "Goddamn, there stands that traitor Riley and his micks! Look under that green banner!" It was sure plain to see, a big green flag, distinct from all the others. A green banner for Ireland, is it! Having no telescope I couldn't make out Mr. Riley himself at such a distance. But it has inspired a fury that this little Army is going to need, against such odds.

There go our cannons! Off to our right, on the road. Raking the Mexicans coming on the road. What noise, I'd near forgot how I hate such noise! And the murmur of countless voices talking is now the roar of thousands of voices yelling.

Must quit writing. Indiana regt. starting to move. Must see what I can and draw if I can. Holy Mary Mother of God pray for us.

CHAPTER XVI

Saltillo, Mexico in hospital ✳ *March ? 1847*

WASN'T SURE I would ever try to write in this diary again. After what happened to me on the battlefield, I didn't care to write, to think, barely cared to live. I was in too much pain, then fever, to think.

Sure and I'll not be going to soldier when I come of age. No one needs a one-armed soldier.

Really shouldn't be trying to write even now. Words make me feel like I'll scream.

In hospital, Saltillo ✳ *March I suppose. 1847*

ON THE OTHER hand, what else can I do but write? And draw?
"On the other hand."
What other hand?
I may try again another day. Damn it all!

Camargo, Mexico, on Rio Grande ✳ *April 4, 1847*

WAITING HERE FOR a steamer to take us down to the Gulf coast. I'm picking up the pen and pencil again. I might as well. Need something against the tedium and misery.

Some of the wounded from the Battle at Buena Vista are still dying, from festering, flux, bad lungs. Now and then one kills himself.

I can't bear to write about the battle. Seems better to forget it. If you saw several thousand people funneled through a sausage grinder, why would you want to preserve the memory of it?

Gen. Taylor claims we won the battle. I'd call it a draw. Near a third of our soldiers casualties.

Mexicans likely lost more, but a smaller proportion of their Army.

Full battle went on all the day of Feb. 23. Expected to resume next day but by morning Gen. Santa Anna's Army was gone. Probably left for to defend Mexico City from Gen. Scott's invasion.

Lieutenant Wallace of the Indiana Volunteers talks to me when he comes to visit wounded soldiers from his company. He will be mustered out. He says he's composing an account of the battle. He urges me to finish the one drawing I had started before I was hit. He hopes it could perhaps go with his battle story to that journal in Indiana. Lt. Wallace came two days after the battle, so he didn't see it. But the Indiana Infantry is faulted in Gen. Taylor's battle report for failing and falling back, almost losing the whole battle. The Indiana officers say the General's report is unfair, that it doesn't tell how they rallied. Lt. Wallace is mad at the Gen. and is interviewing everybody to write a more glorious account. Mainly, trying to defend the reputation of his Indianans. He believes them, not the general. Mister Wallace has faith in his own writing power. He thinks Gen. Taylor is out of favor back in the United States and won't be believed once the account is told true. That could be, seeing as how Pres. Polk gave most of Taylor's Army to Gen. Scott. And Gen. Taylor's own pluck is being questioned. Some officers wonder why he didn't go chase after Gen. Santa Anna when he retreated.

Well, I'm damned if I quite understand this, when you have to bury several hundred soldiers in blankets because there's not enough wood for coffins, when several hundred more soldiers lie here in pain, eaten up by fleas & festerations, getting amputations, dying of fevers, puking to death, when all this wretchedness is here, why is it important that some officer or another gets hurt feelings, or a stain on his reputation, or a better account in the newspapers?

Wears me out to write. I am already worn near to death with pain, and all the misery in this dismal place. One doc leaves some infections undressed, open to flies. Says it's because their maggots eat the infection away from the good flesh. Maybe so, I think I'd rather have the infection. Thank God I don't.

From reading the newspapers you'd think all this slaughter and misery was just for seeing whether a Whig or a Democrat is the next President. Pres. Polk undercut Gen. Taylor to deny him political glory. I hope the President of the United States feels a great burden of remorse, as this was all his doing. I fancy myself and a score of these veterans here all raising a salute under his nose with the stumps of our limbs.

John Doherty has found me here & he smuggled in a quart of decent rye for me, may Saint Patrick bless his soul! This ought to dull the ache a mite.

Camargo Mexico ✳ April 6, 1847

BEYOND THE SORE stump, I often still feel my hand, although it's not there anymore. In my mind I imagine grasping with my fingers, and feel myself doing so, though there's no fingers.

I've heard of this, by being around soldiers so much. They call it Phantom Limb. There are tales of fellows getting drunk enough they forget they haven't a leg to stand on, and fall over.

(That also happens to some drunks who still have both legs, too. I've seen it often enough.)

Camargo, on the Rio Grande, Mex. ✳ Apr. 7, 1847

WHAT I HEAR told is, more of us got killed and hurt by the Irishmen's cannons up on that hill than by the rest of the Mexican Army together. Their 24-pounders and 16-pounders could reach just about anyplace on the battlefield, and their smaller guns just deluged our infantry with grapeshot. Sure I remember, there was never a moment when there wasn't smoke and fire and iron coming off that place, up there where the green flag was. It's said that Gen. Taylor was so furious it was the deserters' battery chewing up our Army, he sent a troop of dragoons against it. Sure he remembered letting those very gunners march out of Monterrey last fall! Those dragoons didn't quite get there.

After the battle our officers found 22 of Mr. Riley's gunners lying dead up there. All were recognized as deserters. If any had been left behind wounded it's sure they'd have been hanged. Whatever wounded they had they carried off with them, and I don't doubt it was many. Our own artillery officers were astonished that so many big guns and so much shot and shell could have even been toted and hauled up onto that height, in that short time they had to do it before the battle started.

I hear that Lt. Braxton Bragg did fine gunnery for our side. That's well and good. But think of all the good Irishmen he drove over to the Mexicans by his meanness, and them up there manning Mexican cannons instead of ours, well, it might overweigh whatever good he did with his own battery.

Now and then I thank God for sparing my writing hand.

The surgeon who took off my left hand said that it was not ball, grapeshot, or shell fragment that smashed the hand, that it might rather have been some part of a soldier, likely a chunk of skullbone. He said he took other pieces of bone out of several wounds in my side. He reckoned about half of bombshell wounds aren't from metal, but pieces of other soldiers.

What hit me I never saw coming. I recall little from that chaos. The Indiana Volunteers were protecting one of our artillery batteries. An awful number of Mexican infantry came out of a gully in front of us, like a thicket of bayonets coming closer. An awful storm of cannonfire was coming down on us from the elevated place where the Irishmen's green flag flew. Smoke and dust were so dense that one couldn't really see. In some places the bodies of dead horses and writhing soldiers lay so deep they had to be climbed over in order to advance. I quit attempting to sketch anything, just shaking too hard. I was deaf from shellbursts and was wet with blood and gore from dead and wounded soldiers being hurled upon me by explosions. Frankly, I had given up and was kneeling in a low place in hopes that the action would move away. I was looking to see if the enemy bayonets were closer when a shell burst nearby and things hit me and knocked me over. If I believe the surgeon, it was pieces of some poor Indiana bastard that trimmed me up like this. I can write it down here, but sure I don't care to think on it.

I believe it was then that the Indianans turned and ran. As for me, I reckon I just lost my senses.

CHAPTER XVII

Port Isabel, Mexico ✳ *April 10, 1847*

H ERE I AM back down the Rio Grande to the Gulf coast. A year since I arrived here in Mexico a picksnot urchin following an army. Now I am still the same, though now five fingers less, and a few lessons learned. I've been walking the shore in the wind, waiting for berth on one of the steamers. The wind keeps shifting the sands, and thus the bones of last year's soldiers (all who died of sicknesses, before the war started), those bones keep rising from the sand. And as they come up, others are buried, for some are still dying after the Buena Vista battle, all these weeks since. They'll never get home. And many more won't, either, many of those that have gone on down in Gen. Scott's Army for that campaign. I should like to believe that Our Good Lord has some reason for events the like of this. Perhaps at some great age I'll get an understanding of it all. But I doubt I'll ever feel older than I do now.

I have a bottle set in the sand beside me. I'll try to draw a picture of one of these rising dead. But with the shore wind it would be difficult even with two hands to manage a sketchbook.

Now there's a task for me: engineer a means to secure a writing portfolio or drawing board onto my stump. To hold it steady when I write or draw. Buckled straps might do.

One of last year's dead soldiers
rising from the grave at
Port Isabel as the
wind blows the sand
away, April 1847.
My whiskey in the
foreground, Gulf of
Mexico in the background.
Drawn by P. Quinn

Port Isabel, Mexico ✳ April 11, 1847

NOW A NEW matter at hand, changing my course:

A letter arrived here from Col. Harney's staff. It directs that I not sail back to New Orleans, but be put aboard a vessel for Vera Cruz; that my good Ma has somehow made her way to that place, and that if I am found I should be sent to meet her there.

By the Harp of Erin, how has she got herself on the road of the old Conquistador! As Lt. Wallace calls it. While he is himself being mustered out and returned to Indiana, never to see that fabled road.

Mister Wallace took with him several of my drawings. Among them was a well-finished illustration based on the one shaky sketch I did on the Buena Vista battleground. He hopes to have it as a pictorial enhancement of his account of the battle, for it does depict the Indiana Volunteers in honorable action. Saving their reputation seems to be his prime purpose, in the offing.

He promised that if the picture earns anything by publication, he will bank it in a trust to be held for me, there in Indiana. He took also the three portraits I sketched, of himself and two company officers.

So! If I survive the rest of this war, as I surely shall under the protection of my doughty Mum, I shall be able to travel to the State of Indiana, a land of duly honored regiments, and there find in a trust fund perhaps enough money to buy me a fine bottle of whiskey! And while there of course I won't neglect to call on Mister Lewis Wallace, to inquire into the progress of his great novel concerning an earlier conquest of Mexico.

Perhaps I'll even take to him some descriptions and drawings of the Road of Cortez, which I shall have seen, and he not!

How I enjoy to sit here with this diary and my bottle, and write my thoughts, while I may. For I expect the rest of this war will interrupt such pleasures. And what will it be like, I wonder, to have a parent trying to preside over me again, after all this eventful time on my own?

Sure and she'll be proud of my progress in writing and drawing. But she'll not be so proud to see how well I love the bottle at this age.

I do dread to see her face as she finds me short a limb.

I'll love to see her dear face however. Sure she'll be a bit changed, too, from what I remember. Nothing is easy for us the Irish poor folk. She will look old, I reckon. She's past thirty years by now.

BOOK II

The Southern Campaign

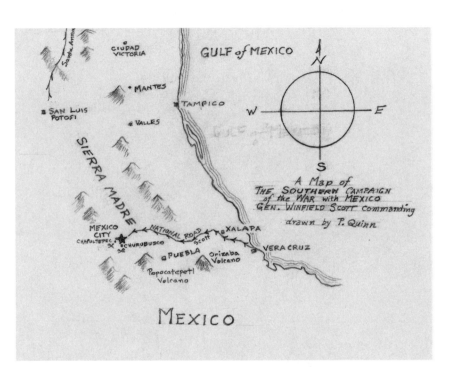

AGUSTIN JUVERO
SPEAKS WITH THE JOURNALIST
ON THE ROAD TO OUR LADY OF GUADALUPE
IN SPRING OF THE YEAR 1861

I T IS A new experience in my life, *Señor.* I have never made this
pilgrimage with another pilgrim alongside me. Certainly I have
never gone along day by day relating my narrative of that war, to a *Yanqui* who crawls on his knees in agony and humility!

Oh, it is good to see a *Yanqui* crawling on his knees in agony and humility! You people should do it now and then. It would alleviate your national disease—overweening pride.

And it is good to see a *Yanqui* asking instead of telling! That is another thing you should do now and then. Your United States is such a young country, a child among nations. Less than a century in age. But like a willful child who will not listen to the wisdom of your elders.

I am not happy to be deaf, *Señor Periodista.* Before your bombshells deafened me, I loved music, the sounds of birds, and voices speaking, and fountains in the courtyards, and mountain rivers dashing through the rocks. And of course the bells and the choirs and cantors of our holy religion. But it is appropriate that I cannot hear you, that you hear me. Now I am like the grandfather, who cannot hear the cries and silly questions of the children, and thus tells them what he knows, instead of the things they would like to hear.

You and I have now shared food and drink, shelter and the lack of shelter, the pain of penitence, and the pleasures of resting together in the niches and sanctuaries along this beautiful and tragic road. We have come about half the way. This has been a more tolerable sharing than I expected. You listen well and pay attention. You write and draw by candlelight where there is candlelight in the evenings. You are hardy, and not a complainer. If your *Yanqui* nation had more like you, it would perhaps be a better country than it is.

Now, *Señor,* in this year of 1861, your ignorant young nation is beginning to attack itself from within. You will feel the great sadness familiar to Mexico, of your own citizens killing each other. This is happening because your nation became too proud, and would not listen to the wisdom of those who were older and more wise.

As we have come along this hard road together, *Señor,* I have been telling you how we felt, losing our pride as your nation grew more and more proud by winning.

My people are brave and patient. We have seen tragedy and defeat for so long that we are not very susceptible to being astonished. However, in that last war, *Señor,* the one that hurt us in so many ways, we were astonished by the madness of your president, and by the recklessness of your generals. Your General Taylor had victories in northern Mexico because he was courageous and steadfast, not because he was a brilliant tactician. And as a hero, when he went home from Mexico he became your president for a little while, until he died in the office. You know all that, of course.

If General Taylor had remained in command of the war in Mexico, it is certain that Mexico would have defeated and humbled you. Zachary Taylor would have marched southward down the long, long road, five hundred miles through our uplands and mountains from Saltillo, and his supply line would have been eight hundred miles long by then. But your army would have perished long before then. I am speaking as a scholar of war, you see.

Your General Winfield Scott, though, was a genius. The world's greatest general, the duke of Wellington who had defeated Napoleon, said that General Scott was the greatest living general of his time. Alas for Mexico, it was General Scott who conducted the rest of the war for you. Because it was he, Mexico was doomed. For as you know, he chose the road by which the first invader had conquered Mexico.

The road of Cortéz.

PADRAIC QUINN'S DIARY

Aboard Steamship Naiad *Port Vera Cruz, Mexico* ✳ *April 17, 1847*

VERA CRUZ. MEANING, the True Cross.

Again I see the real bigness of a war, now I see ships in a port. So many big sailing ships are anchored here and at the docks, their masts look like a forest, as it does in winter when there are no leaves on. And the steamships, with their coalsmoke billowing up. Some ships are both: sail ships with paddle wheels on the sides. The ships are so huge! And they just keep bringing soldiers and supplies for General Winfield Scott.

This place is just docks and a sort of rough jetty, not a good harbor. Most of the ships stay at anchor offshore, waiting for dock space. North of the city there is a fort on a rock, which covers the port with cannons. A sailor told me that Gen. Scott had to land his army by rowboats farther down the beach out of range of that fort's big guns. All the men and supplies had to be put ashore in rowboats. Even their big cannons! Imagine rowing a boat with a cannon in it!

CHAPTER XVIII

*Vera Cruz, Mexico * April 18, 1847*

I AM GLAD to be off that ship but this is an unhealthful hot and low place. Almost everybody here sick with El Vomito. Town hundreds of years old, and not too ugly when you get away from the dock area. Somewhere around here is where that conquistador Cortez landed his ships. What breeze there might be is blocked by dunes and the town walls. Parts of the wall have been all battered down by Gen. Scott's cannons during the siege. They say the American artillery even borrowed big cannons off the battleships and put them up in the dunes. It was a scheme thought up by an Engineer Captain from Virginia, named R. E. Lee. He's famous for it here. Forced the town to surrender pretty quick. I never heard of him before, but hear of little else now.

I got off the ship with my letter from Col. Harney, to look for him & my mother. Now I find the whole Army's already marched off up the Mexican national road toward Mexico City. The Army clerks are arranging now for me to ride up with a supply convoy.

From up on the dunes you can look west and there's a volcano mountain with snow on it even in this weather. Called Orizaba. Said to be more than fifty miles but it's clear to see in morning light. Looks like silver.

Had a good supper of fresh fish and rice, in a shop. The cook spoke English and was good to me, wondered about a fellow my age being alone. I explained. He said he was happy to have a Catholic American in his place, was sorry about my hand, and all that. He told me about a whaling ship harpooner who had been here before the war, while his ship was being repaired, a harpooner whose hand had been torn off in a kink of rope pulled by a whale!

I bought a liquor he had there, made from the agave plant, and we talked about whales and whale oil. The light of the world, he said, pointing at the lamp in the shop. He said the one-handed harpooner had been at sea two years, while his family waited for him in their home on an island not far from Boston. He seemed to love saying "Boston." Wondered how a man could stay away from a wife for two years. I told him that soldiers had to do that, too. He said Yanqui soldiers who came here complained that he had rice instead of potatoes. I told him that my Irish forebears hadn't had anything to eat but potatoes, so we tend to like them. Then he told me there never was a potato in Ireland until they were sent over from South America. I was surprised. He said, yes, and maiz. He meant corn. No corn anywhere until they found it here, he said. He was proud to tell me that Mexico had fed the world.

I paid him for the meal, and then drew his portrait and gave it to him. He was so grateful he poured me another glass of the liquor. So then I drew a picture of his wife and he gave me another glass.

When I woke up I was on a pallet on the floor of his place, and he served me a free breakfast before I went back to the Army headquarters. I checked in my wallet and every penny was still in it. The last thing he told me when I left the shop was that if I couldn't catch up to find my mother, come back to Vera Cruz and he and his wife would take care of me. Good that they spoke some English. I still don't hardly know Spanish well enough to be traveling in their country. Shame on me for that, as I've been in their country a year now.

Vera Cruz, Mexico * April 20, 1847

ANOTHER VICTORY! Gen. Scott got into a battle up toward the mountains, against Gen. Santa Anna, and won it. Santa Anna was forted up on a mountain covering the national road to Mexico City. But our Army flanked him and drove him off. Col. Bill Harney led the flanking charge, I hear. I will want to find out more about that. That vicious bastard's a hero again.

To my mind, what's most remarkable about all this is that Gen. Santa Anna could even have been there for that battle! It's less than two months since his Army fought Gen. Taylor in northern Mexico, way up there at Buena Vista, where I lost my hand. That is seven or eight hundred miles of deserts and mountains to move a whole Army through, by the maps I've seen. And in no longer than it took me to heal and come down to Vera Cruz by boat! But no one can march like Mexican soldiers. That we know.

Rumor is, it was a real slaughter, and a rout. More than a thousand Mexican soldiers dead. Three thousand made prisoners. Such a rout, they say, Gen. Santa Anna himself left a cork leg in his camp. Don't know if that's true yet. It's the kind of a yarn soldiers hoot about, for it ridicules their enemy. Whether it's true or not, it's raising the spirits of all the soldiers here at Vera Cruz. Hear soldiers laughing, and that's likely what they're talking about, that false leg.

They need something to make them laugh, for they're dropping sick by hundreds here, down with El Vomito. For every Mexican soldier we kill, we lose one of ours to sickness. They say it's from being down here on the coast with the hot weather setting in. Most soldiers say they'd rather be up in the high country with Gen. Scott than down here. I had rather die by bullet than by puking, a soldier told me.

There is a convoy going up that way tomorrow, and I get to go with it. An Army clerk confirmed that my mother has already gone up, with the civilians following the Army.

I heard the Death March today, funerals out at the Army camp. Sure if there are mockingbirds in this part of Mexico, they'll be for learning to sing it soon.

On National Road, Mexico ✳ April 21, 1847

OUR SUPPLY WAGON convoy made maybe 15 miles on the national road today. Gradual uphill. Up away from that coast, but still hot scrubby country. We were slowed by meeting Army wagons taking wounded soldiers down to Vera Cruz. There's said to be near four hundred hurt bad. Around seventy killed.

Awful to see those poor soldiers all filthy and wrapped in bloody bandages, swarming with flies. One wagon load stopped by us. Such as could, got off the wagons to piss by the road. One all pale in the face stayed aboard, stood up and pissed over the side of the wagon. He had a big bloody wad of bandage on his left arm and then I saw it was just a stump of arm, looked like he had lost about as much arm as I did. He was white as chalk and slick with sweat and all pained in the face, but he saw me watching him. I sort of saluted him with my own stump, and he looked right surprised. "What happened to you, boy?" he called over. I called back and answered, it just came into my head to say it, "John Riley's cannons!" Which I reckon was true.

Said he, "I'll be damned! Me too! Saw his goddamn green flag! Goddamn traitors! But we got them, by God! Killed a mess of them. Took their heavy cannons. Hey, I got to sit down." He kind of crumpled down inside the wagon, breathing shallow through his mouth with his eyes shut. My heart was a-pounding. I went across the road to his wagon and stood up on the wheel hub so I could see in. There were four or five soldiers on the wagon floor who looked dead, or near to it. I said, "Sir, did they kill Mister Riley?" He blinked his eyes open, saw me, said, "Sorry, I think not. They was seen hightailing out, with their goddamned green mick flag. Hey, lad, it's a bother unbuttoning the breeches for a pee, ain't it, with just one hand?" Then he shut his eyes and said, "God, I think I'm about to faint."

Many of the wounded soldiers had keepsakes from the battlefield, Mexican shakos, bayonets, epaulets, canteens, cartridge boxes, peso coins, gold crucifixes, banners, fifes, just to name things I saw. Some had cut off an ear or a finger of someone they had killed, or said they had killed. One man had a scalp of black hair. He bragged that he had other scalps, from the war on the Seminoles. It all reminded me again of all those yarns about Chief Tecumseh's skin on razor strops and all that. The wounded soldiers were wretched, but they would most of them roust their spirits when the subject of Santa Anna's leg came up. It did, often. A few soldiers said they had seen it themselves, in the possession of some officer.

Another thing they laughed and jeered about was Colonel Harney's new whore. They said who but old Horny Harney could find himself a big brass-plated bawd right in the middle of a campaign? That one of his dragoon supply wagons had been fixed up fancy for her to ride and abide in, and another to carry her baggage.

That was no surprise to me, for it was likewise when I was with his troop in Florida. Elsewhere in this journal I made account of his lechery as I saw it with my own eyes, and his long reputation for goatishness.

Those rumors make me uneasy. My phantom hand is bothering me tonight, maybe because of that soldier on the road with his new amputation, for, O how well I remember how that felt for so many days after it happened!

Sure and it turns me thinking about John Riley pretty strongly. As, shouldn't I be for justly hating a man who shot off my arm? And countless others' arms, and legs, and heads?

The wagoneer captain expects we will pass the battlefield tomorrow. At sundown today we gazed on a dark mountain far ahead, which is said to be the one where Gen. Santa Anna dug his Army in to stop Gen. Scott.

In vain, it was for Santa Anna. Now with his Army routed, it is but a bit over 200 miles on to his capital at Mexico City. Here I am upon the very road old Cortez took to the same place! Someday I might go to Indiana and sit with a good bottle and tell Lt. Lew Wallace about this road to Montezuma, as he calls it! God willing, I'll get back there for that. And maybe I can help him describe Cortez's road, for his romantic Christian novel.

Begorrah, I'll drink to that!

Cerro Gordo, Mexico ✳ April 22, 1847

CERRO GORDO MEANS fat hill, or big hill. General Santa Anna's Army fled through this little town after our forces broke their defenses. North of the Rio del Plan are two mountains, called El Telegrafo and Atalaya. Road runs between Telegrafo & the river.

You see the shambles of the rout. Everything an Army uses is scattered along the road, broken. Cannon wheels, wagons, kettles, crates. Parts of blue uniforms all over the ground. Our soldiers are digging shallow graves and dragging Mexican corpses to them. Dead horses lie all about, rotting in the sun. Enough buzzards to give shade, not to exaggerate by much.

Some soldiers paused from their burial detail to point out to us the lay of the battle. Plainly, Telegrafo dominated the road, and the Mexican general expected our Army to come up the road and be trapped under him. But that Engineer Captain, Lee, scouted a route between the two mountains, and sappers cleared a path through its thickets. The path skirted Santa Anna's weakest defense, and Gen. Scott's Army attacked through it. The gravediggers pointed at the steep and distant Atalaya mountain. Americans took that peak and put cannons up there. Santa Anna was outflanked and enfiladed. Even so, said the soldier, it was a bloody awful fight and all steep uphill, and if we hadn't outfoxed old Santy Anny we'd all be dead.

I am sketching a map to send to Lt. Wallace, though I'm sure there will be better ones in the battle accounts in the periodicals, long before I can post mine to him. War news gets home so fast, the whole United States should soon be laughing about the Mexican commander's captured leg!

I asked Mister Wallace, before he went home, how the news does go so fast. He said it goes by fast boat to New Orleans. Newspapers there, like the *Picayune,* support express riders, who gallop off day and night to relay the print. Somewhere they get to the telegraph line that's being extended out of Baltimore, and then it's all up east in those periodicals in just hours.

I sure do find that interesting. Somebody sees a battle in one country, and in days people in another country can read what he saw. Mister Wallace gave me an instance of how important that hastiness can be. He told me the famous Battle of New Orleans was fought fifteen days after the treaty that ended the War of 1812, because neither side knew about the peace treaty. Two thousand casualties because news was so slow! That wire telegraph thing, that could do good. Lt. Wallace had some cards with the telegraph code printed on them and gave me one so I could learn it. I haven't yet, but ought to. Might be a good skill to have someday.

They don't have any wire telegraph anywhere in Mexico yet. This mountain is called Telegrafo because it was a signaling place so high it could be seen for many miles, and helped relay flashing signals between the coast and Mexico City.

Morse is the name of the wire telegraph inventor. Lt. Wallace said Morse was an artist before he invented it. An artist, like me. Probably better. But I'll wager he wasn't better than me at my age. I practice at it as much as I can. My Ma will be impressed, sure enough.

Lt. Wallace told me an odd thing about that Morse: that he is one of the worst of the "hatemongers" against Catholic immigrants. Started when Mr. Morse was in a crowd at the Vatican and didn't take his hat off for the Pope, so a Vatican guard knocked his hat off. So then Mr. Morse wrote some really vicious anti-Pope books, about ten years ago. Well, that really started something. After Mister Morse's books there came hundreds of such books and periodicals about the Papists trying to take over America, and Irish Catholic criminal elements corrupting American cities, and suchlike. Mister Wallace said most of the officers have read this "flood of vitriol" and believe it, and he said it's a major cause of their contempt and cruelty toward the Irish soldiers. Also a reason why an Irish soldier's got little chance to rise in rank. I remember when I was little, other children would say they hated me because Catholic priests and nuns ate babies and drank human blood. They had drawings they would show of nuns being mounted by goats, and priests mounting sheep, and demons dancing with nuns who didn't have anything on but their cowls. Really strange and awful drawings. I remember the one time I tried to tell my mother about them, she said she already knew about such things, that they weren't true at all and I shouldn't mind them. She said people were getting hurt and killed in big cities where mobs attacked and burned down Catholic neighborhoods and churches, and it was all caused by the kind of lies and pictures those children were showing. She said don't hate them, just ignore them, and not hit anybody first.

But she said, "Don't ever let anybody hit you a second time."

I went by her advice, and after a while it came to be that hardly anybody would try to hit me anymore. One bigger boy kept at me, a sergeant's son, but then my mother caught him by his topknot when he was after me. He was bigger than she was, but she spun him around and punched him on his snot horn, & he was polite to me from that day on.

I expect we'll catch up with the Army tomorrow, and I'll see her. Soldiers here say the army is encamping up the road at a goodly-size town called Xalapa. It is well up out of the fever country, saints be praised.

And I couldn't bear to camp one more night so close to this battlefield. Stink of death. Dogs and buzzards feeding on dead horses. There are dead horses by hundreds, and sure nobody bothers to give a horse a funeral, even a burial.

Xalapa, Mexico in camp ✴ Apr. 24, 1847

MAY THE GIANT holy fist of Saint Patrick close around Col. Harney and squeeze the gleet out of him, for the ass-pimple he is! Damn *damn* damn him!

What could be worse than this I sure don't know! I am near too ashamed to put it on paper here, though it's no fault of mine.

Or maybe it is. I might have warned her when I wrote to her: Ma, keep a distance from the colonel for he's nought but a two-legged cock-stand and will smirch your reputation just by looking at you. And cruel besides!

Yes, sure and she's the one those soldiers called the brass-plated bawd that Harney's taken into his wagons. Horny Harney's whore, they said. I'd never guessed it was her. If I'd foreseen this, I'd not have come up from Vera Cruz. If I'd known this I might have just followed the Mexicans and thrown in with John Riley, as his errand boy or something.

No. That would leave her at Harney's mercy. She must be warned what a lethal brute he is.

How I found it out is when the wagons came up, there was that old corporal, Barton, from Col. Harney's Seminole War regiment. He saw me and yelled, "B'God, it's our catamite! The Quinn lad, him who don't know his Pa's name! How ye been farin', boy? And might the Colonel's lady Quinn be a relative to ye?"

Of course he knew she's my Ma. They all know. When they directed me toward the regiment camp, they greeted me, but they all had a leer on. I was in a fit of rage and shame by the time I reached her wagon, & there she stood awaiting for me, her mouth open.

I guess she saw my empty sleeve instead of whatever was showing in my face. Sure and she didn't know I'd heard her called Harney's whore. So she seized me in the first hug I'd had since I was eight or nine, near smothered me and was quaking with sobs. I was affected, I admit, and guess I sniffled at her bosom even as I was smothering in it. It probably was a good thing we got through the first minute or two of our reunion that way, instead of seeing each other's faces, for it was such a comfort,

I felt it weighed more than the shame. And I will say it was a damned blessing that Col. Harney was away at his headquarters instead of present at our greeting. I don't know what I'd have done if that son of a bitch had been standing about. Before that hug mollified me, I might have gone a berserker and gelded him with my rattlesnake knife.

As it was, the first thing I told her when we sat down was that I would be camping separate and didn't want to see the colonel or talk to him. I didn't even give her time to inquire about my arm. I implored her to gather up her mere necessities and we would get away from Harney's dragoons, and set up amongst the camp followers in Little America. Or find passage back to New Orleans. She wanted instead to learn what had happened to me. She kept reaching toward my arm, with tears welling. But I drew back and kept urging her to get away from Harney. After a bit of that, her temper started to rise up, those signs I knew, her nose and cheeks reddening, eyes getting narrow. She said, "Padraic, this is a good situation. Colonel Harney treats me well and sees that I want for nothing. I won't be for having you meddle. You and I only just found each other after years of hardship, and rather than let me rejoice, you scold me! If you don't like Bill Harney, then get to know him better. He'll treat you well. He remembers you from Florida and has said only good about you."

That is what she said. What I said then was that the colonel is a murderer, and a raper and torturer of little Indian girls. And that he disciplines his soldiers so brutally that his is one of the worst desertion problems in the whole Army. I told her that he is especially brutal to the Irish, which ought to mean something to an Irish-born woman. Here she interrupted me to protest that Harney was himself an Irishman, and she didn't believe me. I said, "He scorns the immigrants, for he's a born American and believes the newcomers disgrace him and others like him!"

It was at that moment when one of Colonel Harney's Irish dragoons went by, leading a lame horse, and overhearing, he said, "The lad speaks true, Ma'am. I can show ye the stripes on my back." She pointed at him and said, "I can report you, soldier!" Well, he halted and turned to reply, "If ye must, Ma'am, go right on, as he'll be a-whippin' me anyway for letting me horse go lame." Then he went on, beginning to whistle quite beautifully the song called I Wish I Was Married Again Again.

She was speechless for a moment. Then she turned to me and said, "Paddy, dear Paddy, come sit for tea with me and let's be kind."

And that we did. I was relieved. I told her of my arm, she kissed the stump scar with tears in her eyes. I showed her some of my sketches and she was astonished by them—not merely a mother praising a son. I told her of Lt. Wallace and his kindnesses to me, and about all he had taught me of newspapers and other matters. I told her of the novel he is writing, and that we are now on the historic road of the conquistador. She said she was pleased by all my education that I had gotten without school. Now and then her eyes welled with tears. Who knows what troubles she has endured between Michigan and Mexico, but she appears little older than I remember. I observed that soldiers tend to stray toward her for a close look, and I do suspect it's not merely curiosity about their colonel's companion.

I drank more tea and restrained myself awhile from badgering her to leave the colonel. I kept watching about, intending to have gone before he arrived. She said she would prepare a place for me to put my bedding down in the other wagon. But I told her that I would be for finding another place to sleep. She protested very little, I guess because of seeing how strongly I dislike the colonel. As the sun sank, I began moving to leave. She urged me to stay and have supper, of good fresh beef she was stewing over her cookfire. I excused myself, saying that I had friends I wished to visit in the 4th Infantry. And it was true the urge had risen to find Lts. Grant and Maloney and show them I am still alive.

She assured me as I left, that she knows how to keep a man from hurting her.

Can a son know what his mother is thinking? I believe that she is planning how to persuade me to live with her. And, that Colonel Harney bears watching, for those great faults I spoke of. I want her to imagine the Seminole girls he raped.

So I left her, after that long-awaited reunion, and went looking for the 4th Inf. Both lieutenants out on patrols. I'll go back tomorrow evening. I went into Xalapa, found the townfolk polite, curious about me. Bought spicy meat in a fritter. Good.

I came back after dark and bedded down not far from her wagons, but stayed in the shadows. Soldiers were singing and laughing near their fire, and part of their song was this:

Colonel Harney, Red head Harney,
Full o' lechery and blarney!
Within earshot of War's trumpet,
Old Bill Harney beds a strumpet!

I confess, to this diary in the place of the priests we don't have, that the demise of Col. Bill Harney in this poor Catholic land would not sadden my heart.

Xalapa, Mexico ✳ *April 25, 1847*

LT. GRANT WAS reeking whiskey and cigars but seemed happy to see me. My stump arm moved him to rant on this "unholy war," which maims children and loots cathedrals and so on. The lieutenant is generous with his whiskey and cigars, and shared with me despite my minority. When Mick Maloney frowned on that, Sam Grant surprised me by retorting to Maloney that he deems me a veteran, age be damned. They both drank to that, and my head swelled so, I could've worn two hats!

Inspired by the whiskey, the officers blew steam about two things mainly. Which general, Taylor or Scott, would likelier be the next U. States president. And whether the rest of the campaign on Mexico City is to be a bloody ordeal or a promenade. The battle here was such a drubbing that Santa Anna probably is sunk in disgrace and unable to mount a defense of the capital. Mister Grant disagreed. "We've invaded their country, damn it, so I expect we'll pay a steep price for every inch." He lamented the loss of several thousand volunteers who were going home because their enlistments had expired, and no sign of reinforcements yet. "This Army proved itself there at Cerro Gordo," Mister Grant said. "But if we ever meet their Army head-on, instead of finding a way around, well . . ." He stopped and shook his head, and the talk fell off, and we got so grogged I woke up cold on the ground under a cot, with officers snoring all around in the dark. My last cigar had burnt a hole in my shirt and I hadn't known it.

Avoiding Col. Bill Harney could be the death of me yet.

✳   ✳   ✳

Noon today I went like a good son to look in on my mother. Found her in low spirits. Col. Harney had argued with her last night. He was criticizing me. Said what kind of a boy is it that won't stay with his mother in camp, or won't even come to pay his respects to an officer who protected me from Seminole Indians in Florida, and who got me passage to come find her. Being as she is, she told him right out that I don't much care for him. She said he colored at that, and asked her why not. She told him she reckoned I thought he wasn't good enough for her, as a son might think about his mother. She said he swelled and called it an impertinence when a damned camp urchin looks down on a colonel of the United States Army and he would damned well like an explanation of it from me. He said if I couldn't show proper respect he might just bar me from the camp or ship me back out of Mexico altogether. She told him she would advise me thus, if she saw me, but warned him not to think of laying a rough hand on me. He said by God he never had. I told her, that's true, for I never gave him cause. I told her also that he never protected me from Seminole Indians, either, unless those little Indian girls had meant to do me harm before he ravished them and rendered them harmless. She looked hard at me then but didn't scold. So I guess I've got her looking at him a little slaunchwise now. Or could it be that she's heard his dragoons sing their little ditty about his lechery? I hope not, for it sure demeans her as much as him.

I told her I would stay near, and if the colonel came, I'd face up to him. That lifted her mood. We ate together, and talked. She had made a straw pallet for me in the other wagon, and I put my pack and blanket in on it. Then we drank tea and talked some more while she mended the burn hole in my shirt. It was chilly sitting there with my shirt off, and whenever she looked at the stump of my arm, she'd bite her lip and blink and go back a-sewing.

After a while like that I said, "This isn't so bad, not if you saw some of the fellows in the hospital with me after the Buena Vista fight." She shut her eyes and shook her head. I showed her my other scars, and told her that what had hit me was probably pieces of a soldier's skull. She shuddered so hard I could see it, and burst out, "Damn it, Paddy, why were you on a battlefield anyway!" So I explained about being there to sketch the combat of the Indiana troops for Lt. Wallace. "Well," she said, "you're no soldier, you're my very young son, and I forbid you to go into a battle again if God forbid there is one."

I said, "There will be. My friend Mister Grant thinks we're in for something awful, when we go for their capital, for it's sure to be walls and forts and strongholds all over." She said, "Friend? Ah, sure and would that be the Lieutenant Grant that gives a child whiskey to drink and cigars to burn himself up with, now?" And then all at once we both just started laughing. It was the first we'd ever laughed together since I was little, sure and it was that, and it felt so good. We just went on and on laughing. Some soldiers nearby looked at us, curious, and began to edge our way as if to hear what was funny. Sure she is an object of their own base humor, I know, so it's fair that they're puzzled by our laughter. And I reckon many of them envy the colonel her company, too, a body can tell that by the way they look at her. This isn't easy for me, but like any misery, laughter eases it.

Late in the day, Col. Harney came up, as I knew he would eventually, both smiling and scowling at once, I swear he was. He greeted me as his good lad, which gnawed in me, but for her sake I was polite. He gave a nod and a wince in respect to my empty sleeve, as a proper soldier will. Then he eased past me toward my mother. However they might usually greet each other, they were proper as churchmice in my presence. And good for him, because if he'd so much as patted her haunch I might have amputated his hand with my Mexican knife, or perished in the attempt. He is a man to be feared, I'd learned long ago, strong and quick and mean-spirited. He is a hard-faced redhair. What charm he ever resorts to doesn't come from as deep as his heart, it's just blarney, to gain something. Not many soldiers really like killing and hurting, but I'm sure he does, and that's why I pray my mother will get over her attachment to him. She sure will as far as it's in my power.

We sat a moment for tea, though any of us would have preferred liquor, if we weren't trying so hard to make good impressions. I felt there were some invisible people present with us as we sat there. I mean the Seminole girls. We all three knew of them. Perhaps the colonel knew that I had told my mother about them. Maybe she had asked him about them. I doubt it. Probably she will keep that knowledge to herself, like a hidden weapon to use on him if ever need be.

Colonel Harney's preferred mood is anger. Today he had cause for it, without directing it at me. He soon began complaining about deserters. Two more of his own dragoons had vanished last night, and scores had left other units here at Xalapa. My mother inquired, in an innocent-sounding manner, whether a soldier would ever be whipped for letting his horse go lame. The colonel drew up tall and said yes. She said, "Has any been whipped lately for it?" He replied, "As a matter of fact, yes." She said, "Is that whipped soldier one of the recent deserters?" Well, the colonel's face went as red as his hair and he admitted that it was so. She said, "Was he an Irish soldier?" All this she pursued as mild discourse. At length the colonel drew from his coat a folded document, shook it open, and handed it to her. "It's the damned Mexicans and their print-ing mill," he said almost in a shouting voice. "These are coming as thick as snowflakes!"

I remembered the pamphlets and broadsides that had been distrib-uted at Fort Texas, and could scarcely contain my eagerness to compare this new one. So I contrived to have it in my possession by the end of our visit. It is most eloquent, and bears the signature of General Santa Anna, who apparently remains in power despite his defeat in the recent battle. It was from Mexico City, and here follows its text:

MEXICANS TO CATHOLIC IRISHMEN

Irishmen—Listen to the words of your brothers, hear the accents of a Catholic people.

Could Mexicans imagine that the sons of Ireland, that noble land of the religious and the brave, would be seen amongst their enemies?

Well known it is that Irishmen are a noble race; well known it is that in their own country many of them have not even bread to give up to their children.

These are the chief motives that induced Irishmen to abandon their beloved country and visit the shores of the new world.

But was it not natural to expect that the distressed Irishmen who fly from hunger would take refuge in this Catholic country, where they might have met with a hearty welcome and been looked upon as broth-ers had they not come as cruel and unjust invaders? Sons of Ireland!

Have you forgotten that in any Spanish country it is sufficient to claim Ireland as your home to meet with a friendly reception from authorities as well as citizens? Our religion is the strongest of bonds.

What? Can you fight by the side of those who put fire to your temples in Boston and Philadelphia? If you are Catholics, the same as we, why are you men, sword in hand, murdering your brothers?

Are Catholic Irishmen to be the destroyers of Catholic temples, the murderers of Catholic priests, in this pious nation?

By conquest you can take the cities and towns, but never possess two feet of ground unmolested as long as there is a Mexican.

But our hospitality and good will towards you tenders you without force as much property in land as you require, and this under the pledge of our honor and our holy religion.

Come over to us: you will be received under the laws of that truly Christian hospitality and good faith which Irish guests are entitled to obtain from a Catholic nation. Our sincere efforts have already been realized with many of your countrymen, who are living as our own brothers among us.

May Mexicans and Irishmen, united by the sacred tie of religion and benevolence, form only one people.

ANTONIO LÓPEZ DE SANTA ANNA
President, Republic of Mexico

This eloquent appeal I read and reread by candlelight in the wagon tonight, and now write this summary of a day which has been difficult for me. In the other wagon a few feet away are Colonel Harney and my mother. I prefer not to think of them. I do wish that General Scott would execute a policy forbidding his officers from such behavior. Old "Fuss & Feathers," as Gen. Scott is known, is said to be such a Prig, that he would not abide the colonel's wantonness. Mr. Grant said Gen. Scott despises Harney anyway, knowing him as a crony of Pres. Jackson. More politics!

But we are deep in a hostile country. Colonel Harney is the sort of officer Gen. Scott needs here. Even if Gen. Scott knows of this, as he probably does, he would not vex a fighting officer by caviling with him over his morality.

I would very much have liked to needle the colonel this evening,

Colonel Wm HARNEY
commander of
Cavalry
"The Red Devil"

drawn at
Xalapa, Mex.
1847

by P. Quinn

during his rage over desertions, by telling him of my friendship and admiration for Mister John Riley. O How satisfying it would have been to say, Colonel, I know a gunner from Galway who is worth about twenty of you.

But of course I am no such a fool as all that.

And I must keep faith that my mother can handle a scoundrel well enough her own way as long as she's near him, which will be only until I can devise to drive the bloody villain off her. I can't do that by staying away, so that means I have to suffer being around him for the while.

I drew a picture of him after having to look at him through a whole supper, drew him the way he looks at me. I showed it to her and said, "See those evil slit eyes? Is that a mean bastard or not? Be frank, Ma."

She huffed and said, "A man can't be blamed for the phiz God gave him!" I said, "It wasn't God made his eyes mean. That's his own doing."

CHAPTER XIX

AGUSTIN JUVERO
SPEAKING TO THE JOURNALIST
ON THE PILGRIMAGE ROAD

I T WAS AN excellent breakfast, *Señor Periodista. Gracias.*
Before we return to our *peregrinación,* I will show you some papers that you should find to be of much interest.

These papers bear the handwriting of a certain person. Never mind how it is that they are in my possession. They are of some historical importance.

These have been marked with dates that indicate when they were composed. You will observe that they are from the spring and summer of the year 1847. That is, after our army's defeat at Cerro Gordo. By that time, *Presidente* Santa Anna was back in Mexico City, with his headquarters in the Citadel where I was continuing my military education. You may try to imagine the anxiety. *El Presidente* was not in disgrace for the loss of that battle, despite what you might have read in your country's periodicals. The desperate defense of the heart of our country made him instead, in the eyes of our people generally, still more our savior. It is true, some political opponents were critical of the failure at Cerro Gordo, and the status of certain generals under his command was changing. General Santa Anna was always adept at assigning blame for any failure to his subordinates, whom he would blame as traitors. By condemning them, he would elevate himself in the eyes of the people still further.

We watched your advance closely. Guerrillas were everywhere around your army. They sent us reports sometimes encouraging, sometimes not. General Scott's supply line from Vera Cruz to Xalapa was over-extended. Thousands of your volunteers had gone home. Thousands more were ill and dying. General Scott was attempting to supply his army with food taken from our farmers in the vicinity of Xalapa. When that met resistance, he made arrangements with the *alcaldes* and other leaders, and began paying for the food. We did not brand those suppli-ers as traitors to Mexico's defense, for we knew they had little choice in the matter. And General Scott was fair, plainly an honorable and judi-cious man, although he served an aggressive and corrupt government.

But the signs were ominous that he would be coming on toward our capital. Those Irish and German Catholics who were deserting him in such numbers, they carried rumors that he was preparing to march on from Xalapa to Puebla, a giant stride, halfway to our capital. In a way, that gave us some hope, for it meant that his line of supply would be perhaps stretched beyond its capacity. In the classroom, our *Colegio* in-structors were by then discussing the strategies of the current war in-stead of military history and theories. The times were exciting. We grew ever more patriotic. We spent more time drilling and practicing for combat. I remember that we would gather on the parapets of the castle of Chapultepec, small groups of cadets, gazing out over the spires of Mexico City and the lakes and mountains beyond, and imagine the day when General Scott and his *Yanqui* army would appear from the east. Sometimes we would see *el Presidente* move between his door and his carriage. He was always surrounded by officers and dignitaries. Some looked to be English or Americans. There was a rumor, *Señor,* that your President Polk had sent a diplomat to negotiate secretly with *el Presi-dente* Santa Anna for peace. It was thought that your president did not really want General Scott to succeed in capturing Mexico City because the general was of different politics and might return to your country in triumph and defeat the president's party in the next election. There were such intrigues and subterfuges always going forward, as the his-tory of the war proves. And we the cadets believed that we saw the plot-ters, though we seldom knew which were which.

Then there was a day, *Señor,* that I shall never forget. It was when a great many of our military officers came up to meet with *el Presidente,* and one of them was Don Juan Riley. He was a captain by then, much decorated for his artillery service at Buena Vista and then at Cerro Gordo. I was one of the cadets who were sent to attend the horses of the visiting officers. There I saw the great Irishman, and his commander, Major Moreno, who as I told you was a friend of my family. They had in fact sent ahead a request that I should be among the cadets attending their horses, so that we could greet each other.

Capitán Riley appeared most splendid in his uniform and medals. His face was tanned by sun and weather, and his black hair, long and curly, burnished with red from sunbleaching. He and Major Moreno flattered me with warm and sincere attention, which thereafter was to enhance my prestige in the academy, but also was to exacerbate the envy from certain older cadets. Both officers relayed to me my mother's greetings. From that I presumed that she and *Capitán* Riley were again in company with each other, much to their mutual happiness, I suspected. The captain explained very briefly to me that General Santa Anna had summoned him to bestow another promotion upon him and upon other of his Irish gunners, but also to employ him further in the enticement of Catholic soldiers away from General Scott's approaching army.

"I have become his example," *Capitán* Riley told me with a smile. And Major Moreno said to me, "We are still doing what you helped us do so well, Agustin, so many months ago when you so bravely carried our noble appeals across the Rio Bravo to General Taylor's fort." Some of my fellow cadets heard those words, to my considerable satisfaction.

Now, as to these papers that I mentioned. These, *Señor,* are in a hand that may be familiar to you. I have shown you already another thing that he wrote. You doubted it was his. These are various drafts of a broadside that President Santa Anna asked *Capitán* Riley to compose in his own words. It is a rather handsome script, is it not? Much better than the contemptuous West Point officers would expect from what they liked to call "ignorant Irishmen." Read it, *Señor.*

TO MY FRIENDS AND COUNTRYMEN
IN THE ARMY OF THE UNITED STATES OF AMERICA

Actuated by only the purest motives, I venture to address you on a vitally important subject.

The President of the Republic of Mexico, in hope of giving every opportunity to Foreigners in your army, through a sentiment worthy of his high station, and through motives of pure friendship towards the misguided natives of other countries (than the United States) who have foolishly embarked in this impolitic & unholy war, once again offers to you his hand, & invites you, in the name of the Religion you profess, the various countries in which you first drew breath, of honor and of patriotism, to withhold your hands from the slaughter and invasion of a country whose thoughts or deeds never injured you or yours.

My Irish Countrymen! I call upon you, for I know well your feelings, for the sake of that chivalry for which you are so celebrated, for that love of Liberty, for which our Ireland has so long been contending, for the sake of that Holy Religion which we have for ages professed:

I conjure you to abandon a slavish hireling's life in an army which in even the moment of victory treats you with contumely & disgrace. For whom are you contending? For a nation which, in the face of a disapproving world, trampled upon the holy altars of our Religion, set firebrands to a sanctuary devoted to the Blessed Virgin, and, even while boasting of civil and religious Liberty, trampled in contemptuous indifference everything appertaining to the dearest feelings of our country. My brave Countrymen! I have experienced the hospitality of the citizens of this Republic; from the moment I extended them the hand of friendship, I was received with kindness; though poor, I was relieved; though undeserving, I was respected. I pledge to you my Oath, that the same kindnesses extended to me await you also. ~~if you will attend your conscience and~~

I join my voice with that of the President of this Catholic Republic of Mexico, inviting you to leave those ranks which are unworthy, and to come over to ~~this side of~~

And so you see how he would strike through and begin again. This was the work upon which the president engaged him, in addition to his exemplary soldiering, and it is evident that he worked and reworked his words, hoping to move Irishmen to this cause, in which he fully believed. Look at these papers. Imagine him.

Perhaps you might imagine our excitement and our anxiety in those times, *Señor.* A formidable enemy was pressing close to the heart of our country, our magnificent and ancient capital city. They were *heréticos, bárbaros, violadors.* They scorned our religion, mocked and ransacked our churches. They were soldiers who somehow always surprised or outwitted us and won battles they should have lost. We who knew the history were reminded of the Spaniards of Cortéz who had come here by this same road so long ago, with so few soldiers, the unstoppable *invasor.*

But this time we were armed with cannons and muskets and cavalry, the same weapons possessed by our *invasor.* And now we also had turned our faith to the powerful God of the *conquistadors,* and we prayed to him. We had as our *presidente* and *commandante* a glorious man already famed for heroism. He had rebuilt the Mexican army still again, and encouraged us to believe that the defense of Mexico City was not a battle that could be lost. This time his parades and reviews were held not in distant San Luis Potosi, but here in our greatest city, where we, the citizens of our *cuidad capital,* could see and admire them, the thousands of them, all in their beautiful and colorful uniforms with gleaming weapons, under the brilliant banners of their regiments; we heard their bands and drums, the clatter of thousands of hooves of the cavalry on the old stone streets, the rattle of the heavy cannons with their steel-rimmed wheels over the cobbles. Always we were seeing those soldiers and horses and guns going out to form their defenses on the heights guarding the roads. In our foundries, more cannons had been forged to replace those lost at Cerro Gordo. And now we had so many superb artillerists, many of them trained to a new level of alacrity by our adopted Irish patriot!

And close around him, devoted to him, and to Mexico, were his batteries of Irish and German cannoneers, the big, sunburned men we called *Los Colorados,* the Red Ones, or sometimes the *San Patricios,* or *Los Gringos Irlandeses,* so many names for them because we so loved to speak of them. They were proud and fierce under their banner of green silk. We knew of many of them who had become betrothed to lovely women of our city, and meant to marry them after the war was won. Many of the Irishmen were great athletes, lifters and wrestlers, runners and boxers, whose contests our people loved to watch. Some danced mightily. Some were champions in drinking, some were glorious singers. Their time in Mexico City, waiting for the Americans to come, was not long, but they seemed like a small *circo,* a visiting circus, not to be forgotten. And, as they were our protectors, everything we saw them do well gave us heart. *Sí,* even the drinking, for some said, if they can drink like that and not fall, they will not fall in battle! *¡Viva Los Colorados!*

Here is an irony that you might not have thought of: As a military scholar, I know that it was General Scott himself who had modernized the artillery of the United States Army. Before the war, he had studied war in Europe, and brought their new gunnery tactics over. He developed the flying batteries.

And then it was exactly such tactics that *Señor* Riley and his Irish gunners adopted, and turned with such deadliness upon General Scott's own army when he invaded Mexico! Irony is bittersweet, is it not?

PADRAIC QUINN'S DIARY

Puebla, Mexico ✳ *May 27, 1847*

WE MOVED TO this big city from Xalapa with almost no resistance. Col. Harney's cavalry met guerrillas and skirmished but they'd usually just fire a volley and then tear off in retreat.

I enjoy a wicked satisfaction lately at Col. Harney's expense. His dragoons now joke that their tyrant is himself being browbeaten, that he is like a meek husband. In short, my mother has got the upper hand. The son of a bitch has met his match. A bully can't dominate someone who has no fear, and she has no fear.

I'm glad that I warned her of his reputation. That put her on her guard, and cleared any illusion she might have had. Then, whenever it was that he went a mite too far, she must have brought him down real hard. She might have done it with that sharp tongue. She might, too, have had to inflict some bit of corporal pain, to get his full attention.

But I'll fear for her until they've quit each other.

I keep my distance from him. She excuses me. She pampers me, keeps me well fed and clean and mended. I still do a few errands, to keep pence in my wallet, but not having to scramble and scratch for my upkeep like I did before she came, I have more time to practice my drawings, both pencil and ink. And I also learned Mr. Morse's telegraph code, from the card Lt. Wallace gave me. Sure and it's useless as yet, for there's no wire telegraph in this Army, to my knowledge, nor anyone I know who can understand the code. Still, it isn't a waste of time. Someday if I become a correspondent of war, it's a skill that might serve me well.

Until then, I enjoy thinking in words made of dots and dashes. And if I wanted to put something in this diary that no one should understand, I could write it like this:

```
....    .-   . ..   -.  .   .. ..

....    .-   ...      -.  . .

-...    .-   -    -    ...
```

General Scott's Army received reinforcements bringing us up to near 14,000, which he thinks is sufficient to push farther toward the Capital. The scouts and spies found this city of Puebla all but undefended, only residents here, none of Gen. Santa Anna's Army. An astonishment to us all. Here we wait and build up. The troops are encamped in various plazas and commons within the city. A beautiful old city. The Cathedral so elegant inside it's hard to believe God didn't build it Himself, for how could mere people have done it? The habitants of the city treat us neutral. All polite, and Gen. Scott keeps the troops from being too obnoxious. He went with a number of officers to visit the Cathedral, to give the Pueblans an assurance that the United States doesn't scorn the Catholic Church. From my experience I would say that is false, but it was a wise thing to do.

Col. Harney usually out, his cavalry ranging the countryside for signs of a Mexican Army. Now and then they skirmish with guerrillas, but no more than that. He believes Gen. Santa Anna is either out of power, or fixing to make a stand at their capital. Only about a hundred miles from here to the capital! Some officers are uneasy. Lieutenant Grant worries that we're so far from Vera Cruz and our line of supply and communication could be cut clear off by as little as a regiment of Mexican cavalry, if they wanted to do that. Some who have fought Indians say this feels like being drawn into an ambush.

When the Army stops and sits any time, rumors get going. One going strong now is, President Polk wants to get a peace treaty with Gen. Santa Anna, before we get whipped. There's a civilian here who's supposed to be an emissary of some sort, came up from Vera Cruz awhile ago. Rumor is that Gen. Scott won't talk to him because he smells a political rat. Gen. Scott is a Whig, and if he takes Mexico City, he could go back to the U.S. and win an election against President Polk's party, the Democrats. I don't understand that much, but that's what some of the officers are making of it. Gen. Taylor, too, maybe. Another Whig.

Col. Harney is feeling put upon, too. He hates Gen. Scott because he thinks Gen. Scott hates him. Well, who doesn't? Sure and the general could not condone his moral ways. The colonel mocks Gen. Scott as a prig and a Whig, so the politics may be a good bit of that, too.

Not sure I want to become an adult man. I doubt I can acquire enough prejudice and foolishness to be one. That is a joke, of course. I'll be a man all too soon.

```
 -    ..    -
-..   .-.   .   .-   --
.-   --.   .-   ..   -.
 -    .-   ...   -
-.   ..   --.   ....   -
```

CHAPTER XX

PADRAIC QUINN'S DIARY

Valley of Mexico ✳ *August 11, 1847*

S OME DAYS I can scarcely believe what I see.
Crossed over the mountain road today in a cold wind and
looked down off to the west. Greatest landscape I ever saw in my life, a
valley, must be fifty miles wide, mountains beyond with snow still on
in the middle of summer!

Valley is more than I can describe—ranches, towns, lakes, marsh-
lands, woods, forts, and castles. Roads so distant they look like threads.
Far over toward the mountains is a pale and hazy spread of buildings
and walls and spires, and they say that is Mexico City.

We have got right into the heart of their country!

Our Army spending most of this day crossing over the height. Soldiers panting for breath and shivering at once. Then they look out over
the valley and sure they look like they see a miracle. I'm for guessing it's
joy and fear they're feeling. They're conquerors, just like old Cortez
when he stood up here looking down over all that. But they also see the
size and expanse of what they've got to conquer. Myself I pray the
rumor is true that a truce can be made by the diplomats, but I'm sure
not counting on it. I wager Gen. Santa Anna has got cannons on every
height, aimed down every road to that city. Judging by what I've seen
and heard so far in this war every third or fourth one of these soldiers
will get to feel canister or grape or musketball before this is over. I do

reckon Mister John Riley stands a-waiting for us with his guns and gunners. I hear Col. Harney cussing and damning the Irish "traitors" every day. Says just getting to hang them by their necks will make the whole war worth while. Makes me sick to listen.

I can sure imagine John Riley's own sentiments as well. If there's no truce and Gen. Scott attacks the city, it's not likely the deserters will escape again. Sure and he must expect to win or die before much longer. I remember his feelings about the West Pointers, and I would not want to be an officer in his sights. They're plain targets for certain, with their dark blue coats so distinct from the soldiers' pale blue.

But likewise Mister Riley's a choice target, flaunting that big green Irish banner as he does. It's a wonder he's still alive.

Colonel Harney's horse patrols rode ahead down into the valley already yesterday. Now Harney has another thing to grumble about: Gen. Scott put that Engineer Captain Lee in charge of scouting the roads, with authority over one of Harney's majors. The colonel resents that, never mind that Capt. Lee's scouting is credited largely for the victories at both Vera Cruz and Cerro Gordo. I suspect Harney just hates to see anybody but himself get any glory. I opined that to my mother today, and she didn't argue it with me. She seems to be glad to have him gone awhile, even though his troops are gone and we have to drive the wagons ourselves on such awful steep roads. It didn't take long for her to get the measure of him and put herself where she belongs, where she's using him instead of him using her. God only knows where we'll all end up when this war is over and done. But this I believe, that if we mortals are ever to understand what God has in mind for us to understand of the Mystery, the lesson is being taught to us in this glorious old country. I really don't know quite how to say it. But for all the discomforts of desert heat and mountain cold, for all the fevers and the shits, for all the blood and lice and sand and ice, for all the brave men and the scoundrels, I do thank God that He put me here in this place and this time, to make me what He means me to be.

And I never thought I'd say this, but I'm so glad my Ma came down here after me. I could give her a kiss on the cheek. Old Bill Harney's dragoons lately salute her when we drive by!

That provides me a chuckle now and again. But it's a worry, too. If

My Mother Moira Colleen Quinn drawn at Puebla, Mexico 1847

Red Devil Harney understands she's making him a laughingstock, he's more likely to harm her when the time comes. I keep badgering her to get shed of him. But she's a bad mix: fearless and stubborn.

AGUSTIN JUVERO
SPEAKING TO THE JOURNALIST
ON THE PILGRIMAGE ROAD

The castle of Chapultepec, *Señor*, is a *mirador*. From its height one can see almost everything. And so it was that we the cadets of the *Colegio Militar* for a moment in August of 1847 were like little gods on Olympus, looking down as the smoke and thunder of man's strife moved about over the panorama below.

We watched eastward, at first. Your army had come down from those mountains and into the Valley of Mexico. *El Commandante* emplaced many batteries on the hill called El Peñón between the Lakes Texcoco and Xochimilco, aimed to cover the National Road on its approaches to the city. As you know, an army must move on causeway roads to come to the city, because the ground is too soft and wet for moving wagons and cannons. The great road passes close between the hill and the lakeshore, and it always has been a natural place for strong defense. An army approaching that way is in the open for miles as it comes through the gauntlet. It is one of the great defenses we studied in the academy. *El Commandante* Santa Anna expected your army would come straight up that road toward the city and be destroyed in a gauntlet of shot and shell.

But he had learned a lesson at Cerro Gordo, when your army went around his flank instead of into his frontal defense. Knowing such a tactic might be used again, the general put artillerists in emplacements along the other roads. And around the city he deployed reserve units that could be rushed to any roadstead where your regiments might appear. His plan was not to defend from within the walls of the city, but rather to keep you miles away from it. The city is itself a great fortress, in the event that you could get to its walls. But he intended to keep you from getting that close. There are many natural defenses all around Mexico City, and he was prepared to man each one as it was needed. He set cannons at bridges and crossroads. And we dared hope your long supply route would fail.

Our studies in the *Colegio Militar* became very much changed as your army approached. We studied less the old theorems and histories of distant wars. The officers of the faculty now concerned themselves, and us, with the history and geography of our great city itself. All the academy had become concerned with the imminent conflict. Our studies became immediate and exciting. We were patriots before, but we became *fanáticos*. We had imaginative *escenarios* of fighting to the death to defend Chapultepec Castle from troops of the *herejes*. Some of the faculty mocked us for that notion. They said there was no reason for the *Yanquis* to make an assault on this archaic stronghold; that it would be a waste of lives for no strategic purpose, since the Citadel could not block an invasion of Mexico City.

And so you can imagine, *Señor,* how our lives as students changed. We no longer thought as we had before. The offices on the Citadel were always swarming with officers coming and going. We would gaze over the parapets toward any distant road and see soldiers marching and wagons and cannons rolling, hear bands and cheers. And we were always listening for the first cannonades.

But when it began, it did not begin east of Mexico City at El Peñón.

Instead, it began in the south. Your generals had moved down between the Lakes Xochimilco and Chalco—we on the Citadel had been able to see them marching south across the causeway—which meant they were to take the road to San Agustin. That town and I are named for the same saint. From San Agustin, their route could be nothing other than straight north up the great road through Churubusco, then across the Churubusco River bridge and north four more miles to Mexico City's southern limit.

¡Diga! It was an approach even easier to defend than the National Road, because of the bridgehead, and the old monastery, which was a strong fortress for artillery, covering that road. The other road coming up to Mexico City from the south was through Padierna and San Angel, a less likely route, but *el Commandante* put artillery and soldiers at Padierna as well. It was a brilliant defense! Both those roads met under the guns of the monastery, and therefore General Santa Anna emplaced his best cannoneers there: the *San Patricios!*

You know the history of the battles down there of course, *Señor.* Therefore I don't need to describe all the maneuvers. You already know how your remarkable engineer captain Lee went scouting and found a way to sneak your army through the wilderness of the lava field known as the Pedregal, which was believed by all to be utterly impassable, and thus brought one of your divisions up behind the Padierna defense. You know of that, yes? And so I shall only tell you of how it was perceived by us.

I could tell you all the history of that defense, for I have studied that war in all these years since. Because there is little more I was able to do, after your soldiers did this to me.

I do remember that there was a long and heavy downpour of rain the night before the battles erupted, and that we took satisfaction in the misery of your army out in it without shelter. Not that we were pitiless, but we know that miserable soldiers have poor morale, and soldiers with poor morale are less able.

I remember that the first sound of battle was so faint that we had to shush each other and cup our ears to be certain were really hearing it. Musket fire from five or six miles distant in that kind of damp air is a dull noise, like water beginning to boil in a tin pot. That morning we were sweeping the paving stones near the gate on the south wall of the

Citadel, and we stopped our push brooms and ran over to the parapet to listen. Officers were rushing to the wall, listening and peering southward.

The musketry rose and ebbed for perhaps an hour. We guessed that it was down near Padierna, as it would prove to be.

That noise diminished and ceased. We were still standing, listening, when a sound like faraway thunder began to throb, and it was presumed to be the cannons of General Valencia down at Padierna. Or those of Major Riley at Churubusco. Or perhaps both at once, we thought at the time, but soon enough we determined that it was General Valencia, who had espied your division making its road through the great lava field, the Pedregal, and begun bombarding you in that wasteland. I have read interviews in which some of your veterans recalled that they thought they must have died before the shooting began, because they appeared to be in the *infierno* already! If you have never seen that place, *Señor,* I recommend that you should, because it was probably the key to your victory over our army. Although other battles were yet to be fought in your push to the city, we were stunned when you marched out of that desolate wasteland and cut General Valencia off from the rest of the defenders. If my appraisal is correct, and that surprise was the mainspring of your momentum, then it must be postulated that the success of your invasion was assured by one mere captain of engineers, that Robert Lee. For it was he who circumvented our defenses three times: at Vera Cruz, at Cerro Gordo, and here.

And now, *Señor,* as your United States disunite themselves and begin a war between your North and South, I understand by my reading that he, that same genius, is to be a general on the side of the seceding states. That must be disconcerting. Of course, you have brilliant generals on your side, too. So many learned their lessons of war in the invasion of Mexico, in that time of which we speak. The brave soldiers of Mexico taught them well.

And when I think of that General Lee, and of those other bold generals taking up arms against your government on behalf of the slave states, I smile to think of the irony: that so many officers who condemned Don Juan Riley as an archvillain, for deserting a country of which he was not even a citizen, have now deserted that nation to take up arms against it! Is it not the same crime? If he was a traitor, are not

General Lee, and those many southern officers now serving the Confederacy, traitors also? They are men who held high rank in the United States Army, who were privileged citizens of their native country, and they have turned against it. *Señor* Riley was neither privileged, American-born, high ranking, nor even a citizen. Why, then, was he a "traitor," and they not?

Yes, I know, *Señor Periodista,* these are embarrassing questions. Your country is not good at answering embarrassing questions. For example, the matter of slavery. Or the decimation of the original peoples of your country, the Indian tribes. You condemn the Catholic *conquistadors* for their aggression in the New World, their murder and enslavement of our early civilizations, their plundering of our riches. But what did those *conquistadors* do that your own leaders are not now doing? You admonish the Spaniards for imposing their Catholic religion upon the natives here in Mexico and in South America. Yet your government aids Christian missionaries in erasing the heathen beliefs of all the tribes of *Norteamérica.*

True, Catholic *conquistadors* destroyed and stole all the religious temples and treasures of the Aztecan king. Then, likewise, your Protestant soldiers marched through Mexico, and pilfered holy artifacts of our cathedrals, to take home as souvenirs of your conquest. And there was of course that most enormous theft, of our land itself. The Spaniards seized the lands of South and Central America in the name of the Cross. And now your United States government has seized all of North America, including much of Mexico, in the name of Manifest Destiny. Does it surprise you, *Señor,* that I have given so much thought to your country? Why so?

Your country cannot be ignored. It is too great, too aggressive, and too near. When you took Texas, and then invaded Mexico, you focused Mexico's attention upon your country. Mexicans will always watch your country, for we must. We will watch you out of fear, and we will watch you for opportunities.

I sense, *Señor,* that you do not disagree entirely with my perceptions. But we were speaking of General Scott's invasion of Mexico City. We were speaking of the twentieth day of August in 1847. The day that began with the rout of General Valencia from Padierna, and your army's hard, costly drive through Churubusco. I was telling you of the vast field of battle that we the cadets could see from our height on the Citadel of Chapultepec. There is a high watchtower on the Citadel, and it was a vantage point for certain officers. From there they must have been able to see even more than we could see from the parapets, they with their telescopes. But we saw the assault mostly as smoke in the distance, and now and then as vague movements of great bodies of troops, so far that a single man was not distinguishable. We saw the smoke clouds coming northward toward us, and the musket fire grew more distinct. When the breeze was favorable, we could hear the yelling of thousands of men fighting—a strange and terrible drone. A deaf man can remember sounds, still hear them distinctly within.

Near the middle of the morning, with the sunlight growing intense, there was a lull in the shooting, but even more yelling than before, and then we perceived that the movement of those thousands was veering eastward, along the road from San Angel to Churubusco. General Santa Anna's main defensive force was along that road, we knew, but we did not know yet, of course, how it was reeling from the morning's surprise.

When one looks southeastward from Chapultepec, one sees a remarkable view. Four miles away beyond marshes and pastures and cornfields there stands the town of Churubusco. It is named for the Aztec god of war. In those ancient days there stood a great temple. Upon that height a hundred years ago the Franciscans built the great monastery of Santa Maria de los Angeles, with its magnificent domes and massive walls. It is the dominant feature of that place. Just north of the monastery is the Rio Churubusco, which has been straightened by excavation. Just beyond the town, the river drains into Lake Xochimilco, as you know, *Señor*. And so when we looked southeastward from Chapultepec, what we saw was the great monastery with the vast lake stretching eight miles beyond it as a background.

In the middle of the day, the thunder of battles resumed, and it was in the fields around Churubusco. So much musketry there was that it sounded as steady and insistent as rain on a roof. The two parts of your army had come up the two roads, past the Pedregal lava field, to converge on Churubusco from the west and the south, and there our *commandante* was rallying our defenders. Soon there was so much smoke that the monastery was almost invisible to us. And never, *Señor,* have I heard such a thunder of artillery! For the monastery was the dominant place for the cannons of our defense, there at the junction of the roads and the bridge, and our army's finest gunners had been placed there. By that you know what I mean, *Señor: Sí,* the *San Patricios*!

Of course, I did not know at that time that our Major Riley and his cannoneers were emplaced there. I should have presumed it from the fury of the barrage. It was *asombroso*! Even with telescopes we could not have seen his green banner, at that distance, not through the enormous curtains of battle smoke.

It was an example of General Santa Anna's brilliance, that the best gunners were at that place. Your General Twiggs was attacking eastward toward the bridge on that road, and your General Worth was marching northward toward the bridge on the San Antonio road, and Major Riley's batteries on the monastery covered both roads. Our infantry was all around Churubusco, with regiments in reserve on the other side of the bridge, guarding the road to Mexico City. I am certain that you already know of the carnage the Irishmen's batteries were inflicting upon your army. It has been told in the reports and the histories. Your advances slowed to a halt and your soldiers dropped down behind the bodies of their fallen comrades in the fields of corn and marsh grass, but there was no protection from the deluge of canister and grapeshot, or from the volleys of musket fire from our infantry. It is almost a certainty that your soldiers, brave and able as they were, would have been stopped there and finally defeated there, four miles south of our great capital city, except for one thing. And once again, as you surely know, I speak of that man Lee, the captain of engineers.

We must compare our historical knowledge of that day's battles, *Señor,* you and I, at our leisure sometime, and with maps. The legend says—and it is a legend in your army, I believe—that *Capitán* Lee did not go up the road with General Twiggs's main force. Rather, he went scouting again, and led General Shields over a small bridge more than a mile west of the battle. And when Shields's force turned east, it was on the *north* side of the river, coming upon the flank of our infantry above the bridge. I believe, as do the other scholars, that our defense would have held, except for that sally, catching us by surprise yet again.

Of course, one cannot say with perfect certainty that one single thing, or one person, changed the course of such a mighty tide of fury as a battle is. But I venture to say it of that day.

And so, *amigo,* I suggest that your army, though manned with heroic soldiers, won the battles for Mexico through the intelligence of one *sobrehumano,* Robert E. Lee, a mere captain at that time. And his own *commandante* General Scott was to give him just such praise for his crucial sorties. I would drink a toast to a soldier like Lee.

I would also like to make a toast to one whom I call the other *sobrehumano* on the battlefield that day. I do not mean General Santa Anna. Nor do I mean the countless other brave soldiers and officers who so valiantly and in vain defended the heart of their homeland that day.

No, *Señor,* I wish to raise my glass in tribute to one who fought with ultimate skill, fury, and courage to defend a country that was not his native land, but became his land by virtue of his pure and noble conscience. I mean of course that gallant Irishman whom you call an archtraitor: Don Juan Riley! Please drink to him with me, then, even as I tell of that tragic battle, which was his last. *Gracias, Señor. ¡Viva Riley!*

Would you now like to hear the true account of his last day of combat? I know it all very well. I told you in the beginning that you came to the right man to learn the truth of this story. I can tell it to you as no other man now alive can tell it to you. I swear that to be true. The *Yanquis* who made their reports on it did, of course, bend the truth to their own advantage. As you know, I myself was not a witness to his last fight because I was four miles away, among my fellow cadets at Chapultepec. But the story I shall now relate to you is as if seen through the very eyes of Don Juan Riley. Here is how it came about that I have seen it through his eyes. Let us tarry here for another little refreshment. You may want to sharpen your pencil while I pour. The disbelief in your face amuses me, *Señor.* But you will believe, soon enough.

And you deserve to rest your poor knees, *Señor.* You are not so accustomed to crawling on stone and gravel as are we *penitentes* of Mexico. I have here a balm made from one of our desert plants, by a recipe my mother knew. Massage this into your knees, and we will sit here in this pretty spot and drink to our heroes, your Lee and my Riley.

I don't mind pausing again like this. Our Lady of Guadalupe will still be there when we eventually arrive. She has eternal patience. Have I not told you that the great lesson a *Yanqui* learns from Mexico is that patience is the greatest strength of all?

Probably I have told you this before:

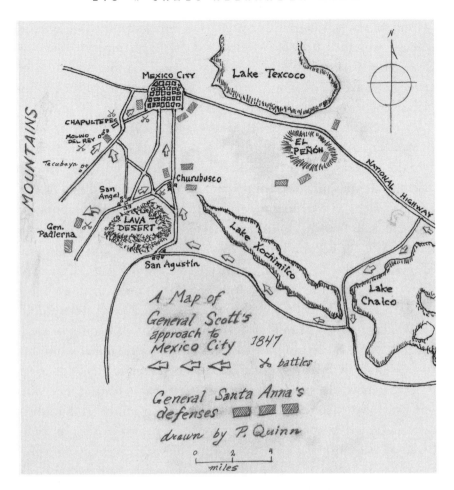

A Map of General Scott's approach to Mexico City 1847

✳ battles

General Santa Anna's defenses

drawn by P. Quinn

Major Riley and his cannoneers knew when they deserted from your army that they had crossed *un borde irrevocable y mortal*. They expected no pardon. If they did not win in the battles, they would die in them, or die on the gallows. They had vowed not to surrender. In all the defeats of the war, on the Río Bravo, at Monterrey, at Buena Vista, and at Cerro Gordo, they had carried away their wounded to save them, and escaped to rebuild their batteries for the next battle.

At the monastery at Churubusco, there was no escape for the foreigners. The Franciscans had built a place of peace and holiness upon the old temple of the Aztec war god, but on that August day it again became a temple of war. General Manuel Rincón with twelve hundred infantrymen and Major Riley's battery had been ordered to defend the bridge, and the two divisions of Americans were closing on both sides of the monastery. The cannoneers watched them come on, until they could distinguish the dark blue frock coats of the officers from the light blue uniforms of the soldiers. Major Riley raised his green banner above the parapet, went from gun to gun reminding his Irishmen and Germans of the tortures and humiliations they had suffered under those martinets, and told them to commence killing. They set to it with vengeance, fury, and terrible accuracy. So many *Yanqui* officers fell at once that it was understood that this was not just defense, it was revenge.

Only once in my life, *Señor*, did I ever feel the murderous passion that those gunners must have felt. I shall tell you of that, in its time. It is so different from every other state of being that, even though it is the greatest and worst passion in any man's life, it is hardly possible to remember it, once it is over. Soldiers have to bring themselves to it by the force of their own minds and hearts, or they cannot overcome the natural fear of pain and death. But I am digressing from the tragedy at Churubusco.

It went on for two or three hours in the terrible heat and deafening din. General Twiggs's soldiers surely were as infuriated by Major Riley's green flag as his were by the West Pointers' dark blue coats. The *Yanquis,* though they could not stand up and march through that hail of metal, they could crawl through the corn and grass, shooting while lying on their bellies. The road and the fields were strewn with the bloody dead and dying. American artillery eventually came up, and returned the *San Patricios'* cannon fire. One by one, the Irishmen and Germans were hit, and their bodies stacked up within the emplacements. The cannons were sizzling with heat, the smoke was blinding and choking the gunners, and they were so blackened by gunpowder that they looked like coal miners. These are the sights and sufferings as they were experienced by the great Irishman himself, that *sobrehumano.* As I have said already, I was myself seeing it from another high place, four miles distant, and to me it was just a rumbling cloud of smoke, both thrilling and squeezing my heart. But I can tell you how it was for him because I relived his last battle myself. You doubt. But you will see.

Eventually, three of Major Riley's cannons were hit by your artillery, more than half of his soldiers were dead or wounded, and his shot and powder were nearly exhausted. His soldiers took up their muskets and fired out through embrasures. *Yanqui* snipers brought more of them down with their long rifles. The Mexican infantry under General Rincón had expended almost all of their powder and ball, and General Worth's division was gaining control of the bridgehead. When the fire from the monastery waned, the infantry of General Twiggs rallied and charged the parapets with scaling ladders. The *San Patricios* fought them *mano a mano.* As Major Riley was loading his one last cannon with grapeshot to sweep the *Yanqui* soldiers off the wall, a muzzle flash or something ignited the remaining gunpowder and burned several of his men. They fell among the bodies in the courtyard, and their comrades smothered their flaming clothes. His last load of grapeshot tore into the attackers, and then he pulled down his green banner and ordered his remaining men in through the doors to the inner rooms of the monastery. The remnants of General Rincón's infantrymen were already inside. The *Yanqui* infantry charged across the courtyard with bayonets, battered the doors open, and poured into the building.

For the next half an hour or so, *Señor,* it was inside that religious place the most violent chaos—shooting, bayoneting, stabbing, clubbing, fists and boots, down the corridors, from room to room, up the staircases . . . the kind of murderous brawling at which Irishmen and young *Yanqui* men excel. *Señor* Riley said it was like—it was an Irish term—like Donnybrook Fair. But desperate and full of true hatred. The American soldiers knew that these were the *San Patricios,* and the *San Patricios* knew their fate.

They had carried the green banner into the building, and it inflamed the *Yanquis.* Some Mexican soldiers were mixed into the fight, and many of them were killed in those rooms. At least twice, some of the Mexicans wanted to surrender, and waved white cloths. But the Irishmen snatched the cloths from them and threw them on the floor, and kept fighting. An Irish gunnery officer with his saber was fighting several soldiers who had him cornered with their bayonets. An Irish soldier seized an American lieutenant and in their struggle bit his nose off. Some of the Mexicans and a few *San Patricios* found a corridor and fled down to emerge near the river, where some escaped and others were caught. But the remainder of the deserters, about eighty of them still alive, were forced into a *calle sin salida*—a, a cul-de-sac—and cornered. Senor Riley refused to surrender to anyone less than a general. But of course no general was that close to the fight. So he fought on, choking in smoke, wet with blood. The corridor roared with curses and screams and pistol shots and the clanging of metal. Then all went dark for him.

There is a reason why I can relate so vividly what his defeat was like, *Señor*. It is that I, a few days hence, would endure the very same. The very same.

But I must not get ahead of the story you came so far to hear. I was speaking of Don Juan Riley's last battle.

Señor, I am so little a believer in miracles; I have seen too many instances in which miracles were needed but not provided.

It was, though, much like a miracle that Major Riley and his *San Patricios* were not all killed at once on the bayonets of your soldiers who captured them in the monastery at Churubusco on that terrible day. Almost every one of your soldiers wanted to do so. They were mad for vengeance and seething with contempt, for hundreds of their comrades-in-arms had been torn to pieces that very afternoon by the shot and shell of those cannoneers—those who once had served right alongside them in the American ranks. It was only by the orders of their captain, screaming over and over above the din, that the *San Patricio* prisoners were spared an immediate massacre.

Most of them had been wounded, some severely. They were of course given no medical care. Already there were too many hundreds of *Yanqui* soldiers lying in the fields around the monastery bleeding to death and screaming in pain. An army never has enough surgeons or healers to handle even a few casualties. General Scott's army had sustained more than a thousand. Numbers of course are meaningless in the measure of suffering. But the injuries of those few dozen *San Patricios* were their just desserts, for the carnage they had caused, and who was to pity them? The more they suffered, the more justice, the *Yanquis* felt. They were dragged out into the battery where they had fought before. There they lay amid the corpses, the blood, and the excrement. Yes, *Señor Reportero,* if you have been on battlegrounds, where bayonets and cannons have been used, you know about the excrement stirred in with the glorious gore.

In the evening those who could stand were made to get up and form ranks, to be shown to your *commandante.* General Winfield Scott was led in by a flock of junior officers. In the torchlight, he glinted and shone with as much gold braid and ornamentation as if the day had been a parade instead of a *matadero.* You know the war-like visage of that old *Martes.* Here was your god of war, come to the old temple of our god of war. The *San Patricios* were such a prize, they had to be displayed to him. Those proud captors had thought General Scott would give them permission to execute the deserters then and there. The old general looked at them but said nothing to the prisoners. The prisoners said nothing. They all had agreed to say nothing; they were not replying to insults. They had agreed not to be provoked. They defied in silence.

General Scott spoke instead to his officers. He told them they must prevent the guards from attacking the prisoners. More officers, he said, to keep order here. Your god of war was *un abogado* by profession. And that perhaps was the miracle! For even in victory, your General Scott meant that there should be law if there could be law. *Señor* Riley heard the general tell other officers that the fate of these traitors must be determined by courts-martial. For, he said, civilizations were all watching, and none was in approval of the invasion. There must be no massacre of the prisoners.

I believe, *Señor,* they would have been killed that night, but for his visit with them. The prisoners were held without water or food or care for their wounds, for the rest of the night, among the corpses of their comrades. In the night there came a long, cold rain that at least washed off the soot of battle and faded their bloodstains. A few bled to death. One with both legs shot off was somehow kept alive by the care of the others. The thought of that one returns to me often even after all these years and moves me to *empatía,* because . . . well, *Señor,* as you see. The worst sufferers were those who had been burned by the exploding powder. Many of the *San Patricios* would have died of thirst that night, if the gift of that rain had not come, for them to collect and drink. Though some died of it from the chill. The *Yanqui* soldiers set to guard them resented such duty, and some prodded them with bayonets to add to their suffering. One soldier was heard to say to the prisoners, "Why don't you try to escape, you filthy micks, then I would have an excuse to put this bayonet through your foul guts!" But the guard officers had their orders not to permit that to happen. *Está milagro!*

At that time, of course, I was in the cadet barracks at Chapultepec four miles away, knowing only that Churubusco had fallen, and understanding that the last good defense south of Mexico City had fallen. Our anguish, in the academy, cannot be described.

I did not yet know that General Scott's losses on that day had so stunned him that, for the moment, he was afraid to go on and attack Mexico City. It was by good fortune that an emissary of your government, one *Señor* Trist, was with General Scott's army. He had been in correspondence with English diplomats in Mexico City. An overture for a truce was brought down the road from Mexico City and presented to General Scott. Thus the negotiations for an interval of peace began, and two badly wounded armies, within five miles of one another, drew back to lick their wounds.

We, the boy cadets up on the Citadel at Chapultepec, we knew only that the thunder and smoke of war had stopped, that a quietness had descended with the dusk upon the Valley of Mexico. We were left to wonder.

What was to be the fate of our country?

CHAPTER XXI

PADRAIC QUINN'S DIARY

San Angel, Mexico ✳ *Sept. 5, 1847*

... . .

‒ . . .. ‒... .

JOHN RILEY TODAY was sentenced to be hanged!
A court-martial here sentenced him and 28 other deserters to
hang four days from now. It will be done here. Gen. Twiggs is to oversee it. Probably because his troops captured them. And suffered the
most casualties by the deserters' cannons.

That is a total of 70 of the San Patricios sentenced. The others were
court-martialed up at Tacubaya and are to be hanged on Sept. 13th,
with Col. Harney in charge of that execution.

... . will probably enjoy it. He told Ma he wishes he
could hang Riley himself. She said, "Maybe killing 43 will be so tiring
you'll be glad not to have another, Bill, dear. Mustn't wear yourself out."
I can hope she will find him so repulsive as an executioner of Irishmen,
she'll leave him. She's not forgot where she was born.

I don't know why Gen. Scott put Harney in charge of the hangings.
They hate each other. Different politics, for one thing. Col. Harney
says the general isn't letting him hang Mister Riley for that very reason—that he hates him.

Gen. Scott took advantage of the truce to get these courts-martial over with. The trials need a lot of officers, and this army is kind of short on officers because Mister Riley's gunners killed so many of them.

I wish I could have heard the trials. Only certain people could be there. I was outside where they tried him. He and the other prisoners were being guarded in a big dirty storehouse kind of place. Very heavy guard. I got to see him from a distance as they took him over to the court. They hadn't let him wash or shave. Still had on his Mexican officer uniform, I guess so he couldn't deny he had been fighting for Mexico. He was in chains, powder-smudged, had blood caked all over, his coat tattered, and a dirty, bloody bandage on the left side of his head. None of that kept him from walking proud, though. He was in there for hours. I saw them take him out and back to the prison building. He didn't see me. Too many guards around him. There were some newspaper correspondents who came out and it was by following them and listening that I heard he had been found guilty. The correspondents were so satisfied that you would have thought he had killed somebody in their own family. They were making mockery of his testimony, from what I could hear, some yarn about the Mexicans capturing him when he went to Mass near Matamoros, and forced him to join them. I don't know whether he actually told the court that, as his excuse, or if the correspondents were making it up. I saw Capt. Merrill and Capt. Chapman of his old 5th Regt. who had been in there as character witnesses but couldn't get near them, either, for the correspondents and other officers all around.

So then I just walked away from all that. Feeling so low I just can hardly bear it.

My poor Ma & Col. Harney are up at Tacubaya, closer to Mexico City. That city sure is beautiful, with churches pointing up everywhere. There are Catholic churches in all these little towns, like this one here. I would go in and get my feelings in order, but all the churches are where the officers idle and smoke and have their officer meetings. Gen. Scott has the Bishop's mansion.

This truce is a strange thing, just about more than I can understand. Here these Armies have been killing each other and now they're not. In fact, our Quartermaster company is allowed to take wagons into the city and buy grain and meat for our Army! In our part of the bargain, we don't bother the farmers and ranchers going into the city with their stuff. Gen. Scott seems a shrewd man.

Neither Army is permitted to make defensive or offensive improvements while the diplomats work out peace terms. But some of the Quartermaster troops say they saw the Mexicans hauling cannon batteries through the streets. Of course we're cheating, too.

A rumor is that one of the terms Gen. Santa Anna keeps demanding is that the San Patricios must be released back to him. Sure and that isn't going to be done! It must work like that; you keep back at least one thing you know you can't agree on, so that when you're set to break down the truce, you bring that up to do it with. From all I've read and heard of politics, this truce thing is a kind of politics. I expect the war to start up again as soon as everybody's rested and all the amputations and buryings caught up with, and all the cheating on the truce terms.

There are officers who are mad at Gen. Scott for stopping for this truce just when we had broken the Mexicans and chased them into their capital. I hear officers say the whole war could have been finished off the day after Churubusco if Gen. Scott hadn't stopped to negotiate. Then there are others who say if we had gone in after them, we'd all be dead by now.

I don't reckon those officers know what the President wants done, any better than I know. He did send down that ambassador. Gen. Scott knows things they don't know. From what I've heard of him, he's not one to think out loud. Some speculate he wants to go home and be put up for Presidency. But others say he wouldn't have the job if you served it to him on a gold tray.

The surgery is close by here and you can hear screaming most any time day or night. There's a pile of arms and legs outside always black with flies. Yesterday a scrawny Mexican hound ran past me with a bloody hand in its mouth. Almost made me vomit. Made me wonder whether some cur ran off with mine after Buena Vista. Col. Harney was haranguing me the other evening when he was drunk as usual. Said I need only one hand for my one knack, pulling my inchworm. He really thought that was wit, and laughed till he nearly choked to death.

.−−   ..   ..

....   .−   −..

San Angel, Mexico ✳ *September 8, 1847*

END OF TRUCE!

Bloody war started back up. Another 700 or 800 American casualties—all to capture a cannon foundry that existed only in a rumor! Another victory more costly than it was worth. And it didn't get us any closer to winning Mexico City. Lt. Grant said another victory like these last two and we won't have anybody left to occupy Mexico City.

It got the Army's spirits down low. Something else got them down about as bad. It's another rumor, yet to be seen—that John Riley won't hang tomorrow after all! Can't say I'm depressed by that news. Here is the rumor:

Gen. Scott being a lawyer by profession reviewed all the deserters' court-martial verdicts. Law is, the penalty for desertion is death only if war has been declared. Mister Riley crossed the Rio Grande to Matamoros a whole month before Congress declared war! Most of the Army furious that the Arch Traitor won't hang, while those who followed him and served under him will.

A few others escape the noose for the same reason. Some for various other reasons perceived by Gen. Scott.

He is visited all day by Mexican officials and priests petitioning for him to pardon the deserters. And many women from round & about have come crowding to his headquarters to plead mercy for the San Patricios. The newspaper correspondents are angry about everything that is being done to save the "Irish Catholic turncoats." I can innocently edge up next to any correspondent and any officer he is interviewing, and in half an hour I know the kind of impression the reporter's story will aim to make upon his readers in America. They are gloating over the example of faithless, immoral, violent Irish Catholics that can be made by these trials. This confirms what their newspapers have been saying. Now I can see that Gen. Scott will pay dearly in public sentiment at home, for sparing John Riley the noose. Such scrupulous lawyering will assure that the Nativists in the United States will all be against him, even if he goes home the conqueror of Mexico.

Even that is in doubt, after the futile bloodletting which took place this morning at the imaginary cannon foundry.

That attack did seize control of a number of mills and ironworks within 500 yards of the old Castle of Chapultepec. The castle is deemed to be impregnable. It is said to be Gen. Santa Anna's summer home though I doubt he is there after today. The Mexican Military College is also within its walls, which I suppose is their West Point. I look at that castle up there, even from this distance, and pray that Gen. Scott is not fool enough to try to attack it! It is beyond cannon range from Mexico City and would not interfere with our invasion of the City. Can't see any object at all in attacking it.

I find myself in a bad state of mournfulness and dread. Half a bottle of the tequila liquor standing here by my candle. I suppose it will determine whether I am able to go over to the new gallows tomorrow and witness the executions. Still can't imagine they won't hang Mister Riley and reckon I won't believe anything I don't see with my own eyes. Probably I should take my sketchbook, maybe one of those famous correspondents would want a picture to send along with his story celebrating the justice inflicted upon these "Traitorous Papist Paddys and Malevolent Micks," as they so like to describe them in their dispatches. One drink only.

Yes, that decides it for me. I must be there. Of the events I have been given to witness in this short lifetime, what could be more important than the fate of the best goddamned Irish patriot I ever knew of?

Sure and what kind of Irishman would I be if I wasn't there for him at such a time!

San Angel, Mexico ✳ Sept. 10, 1847

FAITH AND IF I live a hundred years, may I never, ever see again such a show of vicious hatred as that I saw today. I would never have imagined that men who deem themselves civilized could take such delight in their cruelty.

It was indeed true that General Scott had adjudged under the Articles of War that John Riley, and six others who likewise deserted before the declaration of war, could not be executed like the others by hanging. But Gen. Twiggs and the officers and soldiers in charge of the punishments were determined to punish him to death anyway. They had said so, and sure they made it plain.

This is a personal diary, in which I put forth my beliefs and my feelings, such as those above. Of this occasion, an historic event witnessed by my own eyes, I'll try to write as a journalist. I've also made pencil sketches of the proceedings. The drawings, and a hand-copied script of the following account, is in the hands of a correspondent of the *New Orleans Daily Picayune:*

The sixteen deserters condemned to hang were marched to the town plaza of San Angel soon after sunrise, their hands tied, under guard of American soldiers with bayonets fixed. Another line, of six deserters, marched in separately. John Riley was one of these, who were to be flogged and branded instead of hanged.

The cobblestones of the square shone with sunlight flashing off puddles left by a nightlong deluge of rain. Hundreds of American soldiers in ranks faced into the plaza, where a long gallows of timbers had been erected, strung with sixteen nooses. Brig. Gen. David Twiggs, the executioner, sat his horse near the gallows, erect and still as a statue.

Hundreds of Mexican civilians, men and women, filled the margins of the plaza and the park, many of them crying, and displaying their rosaries. Some held crucifixes high overhead. This demonstration of Catholic religious pity appeared to annoy many of the soldiers, but discipline held them rigid. The soldiers' greater attention was upon the prisoners, and naked hatred was intense in their expressions.

John Riley and his six fellow prisoners were taken to a row of trees in front of the church. Their hands were untied, their filthy uniform coats and shirts were stripped off, several of the shirts bloodstained, and then the seven were tied up by their hands, facing the trees, their backs to the gallows. Their bodies were pale and thin in the harsh daylight, and many were marked with cuts and great expanses of bruising, testimony to the violence of their capture in the monastery at Churubusco. A sort of moaning arose in the crowd of Mexicans, at the sight of their condition. The prisoners had been chained hand and foot since their capture, unable to wash, shave, or groom themselves for three weeks, and they could hardly have looked worse for this public spectacle. That would seem to have been the Army's intent, for by contrast the Americans were clean and shaven, although their pale blue uniforms are still dingy and stained from the recent battles.

While the seven were being tied to the trees, the other sixteen were lifted onto the beds of eight mule-drawn wagons parked under the gallows, two prisoners in each wagon, thus elevated to stand where the nooses could be put around their necks. The hangman on each wagon held two cloth hoods. The prisoners were turned to face rearward, and their hoods left off in order that they would observe the flogging of the others. They were quite stolid, some even appearing haughty. To a well-placed observer, it seemed that they were looking into the faces of the Mexicans. Surely those would have been the only kindly faces they could see. A few times, these men with slipknots around their necks turned to look at one another, to say something. Their words could not be heard over the murmur of weeping and praying Mexicans, the rattle of trapdrums, and the orders being given by Gen. Twiggs in his barely comprehensible Georgian dialect, but whenever they did speak, they were answered by sneering and growling from the American soldiers, who seemed to want them in utter abjection.

I, the writer of this account, not being tall enough to see over the heads of civilians and soldiers, and having no license to pass within the guard lines, made myself a perch in the fork of an oak at the edge of the park, where I sat in the company of several Mexican boys who were already in the tree and who, seeing my handicap, moved up out of my way. Their attention then was to be divided between my one-handed penmanship and the events I was recording as they occurred, all too vividly, close below me.

At a little distance from the tree a wood fire was burning, attended by several soldiers, and its smoke rose up, a very fragrant wood. The smoke now and then veiled the scene, but mostly the view from the tree was very advantageous and clear.

My attention was mostly upon John Riley. He was not singled out by name from the others, as their leader. But most of the spectators and soldiers knew which was he. He passed his gaze everywhere he could see. In his eyes was a look betraying no fear, nor shame. Now and then he would pause at a face, and nod. It's likely that any Mexican who was thus acknowledged felt honored. Mister Riley even nodded to several soldiers, who flushed or grew pale but probably dared not respond. Many of the soldiers in the detail were indeed Irishmen, I realized, really looking at them for the first time. Probably this spectacle was intended to be partly a discouragement of any American soldiers who might be contemplating desertion. It was becoming apparent that Gen. Twiggs had planned all aspects of the event with that kind of theatrical attention to dramatic detail that prevails at military ceremonies.

When Gen. Twiggs called forth seven men with whips, they were not noncommissioned officers, as is the custom, but Mexicans! They were muledrivers. The cunning general executioner had chosen them, it was explained, to deny the deserters the distinction of being whipped by American soldiers. The Mexicans were not merely a lower form, but being muleteers they could apply the whips expertly and tirelessly. Their whips were the muledriver's usual long whip, not the Army's customary cat-o'-nine-tails. As the muleteers took their stance, and measured the length of their strokes by flicking the long whips over the prisoners' bare backs, Mister John Riley took a final look about, and this time his eyes came to the Mexican boys up in the tree above me, and he nodded at them with a slight smile on his lips! And then his gaze, I am certain, stopped upon me, and he gave another smile and a nod. All of us, this tree full of boys, looked at each other and nodded also, most gravely.

One of the soldiers tending the fire below said, loudly enough that I heard him over the dreadful murmur of the crowd, he said to another, "There's to be extra pesos for the Mex if Riley dies under his whip!" When I looked down at the soldiers, I noticed what the fire was for. The long handles of branding irons stuck out from the fire.

General Twiggs bellowed out, "There shall be fifty lashes. I begin my count—*one!*"

A translator called, "Ahora mismo . . . *uno!*"

Nothing ever done with a razor strop—even one with Tecumseh's skin on it!—could be as bad as what those whips do. You can get welts from a strop. But a cat-o'-nine or a bullwhip cuts up flesh. I've seen those bloody floggings enough in the Army that I can hear that sound in my memory. It's a hiss and a slap and a grunt all in one, and usually a scream. In this incident at San Angel there was another sound that I'll never forget. It was a woeful cry from the Mexican civilians in the crowd. It just squeezed my heart. I don't pretend to say Mexicans are strangers to cruelty. They have it in their bullfights. The discipline of soldiers in the Mexican Army is brutal, from what I've heard. And there's that Spanish thing about bleeding and pain that you see in their church paintings and statues. But as the count of Gen. Twiggs started, what I saw in the Mexicans' faces was pity. That I guess is what's in all their gory crucifixes, is pity, like the feeling that cruelty should not be, it just is. What I saw in the faces of most of the soldiers was not pity, but satisfaction. They hate the deserters, and what they were seeing was right and just.

At the moment of the first stroke I was watching Mister Riley in particular, as I reckon most of us were. He lurched, but made no sound. One woman up on the church steps gave the most heartrending scream I ever heard. Mister Riley shuddered, opened his eyes, and I do believe looked right at that woman, as if he knew her to be there. He sort of shook his head, then squinted his eyes shut to brace for the second lash. The woman was in black with a shawl and a veil, as most of the women there were, a tall woman, and her hands were over her mouth. I don't think it was my imagination that something passed between them.

I will say it's merciful that he was facing her so she couldn't see his back. Even before the shout of *dos,* his back was welling with blood from the first cut. The second lash made a red spray of that blood, and another deep cut. The whip itself was already red.

A flogging of fifty lashes just leaves such a bloody mess, it's a wonder it can ever heal. For the whipped, the pain gets worse with every stroke. I have heard soldiers say that. They say it's not like most kinds of pain, that go numb. The only way past it, they say, is when God takes mercy and makes you pass out. And they say you can't count on that.

So it went on and on. There were the numbers being shouted, and people sobbing, the whipped men screaming and groaning, the priests chanting prayers. It was sickening. The deserters on the wagons with nooses around their necks, some of them were growing pale, but others were getting red-faced with anger, watching their comrades suffer. Now and then one of them cursed Gen. Twiggs, which would result in a blow to his face by the hangman.

Mister Riley still didn't cry out. I guess some of us there were praying he wouldn't. But I'd guess that many of the American soldiers, on the contrary, really wanted to hear him scream. But he didn't. As it went on and on, the muleteers' sleeves and smocks turned red from all the spraying and splattering blood. Two or three of the men sagged on their ropes, having fainted. The general counted slowly, making the punishment draw out. And after about twenty-five lashes, he stopped calling out numbers. The muleteers paused, waiting for him to go on. He told the translator to tell them to keep on. He said he had forgotten the count and they should continue until he remembered. It was about nine or ten strokes later when he grinned and shouted, Twenty-five! and then went on from there. The Mexicans in the crowd realized what he had done and their murmurings rose up to an outcry. One could see that Mister Riley even in his agony understood what was happening and it was plain he tensed himself to keep bearing it. Only he & two others were still conscious when that old general reached the end of his count & the muleteers let down their bloody whips.

Then Gen. Twiggs called for the branding irons. Those seven soldiers near my tree pulled the irons out of the fire, so hot they were a-glowing yellow, and I could smell that hot iron smell like in a blacksmith's. The brands were a big letter D, meaning Deserter. The American Army keeps itself in such equipment. I knew several soldiers with the HD scar on their hip, the brand for Habitual Drunkard. If an officer is especially vicious, he'll apply that brand on a man's face instead of his hip. I've seen that done. But one seldom sees a branded Deserter because they're mostly gone out of the Army.

The soldiers hurried over to the trees, and as Gen. Twiggs announced the process, they each held a man by the hair of his head and shoved the left side of his face tight against the tree, and pressed the hot iron against his right cheek and burned that letter D in deep. It was awful. There were screams from the victims. Two that had passed out were brought awake by the burning, and there was more crying from the crowd of Mexicans, who held up their rosaries and crucifixes as if to protect themselves. Some people were getting sick on the ground, some just turning away and hurrying off. I watched the smoke curl off Mister Riley's face and his whole body writhed. But even then he didn't make a sound. I was crying, and I sure was not the only one. If I'd had a pistol I guess I would have just discharged it into Gen. Twiggs without a thought for the consequence. One of those correspondents was actually laughing, and if I'd had another pistol I'd have shot him, too. Maybe this shouldn't be in a journalism story, but I mean it.

When they took the brands off I could smell burnt hair and seared

Drawn by P. Quinn an eyewitness

John Riley flogged and branded at San Angel, Mexico September 10, 1847

flesh and was about to throw up myself. When the soldier let loose of Mister Riley's hair, he turned his head to look up where that tall woman was. I looked over there and some people were holding her up. Her head was lolling as if she had maybe fainted. There was just a full up-roar of voices, but still the ranks around the plaza hadn't moved. The Mexicans with the whips had left. The mules were nervous under the gallows, but their drivers held them quiet. Priests were chanting like crazy. Then Gen. Twiggs finally got down off his horse and started coming up the line inspecting the branded faces, being careful not to get blood on his fancy uniform from those poor sufferers. He stopped last at Mister Riley, probably real disappointed that he was still alive, and not only alive but awake. He looked at his cheek and said to the soldier, "Damn it, that letter is upside down! This man is sentenced to be branded with a D! That's not a D! Turn him around! Put a D on him, a good plain D if you have to burn his damned head off to get it right!"

So again that hot iron sizzled, on his left cheek this time, and I guess Mister Riley wasn't ready enough, for he gave a deep noise like a cough, and fainted. The whole crowd moaned.

The general nodded and smirked at the soldier with the branding iron. I know I saw that. Whatever the pain and turmoil in me at that time, that was not of my imagination.

Now that the men in nooses had been forced to watch their comrades be whipped and branded, it was time for those to watch the others hang. Cold water was dashed on them to bring them awake. They were cut away from the trees, shaking and groaning with pain, and their hands tied again. The blood on their shredded backs was drying, flies were swarming on them. The big letter D on every man's cheek was blistered and seeping. Soldiers with bayonets marched them in line, knocked them down close behind the wagons. Several priests with a large crucifix had followed from the church. They went from one wagon to the next, giving last rites. I had climbed out of my tree, almost too weak and shaky to walk, and went as close to the gallows as I could. As I arrived, hoods were being pulled over the doomed men's heads. A drumroll started up. One fine-looking prisoner, still wearing his dark blue shortcoat and insignia of a Mexican army captain, just before the hood was slipped over him, looked down and said:

"Farewell, gentlemen. Farewell, my friend John."

And Mister Riley, raising himself up on an elbow, replied,

"Godspeed, Cap'n Dalton. My good men all, Erin go Bragh . . . Viva Mexico!" His voice was a whispery croak, but I heard those words, and I pray those sixteen men on the wagons heard them, too, for the wagons were all driven forward out from under them then, leaving them dangling and twirling and strangling, and those were the last words they heard on this earth.

One would think the most barbaric mind could think of no further humiliation or torment beyond that morning's spectacle.

But when the dead men were cut down from the gallows, those who had asked to be buried in consecrated ground were loaded into a wagon and taken away by the clerics. The remaining nine were to be buried under the gallows. I could not believe my own hearing when Gen. Twiggs ordered, pointing at Mister Riley and his mutilated comrades, "Those six will be the gravediggers. Give them the shovels."

I cannot describe in words the agony of that burial detail. The sweat and the work broke open the drying wounds and they seeped blood until their trousers were crimson. Black flies were all over them. The branding had swelled their eyes shut and they were nearly blind. But they dug the nine graves without a word or a whimper. They laid their comrades in and covered them while the hundreds of American soldiers held back the Mexicans who were asking to finish the task. It took a long time. I stayed and made a drawing, from a little distance. I over-heard a correspondent and an officer, who were talking of the mishap of the inverted brand, which had made the second necessary. The offi-cer laughed. He said, "Mishap, you think so? Why, General Twiggs had this entertainment arranged down to the last jot! I wager that soldier had instruction to make that misprint!" The correspondent joked, "Ah! Like in Scripture, Turn the other cheek!"

It was what I had suspected myself, such a skeptic this Army has made of me already.

The day was nearly done, but the entertainment not quite over. Mis-ter Riley and his five gravediggers, by some unbelievable fortitude, some Irishness I suppose, still standing tall, were forced to kneel by the graves. There, soldiers who had been supplied with razors were ordered by the General to shave their heads, and be quick about it. While the regimental fifers tweetled that ugly little song The Rogue's March, the deserters' heads were shaved down to their bloody scalps. Their hair was thrown on the graves.

And thus, General Twiggs's day of righteous theater and morality play was over at last. He'd only smiled once: at the branding. The pa-rade back to the prison cell was to that same song, on fifes and drums. There was left a kind of feeling on that plaza that was so evil, that I reckon it will linger there like a demon ghost for a hundred years after every witness is dead and gone. I looked toward the church, and several stately figures in black were mounting the steps toward the church door. They were not priests. Several were women, and in the midst of them, I thought, was that tall woman whose eyes Mister Riley had met.

Their backs were to me, and I couldn't be sure at that distance, but I'm sure it was the one.

I have taken almost all night here, to write down as best I can, the worst day I have ever had.

Likewise I am sure it's the worst day my good friend John Riley ever had. Even if they devise a way to kill him yet, as they'd sure love to do, that wouldn't be as bad a day for him as this was.

Now to finish that bottle of agave liquor. Sure I'll not get to sleep without it. A toast. One boy with one hand to raise a toast, in solitude. Viva Riley!

And goddamn all of those who think they're his betters!

CHAPTER XXII

Agustin Juvero
Speaking to the Journalist
on the Pilgrimage Road

TODO ESTABA A REVUELTO. Everything we knew was in disorder.

Your country's invasion of my country had come so close now, *Señor Periodista,* that we could hear your army even when the attacks were over. I have already mentioned to you that all sounds would rise up on the warm air, to our height on the Citadel of Chapultepec. Where we had used to hear church bells, music, laughter, dogs barking, wheels and hooves on cobblestones, the cries of vendors and the noises of workmen's tools, now we could hear all the sounds of your army drifting up to us from less than half a mile away, in the buildings of the Molina del Rey. We could hear your shouts and commands, your *ambulancia* drivers, the cries of your wounded. We could hear gravedigging, and on the hot breeze that came up the slope of the Hill of Grasshoppers, we smelled the dead flesh of your soldiers and ours. We were high enough that we looked *down* upon the backs of drifting vultures, *¡allá abajo!* The truce had failed, as we had known it would, and your soldiers had thrown themselves against an army you thought you had already defeated.

You won again, eventually; somehow you always won. But your army was decimated further, and still you faced the fortress of Chapultepec and the walls of the Ciudad de Mexico itself. We were beginning to believe our *commandante,* that you could afford to come no farther.

Two days after your attack on the Molina del Rey, a letter came to me from my mother. I hardly recognized her handwriting, and I knew before I read a word that she was distressed greatly.

Her letter said that our friend the Irishman Juan Riley had been captured at Churubusco, with eighty of his battalion, a fact that I had already known, that he had been tried for desertion in a military court and sentenced with most of them to execution upon the gallows. Then, something like a miracle: *por una cuestión formal* under their military law, their commanding general had commuted that sentence, adjudging that those few who deserted before the war was declared could not be executed. That judgment so infuriated your army that there might have been a mutiny, in an army less disciplined. She wrote that the journalists of many countries spread the news quickly, and that foreign diplomats in Mexico City began pressing your general to pardon all the *San Patricios,* and return them to the Mexican people who loved and admired them. Much of the society of the towns in the district also went to the headquarters to plead the same. But the punishments had been set. The general himself wanted the severest punishment, to discourage more desertions. Thus the punishments were set, to be done, one at San Angel, the next at Mixcoac a few days later.

In the letter, she said that she went to San Angel with relatives and friends from the city. Among them *Tío* Rodrigo. He had advised her not to go. That she should not see such things, which are worse than the *corrida de toros.* But they went, early in the morning. She said she had to be there, and that *Señor* Riley should see that she was there. She said that he had become most dear, a greater affection even than before, while he was in Mexico City between the battles of the war. While I was in my studies at the academy. As if I had not known.

So she went to San Angel and she believes that he saw her, that he knew her even with the veil. And of course he would have seen Rodrigo, to know she was with her brother even if he could not see her face.

Thereby, she was glad that he knew she was there. But then she worried afterward that he might have been ashamed for her to see the humiliations done to him, the mutilation by the whip and the *hierro.* She worried that Don Juan Riley would think himself too ruined. That even if they let him live, she might not want to associate with a branded rogue. In the letter she told me that she would try to find ways to visit him in the military prison. She was desperate to have him know that she would not abandon him. She said there were associations of women in the neighborhoods and the towns who would go and take delicacies to the *San Patricios* in their prison, so that they would know how Mexico loved them for their brave and patriotic defense. And the women would also use all their influence to make the officials and the diplomats press General Scott to release them. They had already taken their punishment. They were not even citizens of the United States, and should be released into the care of a grateful people. Those were the causes of the women. Their husbands and relatives in the meantime would be working in their own ways to influence the American commander. And they all did those things. It became a cause for the people of those classes, those who were aware.

As you surely know, in Mexico there are those who have education and know what is going on. There is a larger class of those who farm and labor, who are not aware, those who do not understand why an army comes through. There have been so many armies going through Mexico, and often nothing changes, so those people just endure and keep working. Unless a war comes through that requires their sons to be taken away and put in uniforms, to carry muskets in the infantry, to come home maimed, or not come home at all. Unless that happens to them, or a battle takes place nearby and destroys their homes and fields, or their livestock are taken from them to feed an army, they have little to hope for or to fear from a war. The people who are aware, those who have something to lose, those who have been educated in Mexican history and the ways of the world, those are the ones who grow impassioned at the progress of events. They are the ones who support this leader or that one, who become army officers, who become patriotic. They find causes, and talk about them with passion, and take sides. A distinct part of that class is the hierarchy of the Catholic Church. They listen, and talk, and they can influence the great movements in this country, whether they are wars or revolutions or reforms. Conversely, they can resist change. That is often their role.

¡Perdón! Señor, I have gone on about how we Mexicans are, when I meant to be telling you what we did. My mother and the people who took up *Señor* Riley's cause were patriots, who love the country and the

beautiful and tragic myth of it. And they loved Don Juan Riley and his soldiers as they would have loved the knights of Europe, in those chivalric stories, who come to serve bravely and nobly only for ideals. They believed in Santa Anna sometimes, but they knew too well his ambitions to love him simply, as they loved these *San Patricios.*

They could not stop the invasion, but perhaps they could stop the punishment of those paladins.

I was left to imagine just what had been done to our friend *Señor* Riley, for my mother, being of such *hidalgo* breeding, would not specifically describe brutal acts. But within hours of her letter there came my uncle, up from the city in a rush of some military business, and he had me called from my duties, to speak to me in private.

I smile when I say "private" because the Citadel was teeming with soldiers and officers and clerics, consuls, village *alcaldes,* and officials of the city. Rodrigo was in a most earnest state, and we stood in a corridor trying to keep from being trampled by workmen carrying desks and crates up and down. He told me in brief manner the abominations done to our noble friend and the other *San Patricios,* there at San Angel, and of my mother's anguish. My heart was sick with grief and hatred and pity, of course. He told me of the other thirty *San Patricios,* whose trials had been conducted at Tacubaya, and who were yet to be executed by hanging, at the village of Mixcoac. Mixcoac lay so close below, to the southwest, that one could see people there, without a telescope.

Tío Rodrigo put his hands on my shoulders and looked into my eyes with such an intensity that I felt for a moment he was seeing me through my mother's eyes instead of his own, and he said, "*Querido sobrino,* it is believed that the *Yanquis* are preparing to attack this place. I can get leave to take you from here. Your mother wants the choice to be yours. Tell me now."

I chose to stay. My uncle left, sad but proud. For he, too, had been a soldier. Oh, I was so afraid, *Señor*! But also I was fiercely eager to take up my musket and shoot at the foreigners who were invading the heart of Mexico, those who had tormented and mocked a noble man, and hanged his comrades. Often already, we cadets had stood on the ramparts of that fortress and foreseen ourselves defending it. In our hearts we deemed ourselves soldiers, even though we were just boys. For months we had yearned to be within musket range of those *herejes.* We were always anticipating, and dreading. Because your army had attacked east from San Angel to Churubusco, instead of coming on northward toward Chapultepec, we presumed that your plan was to bypass this stronghold and proceed straight up the road to the south gates of Mexico City. *El General* Santa Anna thus concentrated our defenses there. We saw no cause for you to waste more American soldiers on this fortress, when Mexico City was what you wanted, and lay open before you.

But then your General Scott, true to his ways, chose to make a feint toward Mexico City, and catch Chapultepec off guard. Taking Chapultepec would be a symbolic victory for you.

But our *general* had grown wily. He sent General Bravo with a thousand soldiers to defend our Citadel. Soon our castle became crowded with our veterans. Almost all of our soldiers were veterans by that time. We the cadets were proud to be among them. We helped them as they set up defenses. We carried water and powder and shot to the ramparts. We helped them place the cannons. Alas, we no longer had the gunners of the *San Patricio* battalion. But there were many cannoneers whom *Señor* Riley had trained, and they were worthy of confidence.

Much of our defense we concentrated on the western ramparts. You know the Citadel, *Señor,* how it stands. It is too steep on the east to be assaulted there. Your infantry could only attack by way of the long slope from the west, up from the Molina del Rey that you had captured those few days before. We placed defenders all the way from the cypress woods on the Hill of Grasshoppers to the high battlements. We felt that the *Yanquis* would storm the Citadel only if they thought it was weakly defended, and so we made our defenses very much under cover, so that if they did attack the castle they would be met by more fire than they expected. Chapultepec is a sacred place to my people, *Señor,* once the seat of Montezuma the ancient king. We would make you pay for the sacrilege of attacking it. Between the castle and the city lay a well-defended road. *El General* could send reinforcements from either place to the other very quickly. We knew that your army had been too much reduced to assault both places at once. *En realidad,* we thought that you must be mad to assault either.

But, on the other hand, we knew you *Yanquis* were indeed mad.

Otherwise you would not have come to Mexico and charged to her center, as you had done. We felt that whatever the outcome of these battles, you were already in the belly of Mexico, and she would digest your little army. Mexico is very old, and has a patience your country does not understand. Anything or anyplace you might have taken by conquest, or were yet to take, eventually it would be ours again. How did we know that? Why, we had already swallowed and digested those *conquistadors* of old. And they had been even more mad and more ruthless than you!

And so we the cadets of the *Colegio Militar de Mexico,* with *patriotismo* surging in our veins, we found ourselves alongside those solid *paisanos* of our infantry for whom, though they were of a lower class, we felt a deep love at that time. I let some of their officers know that I was a friend of Major Riley, and I was awarded respect.

We listened to their talk and their singing, and waited to see what you madmen would do next.

I will never forget the date of September 12, the year 1847. It was my thirteenth birthday, but it seemed also to be the day I was destined to die.

Your first shell came shrieking up soon after daylight when we were marching from the chapel after our *maitines,* and burst on a wall above the parade ground. Bits of stone showered down on us just as the sound of the cannon shot reached our ears. Before we could do more than cringe, we heard several more rounds slam into the walls below, making the flagstones shake under our feet. Our soldiers were grabbing up their muskets and shouting. Stone dust rose and drifted in the morning sunlight. All was deafening.

That battering kind of fire, we knew, was meant to break down walls. It meant that a charge of infantry would be coming, when the walls were sufficiently reduced. Knowing the massiveness of our Citadel, we believed it would be futile for the Americans to try to breach the walls with cannonballs. We were excited and frightened of course. But we were ready to endure, and we hoped the *Yanquis* would soon cease their cannonade and come marching in the flesh so that we could begin shooting them. Cannon bombardment very quickly crushes one's courage. It is too massive, like a volcano, and one feels helpless. A human being grows smaller and smaller.

Then the howitzer and mortar shells began coming down from the sky. The first one exploded among the infantrymen. Particles of something sang past me too fast to see and cracked against a stone wall. I looked and saw dust and stone chips in the air and specks and blots of crimson. I heard soldiers screaming. We were ordered to run toward a door, and as we started to run, another shell exploded. If you have heard a mortar shell explode nearby, *Señor*—ah, you have, yes? Of course—remember the noise, that *trueno de arma*? Yes, as you say, like a clang and a boom at once in your ear, but also a jolt of concussion? There are more kinds of explosions in a war than kinds of thunder in the sky, no?

But I was saying, *Señor:* At the explosion of that second *bomba* the boy running just in front of me became instantly a fountain of blood and began falling sideways toward the wall. Then as I leaped to avoid stumbling over him, two other cadets ahead of me also staggered and fell. The wall was spattered with blood in many places. The door was not far ahead, and perhaps there would be safety inside it from the fragments of broken iron that those bombshells threw in every direction. But the cadets who had fallen were *compatriotas,* even two of them whom I had never liked very much. And so I stopped running and turned to stoop near the first who had fallen. He was still tumbling, and when he stopped he was lying on his side with his back against the wall, and blood was spurting from his throat in jets so high they hit my face. *¡Dios mio!*

Blood sprayed on me, at each of his heartbeats. I threw myself back away from him. Perhaps I screamed. Or perhaps the scream was that of another bombshell coming in. More explosions, more iron bits shrieking and hissing through the air and smacking the walls and whining off the flagstones. I remember a soldier's shako tumbling by. I remember a musket whirling through the air, to shatter against the stone and fall clattering. Many such things I can recall with supreme clarity, but what I did in those moments I recall only vaguely, as when one is waking and remembers only parts of a dream. I do remember looking out and seeing soldiers in smoke close by, some lying, some sitting, some falling, some still standing, and a terrible din of yelling and screaming. I remember one who had fallen dead within reach of me, and that, by the look of his face, he was little older than we the cadets were. He was brown and round-faced, *un indio*. So many thousands of his kind you killed in that war, *Señor*! They who did not even understand why you had come down to kill them! The older ones, who had been in the army since the preceding conflict, presumed that you must all be Texans!

Oh, *Señor,* the ignorance of soldiers about why they must die and kill—how pathetic that is! It always has been, and surely it always will be so. They are told something, then they are told that their honor lies in their willingness to die for that something, even if, in their ignorance, they had never thought of it before. The one true reason why they must die and kill is that some other army has been given a cause to go against them. The making of those causes is the constant work of ambitious men. It has been so since the pharaohs, Caesars, khans, and the *conquistadors,* to the European kings, to Napoleon, to your President Polk.

But on that birthday of mine that I was speaking of, we were not considering why to die, we were just doing it. Your cannonade went on much of the day, a bombardment too terrible to recount. At the end of the day, scores of the soldiers were dead. Others lay wounded in the long corridor that had become our hospital.

How can it be imagined? The blood everywhere, the weeping and groaning, the pile of amputated limbs, the priest giving rites . . . you have been in hospital after battle, *sí*? I need not describe it. I was one of about forty of our cadets still fit for duty. Most of the night I spent helping with hospital chores. Then when I should have lain down to rest I was instead put on the parapet as a sentry, looking down into the darkness and listening. Too much in my mind and spirit had been shocked and horrified, and so it required all my strength and discipline to hold myself together. At times during the night I must have slept standing; at times I nearly strangled in my effort not to weep or scream. Even my prayers were in chaos. By morning I had passed from boyhood to old age, without having ever been a man.

And then that morning came your army's assault on Chapultepec. If I am to tell you about that day, I must fortify myself. How much have we left in our bottle, *Señor Periodista*?

PADRAIC QUINN'S DIARY

Mixcoac, Mexico * *Sept. 12, 1847*

TODAY THE SHELLING of the grand castle on Chapultepec began. Gen. Scott thinks we can take that place! Or is this a feint?

Lieut. Mick Maloney saw me, and called me to him, with a big smile that showed he was really glad to see me, or that he was generally in high spirits, with another good fight looming. He recalled to me a conversation we had long ago, by the Rio Grande, concerning the disgrace being reflected upon Irishmen by the desertion of such as that John Riley of the 5th Infantry. Did I, pray, remember that? I confessed that I did, whereupon the brave lieutenant asked me, had I enjoyed as much as he had, the fair punishment lavished upon that scurvy rogue Riley? Lt. Mick Maloney had seen me up in my tree observing the entertainment, as he called it. He hoped that I as an Irishman had felt absolved of a bit of shame by that fine display of justice. "*Perfect* justice, though, would have hanged him! Had he stayed loyal," Lt. Maloney said, "he might be a lieutenant!"

I thought: In the Mexican army he rose to Major. But I carefully replied, "Did I enjoy the entertainment as much as you did, Sir? That would be hard for me to say, as I can only imagine how much you enjoyed it. May God keep you, Sir." Upon that, I saluted him with my only hand, and excused myself, for I had just purged one Irish hero out of my heart, one who'd gloat over another's suffering. And I who had so lately basked in any attention Mick Maloney gave me. I'll be content not ever to see him again.

I learn that Gen. Scott really is planning to storm the Castle! The bombardment today is preparing for infantry to go up, probably tomorrow morning. I look at that place and think the General has gone giddy from too many successes. If I ever saw a place not to attack, that's it. Our cannons on it until it's too dark to shoot, and just one chunk of wall breached at all. Some loads of ladders were hauled up the road at dusk, to be used for to scale the castle wall. Who are the unlucky fellows who get to go up those? Gen. Worth and Gen. Pillow massing on the west side of the castle, Gen. Quitman on the south. Saw Lt. Grant of the 4th Inf., in Gen. Worth's division, and he told me the plan of it. He was more talkative than usual, as if by talking, he'd not have to brood on what's to come. Asked if I still draw pictures. I told him I'm working on the one of John Riley's punishment. That seemed to get him down. He said maybe I should do just portraits and good military scenes, not such awful things. I said well it really happened, and he shrugged. He said I ought to portray Mr. Maloney in his officer uniform. I said I'd already drawn him as a Private, and would remember him as that. Then we talked about that loyalty matter & I told him my thought, that probably Mister Riley feels as secure in his honor as Mister Maloney does. Mister Grant said I should keep that kind of thought to myself or some of these soldiers might whip me for saying it because to their way of thinking Mister Maloney is as high as a body can get and Mister Riley is as low. Lt. Grant said he was himself pretty sorry for Mister Riley, but is glad that those San Patricios aren't up there on the castle with their cannons. Said he's had enough of facing their kind of gunnery for his lifetime. Then he said he won't be here to see the hangings of the rest of them tomorrow, as he will be going up against the castle. He said attacking the castle wouldn't be much worse than seeing men whipped and branded and hanged.

I told him that I was going to the hanging. That I didn't want to see those cruelties again, but it is an important occasion and I intend to make illustrations. That I was going to stay off the battlefield this time. I had promised my mother that.

I didn't tell Lieut. Grant this, but I have just about persuaded her to go with me to the hangings tomorrow. Told her it's something really important that will be in history someday. That it is all about native Irish and she's native Irish and so she should be there. Even more reason, the executioner is her own Col. Bill Harney.

I didn't say this to her, but I sure just damned well believe that when she sees that murderous son of a bitch torture and execute a few dozen unfortunate of her countrymen, and his enjoyment of it, she will sure shed herself of him. What I've told her about him so far hasn't been quite enough for her to give up what he provides. But I can see that whatever affection there ever was, if it ever was that, is about all gone. She looks at him with contempt half the time, and gets like a banshee whenever he's a real horse's ass, that being most of his waking hours. I want her away from him before he kills or maims her. Tomorrow ought to do it. With a headscarf and a veil she can just mix right in amongst the Mexican women and he'll not know she's there. The older he gets, the meaner. It could be that I'm saving my own mother's life. Good way to think of it.

At daybreak everything's supposed to start, the executions and the battle. What a day to expect. Dark out there tonight. Can feel some power in the air. It could be so many thousand people praying all at the same time.

Mixcoac, Mexico ✳ *Sept. 13, 1847*

THE INK HAS dried in this pen several times already as I sit here trying to find words to begin the narrative of this day. There is too much of everything. The great authors of all time, I bet, would have to scratch out a half dozen false starts before they'd find language enough to tell of a day like this.

This is just a boy's diary, not a classical tome of history. The correspondents I guess are writing what will get read about this day. That the American soldiers did even more than Gen. Scott could have expected them to do. That they didn't stop at Chapultepec Castle but charged on up the road and got into the gates of Mexico City! Or so the rumor is.

All I can do is write down what I saw, myself, from right here in Mixcoac. It was hell enough for me. And sure I reckon it was enough hell for my Ma. I doubt Col. Bill Harney will ever see a trace of her again, not if he's lucky. She will surely kill him if he ever comes into spitting distance of her! If I ever had any triumph in my life, this is it: I contrived to make her see the Red Devil as he is. *Viva me!*

The punishments and executions of the rest of Mister Riley's men was much like seeing Gen. Twiggs's show played again: the men on the gallows having to watch the others be whipped and branded, before being hanged themselves. But Col. William Harney is a fiend, where Gen. Twiggs was just a ruthless executioner. I think I said before that the military does its rituals like a dramatic theater. Col. Harney did the theater with a whole genuine battle for his backdrop. That's how my Ma said it. She's been to theaters. I haven't, but the way she explained it sure sounded true to what we saw.

Maybe it was Gen. Scott who planned to have the executions in a place where you could see the battle. The big Chapultepec Castle looms up not very far away from Mixcoac, I'd guess maybe a mile off. Col. Harney had the deserters standing in the wagons with the nooses on by the time there was enough light for the cannons to open up again. Col. Harney got the whipping and branding started, and I watched my Ma's face as much as I watched that. There were Mexican men and women around again, too, but not as many as there were at the San Angel punishments. I didn't see that one Mexican woman today.

Col. Harney yelled to the prisoners that they would stand there watching true American soldiers win a battle. However long that took. He said that when the American flag rose over the castle, the wagons would move and they'd swing. He said they'd be hung without hoods, so they could watch their moment arrive. Then it was that one Irishman with a noose around his neck called out the Colonel's name and in a merry voice said that if they didn't get hung before his dirty old flag was up over the castle, they would live long enough to eat the goose that ate the grass on the Colonel's own grave! Some of the others laughed at that, and red devil Harney got three shades redder, and I feared he would just order them hung right then. I doubt if anybody ever taunted him that boldly before, except maybe my Ma. Well, would a man with a noose around his neck be afraid to sass? What more has he to lose? Also some of Harney's own deserters stood under the nooses, and the Lord knows how his own men hated him. John Riley could have thanked Col. Harney for causing so many good Irishmen to cross over to Santa Anna!

By the middle of morning it was starting to look like they wouldn't hang, if it depended on that flag going up. The American cannons had stopped and the infantry was up there in the woods on the slope, not getting anywhere. The Mexican cannons were still booming, and there was no pause in the musketry, just a continuous rattle of it, banks of gunsmoke drifting. The sun was fierce. It was a wonder those deserters sweating up there on those wagons didn't just faint from the heat and hang themselves by falling. One was almost dead even before they put

the noose on him, the one whose legs had been blown off at Churubusco. He had been hauled out of the hospital and set up in the
wagon bed. Ma kept looking at him, I noticed, and she'd shake her
head, then look at Harney there on his horse.

Her darlin' Bill looked ever more sour and gloomy as the battle
thundered on, so close by it was almost deafening. There were the
priests standing off to the side with their crosses, there were the
whipped and branded fellows, eight of them, their backs all raw meat
covered with flies, waiting with gravedigger shovels. Just pretty much
like the other day at San Angel, but the Colonel had got stalled by his
own grand announcement about that flag way up there, and couldn't
continue his entertainment unless he went back on it.

Sure and it couldn't have been easy for those American soldiers
ranked around the square there, either, in their full uniforms in that
heat. Now and then one of them keeled over. But there they stood useless while their comrades were getting killed a mile or so away. I
thought now and then that if it kept on, these very men might have to
be called away from this spectacle to be reinforcements in that other
one.

Then shouts went up. We could see faintly through the shimmering
heat that our infantry had emerged beyond the woods, was moving in
a mass of light blue uniforms up the steep ground toward the Mexicans'
emplacements at the base of the castle wall. The Mexican defense at
that level was failing. Col. Harney was looking fierce again, and the
prisoners sure must have felt the sand shifting in their hourglass.

It was too far and smoky and shimmery to see much detail, but after
a time an officer with a spyglass cried that they were on the ladders.
Musketfire went on and on. I had my sketchbook out and tried to
sketch the scene broadly, though mostly was wiping sweat away with
my sleeve. I labored that way for a long time. My heart was tripping
and my hand a-shaking. I thought often of what it must be like to
climb a high ladder closer and closer toward an enemy who is loading
his musket to blow you off the top rung. I felt as close to the jeopardy
of those men so far over there—Lieuts. Grant & Maloney surely in the
midst of it—as to these Irishmen on the gallows, who were beyond
jeopardy, fully doomed.

I felt my Ma lay a hand on my shoulder, what an unusual tenderness! and looked up to see her looking at my spattered page. Maybe she thought it was tears dripping on it rather than sweat. Maybe it was that, too.

The sound of the battle was changing. More muffled. The officer with the glass called to Col. Harney, "They've gone in, Sir!" An excited murmur passed through the soldier ranks, and then to my astonishment I heard a clear voice sing out in the brogue,

"Colonel Harney, my dear old Colonel!"

I looked up to the gallows, where the priests had begun moving from wagon to wagon giving the rites, nobody impeding them, and one of the men all bound up and his noose on, was calling,

"Ye know me, Colonel! I served with ye in the old Second, in Flarida! Would ye grant a wee last favor to a doomed man?"

Why, I'd seen that man in the Swamp War! Though I'd not known him by name, well enough to remember it. My Ma and I watched in considerable wonder as Col. Harney rode over to his wagon and asked, "Eh, what is it?"

Said the man in that clear sweet voice, "Colonel, thanky! I knew y'r a kind-hearted man! Colonel, would ye kindly take me dudeen pipe from me pocket—me hands are tied, y'see—and light it for me with y'r flamin' red hair? Just that little favor, Colonel!"

There was a little laughing there among the doomed, but the rest of the soldiery gaped in silence. The Colonel actually got down from his saddle, and climbed up on the wagon bed to face the Irishman. Said nothing that we could hear. But he didn't draw the fellow's pipe. Instead he drew his saber, and with his fist in that big metal hilt he struck the poor fellow so hard on the mouth that sure it broke every tooth the man had. The Colonel sheathed the saber without a word and jumped down off the wagon and mounted his horse. My Ma's hand was on my shoulder as I said, but now her fingers digging in so hard they hurt, and she seemed about to say something to me when that poor wretch spat out blood and teeth, and called after him:

"Ah, Colonel! Y've ruined me for smokin'! How can I ever hold a pipe in this mouth as long as I live? Here's bad luck to ye, Colonel!"

And laughed, he did, like a man at a comedy!

My Ma was tugging me to stand up, and her eyes were fixed on her old beau so cold and hard he surely must have felt it like a knife.

It was that moment when someone yelled for all to look up, for there on the castle, the Mexican flag was out of sight, and the Stars and Stripes rose on the flagstaff, glimpsed through the smoke. A roaring cheer went up from the soldiers ranked around the gallows. And then, what I'll never forget, or quite understand.

Those thirty men with nooses round their necks, loud as a brass band, they gave up a single cheer of their own!

And upon that, Col. Harney faced the gallows, gave the order, the bullwhips cracked, the wagons rolled out from under, and those San Patricios were left to dance and twirl on air. My Ma yanked me to my feet. Said she,

"Come to the wagons, Paddy. We're vacating. And a blight on our tongues if we either one speak the name of that thug again!"

So at the end of this day of days we two are encamped in the Little America, where my Ma found two old friends among the laundresses. They are at this time getting hugely and merrily drunk together in celebration of their reunion, of her riddance of old Horny Harney, and, as they imagine, the end of this unholy war. In which they may be right, or wrong, as we'll know any day now, Gen. Scott having got a foothold inside the gates of Mexico City before the day was over. The ladies began drinking about the time I started this day's journal entry, and are still at it. They expect tomorrow to be a long and hard workday, blood being very hard to wash out. The noise of combat long since gone quiet at both Chapultepec and Mexico City, the only sound now is mostly drunken voices. Though when the breeze shifts I hear screams from the Surgery, and expect that will continue through the night.

Here beside my candle stands a new bottle of rum that I took from the Colonel's wagon. I've not uncorked it yet. I might not. In honor of John Riley who doesn't drink and wouldn't like seeing me do it, I just might not touch a drop of it.

Yes, in his honor, and all his brave Irish gunners! Their suffering wasn't altogether in vain. For I guess seeing it inflicted on them by her Red Devil himself, it may yet prove to have saved my Ma's life.

More honor to John Riley! Viva him and his wild geese soldiers, God rest their souls.

AGUSTIN JUVERO
SPEAKING TO THE JOURNALIST
ON THE PILGRIMAGE ROAD

Here is a fact about me that I can boast of: that I once refused to obey an order of *el General* Santa Anna! It is of course because of that disobedience that I am "abbreviated" in this manner. Is that an interesting story? I will tell it to you. It is next in the story I was telling you, about General Scott's attack on Chapultepec.

You see, when *el General* saw that your army was shelling the Citadel, he sent an order that we the cadets were to leave. He did not want boys harmed by your attack.

The senior cadet among us was eighteen years old, a fine and handsome youth, whose name was Agustín Melgar. *Sí,* the same given name as mine. Cadet Melgar plainly wanted to stay and defend. He did not think of himself as a boy anymore. Others of us declared that we also were ready to stay and defend. And so in the night we took a vote. We all chose to stay. Cadet Melgar took the message of our vote to General Bravo, who was the defender of Chapultepec, another old comrade of my uncle. Bravo. What could have been a more fitting name? For he was a courageous and splendid man. He told Cadet Melgar that *el General* was strict about the obedience to orders, particularly his own orders, but that if he would forgive disobedience to any order, it would be this brave kind of disobedience.

And so, we stayed. And as I said before, most of us spent the night awake, standing sentry and doing chores to prepare for the morning when you would attack.

In a time like that, all of one's soul is intensely in the moment. One expects to die, but cannot believe that one's death can really happen. Beneath the dread and the hurry, there remains a sweet center, a haven, made of the most cherished memories and sentiments. In my case, what was there, other than my country, but my mother? She was always in my center of being. I wanted her to have pride in me, but wanted to cause her no fear. By choosing to stay at the Citadel, in harm's way, I abandoned her to her fears. And in fact made them manifest.

How often that terrible night, I wished I could see her and explain why I had chosen my country.

I saw her in my memory, every few moments. But I also had another image of her. Many times that night, by fireglow or candlelight, I looked at this. Look at this:

In this gold locket is a *retrato miniatura* of my mother, God rest her stricken soul. This little painting is the one my father had always carried. After he was killed by Texans, his comrade-in-arms Francesco Moreno retrieved this locket and brought it back to her. Eventually she gave it to me to wear, as my father had. I shall carry it with me to my death.

It was painted before I was born. She was very young. As for her, she did not care for this as a likeness of herself. She said it was too pretty, that the painter had flattered her. As I remember her, I agree: It is perhaps too pretty. But it is not beautiful enough.

If you wish to make a drawing from this, of this woman at the heart of these stories, try to limn the beauty, not the prettiness.

She wrote to me every day in that tragic time. She tried to express to me the horror of the punishment of *Señor* Riley, which she had witnessed. She was afraid that his captors would go ahead and kill him, or simply let him die, when they took him back to their prison. That even though the punishment sentenced upon him had been fulfilled, they would not be satisfied until he was dead. Women of her society were visiting the *Yanqui* headquarters and clamoring for the release of the *San Patricios* who had already taken their punishment.

She was despairing. She did not believe she would ever see him come out alive. Her one remaining hope was for my safety. In one letter, she lamented so fervently that I could almost hear her voice coming from the paper: "I yearn to have you near me, my son. I have lost too much to those *bárbaros* from the north and I cannot bear to see another dear life thrown to them." She told me that *Tío* Rodrigo would come for me and that I should come away with him. As I have already told you, I didn't. I am forever in atonement for disappointing her. For letting this

Señora Doña Gloria Estrella
Calderon de Juvero.
copied from a locket miniature
by P. Quinn, 1861

happen to me. It further wrung out her fragile spirit, when I stayed at
Chapultepec for the defense.

For that reason among others, you find me on this pilgrimage. On
my knees, of course, *Señor*.

But again I have digressed from the history I was telling you. You
have been patient with my digressions. And with my unflattering opinions of your countrymen. You have been patient and respectful. You are
uncommon for a *Yanqui Gringo*.

I assume that you know, the defending force on the Citadel was a mere
thousand. It was not enough, against your numbers. Until the last
hours, *el Commandante* believed that your shelling of the castle was
only a feint, that General Scott would go up the road from Churubusco
to the south gate of Mexico City, and so his main force he kept there.
Another thousand Mexican soldiers on Chapultepec, no, even another
five hundred, and more gunpowder and ball, and you would have failed
to take Chapultepec. To storm such a fortress as that, one must have a
great superiority in numbers. And you did have. *¡Ay de mi! ¡Desgraci-
adamente!* If you had failed at Chapultepec, you could not have

stormed on into the western gates of the city, where the defense was less prepared. And you would not have gotten into the city, and you would have been defeated, your whole war a failure. You had to win then, or not at all. Your supply line was too long, your army dwindling by deaths and wounds, by sickness, and, of course, by more desertions. So very many of your soldiers saw the heart of Mexico and did not want to leave. If we had had enough men to hold Chapultepec, your General Scott might have struck about here and there for a little while, but then Mexico would have digested much of your army, and driven the rest out. Your Southwest would still be Mexico's north.

Your General Scott took such a perilous gamble, attacking Chapultepec. You *Yanquis* so believe in your invincibility that you forget how desperate you were. I read your histories of that war, and they make me roll my eyes! Your students will never learn the important lesson. The lesson is that you will not always win. You will be a great country only by learning that. I am sorry to say this, but that was General Santa Anna's weakness: He was too much like your country. He thought he could not fail. Even when he did so often fail, he always said others failed him. He was deluded. To use one of your *Yanqui* terms, he was his own Manifest Destiny. Ha ha! I love that phrase, *Señor,* it is one of your country's funniest things. A delusion. No, it is not funny, because it kills and hurts too many.

¡Que rollo! My preachings are a bore! Instead, on with the history.

Before your cannons resumed in the morning, we saw the campfire smoke that showed us where your regiments had moved in, down beyond the cypress grove. Also we saw the gallows, down in Mixcoac, the *San Patricios* already standing in the wagons, ready to die for defending Mexico. We saluted them, but of course they could not see that. We expected to see the hanging begin, but nobody moved. They were waiting for something. Then we saw smoke from your cannons, and the *bombas* came in upon us again. Our cannons below the walls waited in silence for your infantry to come through the grove. What a brilliant morning it was, and the *sierras* off to our right shone white. Your soldiers would be coming with the morning sun in their eyes. Good, for us. A lieutenant reminded his snipers on the parapets to aim low, at the enemy's waists, because they would be shooting downhill. We in the academy had never been taught that, and as I stood waiting, I had to work out in my mind, by the physics of trajectory, why that would be so, and then I was grateful for having heard it, and heartened. To learn just in time how not to overshoot seemed a good omen. I passed the lesson to the other cadets.

For a long time our infantry and cannon down below held your regiments back. So long that we began to doubt they would ever get close enough for us to shoot them. Your artillery stopped, but the grove was a din of shooting and yelling, a roar of fury. We could see very little because of the foliage, but our soldiers in the ditch below the walls we could see, and they were falling dead or crawling away wounded. When we looked toward Mixcoac, the *irlandeses* were still standing in the wagons under the gallows. That mystified us. We did not know that the watching was part of their punishment. We did not understand it was also for the correspondents, to make their accounts more dramatic in their newspapers. To show their readers that deserters, that Irish Catholic traitors, were being punished in very satisfying ways. We learned that later, by reading. We did not know it at the time.

By the late morning your brave soldiers had fought their way to the walls. They raised their long ladders as we shot down at them. But your infantry and snipers were fast and accurate, and any Mexican soldier who leaned over the wall to shoot down was almost certain to die. When your soldiers began to appear at the top of the wall and come over, oh, *Señor,* I cannot describe our fury and our terror! Our fallen *paisanos* lay in heaps on the parapet. We could not load our muskets fast enough to shoot the *Yanquis* as they mounted the wall. Most of our soldiers had expended all their cartridges and were fighting with their bayonets, and we could not shoot then because they were in the way. Our cadet leader Melgar cried out for us to fix on our bayonets, too. We were forced back, toward the doors. *Señor,* I have never seen anything so ugly as the snarling red faces of your soldiers, sooty with gunpowder, their eyes crazed, coming at us like devils climbing out of the *infierno*! In the years since, I have seen them often in nightmares. They are mad with hatred. Killing us is more important to them than staying alive. Nothing can resist such manic force. Irishmen fight that way, too. I suppose that is why the *San Patricios* were so outstanding in their service to Mexico. They glory in fighting. And the defense of Mexico was sacred to them! To die for Mexico was to die for Irish freedom!

A moment, please, to compose myself. Forgive my agitation. When one has such things inside his memory, and tries to speak of them, it is as if it is happening again. It is a reason why I was reluctant in the beginning to grant you this interview. Now I am glad you have been hearing the story. But telling it is not easy. Now, to go on:

The *Yanquis* drove us into the building. They forced us down the long, stinking corridor that was the hospital for those wounded by your artillery the day before. We fought stepping and falling on the bodies of our own casualties. Most of it was with bayonets, with muskets swung like clubs, even with fists. Beside me I saw one of your soldiers use his thumb to pluck out the eye of a cadet who was thirteen years old. Even in that crowded mêlée, some were still shooting muskets and pistols. We were suffocating in heat and smoke. Some of our veterans were still among us, trying to protect us, *los niños*. They kept falling, pierced by bayonets. Cadet Melgar also stayed in front of us, holding our flag. Then he died on a bayonet. One of the cadets grabbed it up, a young boy, even younger than I. We were being pushed back, bayoneted and shot. More than thirty cadets were overpowered and captured. Six were killed. The boy with the flag leaped, or was thrown, from an embrasure and died on the rocks far below. It is the legend that he jumped to keep the flag from the *Yanquis'* hands. I did not see what happened to him, because of the struggle in the smoke. Some of your soldiers shouted about Goliad and the Alamo, their vengeance cry against our *General* Santa Anna. Perhaps you understand now how I could say I knew the feeling of *Señor* Riley's last fight, in the monastery.

We were entrapped, but a few of our soldiers and cadets were fleeing by a narrow passageway. So many of your soldiers had come up the ladders by then that they were a swarm. One of your officers had raised your flag over the castle, though we inside did not know that. The officer's name was Pickett, the histories say. I remember that name because it is an appropriate soldier name. Is not a "picket" in your language a sentry?

One of your officers was close in front of me with a pistol. He aimed it at my face, but I hit the pistol with the tip of my bayonet and when it discharged it went low. My legs gave way and I fell onto a pile of carcasses. His pistol ball had shattered both of my shanks, though I did not know that yet. I remember that a thin and dirty *Yanqui* soldier rose over me and lunged at me with his bayonet. I tried to roll away but felt it go into my side, toward my back. It was not awfully painful, but it was as if I were pinned. Like a lepidopterist's moth. Something exploded near my face. And then all went formless and all the terrible noise went silent.

I returned from that merciful brief death a few days later into a purgatory of pain and fever. A ceaseless shriek was in my ears. I had nearly drowned from the blood and fluid in my lung. My legs both were gone. I was in a long building that had been made a hospital. It was full of wounded and dying soldiers, hundreds of them, and nuns moved among them with pans and white cloth. Doctors and priests were always somewhere in the room. Through the ringing in my ears I couldn't hear any voices.

I did not know yet that Mexico City, as well as Chapultepec, had fallen to your army. Elders of the *gobierno local* had persuaded General Santa Anna to take his army and leave the city while they made a truce with General Scott and the American diplomat, in order to prevent the destruction of the Ciudad de Mexico. I knew that I was ruined.

To keep my heart from breaking, I instead practiced to hate your nation. To avert self-pity, I burned like a *volcán* within. I lay in delirium and dreamed of assassinating your president in the United States—I who could not even get off my cot!—your president who had sent your army to invade my country.

Eventually my good uncle, Rodrigo, found me. Then my mother came. They had thought I was dead. The expression in her face when she saw how I was, that expression made me wish I was dead. But she came every day and stayed, showed me newspapers, talked to me by pencil notes. Soon she told me something that gave me enough resolve to stay alive. She told of visiting, with a society of humanitarians from the vicinity, the Acordada Prison, where our friend Don Juan Riley and his fellow prisoners were kept in chains. She said that those poor men were chained up, their lash marks and brands still raw. That they had around their necks iron collars with sharp prongs. That they were hardly fed. She believed that if not for the attention of the Mexican society and the newspapers, the American army would have had them die of neglect. She said that the women of the society took food delicacies and sweets in to them, and salves, and clean dressings. And that every sort of persuasion was being pressed upon the authorities to ease their suffering, to pardon them, to release them to their adopted country.

Señor, that gave me the heart I needed. If the Mexican people and the Irishmen, both beaten, could still love each other enough to keep helping each other, then not all the good was gone. Though Mexico had lost the war, and I had lost my legs, and I had become deaf as a result of battle explosions, we were still alive and we loved each other, my mother and I, and *nuestro querido patriota,* Don Juan Riley.

Upon those blessings, little by little, I was able to build a dream that he would sometime, if there was a peace treaty, be freed as a prisoner of war. Then perhaps we could be together and begin to heal ourselves of those afflictions your country had heaped upon us.

But had we forgotten that ancient joke, that if you make plans, you might expect to hear God's laughter?

¡Por fin!

We have arrived, *Señor* Quinn. Here is Our Lady of Guadalupe, the destination. I complete the pilgrimage again.

Look at those beautiful *penitentes,* the *viejas!* How beautiful one can become, with enough age and sorrow! What *pecados* can they imagine they have done, to inflict such punishment upon themselves? What power have such *pobres* ever had to do harm? Maybe when they were young, they had the power of youthful beauty, which can be used for mischief. But the beauty of age is only of itself, and has no power.

We, the *hidalgos,* had the power of privilege. When General Santa Anna yielded Mexico City to the *Yanquis* and marched the rest of his army out, he emptied the prisons, to let the rabble assault your invaders with stones and clubs. At that time, there could have been the people's uprising that would have reformed Mexico.

But we the privileged classes wanted to hold our privileges. And so we collaborated with the invaders, to keep everything. That is one thing for which I now do penance, hobbling on these stumps to this holy place.

Of course, I was not responsible myself for that. What had I to do with it, being a boy unconscious in a hospital with wounds? But I do penance for what my kind of people did or did not do then. And later, when I was well and had become an adult, I did the same as they, and in my own small measure kept the people down. Like most in my class, I do it still, even though I deplore it and do this penance for it. I atone not just for the past, but for what I do now and probably will continue to do. You look perplexed, *Señor.* You do not understand time in the way we in Mexico understand time.

Now, before we go in: You have been so kind to accompany me, to interview me under these tedious circumstances. I think it is time to tell you this:

When you joined me, and started with your questions, *Señor,* I disliked you for being *Yanqui.* My intent was to let your curiosity draw you into this ridiculous interview. That you should creep along with me day after day, listening to my stories, writing on that absurd contraption you have on your arm. I was making a mockery of the famed *Yanqui* journalist, and bringing an American down to a very humble level.

But I was also making a mockery of this *penitencia.* For one should not enjoy this, or divert oneself from it, as I have been doing with you. Thus this is an imperfect pilgrimage, not done in pure faith of spirit. I shall have to do another to atone for this one. In this way, I can keep doing these forever! Haha!

Since you have been with me, I have come to admire you in a way I did not expect to admire a *Yanqui.* Especially a *reportero.* I have watched your eyes when I talked of the *San Patricios.* Especially when I praised Don Juan Riley. I have seen that although you are a journalist of the American press, you do not scorn the memory of that Irishman. You admire him. Indeed, *Señor,* you love him, as I do.

And so, you see, I have caused you to do the *penitencia* with me. All you *Yanquis* have much to atone for, oh, yes.

I have more to do penance for than what I have told you. I have been thinking this morning, that if I confess to you the worst I have done to deserve this, then this *penitencia* will be less of a mockery than I have made it. It might compensate, to a certain extent, though only a priest could tell me whether that is so.

The worst that I have done was to my beloved mother. By getting myself maimed. But more in regard to her love of *Señor* Riley. Listen:

While I was mending, *Señor* Riley and the other *San Patricios* who were not executed were moved from the prison in Mexico City to one from which escape would be more difficult.

For, yes, one had escaped from Acordada Prison! He was one who left in women's clothes, in the midst of a group of Mexican women who had come to bring them gifts. Did you never read of that? He was a small man for an Irish soldier, and they dressed him in articles of their clothing, and walked out with him past the guards. My dear mother was among that group. Of course they could not have smuggled *Señor* Riley out that way. He was too big. Too much an object of the army's diligence. And they never unchained him, not even when visitors came.

After the escape, they removed the prisoners from Acordada Prison up to the castle of Chapultepec. The very place where I was shot and put to the bayonet, that corridor of death, that is where they put the *San Patricios* then. All the while, the people and the press of Mexico clamored for mercy and amnesty for those heroes. General Santa Anna kept trying to bargain for their freedom.

You remember, I have mentioned to you certain papers I have, that were written by *querido* Riley, while he was in prison, and after. That they were among my mother's possessions. When I mentioned them, you became very alert.

His letters are in this satchel. They are my treasure, a part of what I always carry with me when I make this *penitencia*. Remember, I showed you one he was writing to entice deserters.

I am ready to show you the rest of them. Come. You can sit on that bench. And as is so often the case, I am thirsty as well as pained and tired. I am so glad my *Yanqui* journalist loves a bottle, too.

A *Yanqui* journalist before you, a few years ago, offered to pay me a large sum for these letters. I said no. Nor would I sell them to you.

Someday I must ask a priest whether it is acceptable to sip refreshment from a *Yanqui* journalist's flask while on a *penitencia*! No, I won't ask, because I do not like the answer I expect him to make. It is very painful to crawl on these poor stumps, so many miles over the stones and cobbles. These wounds have hurt me through all the years since that war. The pain and misery are more bearable if I am *borracho*.

And if it is wrong to make this penance drunk, then I shall atone for it on my next penance. As I say, this can continue as long as I live! Ha! As it should! For who is ever free of guilt?

The page you hold there is the draft of a letter that *Señor* Riley wrote while he was still in prison. It was my mother who took paper and pencil to him in prison, and on later visits smuggled out his letters. That is a fragment that I believe he used in several letters of appeal.

In the month of April 1846, listening only to the advice of my conscience for the liberty of a people who had war brought upon them by the most unjust aggression, I separated myself from the North American forces. Since then I have served constantly for Mexico. I participated in the action at Matamoros, where I formed a company of 48 Irishmen. In Monterrey I did the same, with another company of Mexicans also. I fought at Buena Vista with 89 Irishmen; with them and more I was at Cerro Gordo; at Churubusco I presented myself with 142 Irishmen, all gathered by me. There I was injured and taken prisoner, and my treatment by the American government is well known, indeed, notorious, having received 59 whip lashes and two brand marks on my face, which will always remind me of what I have suffered for the Mexicans.

—John Riley,
A native of Galway, Ireland

Think of it, *Señor Periodista,* as you read the names of those battles! He was in every terrible battle except that of Chapultepec. And in each, he inflicted the greatest punishment on the invaders. Of course you sought ultimate revenge against a soldier who laid so many *Yanquis* low. But it was a grave injustice to torture and disgrace an honorable soldier, to brand him a traitor against your nation. He never was a citizen of your nation! He did desert your army in good conscience. A soldier is a mature man. He is responsible for his deeds. Even an obedient soldier should disobey an order that is repellent to his conscience and his faith! Officers, of course, would challenge that.

Once, *Señor* Riley told my *Tío* Rodrigo, and my mother, that if he had continued to serve the United States in its invasion of Catholic Mexico, he would have been bound to spend the rest of his life crawling on his knees in penitence on the stony road to Guadalupe. He said he owed no repentance to the United States, which was never his country.

Now, that scrap you hold there was a letter he was writing to the English ambassador. He asked for a loan of four hundred dollars to send for the support of his son in Ireland, due to the impoverished condition of that country. You see he promises to repay the ambassador at fifty dollars each month. The request was in vain, of course.

It touches me still, *Señor,* when I remember that plea. To think that he had a son in Ireland. That he had left his son there years before, to earn the pay of a soldier in the British army, because of the poverty of his native land! By the time he was serving Mexico, his son was old enough to write a letter to him begging help! God knows how that letter followed him to Mexico. Perhaps the newspapers in Ireland had written of the *San Patricios* in the war. Surely they had. I thought much of that boy in Ireland, as I lay recovering. I imagined him as I thought a son of *Señor* Riley might look after growing up too impoverished to get good food. I felt brotherly toward him, as if his father should have been my father also. I wanted to help him.

My dear mother, and my *Tío* Rodrigo, were little able to help because after the *Yanquis* took Mexico City, everyone here was without the usual resources. My uncle's military pension had vanished early in the war. Mexico's wealth had all been expended in the defense. When I was at last taken home from hospital, my mother was in shame and distress because there was no food to feed me, some days. She would go out to her society of women, and they would go everywhere to glean food, or *pesos* for food. They would bring only *harina de maíz* to their families. They would bake *tortilla francesa* for the *San Patricios* in the army prison. Some of the newspapers in the city tried to raise money for the aid of the *San Patricios* and their families, in gratitude for their heroic patriotism for Mexico. Some of them had married Mexican women, before the last battles. Others' families were still in Ireland. In both countries, of course, poverty was enormous. Poverty is of course the history of both countries, as it has been since the first plunderers arrived. In my country, the *conquistadors.* In Ireland, the British landlords, eh? And of course our church helped keep us poor.

For a while after the surrender of Mexico City, your soldiers were a scourge here. They drank and looted. A woman was not safe. My mother was followed and insulted often. One day a drunken sergeant stalked her to our very door. When she shut him out, he forced the door open. He found her standing at the foot of my bed with a pistol aimed at his eyes. In English I cried, "Look, Sergeant!" I threw aside the bedcover, showing him my scarred stumps, which were still very hideous. I told him, "My mother wants to avenge what you have done to me!" He heard her cock the hammer of the pistol, and he departed our house so recklessly that he lost his hat. We kept it as a *trofeo.*

After the peace treaty, when *Señor* Riley was released and came to live with us, he liked to put the hat on the floor upside down and pretend it was a spitoon. It was during those times, *Señor,* that he wrote many of the papers you see in that packet. He returned to the Mexican army, but it was a defeated army. Our General Santa Anna was in exile again, and the Supreme Court Justice Peña y Peña was the leader of Mexico. Most of the time *Señor* Riley was with us, he wrote petitions seeking pay for his surviving *San Patricios,* and the land grants Mexico had promised them.

Those were very sad months, *Señor.* Eventually your General Scott brought your soldiers under some discipline, but we were eager for you to go home. The price we paid for sending you home to your United States was the northern half of our nation: the rest of Texas, to California and everything between. Our nation was heartsick and angry. Many wanted to resume the war and drive you out. But we were weak.

It was sad in our house, also. When *Señor* Riley was released from the prison with his remaining *San Patricios,* their heads were shaved again with nicked, dull razors. The brands on their cheekbones were still red and ugly. Army musicians played "The Rogue's March" as they came out of the prison. My mother was there with a bundle for *Señor* Riley, and my uncle had brought a fine horse. The bundle was the dress coat of *Señor* Riley's uniform of a major of artillery, with all its embroidery and epaulets and his medals for valor, and his kepi hat with braid and shiny bill. In the presence of his former jailers he donned the coat over his grimy rags, put on the kepi, mounted the steed, and rode away looking splendid, his back braced. I had been brought to the place in a carriage in order that I might see him set free. I shall never forget that moment. His captors, who had never been able to kill him through battle, torture, or neglect, were chagrined, for he was free of them at last, and in that fine Mexican army coat!

But all became bittersweet when he came to live with us. His pride and shame were intermixed with my mother's pride and shame, and their great love for each other was no longer simple. He thought he had been made too ugly by the brands on his face. He grew his hair long to hide them, and he wanted us never to see the welts on his back. Though he had borne them without shame, he knew they were *estigmas.* She tried to give them the balm of her fingertips, with tears in her eyes she did that. But he misunderstood the tears, and soon he asked her not to touch the scars. That was the first time I knew his words to make her wince.

He also felt that he was bringing her shame by living in the house with her, unmarried. And he was embarrassed that I lay in one bed aware that they lay in the other. He could not comprehend how complete our love for him really was. Sometimes he would try very hard to be merry and gallant. He danced well and sang with a pleasing voice, Irish-language songs that we did not understand but found beautiful. He was touched when his soldiers would come to see him, but if they wanted to drink, as Irishmen do, he made them go away.

But he put more and more of his attention to the welfare of his old comrades, and less to my mother and me. He went among the influential people and called upon them to help him pay his Irish patriots. He wrote constantly when he was at the house. Our trophy hat of the *Yanqui* sergeant then sat on his desk as a pen and pencil receptacle.

My mother tried so hard to seem strong and cheerful, but she was failing within. She wanted him to resign from the army, but he said soldiering was the only profession he knew, and that he was very good at it. He wanted to be called back to active duty because his soldiers in their idleness were getting into drunken disorders, and he had to work all the harder to get them out. He could still be heard, because he and the other *San Patricios* were as yet beloved by the Mexican people.

At last in the summer of 1848 his orders came to rebuild and command the *San Patricios* battalion, and he was promoted to *coronel.* The new president of Mexico was General Herrera, who had been the acting president before the war, and he was was a strong admirer of the

Irishmen. Though the war with your country was over, a government still needed an army. Particularly so as its president was a general whose political enemy was also a general who had also been a president, General Paredes. My mother was grieved that her *querido* was leaving our house, but also I think relieved. He left these papers and his few belongings to assure us he was not abandoning us. When the army began paying him, he would marry her and support us.

¡Ay de mi! He was not out of our house a month before General Paredes attempted a coup, which was thwarted by President Herrera. Because a *San Patricio* officer was under suspicion, *Coronel* Riley was also suspect. He was arrested and put into a military prison at Santiago Tlatelolco. A rumor ran abroad that he was to be shot. We heard it from a woman who was betrothed to an Irish soldier. She ran to our house in the night, distraught, and told my mother. My mother, though pale and trembling, comforted the woman until she could leave. Then she came and sat on the side of my bed to hold my hand.

Surely you can imagine our distress! What to do? I urged her to go to *Tío* Rodrigo at once and tell him, in hopes that he could confirm the rumor, or disprove it, or intervene somehow. She promised me she would. Then she prayed with me and told me to use the chamberpot while she was there to help me up. I did. When I was back in bed she told me to go to sleep. She reached to the chest where we kept the pistol and she got it. I asked her why she was taking the pistol. She said to be protected when she went through the streets to *Tío* Rodrigo's. I was alarmed. I felt she was misleading me.

So then I suggested she should instead go next door and have the neighbor and his son take her in their carriage to *Tío* Rodrigo's house. She said it was a good suggestion. Then she kissed me and told me to try to sleep. I said, no, I could not sleep because of this, and I said I wanted to get up and ride with her to *Tío* Rodrigo's house. No, she told me, she must hurry. Then I said, If the neighbors take you, you can leave the pistol with me. No, she told me. Go to sleep, *niño*.

She shut the door, and I lay in darkness. I listened for her to go out, but did not hear her go. Faintly I heard her doing something near the desk. I heard paper rustling. I thought, I should get out of this bed and make my way to her, because she is not acting right. But I was inert with dread of being scolded. Also I was afraid that I would find her doing something that I wouldn't like. I began to fear that if I made the effort to go to the door and open it I would find she had written a farewell and would be sitting there with the pistol aimed at her own temple. I was terrified to find such a spectacle. Instead I lay praying that it was not happening. I prayed so diligently that I forgot about listening for a pistol shot, or the closing of a door. I said *avemarias* over and over and then I would think that I should be listening for a gunshot, and sometimes I was confused, whether it would be a gunshot executing *Señor* Riley or the gunshot of my mother executing herself. Then the *avemarias* again, with my heart aching, and I went to sleep trying to say *avemarias* and count them at the same time in my head without the rosary.

I was awakened by the iron rims of cart wheels on the street outside and it was becoming daylight, and outside the window a mockingbird was singing a funeral march. There was no sound in the house. I got down out of the bed and crawled on my two hands and a hip toward the door. At that time my stumps were not healed enough for me to crawl on them. In the very dim room I reached up to the door latch and when I opened the door she was lying on the floor beside the desk. The floor was sticky with blood. She was cold. Instead of shooting herself she had cut the veins in her wrist with *Señor* Riley's old razor, the one he had kept in the trophy soldier hat to sharpen pencils and quill pens. The pistol was on the desk lying on a sheet of paper. But upon it she had written no farewell.

Tío Rodrigo found us, when he came to tell us that the rumor was false. *Coronel* Riley had not been sentenced to die at all.

This flask of yours is almost empty, *Señor.* Before you go to find us something else to drink, I will tell you that of my many reasons for penitence, the first is that I lay in bed all that night a coward, her son, who could have, *por lo menos,* summoned a priest for *los últimos sacramentos.*

I suppose that is the end of my story. May I hope you believe it? You have been kind to bear with me, with my cruel and cynical way of making you obtain it. You have done penitence with me, coming along so slowly, swallowing my insults. You have done some sort of penance for your nation, for what it did to Mexico. Now I invite you to enter the cathedral of Our Lady of Guadalupe with me.

Before we make our tipsy way across the plaza, let me show you the piece of paper that I found under the pistol on the desk that night, as if the pistol had been a paperweight.

You see that the only marks she put upon it were these little specks of blood from her wrist.

But on the other side you see that this sheet of paper had been used before. On it is the handwriting of *Señor* Riley, in pencil. We did not have enough paper to waste it. If she had written her farewell, it would have been on a sheet of paper that he had already used to compose a statement. I believe my mother was reading it as she decided to cut herself.

Please turn it over and read it, *Señor.*

I have had the honour of fighting in all the battles that Mexico has had with the United States.

There is no more hospitable and friendly a people on the face of the earth, toward a foreigner, and a Catholic Irishman, than the Mexicans.

I grieve at the deaths of fifty of my best and bravest men who have been hung by the Americans for no other reason than fighting manfully against them. Especially my first Lieutenant Patrick Dalton, from the County of Mayo. His loss I most deeply regret.

Though in the service of Mexico, the banner under which we fought so bravely was that Glorious Emblem of native rights, the banner which should have floated over our native soil many years ago, it was St. Patrick, the Harp of Erin, the Shamrock upon a green field.

EPILOGUE

Spring 1861

TWO PILGRIMS, Agustin Juvero and Padraic Quinn, kneel on the cobbles outside the basilica of Our Lady of Guadalupe. They wait as old *penitentes* climb painfully over the threshold ahead of them.

The cripple squints at the red-haired reporter, and says:

"I regret that I cannot hear your voice or your words, *Señor* Quinn. Though you came to hear me, I am sorry that I cannot hear you. I would like to ask you a question. I believe I know the answer. You and I have met, perhaps, long ago. Do you believe that is true?"

Padraic Quinn nods, and prints on paper with his pencil:

In darkness by Rio Grande when you were delivering propaganda to the Irish soldiers and I was taking whiskey to them. In spring 1846.

"*¡Aunque parezca extraño! ¡Sí!* That is what I have come to believe, also! And so we meet again! I wondered that night whether that boy—you—could have been as frightened as I was."

I had been warned all Mexicans had sharp knives.

"Indeed I carried a sharp knife. But when I saw you, I forgot that I had it." He chuckles, shaking his head.

"The Laughing Penitente"

Agustin Juvero one of Los Niños Heroicos, hops onto a bench on the road to Our Lady of Guadalupe.

Drawn in pencil by P. Quinn

1861

At that time I, too, knew John Riley. Before he crossed to you.

Agustin reads the note. "We were not far into this interview before I sensed that you also knew him. I could see it in your eyes, as you heard me speak of him. *Sí.* It was plain."

"Wait," Quinn says, and writes.

I kept a diary, through the war. I wish you could see it.

"Aha!" Agustin laughs. "Yes. It would be perhaps the only history of that war that I have not read yet."

It led me to this occupation, of correspondent. Probably next I will go to the war beginning in the U.S.

Padraic pauses, then continues writing:

Though I shall regret leaving Mexico again.

"*Gracias,*" says Agustin. "Many who came here for the war chose to stay when it was over. And in the part of Mexico that you took from us, many live under your flag who are still Mexicans in their hearts. California and New Mexico, even Texas, are yours in name only, you should understand. The Mexican people will take all that back, *Señor.* Not suddenly or by force. In the long time. It is yours only for a while. We Mexicans have a patience that you *Yanquis* do not understand. Whatever the laws and the treaties say, all that is still Mexico.

"And now, *amigo,* we have come a long way together, with pain. Now let us go up and into this holy place, and offer candles to Our Lady. Your candle shall be my treat. You are my guest in Mexico. This is the only time I have made this *peregrinación* in the company of another, not alone. I am honored to have traveled it with an Irishman. *Sí.* And a friend of Don Juan Riley, *¡por otra parte!*"

Mexico City
July 14, 1861

To Alfred H. Guernsey
Editor of Harper's New Monthly Magazine

My Dear Sir,

I pray that this finds you prospering, in good health, and that you will remember our correspondence of several months ago, when I set out for this place. To refresh your memory: You expressed enthusiasm for articles I proposed to write and illustrate for your magazine, pertaining to interesting occurrences in the last war:

First, the poignant and tragic fate of the boy cadets in Mexico's National Military College, who fought in the terrible Battle for Chapultepec Castle in September of 1847.

Second, the role of American soldiers, Irish Catholic immigrants in particular, who deserted from our Army and took up arms for Mexico, those known as the Saint Patrick's Battalion. I trust you will recall, Sir, that I was personally acquainted with their principal officer, Major John Riley (also known as Reilly, O'Reilly, & the like in various accounts of that time). I came down here on your generous advance retainer, to do research on his fate and fortunes since that war.

That I have accomplished, my dear Sir, and I do believe that the story of those turncoats is even more interesting now than when we discussed it, considering that most of the ranking Secessionist officers in the present conflict have become turncoats in a like manner, and that those very officers were then among the most severe in condemning the Irish deserters. Hypocrisy, I hope you concur, is a most tempting target for a journal of integrity and truthfulness. Those senior officers who have gone over to make war against the Union were among the most able soldiers in the Mexican campaigns. Among them, I read, are now Lee, Bragg, Longstreet, Jackson, Beauregard, Magruder, Johnston, Pickett, and of course Jefferson Davis as the president of their Secessionist Confederacy.

The periodicals here in Mexico are replete with news of that secession. It is a matter of much interest to Mexicans for obvious reasons, including a certain satisfaction with America's distress, but, as well, they remember many of the officers. The Mexicans, that is the literate portion of them, are also wary of mischief that might spill across their border, with their powerful neighbor in such an upheaval.

Now, Sir, to the matter at hand, my two articles. I have drafts of both pieces, which I shall send within the fortnight, after I pen clean copies of the revisions. I am confident that you will deem both articles even more interesting than they were originally conceived, because of some unexpectedly good fortune I have had in my research.

In brief, I managed to find a young gentleman who was a cadet at Chapultepec, deafened and maimed in that battle, and I have interviewed him at great length, finding him not only full of information but also quite articulate, and something of a military historian as well, with an intriguing philosophical perspective on the invasion and its consequences.

Even more fortuitous, Sir, is that he, too, had an important personal acquaintance with the said Irish rogue Major Riley, during and after the war. You may well imagine my delight and astonishment. The same young fellow was a source, in fact, for most of my findings on Mr. Riley's fate after the war. Furthermore, he allowed me access to certain writings of Maj. Riley, papers and letters that were in the estate of the cadet's mother, God rest her pitiful soul. I have copied those out and incorporated portions into the article, for they reveal an unexpected intelligence and eloquence on Major Riley's part, *and, even better, express in his own words his motivations and tenets of life and service, much at odds with those imputed to him by presumptuous and unsympathetic correspondents at that time. The integrity of this man should be an astonishment to any readers who read of him only as an arch-traitor, vilified by the Army and by the correspondents who were here during the war and his court-martial. Those writers to a large extent adopted the opinions and parroted the words of the American officers whom they accompanied perhaps too intimately. (You'll remember, too, Sir, the rabid anti-Irish prejudice of most periodicals in those days, and the vitriol then being spewed upon Catholic immigrants of any nationality.)*

The gratitude still expressed by Mexico for the service of the San Patricios battalion is touching. I hope to convey that.

I hope also to convey the curious ambiguity these people feel toward Gen. Winfield Scott, he who conquered them, but also he who spared the life of their darling Irish hero. (I read, by the way, that it was Gen. Scott himself who failed to prevent his favorite soldier, Robt. Lee, from defecting to the rebels! Oh, irony!)

Let us hope that the readers' preconceptions of the notorious Riley will not be too rudely overset by the truth now available. It is difficult to alter a long-standing bias. I find that the United States Army now officially pretends that the Saint Patricks and the desertion problem never existed. The Army avers that no records exist of that matter. But it is hard to obliterate a history which had the rabid attention of all the nation's war correspondents and newspaper readers for two years!

I daresay that publication of this account, with the Mexicans' viewpoint involved, might embroil Harper's *in some controversy. On the other hand, the present rupture between North and South probably will overshadow most everything else. The Army itself surely is too distracted to make much of this now.*

To bring this letter to a point, Sir, my forthcoming article will apprise your readers that the notorious turncoat John Riley, upon being released from captivity at war's end, returned to the Mexican Army where he was highly honored and raised to the rank of colonel; was engaged with a noted beauty of Mexico City society (the mother of my informant); then, alas, fell victim to the intrigues which prevailed in the army after his champion, Gen. Santa Anna, was exiled. Suspected of being part of a coup conspiracy, he was in danger of a firing squad with others of his Irish brigade, but so warm was the public sentiment for the "Heroic Irishmen," that they were freed and returned to service. It was by then a peacetime army. He nearly died of the Yellow Fever, and in 1850 was retired from the Army with a pension payout, and embarked from Vera Cruz to Havana. From there, my informant said, John Riley tried to follow Gen. Santa Anna to his place of exile in Jamaica, but found the General already removed to another island. My informant received no direct correspondence from Mr. Riley after that, probably because of his own transience through various hospices and institutions. But he is certain that the Irishman took passage back to his homeland, as he had often expressed a desire to do, having a son still living there in County Galway. The remainder of his Mexican Army pension might conceivably allow Riley & son to exist a notch above starvation in that impoverished place, we may hope. Were it not for our war of secession and my obligation to be involved in journalizing it, I should love to go to Galway and renew our old friendship right now.

In fact, my informant and I have devised a plan for the indeterminate future, to embark together on a pilgrimage to find our mutual friend in Galway. My informant intends to go at his government's expense as the initial envoy to establish a regular delegation that will honor the San Patricios in their homeland. This is his fond ambition, and he is confident that he can arrange it. He is also campaigning for a San Patricios monument to be erected in or about Mexico City. From this you might judge the height of Mexico's affection for those renegades.

All that, Sir, is the issue of my long sojourn here in this bloody and tragic land. Long as it has been, I have not nearly exhausted my expense allowance. Herewith is my accounting.

In my months here, Mexico has been in a series of political tumults, as you surely know. President Juarez seems in firm control and presses his reforms, including the nationalizing of the Church and limiting the Army's political power. I can report on these politics, but doubt American readers would be interested, having their own upheaval to occupy them.

I am reluctant to leave Mexico, but should take advantage of the land's relative political stability to go to Vera Cruz and find passage to the States.

My itinerary there is uncertain as yet. With the Union's Navy blockading our southern ports, I cannot expect to visit my mother in New Orleans. I shall telegraph you from whichever port I disembark in, and then, I presume, go sniffing after gunsmoke for you. I am a journalist, after all, and cut my teeth on war. The battlefield is the deepest circle of hell, but it is where I belong, if I am to be of any use in this life. God knows I won't be among strangers there, whichever side I cover it from, for I knew most of the Generals when they were lieutenants here in Mexico. One such acquaintance likely to be useful is Lew Wallace, now the Adjutant General of Indiana, in charge of recruiting that state's forces, with the intent to lead them. I know of no other officer more able to gain information, or more determined to get into action, and so I hope to establish a liaison with him. I also have special friendships with officers from Michigan, and if a certain U. S. Grant of Illinois shall have attained any prominence in the Army, I can expect him to welcome me. Both those gentlemen know me as an artist, as I flattered them both with portraits when they were in the bloom of youth.

In summation, Mr. Guernsey, watch for my articles on the war past, and I pray that in the event that the current one is prolonged, I shall be able to serve your fine magazine well as an enterprising correspondent and illustrator. Finally I am shed of the War with Mexico, and ready to go on, where "the claret is being drawn" anew. But this time, I pray, for a nobler cause. Good claret should not be wasted.

I am, Sir, your most humble servant,

Padraic Quinn

JAMES ALEXANDER THOM was formerly a U.S. Marine, a newspaper and magazine editor, and a member of the faculty at the Indiana University Journalism School. He is the acclaimed author of *Follow the River; Long Knife; From Sea to Shining Sea; Panther in the Sky,* for which he won the prestigious Western Writers of America Spur Award for best historical novel; *The Children of First Man; The Red Heart; Sign-Talker;* and *Warrior Woman,* which he co-wrote with his wife, Dark Rain Thom. The Thoms live in the Indiana hill country near Bloomington.

This book was set in Garamond, a typeface originally designed by the Parisian typecutter Claude Garamond (1480–1561). This version of Garamond was modeled on a 1592 specimen sheet from the Egenolff-Berner foundry, which was produced from types assumed to have been brought to Frankfurt by the punchcutter Jacques Sabon.

Claude Garamond's distinguished romans and italics first appeared in *Opera Ciceronis* in 1543–44. The Garamond types are clear, open, and elegant.